I0615722

EMBRACING TODAY
© 2021 KAHLEN AYMES

First Edition
Version: 2021.5.11

Cover Design and Formatting by R.A. Mizer of IconicArts Design. For more information visit Iconicartsco.com.

Published by Kahlen Aymes Books, Inc.
ISBN: 978-0-9996713-7-5 (E-book)
ISBN: 978-0-9996713-8-2 (Paperback)

EMBRACING *Today*

KAHLEN AYMES

Dedication

One of my dear readers, Dawn Morrison Brady, lost her husband to colon cancer while I was writing this book and his story touched my heart so much that I decided that I must dedicate my firefighter book to the two of them.

Dawn has been with me almost since the publication of my first book, The Future of Our Past, and over the years she has assisted with book signings, often driving hundreds of miles to do so, and has become a dear friend. I love her dearly and though I never met him, I learned a lot about her husband Barry Brady, a thirty-year fire-fighter and certified arson investigator for fifteen. He became a loving and devoted father to her 2 sons from a previous marriage, and they adored him. I know that he and Dawn shared a special love story.

Brady, as he was called by all who knew him, was beloved in his community and had many friends, he won too many awards and accolades in his home state of Tennessee to mention them all, but enough that the state passed legislation that provides compensation to firefighters who acquire cancer because of their work. It covers four types of cancer and the only requirement is that firefighters get an annual screening. Dawn has said that she receives texts and emails often where firefighters tell her that because of the screening requirement their cancer was found much earlier than it might have been otherwise had it not been for this piece of legislation.

When Brady was on hospice, during the last five weeks of his life, he found out that this legislation would be named after him, and he felt a great sense of honor. Unfortunately, he didn't live to see it become law, but it was signed by Governor Bill Lee just one month after his death. Brady's legacy will live on through The Barry Brady Act and hopefully save other firefighters from losing their lives, as he did.

I love you, Dawn, and I'm so sorry for your loss. I hope this dedication comforts you just a little.

You may notice that Ben's last name in *Embracing Today* is Brady… by design.

Rest in peace, Brady… Heaven is for heroes.

~Kahlen

Xoxo

Since 2002, 2 out of 3 firefighters suffer some kind of side effects from their career as heroes, including cancer. It is my wish that all states and/or the federal government would introduce legislation similar to the Barry Brady Act for firefighters and other first responders who risk their lives for others every day. Please contact your local legislature and share Barry's story.

Learn about The Barry Brady Act here: https://bit.ly/3gfrn89

A news story was done 1 year after Barry's death which explains why, and how, firefighters get cancer from their gear: https://www.facebook.com/watch/?v=729049607862829

Acknowledgments

Special thanks to all of the members of my Dream Team, Review Team, and Kahlen's Angels who help me so often with beta reading and promotion of my books, especially Justin Tevis who manages my reader group, Kathryn Voskuil, Sandra De Gouveia Archangel, Zoë Braycotton, Jaime Billam, & Donna Cooksley Sanderson, who have helped with editing, and the many bloggers who review, blast, post, talk up and feel so passionately about my books… I love you to Mars and back!

To A.M. Hargrove, Samantha Christy, Tina Reber, Ilsa Madden-Mills, Kelly Elliott, Sandi Lynn, Julie Richman, April Wilson, SE Hall, AD Justice, & Lynn Jaxon; I adore you, your books, and your friendship! Thank you from the bottom of my heart!

My heartfelt thanks to the host of authors & bloggers who invite me into their groups to share my books and release events, who help to organize group promotions that give our readers the opportunity to find similar types of books, authors & reader groups!!

To my special friends from the CATB group & the True-R group – I love you and know I can always count on you! You are TRUE & loyal friends!

To my mother and daughter who offer unending support: I love you with my whole heart!

And finally, to my readers… thank you for all of your support, love, tears, and amazing words that you send to me on a daily basis. I am humbled and honored beyond measure. I appreciate, and value, every single review, because you took time the time to not only read my work but share your opinions! I adore each and every one of you!

I couldn't make this incredible journey without any of you. I hope you know that!

Love and Peace…

~Kahlen

xoxo

Prologue

Marin

"Stop, Carter! Don't come near me!"

My shrill scream split the air, but it didn't keep him from advancing on me in his fury.

Over the past two weeks I'd been slowly working up the courage to end things with my boyfriend of almost two years, and I'd decided tonight was the night. The relationship that had started out good turned to crap after my Uncle Leonard passed away a few months back.

After stressing about it all day, I'd come home, gathered my courage, packed up his things and loaded them into my car. Carter didn't have many belongings; just a few clothes, a couple of hats, a pair of New Balance athletic shoes and two pair of work boots. He'd been a bit of a drifter before he settled in Jackson Hole, and that should have been my first red flag.

I was intent in my purpose to be rid of him and had planned to confront him at The Auto Shop, no matter how much I dreaded his response. I couldn't stand to have him inside my home one more night; he'd become violent after I refused to marry him only weeks after losing my Uncle. It was as if he was a different person; mean, short-tempered and violent.

My parents died in a car accident when I was only nine, so I came to live with my bachelor uncle in northwestern Wyoming. It had been rough at first; I was a scared kid who missed my parents and Uncle Leonard had no idea how to relate to, or raise, a young girl. But as I grew up, we became very close and now, I was lost without him. In the midst of my grief I shut down, and Carter hadn't been even a little sensitive to my sorrow. He got drunk after I said no to his proposal and became violent. That was the first night he beat me and the night I knew I had to get him out of my life for good.

I was terrified of what his reaction would be, but I couldn't take one more night of the drunken abuse. I steeled myself against the onslaught of anger that I knew was inevitable.

A lightning storm caused the electricity to short out at the ranch just before I got into my little car and drove the short distance to the family business sitting at the other end of the property. I was determined to tell Carter I wanted to end our relationship, but knew if I told him at the house, he wouldn't leave and more than likely beat me or hurt my puppy just to spite me.

In the aftermath of delivering the news, he wasn't taking it well. My heart was pounding inside my chest, thumping with fear. I realized I probably should have waited until he was sober, but I'd been working myself up to it and wanted this chapter of my life closed. My heart felt like it would fly from my chest as I stood in front of the furious man. I could see him about to fly into a rage and turned to leave my uncle's auto shop before things escalated. I wanted to get home and lock the doors to the house behind me.

"You ungrateful little bitch! Don't you walk away from me!" he shouted viciously as I dashed to the other side of the building. He stumbled. His eyes were glazed over from alcohol; the half-empty fifth of Jack Daniels sitting on his workbench was no doubt the culprit. "I'm talking to you! You can't kick me out! I'll kill you, first! All this should be mine!"

Realization dawned: so that was why he wanted to marry me. It should have occurred to me earlier. I felt sick to my stomach.

Carter charged at me, pushing aside a partially full barrel of waste oil that stood between us and knocking it over. It landed with a loud clang and the thick liquid inside oozed over the cement floor like black blood. He unknowingly walked right through the dirty gunk in his urgent quest to punish me, slipping which made him even angrier. The one thing that Carter was truly adept at was holding his liquor, and terror seized my heart as he charged toward me. He must have had more than usual.

"Just stay away from me, Carter!"

I frantically looked for something to protect myself, but the light was low, and the shop cluttered with a plethora of scrap metal, greasy rags and trash.

My uncle's automotive shop was a mess and to make matters worse, it was dark inside. The one kerosene lantern that sat on the work bench was the only light in the dim space, except when the lightening flashed outside illuminating the premises for a brief moment at a time.

Since Uncle Leonard died six months ago Carter had let the place go to hell. Gone was the orderly and efficient business it had once been; gone were the five mechanics who used to work for us and the steady stream of customers. Carter was the only worker left because he'd run the others off due to his tyrannical ways. I couldn't help but think it was all my fault because I hadn't had the strength to be rid of him sooner.

The shop was now littered with old tires and engine parts, dented bumpers, and other automotive body parts that had been salvaged or discarded. A disassembled motorcycle that was mid-way through an overhaul sat to one side of the garage, and two cars, one with an open hood and another up on blocks, were in various states of repair. Two others were outside the broken-down barn waiting their turn to be serviced. Just a year ago, the lot would be full of repaired vehicles waiting to be picked up, or those about to be repaired.

The locals in Jackson Hole were loyal to my uncle had kept coming after he died because they knew that the shop supported me and the ranch. That alone, accounted for the work that was still in process. The familiar scent of grease and gasoline permeated the air.

The blood rushing madly in my ears was so loud that I could barely hear the thunder booming outside as it rumbled through the northern Rockies; the result of nearby cracks of lightning from the brewing storm.

I lunged away from Carter, narrowly making it out of his grasp as his hand swiped through the air at me. His fingers tangled in my long hair and pulled it painfully as he reached for me, trying to grasp at the back of my suit jacket. My scalp screamed as I pulled away with all my strength. His fist was probably full of my long blonde hair. "

I said get over here!" he screamed, his efforts making the veins in his neck and eyes bulge with his wrath.

I still had make-up covering the residual bruise on my cheek that had been left from the backhand that had landed there only three nights ago, and though it was cloudy today, I'd conspicuously hidden my black eye with large designer sunglasses. I'd come to the conclusion that the shop was a thing of the past and I had to find a new way to support myself. I'd spent the day in town filling out applications at the diner, the police station, and one of the real estate offices.

"Get out!" I screamed at the mad man chasing me. "I hate you!"

I'd never meant anything more. I hated him beyond anything, but I hated myself, too. I'd fallen for his flattery and succumbed to his lies for the past two years ever since he'd come to work at The Auto Shop. I'd just come back from attending Denver University and I was young and impressionable, vulnerable to the attention of a handsome man. Carter had been 26 and unmarried; unlike any of the other mechanics that worked for my uncle, and I'd swooned whenever he flirted with me. It didn't take long until we started dating exclusively.

When Uncle Leonard got sick, he relied more on Carter than the others to take care of the shop, even though they'd worked for him longer. I felt disgusted at the thought of it; guilt filling up my soul because I knew that it was only because he was my boyfriend. It wasn't because he didn't trust the others; Dave, Scott and the rest of them had been there longer and were better mechanics. It was only because Carter had convinced both of us that he loved me and would take care of me once my uncle was gone. But he had flushed my uncle's entire life's work down the toilet in a matter of months as drinking became his priority. He ran through the business's working capital for stupid shit and booze; proving he couldn't care less about me.

There had been a method to Carter's plan; I was just a way to get my uncle's business, the ranch and the life insurance money. Except, I hadn't married him on demand like he thought I would, and then he got mean. I felt like such a fool and completely and utterly alone. I had no friends to speak of, because since returning from college, I'd foolishly spent every waking minute with Carter.

"Get! Ouuuuuuuut!" I screamed again, this time at the top of my lungs. "I want you gone! I want you out of the house and out of my life! Leave, or I'll call the sheriff!" I threatened even as I backed away in utter terror. Undeterred, he advanced.

Carter laughed; a wicked, devious sound. "You can't sur-survive without me," he accused. "Who will run the biz-biznus?"

I scowled at him. "What business? You've run it into the ground!" It was sickening that what my uncle had built over a lifetime was now useless

He lunged again; his arms swiping through the air in front of him, the wrench in his hand flying free and whizzing past my head, barely missing me. My breath stopped as I realized my life was in mortal danger. He was deranged and his anger, combined with the alcohol, could be a lethal combination.

He was pushing aside tools and a floor jack; picking up a fender that had been removed from one of the automobiles and flung it across the room. I searched frantically for something to defend myself with. The fender landed with a loud clang, partially on the cement floor and partially against one of the work benches, and it made me flinch.

There was a long broom on the hook on the wall closest to me, and though it might not do much beyond hold him at bay, it was better than nothing. I raced for it and yanked it down, and turning, I held it up in front of me as a barrier between us. "Stay back!"

Carter stopped and laughed. "You think you can stab me with a broom?" he sneered mockingly. "You really are a stupid little cunt!"

I was used to his vulgarity by now; the face I used to find handsome now repulsed me. "I wish this was a sword, you lousy bastard! I want you to die!" I was crying and frantic, certain I meant every word.

"Do you know what's gonna happen to you when I get my hands on you? I'm going to kill you!" He said, calm as death and then pointed in my direction. "You'll die, not me. I'm going to snap your scrawny neck!"

Suddenly, Carter surged toward me again, but I launched into action, crouching down and pushing forward with the broom with all my might, poking him in hard in the chest. I managed to knock the wind from him, and he lost his balance. Stumbling backward, he fell into the work bench which caused the lantern to fall to the floor. Carter struggled to regain his balance but couldn't, then crashed with a thud and loud grunt, onto the floor.

As I watched the lantern clatter to the floor where the glass broke, it played out in slow motion. It was as if my mind were two steps ahead and I knew the shop would light up like flash paper. It was full of gas and grease, and now that dirty oil was all over the floor, there was no preventing the inedible.

Whoosh!

The sound of the oil igniting combined with the flash of light and an inferno of heat went up in front of me; engulfing Carter in its ferocity.

My mouth fell open amid his horrific screams. He flailed, his arms slashing the air and for a split second I was frozen in shock. His shrieks of pain would mark my soul forever, but there was nothing I could do for him. Adrenaline made me dash outside to save myself. As I ran outside and away from the building as fast as my legs could carry me, a series of explosions behind me signaled the cars inside blowing up when their fuel tanks lit-up; the force of the first one flung me violently onto the ground.

I could barely breathe as I scrambled away, glancing at my own little car so close to the fiery building. Knowing my cell phone was inside, I looked at it longingly, but there would be no retrieving it so I could call 911. My car and the others in the yard would likely explode, too, and within seconds. I had to get as far away as possible before that happened.

Ignoring the blood gushing from my knees and the palms of my hands, I got up and ran. I ran for my life as more explosions sounded behind me. When I was about a quarter of a mile away, I turned, panting, to look at the fire ball that was once my Uncle Leonard's shop. Two of the three cars in front were on fire. For a moment I watched until my Mini Cooper exploded, shocking me back to reality. I turned and ran the last distance to the farmhouse, finding the hidden key and quickly letting myself inside. My puppy cried from her kennel and though I longed to get her out, I had to call the fire department. Thankfully, my uncle was old school, and we still had a landline. I picked it up, but my fingers trembled as I dialed 911.

"Nine-one-one. What's your emergency?" A woman's voice asked almost immediately.

I was out of breath, but I somehow got the words out. "The Auto Shop is on fire," I gasped. "I need help. There's someone inside!" Tears started down my face as the gravity of the situation settled. Carter was dead and it was all my fault.

"Which auto shop, ma'am?"

"It's called The Auto Shop! That's the name of the business. It's out on Old Calloway Road!" I cried.

"Who's inside?"

"Carter Stanton. He is a mechanic who worked there."

"Are you a safe distance away?"

"Yes, about a half-mile," I answered breathlessly, my voice cracking. "Oh, my God! Hurry!" I knew it was already too late to save him or the building. It had been too late before I'd even gotten outside.

"What's the address?"

I told her the address and she affirmed the fire department and EMTs were on their way. "There are no hydrants, correct?"

"No, but we have a lake on the property if they can siphon the water." The suggestion was no doubt ridiculous, but it was all I could think of to help.

"Who am I speaking with?"

"Marin Landry. I own the shop."

"Isn't that Leonard Landry's place?"

"Yes. He was my uncle."

The sirens and flashing lights were already showing up on the horizon. "Okay. They're on the way." I glanced out the kitchen window above the sink of the ranch house. Two fire trucks, an EMT ambulance vehicle, and two sheriff's cars all with sirens screaming and a bevy of flashing lights were coming over the foothills toward me at a breakneck pace.

Honk! Honk! One of the firetrucks blew their horn as they reached the last intersection before the property line. *Honk! Honk!*

"They're already here," I said into the phone, thankful the ranch was so close to the city limits.

"Okay, ma'am. Please be available in case the sheriff or firemen have questions, but make sure to stay a safe distance away."

"I will. Thank you." I was sobbing as I hung up the phone, shoving my bloody feet into an old pair of Vans without laces that I used when working around the ranch. I grabbed one of my uncle's old work shirts off a hook by the door and flung it on as I pushed through the door and started running back toward the commotion. It was painful, but I tried to ignore it.

I could see firemen scrambling to get the hoses out and hooked up to the tankers, and two others in heavy gear rushed into the building as the orange and red flames raged up the sides of the building and set the roof ablaze.

Another group of men were hosing down the two remaining vehicles on the edge of the yard down with some sort of foam I could only assume was some sort of anti-inflammatory agent. I could hear them yelling as I got closer, the one in charge using a megaphone to bark orders to the others.

For the first time, I felt the cold night air and breeze in my hair. I felt a throbbing ache in my knees and elbows, and the burning in my hands and feet where the gravel had ground in and ripped my flesh. I wrapped my arms around myself and slowed to a fast walk as I ran out of breath, keeping my pace quick despite the pain, after seeing the two men rush into the flames, risking their own lives in an attempt to rescue a man who was surely dead.

As I approached two of the EMTs ran up to me with a gurney. "Let us help you," one middle-aged man said, his eyes kind, and no doubt taking in my tear-stained face and assessing the extent of my injuries. "Can you lay down for us?"

I shook my head. "No, please get those men out of there! It's too late to save Carter," I begged. "I saw him die. Get them out! Please!" I begged, almost screaming. "Get them out!" My hand flew to my mouth as I started to sob again.

"I'm so sorry," he said softly. The man who spoke to me nodded, indicating that the other should go tell the fire chief what I'd just said. I sank onto the gurney that they had lowered to make it easier to sit down; the remaining EMT steadying me with his hands. Once I was laying down and covered with a cotton blanket, he ran and got an equipment case, flipping it open and taking out a stethoscope and blood pressure cuff, and then using a pen light to look into my eyes. I started to shiver.

"You might be in shock. I just want to get your vitals, okay?"

"Brady, Danson…. Get out of there!" I heard the voice on the megaphone shout. "Witness says it's a DOA!"

I closed my eyes, silently praying that no one else would be hurt.

BEN

"Brady, Danson.... Get out of there!" I barely heard the captain through the fire's roaring, me and my partner lifting and moving large chunks of metal looking for the victim. Our Turnout gear; the protective gloves, coat, boots, and fireproof pants kept us from getting burned but it was hot as fuck. "Witness says it's a DOA!"

It was an inferno by the time we'd arrived, but if there was a person inside, we had to attempt a rescue, no matter how hopeless. We were probably insane because I knew no one could survive this. My mask was fogging over and mixed with the thick black clouds of smoke, I could barely see a thing. I was used to the weight of the O2 tank on my back and that of my gear. The flames were licking up the walls and over the ceiling, blistering the paint. Soon the roof would probably cave in overhead. No question, we had to get the fuck out, but I didn't want to leave the poor bastard in here. The walls were made of concrete blocks with wooden buildout on the inside, but one had been blown apart by the initial explosion.

"Come on, let's go," Davis shouted. "There could be more explosions! We don't know what else is in here and the roof is about to go!"

The flames were already raging across the ceiling and it could flash in any second. I glanced around and saw the charred form of a man on the floor. He was charred beyond recognition; his features melted, and his hands only stumps on his frozen arms, the fingers completely gone. "I found him!" I shouted, pointing so Davis could see where I was looking.

"The structure was already weakened by the explosions, man!" he yelled back, taking hold of my jacket. "Let's go!"

I shook my head, yelling. "You go ahead. I can't leave him in here. The family deserves something to bury! I'm right behind you!"

I used one gloved hand to pull on the dead man's arm and then bent, to hoist him over my back. It was gross, like a hundred and fifty pounds of charred meat, but all I was thinking of was getting this guy and myself out before the roof caved in on us. The heat was intense; I was sweating profusely inside my gear and my helmet was starting to itch as I carried him toward the opening in the wall closest to me.

Water was already raining down into the guts of the fire on the side that had been blown away by the initial explosion, and the teams from two of the six stations on the scene were getting it under control. I could hear the drops hit my helmet and my coat, but I couldn't feel any temperature difference.

Davis had gone out in advance and there was a black body bag laying on the ground waiting to receive the poor bastard I was carrying. He held it open until the body was inside, then zipped it up. I peeled off my mask, as he had already done, removed a glove and wiped my hand down my face to clear the sweat.

"Cap says it's a total loss. They're just going to control the burn."

"Do they know what happened to start it?" I asked, unbuckling my jacket.

"No. That's the fire commissioner and the sheriff's job to investigate."

I was annoyed that my friend pointed that out because I already knew it, but I was curious if anything had been discovered from questioning the person who called in, though it didn't take a genius to know a place like this was full of flammable substances.

I nodded, looking around. The EMTs were working on someone about a hundred yards away, and instinctively I knew this must be someone close to the deceased. "Be right back," I tossed over my shoulder and began walking toward the open back of the ambulance.

Mitch, one of my team's younger emergency medical techs, was jumping out of the back.

"What's the story?" I asked.

He shook his head. "She was inside and saw the dude light up, from what I gather. She has some injuries on her hands and knees, a concussion from being thrown in the explosion, and her feet are injured from running a half-mile on white rock. We're giving her IV fluids to stave off shock. She lives alone at the ranch house in the distance over there," he pointed. "...so, we're taking her to the hospital for overnight observation."

"Can I talk to her for just a minute?" I asked, taking off my helmet and pushing the hair that was plastered to my forehead back with a clawed hand.

"Sure. Just a minute while we load up the rest of the gear."

"Okay." I climbed in the back and sat down next to the slight young woman under the white cotton blanket. It was up to her neck, and one dirty hand that had an IV line attached to it was resting on her stomach on top of the covers. I could see she was beautiful, despite her smudged, tear-stained face and her tangled, soot-covered hair. Her eyes were closed when I sat down next to her.

"Miss?" I said softly, trying to rouse her.

Her eyes flew open and in the bright light of the ambulance, her light grey eyes were stark against her dirty face and hair. Something inside me stirred. She was so fragile, so sad; her soul seemed to be injured more than her body. My heart broke for her.

When I was sure she could see me clearly, I spoke again. "I just wanted to say… we tried to save the man. I'm so sorry that I couldn't."

"He's dead," she said. Her voice was weak, and I wasn't sure if she was asking or telling.

I nodded. "Yes, ma'am. I'm so sorry." I wanted to ask who he was to her but knew that I shouldn't.

Her face crumpled and she started to sob. Her other hand came out from beneath the blanket to cover her mouth.

"I'm so sorry," I said again, helpless to know what to do for her, or how to ease her suffering. "We did get him out so the family can…" my words dropped off.

She shook her head. "It's not your fault." She swallowed hard and tried to stop crying. "I already knew. I saw it happen."

"Is there anyone I can call for you?" I hesitated to ask after such a harrowing experience. Was the man who had perished related to her? Was he her husband or lover? I didn't want to do or say anything to make her more upset, so I held my tongue. It would be difficult enough to come to terms with his death; she didn't need any extra reminders.

"Not really. My uncle died six months ago. I have no family." She didn't mention the dead man or what he was to her.

"I'm sure there is someone. A friend?"

She cried hard again. "I have a few, but I don't have anyone's number. My cell phone was in my car when it exploded."

My heart fell as silent tears rained from her eyes. I knew what it was like to have no family around. Since my little sister and her son had moved to Atlanta a year and a half ago, so I'd been on my own, too. Sure, I had friends, as this young woman must have, but friends weren't the same as family. Even some of the guys who I worked with had become like brothers back in Billings, but I was new here and it wasn't quite the same. Davis was my only close friend.

"What happens now?" She wiped at her eyes to clear away the tears, but it only served to smear the soot on her face around leaving wet smudges.

"They're going to take you to the hospital to check you out. I'm not sure if they'll keep you overnight, but it looks like you could use the rest."

She began to shake her head adamantly. "I can't!" She was panicked. "Who will take care of the horses and my puppy?" she asked. "I need to feed them and let my dog out. I have to take care of them!"

So, the man who died must have been close to her if she was alone. I cleared my throat, wanting, in fact needing, to help this poor woman in some way. It may have been forward, but I covered her hand with my own in order to calm her. Something passed between us; like an electric charge or connection making a circuit. Instantly, her eyes locked with mine and she calmed down.

"I get off shift in a couple of hours. I know it will be kind of late, but I can do it if you'll tell me what to do. It'll be okay."

She sucked in a shaky breath. "Really? You'd do that? My puppy was crying when I ran from the house."

I smiled. "Sure, if you'll tell me where to find the food. Were your keys in the car, too?" My mind raced, wondering why she'd leave her purse, phone and keys inside the car when she went inside the now burned down shop.

"They were, but there is an extra house key in the blue flowerpot by the back door at the ranch. Just up the road from the shop. I can't remember if I locked the house after I called you guys from the landline."

"Ben, we're rolling up the hoses. Can you help us?" One of the others shouted from twenty feet away.

"I have to go, but don't worry, I'll take care of it." I smiled and patted her hand again.

"My-uh-my dog; Gem; she's just a puppy. She cries if she's left alone at night." Her face crumpled again, and she began to cry again. It was heartbreaking to watch.

"What breed is she?"

"A black lab. She's just ten weeks old."

I nodded, happy to help out. I knew that I'd be taking the pup home for the night.

"Don't worry, miss…?"

"Oh, my name is Marin. Marin Landry."

"Bennett Barry, at your service." I wanted to say it was nice to meet her, but considering the circumstances, it would make me seem insensitive. "I'll pick up your puppy and feed and water your horses. Don't worry about them, tonight. Just concentrate on getting some rest."

For the first time, the hint of a smile graced her mouth and I found myself anxious to see her without soot, blood or sadness covering her face.

"How will I find you?" she asked.

"Mitch and Stan, the EMTs who worked on you, know me. One of them can give you my number. I gotta go help pack up the equipment."

Marin's hand reached out and grabbed the sleeve of my coat. "Thank you. You're a lifesaver. I'll never be able to repay you."

I paused to meet her eyes again. *I wasn't tonight*, I thought regretfully. But I was glad that I could help her, if only in some small way. "No need for that, ma'am. Happy to help."

Chapter 1

BEN

The puppy was crying pitifully from her kennel and had been since I'd brought her back to my house. She didn't eat when I tried to feed her some of the canned puppy food that I'd found in a cupboard in the utility room of the young woman's farmhouse.

I wondered if she had to go to the bathroom.

Dogs didn't shit where they live.

That's what my grandad used to say, and why we'd always used kennels to house train our pets. I could still hear him say it like it was yesterday. Knowing there was nothing left to do but take her out again, I pushed back the covers and padded into the adjacent bathroom where I was keeping the small kennel I found her in at the farm, after I'd fed and watered the horses three hours earlier.

I crouched down and carefully unlatched the metal door.

Bowww, bowww, bowwww! she wailed. *Booooowwwwww!*

"It's okay, honey." I swung open the door to the kennel. "Come on! Come on out," I said in something akin to baby talk. "Do you have to go outside?"

I wanted to reach in to get her, but she was scared, and I wanted her to trust me. She was in a strange place and missing her people. There was a white T-shirt inside the kennel that I hoped she'd snuggle into, but there was no such luck.

The pup peered at me and wailed again. "It's okay. You're okay," I said in a soft voice, reaching in one hand and letting her get my scent again. "Come on, baby," I cooed at her. "You'll be back with your mom soon enough."

If the guys at the firehouse heard me babbling like this to a dog, I'd probably never hear the end of it. She was a baby, I reminded myself, but still. I had a reputation at the station for being a tough guy and this scene would certainly kill that notion, but I smiled when it occurred to me that I couldn't care less if it did. If only my nephew Dylan and my sister, Missy, were still living with me, taking care of the puppy would have been a piece of cake. Dylan would no doubt have already won the dog's trust, and Missy was such a loving person she would have jumped right in to care for my temporary little orphan.

"You're okay, Gemmy." I tried using her name. She had such a sweet face. Her sparkling black eyes peered at me cautiously and she whined. "Come on. Let's go outside, and then I'll get you some warm milk. Would you like that?"

I tried to use one index finger to pet her small, but very silky head. "You're okay." I probably should have gotten her something to eat before I'd opened the kennel, but her sad cries made food a second thought.

"That's it," I soothed as the little puppy inched her way to the open door. By now I was sitting with my legs crossed on the floor, starting to rub behind her ears. Her tail started to wag and soon she was on my lap. I stood up holding the puppy close to my chest, then bent and kissed her head. "You're okay. We'll go outside and then we'll get you something to eat."

It didn't matter to me that I was only wearing boxer briefs and a t-shirt. It was late and my neighbors would be sleeping. I moved through the house to the back door off of the kitchen and pushed it open, turning on the porch light; it was so late that I wasn't worried about my lack of attire. I moved gingerly down the steps and sat Gem in the dew dampened grass. She was so small that the grass came up to her belly and she had a hard time navigating through it.

"Man, I guess I need to mow," I muttered to myself. Soon she was walking around, turning circles until she found a place to do her business.

When she was finished, she looked up at me and then waddled the short distance back to me. Before I could even bend to pick her up, she had laid down in a little ball, then rested her head on my foot, clearly intent on sleeping where she was.

My heart melted. "Awww," I said, and bending, I picked up the black ball of fur and nestled her against me with one hand as I went back inside. If I wasn't careful, I'd become attached and then where would I be? I couldn't have a dog because of all of the time I spent at the firehouse, but this precious little thing sure made me long for one.

After I'd poured a little milk in a saucer and heated it slightly in the microwave, Gem was soon lapping it up happily. "Is that good, sweet face?"

My bedroom was upstairs, and the house was dark, so I scooped her up and returned to it. I yawned, contemplating how the puppy's owner was doing in the hospital. I hoped she'd at least be able to sleep.

I placed the pup back in her kennel and she started crying before I even had the door closed. Sighing, I gave into the inevitable and was soon back in my bed with the puppy sleeping contentedly on my chest as I petted her in a slow rhythmic motion. I mean, if I wanted any sleep at all, what choice did I have?

I smiled into the darkness as my hand stroked back and forth over the silky black fur. Yeah, it was the least I could do for the beautiful young woman who'd probably just lost the love of her life. This little dog was all she had to come home to; I reasoned, feeling sad that we hadn't been able to save the man.

The woman's heartbreaking sobs still rang through my mind, as did her smoke smudged and tear stained face. I took my job seriously, and tonight was a particularly grizzly scene. I tried to remain impartial, but this… was worse than most. I could only imagine what it had been like for her to watch the man she loved burn to death. His screams must have been horrific. I'd witnessed something similar once and it still made me cringe to think about it.

I inhaled a sigh of regret as the dog shifted on my chest and smacked her lips a couple of times the way dogs do when they are content and snuggling in for a long night's sleep. I was loving every minute of my time with little Gem and I had to admit, having her with me tonight was nice. I was also looking forward to checking on her owner in the morning… as soon as it would be acceptable to do so. She'd just lost someone dear to her, but something deep inside me longed to know her better… The caveman inside me roared. I felt protective of the frail, broken young woman. I wasn't sure if it was because I'd failed to rescue her partner, or if it was another deeper connection that would have stirred regardless of how we might have met. It struck me that, somehow, she would be a big part of my future.

Marin

I was looking forward to getting out of the hospital. The house would be empty; a screaming reminder of what had happened, but then, so was being in the hospital. The horrific image and sounds of Carter burning would haunt me forever. It was awful.

My injuries from the night before were relatively minor, though I'd been given IV fluids and some type of medication to sleep. They discovered two cracked ribs from one of my scuffles with Carter. I tried to hide it, but I'd winced during the initial examination, so they'd ordered x-rays. Hiding any injury had become such a habit over the past months, it hadn't occurred to me that without Carter around to threaten more abuse, it wasn't necessary to lie about it.

The physician, who self-proclaimed himself the hospitalist, visited around 6 AM. I'd been anxious to leave ever since, as the gravity of the situation hit me. I was totally alone in the world but at least I had the ranch, the horses, and my little baby dog. Carter was a bastard, but at least he was someone to go home to. I was so devastated after Uncle Leonard died, I was ignorant to Carter's motives.

I sucked in a deep breath, shaking my head in an effort to rid my mind of such thoughts. As the television droned in the background, I wondered what needed to be done about Carter's funeral and how to find his family. I didn't have time to feel sorry for myself. Thankfully, Uncle Leonard's life insurance had a nice payout though I hadn't touched a cent of it. I would be able take my time and find a job I really wanted, and I'd have the money to cover the funeral.

Maybe I'd go to back to school for my MBA. I hadn't done so before because it was just assumed that I'd keep working at the shop as the business manager. Uncle Leonard taught me the billing duties when I was sixteen, so I had some practical experience that I could build on. My uncle loved having me involved and I wanted to make him happy.

The pert young nurse who had worked the overnight shift popped her head into my room. She was dressed in the hospital RN uniform of monotone dark blue pants, top and long-sleeved jacket. The employees wore color-coded uniforms to easily distinguish their role in the hospital.

"You've been cleared to get out of here, Marin. The discharge papers have been signed so you're good to go! Do you need help getting dressed?" She smiled her encouragement.

"Um…" I hesitated. "I don't really have anything to wear home. I just have the clothes I came in here with and some of them were cut off in the emergency room. Is there a gift shop?"

She looked at me sympathetically. "Sure," she said. "If you want to dress like you're sixty and spend a boat load of money to do it. Those ER doctors just get down to business after an accident without thinking about stuff like that. Thankfully, you weren't hurt too badly."

I glanced at the white board on the wall to recall her name; Gina. "It's understandable how they do it," I answered, though I was worried. I couldn't go home in a hospital gown.

"Do you have anyone I can call to get you some clothes or to pick you up?" Obviously, she'd noticed I didn't have any visitors during my brief stay.

"I don't have anyone. I spend most of my time with my animals, and our place is out in the country. Growing up, I pretty much kept to myself." I'd had one or two high school friends, but they'd left Jackson Hole after graduation and never returned except an occasional holiday. I knew some of our neighbors, but they were more friends of Uncle Leonard than of mine. I ran a hand through my still dirty hair, realizing how gross it felt. "It sounds pretty pathetic, doesn't it?" Tears blurred my vision and began to sting my eyes.

"Not at all. I love animals, too. I have a dog, and three cats."

"I have a few horses and a new puppy." Thinking about Gem crying from her kennel when I was calling 911 and how I had to leave her there, hurt my heart and made me anxious. I hoped the fireman who had volunteered to take care of her was good to her. He seemed like he had a big heart and a certainly had a kind face. I could tell he was handsome, despite the soot that was smudged all over it.

"I was very sorry to hear about your boyfriend," Gina said softly, coming into the room now.

"Thank you," I wiped at my eyes. I wanted to tell her that I was actually relieved, but guilt stopped me short.

"I get off in about an hour and I could run home and get you something to wear. You can borrow something of mine… we look about the same size. And then I could take you home, if you like."

"Really? That would be amazing and very kind, thank you." I dabbed at my eyes. She seemed close to my age and I felt a pang that she was so established in her life and I wasn't.

Gina smiled warmly. "It's my pleasure. I'll let my replacement know you're waiting for me to come back during our shift change."

"Thank you, Gina. I really appreciate it."

As she was leaving, a large masculine frame appeared in the doorway, hovering.

"Hey," he said gently. I recognized his eyes from the night before. In the harsh light of the back of the ambulance, the cornflower blue color had been striking against his soot and dirt covered skin. I couldn't help the way my heart leapt inside my chest. He was so good-looking my breath caught. Tall, with a muscular frame that had been hidden by his bulky gear, and dark blonde hair that was short in back and on the sides, but a tad longer on top.

"Oh, hey…" I felt a small smile settle on my mouth. I wasn't expecting him to drop by the hospital, and thought I'd have to go by the several fire stations in Jackson Hole, to find the one where he worked, in order to get Gem back.

"How are you doing?" his deep voice reverberated in the small, stark room.

I felt self-conscious of my surroundings and the hospital gown that I wore. I nervously began to fiddle with the edge of the rough cotton blanket that covered me to the waist.

"I'm a little sore, I guess. How is Gemmy? Did she keep you up all night?"

"She did a little, I can't lie, but… she's amazing." One side of his sensuous mouth tugged into a lopsided grin. He was so disarming. "I don't think I want to give her back," he teased. "She had some warm milk last night and then we had oatmeal and peanut butter toast for breakfast."

"We?" I smiled gently.

"Oh, yeah. I shared mine with her. You should have seen the way she went to work on it." He stood, towering over me at the foot of the bed. "Sorry, she didn't seem to like the puppy food I grabbed from your house."

"I'm sure she loved it. Thank you, again, for taking care of her; I don't know what I would have done without you. Would you like to sit down? Forgive my lack of manners."

"You've been through an ordeal," he said, understanding lacing his voice. "I can't stay long."

He was right, I had. "But, still, after everything you've done to help me, I should be more thoughtful."

It felt weird to be equally intrigued and yet have the inherent fear of the male sex which Carter had instilled into me over the past several months. The man's face twisted ironically, as if to say he didn't consider me in anyway rude.

"I'm glad to be of help'. He eased his long body into the one reclining chair next to the window after he moved a pillow from it. "So, you're getting out of here today, then?"

"Yes. As soon as my nurse comes back with some street clothes." I felt embarrassed by my pathetic circumstances.

"Ah." His amazing eyes seemed to look right into my soul. I could sense the questions behind the blue depths. Surely, he was wondering why I had no friends or family who could take care of my dog or bring me clothes. "I went out to your ranch this morning to feed the horses, but the puppy cried when I put her in the house and in her kennel. I figured the same thing would happen at my place; strange place and all. So, I thought I'd take her with me to the firehouse for the day, if that's okay?"

"Oh, I don't want to burden you. I'll be home in a couple of hours."

He nodded his understanding, but his brow wrinkled as if he were pained. "Yeah, but they say an hour to a dog is like an entire day to a person, and I just can't stand leaving the little thing alone that long. Or… at all," he said with a sheepish grin. "She'll get to run around, and everyone will love her. I promise I'll take good care of her."

I was looking forward to seeing my fur baby, for that's what she'd become in the short time I'd had her, and it was sweet that in one night this big, tough fireman had fallen under her spell as well. "It's so nice of you, but you've already done so much. I can see if Gina can bring me to the station to pick her up on the way home."

"I can bring her out to your place tonight after my shift. I only have a partial day today. I picked it up for some extra cash. Then, I can take care of the horses, too."

"Oh, Ben, you don't have to do that," I protested. I felt like I was sliding down in the bed and tried to shift up to get a better position but winced at the pain that shot through my mid-section. "I'll be home by then."

His expression was concerned. "Marin," he said in mock sternness, proving he'd remembered my name as well. "By the looks of things, you're in no shape to do chores just yet."

I'd done chores in worse shape than this, but I was ashamed of the situation with Carter and I didn't want to tell him I was used to working with injuries. "I'm okay," I said, instead. "I'll be fine."

He stood up, shaking his head. "You're dealing with a lot, and probably not just physically. Let me help you out for a few days until you get back on your feet. It's the least you can do in exchange for your pooch keeping me up all night." Ben offered a wink.

I could feel my skin flush at his teasing. I had a rush of guilt that I found him so charming, but I couldn't help it. "Well, since you put it that way," I agreed, a warm blush of happiness washing through me.

"The fire commissioner will probably be around the burn site to do some investigating later. They might have a few questions for you, too. It's standard procedure," Ben assured seeing my shocked expression.

I tried quickly to hide my fear.

"I just didn't want you to be scared if you saw vehicles or people snooping around out there. If you need more time before you speak to them, I can put in a request that they wait a week or two for your statement, but they'll need to get on-site today."

Panic spread through me. I was responsible for Carter's death. If only I hadn't gone out to the shop. If I'd waited to talk to him, he wouldn't be dead. It weighed heavily upon my conscience and now… would I be held accountable? Would I face charges? "I'd prefer some time before I speak to them, yes." Was that squeaky, meek voice mine? Inwardly, I was freaking out.

"Understandable. I'll pass that along. Don't worry," Ben said, knowingly. "What happened was an accident and they just have to follow procedure."

"Okay," I said, my trepidation only slightly appeased.

"Listen, your little girl is in my truck by herself so I'm gonna head out." He pointed toward the door of the hospital room and flashed a brilliant smile. "No doubt, she's crying her head off."

In light of such an onslaught of kindness, I couldn't help but smile at the mention of the puppy. She'd been my one true source of solace, though I'd had her such a short time.

"Which station did you say you were at? In case you try to kidnap Gem, you know." I laughed softly but still enough to feel it in my ribs. "Ugh," I wrapped my arms around my midsection as if cradling it would make the pain stop.

"Oh, yeah, clearly you're ready for hauling bales of alfalfa. Just rest and I'll bring her out. See you later, Marin."

"Ben?" He'd started to leave, and I stopped him, causing him to glance over his shoulder.

"Thank you, again." I meant it with all my heart. He was such a dramatic contrast to Carter's awful and unkind personality. My heart fell when I realized that when Carter had first come to work at the shop, he'd seemed kind and caring, too, and I fell for it. I wanted so badly for Ben's words to be genuine.

He lifted a hand and put it over his heart, barely stopping his stride. He offered a gently grin. "No problem."

"Bye," I said. He left me smiling, but the starkness of the room became overwhelming after his commanding presence, which had just so completely filled the space, had vacated. I was left bereft; the prospect of my future seemed bleak.

Ben's kindness was amazing, his smile infectious. For a just moment, I'd almost forgotten that the night before when I'd killed Carter. Then the guilt set in again, and just like that, I broke down into painful sobs.

Chapter 2

BEN

I couldn't understand how such a beautiful and kind young woman, who I now knew as Marin, was so alone in the world.

She seemed so distraught, and I couldn't wrap my head around why she didn't have anyone to help her. Her situation tugged at my heart so much because my father split when my sister, Missy, and I were just kids. Other than Missy, I'd never wanted to protect someone more.

Marin must be lost without the man who died in the fire. After all, he was all she had in the world after losing her uncle. The responsibility of the ranch and auto shop had to be intimidating. It would be for anyone who'd recently lost so much. I just wanted to make sure she was okay and ease her burden; even if it was just helping out with care of the horses.

When I arrived at the fire station, little Gem and I made our entrance to a round of cheers and happy greetings. The guys and the captain had discussed adopting a dog for the firehouse, but we'd never gotten around to it, and so they were enthusiastic about this little lady's appearance.

"What do you have here?" Davis asked, bending to play with the puppy. "What a cutie! Is this for us?"

"That's Marin's pup—" I paused at the familiar use of her name. "You know, the woman from the shop fire. Last night," I said awkwardly. For some reason I felt the need to explain.

My friend's eyebrows shot up. "Marin, huh?"

"That's asinine to imply, Davis. As you know, Marin Landry was injured and taken to the hospital, so this little thing was left kenneled inside her home without anyone to take care of her. What was I supposed to do? Let her go hungry and leave the poor thing to sleep in her own crap?"

"Uh huh. Don't forget, I saw her, too. Even bruised and bloody, she was beautiful."

I was annoyed at his crass suggestion and the protectiveness inside bolstered. "Yeah, I noticed," I said honestly. "Have a little sensitivity, please. The woman just saw someone she loved burned alive, so why don't you grow up? She's off limits. I'm just helping her out with her animals. From what I gather, she's not long on friends or family."

He nodded and smiled, then punched me softly on the shoulder. "Fine, you be her *sensitive friend*, Ben." Davis emphasized the words with sarcastic humor. I liked him in many ways, but my sister's abusive situation with her first husband had taught me to be more sensitive to hidden pain than the average guy.

"I will," I said, feeling uncharacteristically indignant.

"Good," he retorted, picking up Gem and scratching her head. The pup wagged her tail and nipped at his fingers playfully. "Let me know when she's ready to date again, and I'll call her."

"Humph," I snorted and shook my head in disgust. "Don't be a dick. Leave her alone."

I wasn't sure if he was pissing with me or serious, but I flashed him a pointed look. I also wasn't sure if his callousness was what was making me furious, or the prospect of a man, any man, trying to move in on Marin when she was so vulnerable.

In that second, I made it my mission to find out the rest of Marin Landry's story. It was unclear why I was so fascinated by her, or why I was feeling so protective, but something told me she was fragile for a reason. It became my new mission to befriend her and make sure she was on a solid road to recovery.

The others all adored having the puppy at the firehouse and she spent the day frolicking among the crew. I was worried that she'd get sick when they all started giving her bites of their lunch.

It was turning out to be a quiet afternoon and the station was fairly silent. With the puppy snuggled next to me on my assigned bunk, I did some research on the subject of my thoughts. I found her uncle's obituary, and noticed he was preceded in death by his parents, and his brother and his wife, who must have been Marin's parents. More digging found their obits and a news article about a car crash many years earlier.

Poor kid, I thought. So, she had no family, but why no friends? And why was this woman hanging out in my head all day? I was going to help her, but that was already settled. I shouldn't be so preoccupied with her predicament. This wasn't my first rodeo with helpless victims, but this time I wasn't able to compartmentalize as well as I had in the past.

I was tired due to my late night and early morning. I closed my eyes, deciding to take a short nap, all the while petting the sleeping puppy who had climbed up and settled on my chest, resting her head beneath my chin. As I started to doze off, I was surprised how quickly we'd bonded. Maybe I'd have to get a dog of my own. I'd been lonely since Missy and Dylan moved to Atlanta the previous year.

I'd long-since learned to sleep in the midst of my fellow firefighters milling around the station and quickly nodded off.

It was unclear how much time I'd spent sleeping when I was startled awake by something hitting the bottom of my foot.

My eyes opened and I craned my neck to look down my body toward the bottom of my bunk. Captain Connors was leaning in and down peering at me. His bright blue eyes were shinning out of his weathered, but smiling, face. "You got company."

"Oh, hey, Cap," I mumbled sleepily. I rubbed my eyes with the thumb and index finger to clear them. "Who is it?"

He only chuckled. "Just get your ass up, boy," he grumbled in his signature good-natured way. "Hurry up. In the garage."

My arm wrapped around the puppy who was yawing in protest as I started to remove both of us from the bunk and begin the walk out of the second-floor bunk room to make my way downstairs. The pup was way too small to navigate the steep stairs, so I continued to carry her in my arms, but she started wiggling like crazy and then whining.

When I walked through the station there weren't any of the guys in the kitchen or lounge area, which was unusual. Passing through the archway into the garage where the three engines were housed, I noticed a crowd of dark blue uniformed people standing in a semi-circle near one of the open doors.

As I got closer, I could hear murmured statements of condolences and I realized Marin must be here.

I wove through the dozen or so men and two women, who had stopped their work cleaning the engines and packing up gear, to hover around the fragile young woman and another; the nurse I recognized from my earlier visit to the hospital.

Davis was right up in there talking to her, though he was respectful.

"I'm very sorry for your loss," he said.

Marin nodded somberly. "Thank you."

The bundle of fur in my arms started to yip and wiggle more the closer I got to her.

Marin's face lit up. "Gemmy!"

I moved closer to hand Marin her puppy, who instantly began licking her face. She reacted by pulling Gem close and kissing the top of her head. "Hey, baby. I missed you!"

I glanced around, silently communicating that everyone should scatter. I met Davis' gaze and he offered a slight nod and moved away to get back to work.

"Hi," I said. "Are you sure you're ready for her? I thought you were going to rest today, and I was supposed to come by tonight."

It occurred to me that by coming here, Marin Landry was going to collect her dog and tell me to buzz off. A veil of panic settled over me, and I frowned awkwardly. "To help with the horses." I felt completely out of my element. This bruised young woman had affected me in a way that no one had before. I cleared my throat.

"Marin, I'm just going to wait for you in the car," the red-headed nurse said, pointing in the direction of her parked car and backing away. "Nice to see you, again," she said to me.

"You, too," I nodded, feeling rude. "I'm Ben." I held out a hand to her.

"Gina," she said, offering her hand in a brief handshake. "Marin?" she pointed to the car again.

"Oh, sure. Thanks, Gina. I'll just be a minute."

The jeans and blouse Marin wore looked a size too large and hung loosely on her small frame as she stood before me, still cuddling little Gem.

I put a hand up and rubbed the back of my neck. "So, I'll still come out about six to feed and water the horses."

"Oh," she hesitated nervously. "I feel so bad asking you to help me. I'm sure I can manage."

This was what I was afraid of. "You're not in any shape to open new bails of alfalfa and that's what is needed." I didn't want to sound chauvinistic in my comments, but it would be tough for any healthy woman. They weighed up to seventy-five pounds each. "Besides," I continued gently. "You're injured, and I'm happy to help."

She winced a couple of times when the puppy got too rambunctious in her arms and there was a yellowish bruise on her face that was too old to have happened the night before. My jaw flexed as I clenched my teeth. Did the man who died abuse her? Was she a battered woman like Missy had been? Rage burst inside my chest, and the image of the charred man on the shop floor suddenly wasn't so horrible to me. The bastard probably got what he deserved.

Marin's grey eyes were stormy. "I just feel so bad asking," she began.

"Hey, you didn't ask. I volunteered, okay? I love horses and I always wanted one as a kid. Really, it's you who is doing me a favor." The corner of my mouth lifted in the start of a grin.

"Alright," she said with a small smile. "I do appreciate it."

"Sure." I felt my smile deepen. "Is there anything you need? Groceries? Should I pick up dinner?" I groaned inwardly. I didn't mean for it to sound like I was inviting myself for dinner, however, she had to eat, and it would be hard to cook in her injured state. "I mean, you should have some stuff that's ready to eat in the house. For a few days at least, right?"

Marin bit her lip and hugged Gem close. "Okay," she agreed reluctantly. "I don't feel very well."

I licked my lips and swallowed. "It's settled then. See ya, later." I took two steps forward and rubbed the puppy's head. "You too, sweet face."

Marin's head cocked and a surprised look dawned on her face.

I was concerned. "What is it?"

"Nothing. It's just... that's my nickname for her. Did I tell you? Is that how you knew? I was sort of out of it last night."

I shook my head and smiled. "Nope. But she *does* have a sweet face. Gem certainly suits her. I think I'm already in love." I winked, casually. "I should get back to work."

Marin nodded and started to walk toward Gina's car. "See you later, then."

Marin

Gem settled onto my lap and fell asleep on the way out to the ranch. I gave directions to my new friend, Gina.

Once we headed out of Jackson in her dark grey Toyota Camry, she grinned and threw me an offhand glance as she watched the road. "Who's the cute fireman?" she asked. The expression on her face was lit up with undisguised interest. "I mean, I know his name but um..."

I flushed with guilt and an odd sort of jealousy. It wasn't even twenty-four hours since Carter had died. "Um..." I began, almost unwilling to share more. I didn't really know anything, but I felt strangely selfish about him.

Instantly, her expression changed to one of regret. "Oh, I'm so sorry. That was incredibly insensitive after all you've lost."

There was a big part of me that wanted to confide in her; tell her how Carter had abused me and beat me, how I was glad to be rid of him, even if I would have preferred him to just leave rather than dying in the fiery inferno that I had caused. I felt sick to my stomach remembering his blood-curdling screams.

I shook my head, still stroking the silky puppy on my lap. Her warm presence offered a little comfort as my fingers threaded through her soft black coat. "Oh, no, you're fine. I don't know that much about him," I answered honestly. "He was kind last night after the fire. He helped me with this little one and my horses when I had to go to the hospital. He's been so nice."

"He's like some bronze god and if that wasn't enough, he straps on all that silver armor," she murmured, almost to herself. She seemed to regret her words. "I mean, it's great he was there to help you. And then the way he came to check on you, he seemed genuinely concerned."

Her words echoed my thoughts. Ben was physically stunning, but his personality was the thing that made him stand apart. If only Carter could have had just a fraction of the qualities I'd seen in the handsome fireman. If only I'd met Ben instead of Carter. I was always in the wrong place at the wrong time, picking the wrong guy.

I nodded. "Yes," I said softly. "I don't know what I would have done if I'd had to leave my animals stranded out there all night. Ben was a huge help."

"Is this where I turn? Up here?" Gina's face turned toward me when I didn't answer right away.

My eyes started to burn behind my sunglasses, and then I swallowed hard trying to suck up my misery. I pointed to the dirt road in front of us.

"Yes, take a right at the next intersection." She must have heard the catch in my voice.

"I seem to remember my dad bringing a couple of cars out here to The Shop when I was growing up."

Her words, though innocent, conjured so much pain. The true knight in shining armor of my life had been my Uncle Leonard. I put a hand over my mouth as my shoulders started to shake. Sobs racked my body as if a dam had burst.

"Oh, Marin. I'm such a twit yammering on and on about nonsense when you're suffering so badly."

After a few minutes, I was able to curtail my pathetic display. I sniffed and put the back of my hand to my nose, but tears continued to roll down my face. "No, it's just... my uncle was the only person who really cared about me in the entire world and I feel so lost now."

I could see the question flash across her features even as she kept her gaze on the road ahead. She was wondering why I didn't include Carter in that equation.

"What about the man from yesterday?" she began.

I shook my head sadly as tears clung to my lashes and smeared the lenses of my sunglasses. "Carter. His name was Carter Stanton."

Gina appeared shocked. "Wasn't he your boyfriend?"

"We dated for a couple of years, yes."

"And now you have this loss on top of that of your uncle," she said. Her sad expression was filled with empathy.

Once again, the urge to tell Gina every horrible thing about Carter surfaced, but I didn't know her well enough to trust her. Not yet. She might come to the conclusion I'd killed him on purpose. As much as I wanted to believe she was my friend, I couldn't take the risk. I couldn't confess that Carter only pretended to love me, or that it was all a well-crafted act to convince first me, then Uncle Leonard, because he just wanted control of the business. I'd just been too stupid to realize it.

It was humiliating, yes, but I couldn't let anyone know the truth. I was feeling thankful that the ranch house was about a half-mile in front of us and I'd finally be alone. This felt like torture when all I wanted to do was take a bath, and cry. I wanted to put this nightmare behind me and the less I had to speak about Carter, the better.

"Is Carter's family from around here?"

Jackson Hole was a small town, and most folks knew everyone else.

I shook my head. "No. He moved to town and got a job at the shop while I was away at college." I remembered one or two conversations where Carter had mentioned his family, but it wasn't much. "I don't remember him saying much, except he had followed his high school girlfriend to college in Seattle, and then when that ended, he'd been on his way back to Minnesota and passed through here, saw the help wanted sign Uncle Leonard had posted on the bulletin board in the diner, and then I guess, Uncle Leonard hired him."

"You never met his family? In two years?" Gina was shocked.

I shook my head, feeling foolish and somehow ashamed that he'd never taken me home to meet them. "No. They never visited. Thinking back on it, it does seem odd."

"I see. So, we should start looking in Minnesota?"

"Probably. I'll see what I can find online, later tonight."

Gina smiled gently, finally pulling into the long white fence-lined lane for the now short drive up to the house. Gem started to wiggle on my lap as familiar scents of the mixed wildflowers along the ditches and in the pastures, as well as the faint scent of horses in the early summer air. There was a warm, dry breeze blowing as I got out of Gina's car and put Gem on the ground. "Go potty, sweet face," I said encouragingly.

"She's adorable," Gina said, getting out of the car and leaning on the top. I could have invited her in, but the day and the past night was wearing on me.

"She's been a Godsend," I said, letting it slip before I caught myself. "Um, I'll wash your clothes and bring them by the hospital tomorrow."

The pretty redhead smiled. "Oh, just whenever you can, honey."

I nodded. "Thank you."

"Listen, if you ever want to talk, I'm a good listener."

"I appreciate that." It was the truth. I could use a few friends, but I needed to get to know her better before I shared too much. It was better to keep to myself for a couple of months.

"If you need any help with arrangements, food, or whatever… please don't hesitate. I lost my brother in a car accident a few years ago, so I know how hard times like this can be. If I can pick anyone up at the airport—"

"Thank you, Gina. I'll let you know. Right now, I'm just going to rest for a while." My eyes were tired, and I knew I wasn't finished with the torrent of tears that were simmering just under the surface. In the distance, the charred remains of the shop sat as a gruesome reminder of what had occurred, and the faint smell of burning wood still wafted in the air.

She walked around and gave me a hug and I did my very best not to grimace in pain while I hugged her in return.

"Bat, bat!" Gem's puppy barks rang out as she ran around happily chasing a couple of Monarch butterflies that had been feeding on the flowers in front of the house. "Bat, bat!"

"Okay, but if you need help cleaning, cooking, or anything, just call. Even if it's just someone to be with you at the funeral; I'd like to help."

She was so kind, I felt bad for my innate mistrust. "Thank you, again," I said backing away from her car. "You've been so nice. I really appreciate it."

She nodded. "Okay. I'll see you soon, then."

"Bye."

Gina hesitated before she got into the car. "If you need help, please don't hesitate to call me."

I watched her back up the car and turn around before starting the return trip down the lane toward the road that would take her back into town.

We'd exchanged numbers earlier, and Gina was the first person that felt even a little like a new friend in a long time. I had no one to blame but myself. Since I'd come home, I'd been idiotically focused on Carter; brainwashed by his act. I sighed heavily and shook my head at my own stupidity. I'd even sacrificed time with my uncle in those last couple of years.

Fresh tears sprouted in my eyes. I closed my eyes against the pain and turned to sit down on the wooden steps leading up to the porch my uncle had built with his bare hands. I felt his loss so much more than Carter's, but it was useless to wallow in self-pity. Though I knew it, I couldn't help the tears that slipped from my eyes. I felt alone and helpless.

The unpleasant task of sorting through, and getting rid of, Uncle Leonard's things remained. I hadn't been strong enough before, and now I'd have to rummage through Carter's belongings to find any information about his family, but then remembered it all exploded with my car.

In the months that we'd dated, he always brushed off any of my inquiries, saying he preferred to be alone and his family were a bunch of assholes. Over time, I'd come to realize he was probably the cause of the problems. He had me convinced he was sweet and loving until Uncle Leonard died, then he snapped, and everything changed overnight. If they were anything like Carter, I wasn't looking forward to meeting his family, but under the circumstances, I had no choice but to try and find them. Surely the fire had been on the news. If they were anywhere close, then they would have heard.

I sucked in a deep breath as the gravity of what was in front of me settled around me. I still felt grimy from the night before and all I wanted was a hot bath and a nap. Thankfully, Gina had taken me to the Verizon store before we went to the firehouse and I was able to get my cell phone replaced, so in the event that Carter had told his family about me, they knew where he was, or did hear about the accident they could reach out.

I glanced down at the new one and Googled "Fire in Jackson" and there it was plain as day… the headline story on both of the local papers. It probably hit the local TV and radio stations, as well.

Sitting on the top step, I leaned against the railing. I felt so tired as I watched my innocent puppy frolicking in the yard and wished I could be so carefree.

"Go potty, Sweet face," I urged, again. As if she understood every word, the puppy squatted in the grass. "Come on, honey," I encouraged. I reached down when she bounded up the stairs and lifted her on my lap, then stood, kissing her velvety head. "I'm lucky I have you, baby. You're going to make this bearable."

I wondered if Ben had locked up the house after he was here the night before as I pulled on the screen door. It opened, but the one behind it was locked. After I'd managed to find the spare key under the pot, I unlocked the door and went into the house, then straight up to my room, carrying Gem with me. I walked into my room and sat her on my bed. She looked up at me with those soulful brown eyes, as if knowing I felt like hell. I reached out and scratched her head, lovingly.

Crying had made my eyes tired, and a bath might ease the soreness from my body. The air conditioner kept the house cool which was a welcome change from the afternoon heat, but it only emphasized my need for sleep. I kicked off my shoes and then crawled onto the bed, pulling the soft chenille throw over my body. Gem thought this was a fine situation and snuggled into its fluffy folds in the crook of my body as I curled on my side.

The house was filled with looming silence that seemed to boom. I had never felt so alone, and I dreaded the job of contacting Carter's family and making his arrangements.

Chapter 3

BEN

"Uncle Ben!"

The young exuberant voice of my nephew bounded through my phone. I had him on speaker as I drove out to the Landry ranch after my shift ended. We had a small house fire in town, and I was a couple of hours later than Marin expected me.

The gravel roads were bumpy, and dusk was beginning to fill the sky with beautiful colors as the sun started to set behind the majestic Teton mountain range. I loved the scenery and the fresh air that Wyoming offered, but Dylan's call reminded me how much I missed my family.

"Heeeeyyyy, Sport! What are you doing?"

"We're having a barbecue and I played baseball all day! My dad got me and Remi these cool baseball jerseys from the World Series! The *real* one! We're wearing 'em, right now! Some of my friends are at our house, too!" Dylan could barely contain his excitement.

"Cool! Sounds like a great party!" I couldn't help being slightly jealous that Missy's new husband, Jensen, was able to spend so much quality time with Dylan, not to mention how he could lavish all of these amazing gifts on him because he had access through his job. But most of all, I felt melancholy that I was missing Dylan's eighth birthday.

I really liked Jensen when I'd met him a few times over the past eighteen months, though, and I felt good that Dylan finally had a real father figure. After that bastard Missy had married the first time, I couldn't be happier about how things were turning out for them. They had moved away to Atlanta, Georgia for Missy's new job at ESPN and though I had been sad to see them go, things seemed to be working out for the best for all of us.

Shortly after they left Billings, my best friend, Davis, moved back to Jackson Hole to help out his parents after his father's diabetes got out of control. He was always bragging about how gorgeous the area was, so when another spot opened up on his team, with a lot of prodding from Davis, and a solid offer from his chief, I put my house on the market and followed him to Wyoming.

After Missy, Dylan, and then Davis, left Billings behind there wasn't much to keep me there. Billings wasn't huge, but Jackson was only a tenth of the size, the landscape more striking, and I loved the idea of a small-town.

I was still getting settled, but I really enjoyed it here, and as my mom used to say, everything happens for a reason. I wanted to buy a house, but for now, I was living in the upstairs apartment of an old man who lived a few blocks from the station. The apartment was a bit shabby, but the rent was cheap, and I helped my landlord with odd jobs. Harlan Dobbs had become sort of a pseudo granddad to me in a short time. All in all, life was good, even if I did miss the hell out of Missy and Dylan.

"Yeah! My friends all want one!"

"Me, too! Did you get one for me?" I asked happily.

Dylan laughed heartily. "It's not your birthday, Uncle Ben! Geez!"

"It's not? How come Remi got one, then? It's not her birthday, either!" I teased.

"Yeah, but we always get presents on each other's birthdays, now. Her's is from the loser team, though." He'd lowered his voice on the last part.

"Wow! That's still awesome, though! How do I get a gig like that?"

Remi was Jensen's stepdaughter. It was an unconventional situation and the two kids, while not brother and sister, were being raised together.

"I guess you gotta get a dad with connections!" Dylan laughed. My heart filled with joy at the sound of happiness that bubbled from him. His little life had started out so badly, he really deserved this.

"Come on, Dylan!" A little girl's voice could be heard closer than the rest of the background laughs and general commotion. "Jensey said it's time to eat, now. Hurry, cuz I want cake."

"Is that Remi?"

"Yup! I hafta go, Uncle Ben. We're gonna eat and then Dad and Uncle Chase are gonna airplane us!"

To me that sounded like a recipe for vomit. I'd seen what "airplane-ing" entailed the last time I visited them in Atlanta. The kids laid flat on the outstretched arms of the men who then proceeded to zoom them up, down and around like planes all the while the kids made airplane noises amid abundant squeals and giggles.

"Okay, but don't forget to open my present, and then Facetime me tomorrow to tell me how you like it."

"I will, Uncle Ben!"

"Don't eat so much you puke playing that game, Dylan."

"I won't!"

I was driving up the lane toward the Landry house and that big barn to the left that housed the horses. I slowed my truck to a stop.

"Tell Remi and the others I said hello. I'm getting a vacation in a few weeks and I want you all to come up here and visit. We'll go to Yellowstone!"

"Can we ride horses?" he asked excitedly. "Please, please, pleeeezzzze!"

I smiled, as I stepped from the truck and onto the gravel driveway, by boots crunching on it. Ironically, the horses whinnied loudly. There were several dude ranches in Wyoming and neighboring states, but maybe now that I knew Marin, she'd let me bring the kids out to see her horses. "I'll see what I can do! You just start bugging your dad and Chase to bring you guys out here to see me!"

"I will! That will be so awesome!"

"Dyyyllllaaaannn!" I could hear my sister calling her son in the background. "I have your plate ready!"

"I gotta go, cuz we're eatin' kinda late since the game went extra innings!"

"Yeah, you go on buddy. Happy Birthday! Love you."

Dylan lowered his voice again. "Uncle Ben, tough guys aren't supposed to get all gushy like that. It's not manly and stuff," he berated me, wryly. "I'm trying my best to be cool."

I found it adorable and laughed out loud. Someday he might not mind so much. "Okay, see ya, later. Have fun! Hit a homer for me!"

"Okay! Bye!"

I shut the phone off and threw it through the open window onto the seat of the truck, then turned toward the barn.

The horses were surely hungry; it had been more than twelve hours since I'd fed them. When I walked through the open door on one end of the barn, a couple of them eyed me warily, but most of them started whinnying and moving around inside their stalls. The odor of horse manure, alfalfa and leather assaulted my nostrils. It wasn't too unpleasant, and I liked working with my hands.

There was a huge black stallion and a few geldings on one side of the barn and then the mares were stalled on the other. One deep red one with a black mane and socks up to her knees looked uncomfortably pregnant and about ready to foal. She looked at me with soulful, dark brown eyes and I put my hand out to rub her nose and then down her neck. "Hey, how you doing momma? You're ready to pop, aren't you?" She neighed softly and nudged my shoulder with her nose. "Poor girl." Taking care of the horses was new to me, but I liked it, and I hoped Marin would give me the opportunity to see the little foal when it was born.

The stalls all had sliding doors open to separate fenced pastures on either side of the barn allowing the horses to come and go as they pleased all day, access the big water trough and wander or run around. They were all back inside their stalls looking at me expectantly for their meal, some getting more rambunctious as their anxiousness increased.

I was met with a chorus of horse impatience and I smiled. "Okay! Okay! Just a minute!" I said with a smile, upping my pace a bit. At one end of the barn were two entire stalls devoted to feed storage. Several bags of oats filled one and the other was stuffed with bales of alfalfa. I started opening a couple of the bales to divide among the horses. Luckily, I was able to google how much should be fed per day or I would have been completely unprepared. Apparently, if the stringy green stuff the horses seemed to love wasn't dry enough or if they got too much, it would cause bloat, which could be fatal.

I used both hands to pull it apart and added about ten pounds of the stringy green plant into each of the feed bins hanging on the inside of the stall walls. Those who got their food first started munching away happily while the others watched me with huge brown eyes, punctuated by a few snorts and neighs that became more pronounced.

After each of the horses received their portion of the alfalfa, I picked up a large scoop from an open bag of oats. It was ingenious; made by removing the bottom and part of one side from a gallon-sized plastic vinegar jug. I added one scoop of oats to the second feed bucket for each horse, giving the pregnant mare a little extra. After all, she was eating for two.

After I'd finished and the horses were munching happily, I made sure both of the round metal water troughs in both pastures were topped off with fresh water from the hose connected to a water pump in front of the barn.

I wanted to see Marin, hoping she might pop outside while I was working with the animals so at least I'd be able to check on her. There were bags and boxes of Kung Pao Chicken, Moo Shu Pork and eggrolls sitting on the passenger seat of my truck. It was surely cold by now, but there was more than enough for the two of us, and I did tell her I'd bring food over.

I walked back to the truck, second guessing my decision. Maybe it would seem insensitive to expect her to share dinner with me less than a mile from where her man went up in flames a day before. The air was filled with the familiar smell of a fresh burn. I glanced at the house once more, and then toward the charred remains of the mechanic's shop before walking around the truck, yanking open the passenger door and grabbing the white bags imprinted with the Chinatown restaurant logo on them.

"Fuck it," I mumbled to myself. I said I'd bring dinner and here it was. If she wanted to eat alone, I'd respect that. I just wanted to make sure Marin and Gem were okay and let her know that the horses were taken care of.

My boots made a hollow stomping sound on the wooden steps as I went up them, and across the porch. As I knocked on the screen door it bounced against the doorframe and I noticed the screen was coming loose from the frame. It would need repair, or she'd have a house full of mosquitos when the weather got a little warmer. No doubt the windows were equally neglected on the old farmhouse if the chipping paint on the wooden siding was anything to go by.

When Marin didn't answer the door, I opened it and knocked more forcefully on the solid door beneath. I sighed heavily, when it went unanswered again. Realizing that she had my cell number from the night before because I told her to get it from one of the guys, but I didn't have hers.

"Shit!" I said, frustrated. I couldn't call her, and I didn't want to scare her by banging harder on the door.

Maybe the door was unlocked, but how creepy would it be to go inside while she was in the house? But what choice did I have? I put out a hand to close around the doorknob, holding the bags with the other arm. I didn't really expect it to open, but it did. I nudged it open just enough to call inside.

The inside of the house was completely silent.

"Marin? Are you here?" I called quietly, so as not to frighten her. The question was met with the small bark and whining from the puppy, but it was distant, so I assumed they were upstairs. If last night was anything to go by, the little puppy couldn't jump down from the bed without help. "Marin?" I said it louder this time. "I'm finished with the horses! Are you home? I brought you something to eat."

More barking was followed by her reply. "Ben?" she called from somewhere upstairs. Hearing her say my name did something to my insides, but I tried to shake it off. I was here to help her when she needed help, and nothing more. I wouldn't allow myself to feel anything for her beyond friendship. "Yeah!" I called back.

"Oh, I'm sorry! I'll be there in a second!"

Her voice was soft, but I was surprised by the effect it had on me. I felt relieved to know she was okay.

"Take your time." I stood back onto the porch to wait, watching through the glass as she came down the stairs carrying the little black dog who was panting her head off. She was still wearing the same clothes she'd worn to the station that morning, but her blonde hair was messy and still stained with soot. A definite case of bedhead after much needed sleep.

Our eyes met through the door and Marin pulled the door open. The bruises on her face were starting to turn yellowish green, and experience told me they were from a backhand or fist.

"Sorry," she said again, indicating that I should come in.

"Bat! Bat!" Gem's little barks made me smile. "Bat! Bat!" I was already learning the differences in the puppy's barks. This was a happy greeting.

I reached out to ruffle her little head. "I missed you, too! Where do you want this?" I asked Marin as soon as I'd stepped inside.

"In the kitchen." She waved to her left. "That way. On the table. Sorry for the mess." I could see she was embarrassed by the clutter. "I should have cleaned up, but I was just so tired I fell asleep."

She moved slowly, trying to hide a grimace, but not quite managing to keep the catch out of her voice. "Are you okay?" I asked, genuinely concerned. Even though I told myself to play it cool, she was obviously in pain and I couldn't ignore it. She'd fallen on her run from the fire the night before, but people didn't move like that from scuffed up knees, or a bruised hip. Her ribs were hurting her, and I knew from experience what it felt like, and what it looked like.

"Oh, sure. Nothing that won't heal in a week or so."

"I think it might take longer. It looks like you hurt your ribs. Did they check them at the hospital?"

I placed the bags of food on worn wooden table that looked like it was half a century old, at least; varnish was missing from the table's edge and from the seats of the chairs, especially one of them, where Leonard Landry had no doubt spent most of his time when he wasn't working. It was definitely a bachelor pad, and one that was in need of repair. My heart felt sad for the little girl who grew up here, even though now she was a young woman.

"Yes. Two of them are cracked," she admitted. I knew every step, every time she sat down, raised her arms, and especially when she laid down and got up had to hurt like a bitch.

The hair on the back of my neck bristled. "Did you get thrown from the explosion? I thought you made it out before it blew."

"Oh, I did. It only knocked me down." Her response didn't explain her cracked ribs.

I picked up Gem and petted her as Marin walked carefully to the cupboard to get plates and glasses. She winced as she raised her hand to barely shoulder level.

"Oh, hey, I got that." I stepped behind her and took two plates out with one hand bringing my body into close proximity to hers. I felt an instant reaction of a quickened heartbeat. Quickly turning away to place them on the table, I cleared my throat, and bent to let the puppy down. "Sorry, little one. I'll play with you later, I promise."

Gem looked up at me with expectant brown eyes, her tail wagging furiously.

"I'm sorry. I guess I'm worse off than I thought." She touched her hair, her eyes widening when she realized it was matted and messy on one side of her head. "Oh," she murmured.

"You probably just need to eat and then get a bath and some rest. I can leave you to it. How did you break your ribs? From the fall?"

Her eyes widened in surprise. "Oh, um… I don't think so. I fell against the work bench in the shop just before, Carter…"

Her voice broke and her tears flooded her eyes and she dabbed at them self-consciously.

"Listen, I just wanted to make sure you were alright, and feed the horses as promised. I know it's been a rough twenty-four hours and you probably just want to be alone."

Marin pulled out one of the chairs and sat down carefully. "Not really," Marin said. Shaking her head. "My brain won't shut off. All I do is replay it over and over in my head and the silence only amplifies everything. I'd love it if you'd stay and share the meal with me. Gem seems to want you to stay, too."

Marin smiled tremulously. She seemed so fragile; I'd seen that look in Missy's eyes many times and knew that the best thing to do was to get Marin's mind off of what happened.

"How about it, Gem, do you want me to hang out for a bit?" I said in my best baby talk voice. Marin smiled and the puppy got up, wagged her tail furiously and began to jump up, placing her two front paws onto my lower leg. "I'll hold you in a bit." I bent to give her a good petting down her little back.

"I have Moo Shu pork and Kung Pao chicken. I wasn't sure if you like spicy or not. I figured if you live on a ranch, you must like meat." I felt myself rambling, so I looked up from my task of removing the individual boxes of food from the large bag to get Marin's answer. "Is that right?"

"Yes." Marin nodded as she tried to straighten her hair with her fingers, seemingly embarrassed, finally realizing how dirty it was. "Sorry, I must look a mess."

"You look like you slept hard and needed it." I winked. "Spicy or mild?"

"Spicy. I love Kung Pao. Uncle Leonard used to take me to Chinatown at least twice a month. It was one of our favorite places to eat."

I smiled, pleased I'd chosen something she liked from somewhere with good memories. Everything inside me screamed to take care of her and I didn't really understand why. She seemed so helpless, but I knew it was probably just because the explosion was less than a day behind her, and she was suffering a traumatic loss. Who wouldn't look a little frail after such an ordeal? I found myself wishing it was a few weeks later when her suffering would be easing a bit.

"I love spicy food, but there is way too much for me. You're going to join me, right?" she asked.

"Well," I began, as my stomach rumbled. "I can always just take some with me, if you'd rather not have me hanging around." I felt so stupid, as if I was mumbling like some adolescent kid with a sudden crush. Heat rising beneath my skin made my brow break out in perspiration and I wiped at my forehead with the sleeve of my T-shirt. I wanted to stay, but I also wanted to respect her space.

Gross, I thought. *Smooth move. Sweat all over the food, why don't cha?*

As Marin watched, I dished up the food onto the plates and microwaved them one-by-one, setting hers in front of her first.

"The silverware is in that drawer, there," she said pointing to one near the sink where I was standing. I turned to retrieve a couple of forks. "Unless you want to use the chopsticks?"

"I never got the hang of it, I guess. You?"

"Yes. I can. Uncle Leonard and I would challenge each other. I always won, but I think he let me." I could see talking about her uncle brought back happy memories.

"One fork it is." I smiled, holding it up.

"I have soda, iced tea and beer in the refrigerator. What would you like?" Marin got up slowly, careful not to hurt herself, opened the fridge door and waited.

"Tea's great, thanks."

Within five minutes we were both sitting at the table with plates of steaming hot food and a glass of iced tea in front of us, an awkward silence looming. Though curiosity about the man who'd perished in the fire was killing me, I didn't want to ask too many questions that would make her sad. Instead, I decided to let her lead the conversation as we began our meal.

"You're not from around here, are you?" Marin asked before she put her fork in her mouth and began to eat. Little Gem was curled up into a ball at her feet. "I mean, originally?"

"No, how did you know?"

"Everyone knows everyone in Jackson. Mostly, anyway, and I don't remember you from school."

"I'm probably a few years older than you, but no, I grew up in Tallahassee, Florida. I've lived in a few places," I admitted. "My mom took my sister and me down there after our dad split when we were little. She worked hard, and she was gone a lot. I had to watch out for my little sis, but it wasn't an awful childhood. What about you?" I asked, picking up an eggroll and dipping it in soy sauce before taking a bite.

"I moved here when I was only nine. My parents were killed in a car accident, so I came to live with my uncle."

She'd had a difficult time, and I felt terrible for her. She lost her parents, her uncle and now, this guy; whoever he was.

"That's rough."

"It was at first. He wasn't used to having a kid, but it worked out in the end. I loved him a lot. He always put me first, even when I was being difficult. I had a lot of anger that my parents died, and I took it out on him."

Admiration and love showed in her expression, but also sadness, and I found myself empathetic.

"How was growing up on a ranch with all of these horses? I bet it was amazing. My nephew talks about horses all the time. He just turned eight, so being nine when you moved here, you must have loved it."

"I did. They basically saved me from misery. I started hanging out in the barn after school."

"I can't imagine losing both parents like that. I'm so sorry, Marin."

Marin contemplated me for a few seconds as she swallowed a bite of food. "It's okay. That was a long time ago. The loss that hurts me now is my Uncle Leonard. It was kind of like that story of Heidi. Remember that from when you were a kid?"

I thought about it for a bit. "Can't say I've ever heard that one."

"Well, it's the story of an orphan who comes to live with a gruff grandfather who doesn't know what to do with her. It was kind of like that. My uncle had no kids, though he was older than my dad, so we had to get used to each other, but he was the best person I've ever known. We were so close, and I could count on him for anything. I never thought I'd lose him this soon. He taught me to ride and I helped him in the shop. I never would have gone to college if I'd known he'd die just a couple of years afterward. I really miss him."

"I'm sorry." What else could I say? She was probably blocking out the horrific burning of Carter Stanton.

Marin sighed. She'd eaten a little but put down her chopsticks. "I'm sorry I'm such a drag."

I wanted to reach out and cover her hand with mine, but resisted the urge.

"I didn't come here to be entertained, Marin. I just want you to know that I'll help with the horses and Gem as long as you need me. From the look of how you move, I know your ribs will give you pain for several weeks."

Her face fell. "Oh, I couldn't impose on you that long, Ben. I'm so thankful you were there last night. I was frantic about my little Gemmy. I—"

I shook my head. "It's not imposing when I'm volunteering. That's the rules. Besides," I scooted my chair back from the table and lifted the puppy onto my lap. "Gem and I have this mutual admiration society going on." I held her up against my chest with one hand and the puppy began licking at my slightly scruffy chin. "See? She loves me."

Marin let out a little laugh. "I do. I think I'm sort of jealous."

"Consider it a favor to let me come out here and hang with her and the horses. You're the one doing me a solid."

Marin's head cocked to one side and a small smile graced her mouth. Her expression softened and she might as well have reached into my chest and squeezed my heart. "That's very sweet of you, but…"

"Listen, you'll break my heart if you make me say goodbye to little sweet face, here." I was joking, but I could see her hesitation. She'd just lost her man, and I didn't want her to think anything dishonorable about me. "You don't even have to see me. I'll come over and take care of the horses in the morning and evenings, and if you happen to let Gem outside while I'm here, that would be awesome. I'll keep an eye on that mare. She looks like she'll be having her foal soon. My mother would never forgive me if I didn't help out a damsel in distress, and she's certainly in distress!"

"Her name is Sriracha."

"Now, there's a coincidence! A fiery red horse with a red-hot name, and her own personal fireman to care for her," I teased.

My words were met with a brighter smile. "Siri. She's my favorite. Uncle Leonard had her bred a few months before he died. She's due in a couple of weeks."

"Two weeks, huh? Ugh!" I bemoaned. "She looks so uncomfortable."

"Yes. The sire was the large black, so the foal will be big. The vet says it might come a little earlier."

"Well, you'll need at least that long to heal and feel more yourself. So, what'd ya say? Friends?" I asked. I wondered what on earth could make such beautiful woman so shy. I looked forward to the day when she might trust me and feel more at ease around me. "I'm new to town and I don't know a lot of people. I could use more of them. Would that be okay?"

Marin's smile became more relaxed. "Yes. I could use more friends as well."

"Cool. I can't promise I won't steal your dog, though." I made a little ball of rice with my fingers and added a piece of the pork from the Moo Shu. "Is this okay for her?"

"It's okay, but not too much," Marin returned. "I don't want her sick in the middle of the night."

The puppy greedily ate the meat and rice from my fingers as I held her. "Yes, that would be bad. She's hungry. I'll get her dog food and then I'll get going. Did you get my number from one of the guys last night?"

A slight pink hue graced her cheeks. "I did."

I wanted to ask Marin for her number in return but decided it best to let it go. I'd get her number if she ever decided to call me, but that had to be up to her. "Good. Call me if you need anything."

"I will, but we'll be okay."

I stood there gawking at her in the middle of her kitchen, not wanting to leave, but knowing I should. I placed the puppy on the floor and soon she was munching on the dish of dog food I'd set in Marin's laundry room. I picked up the nearly empty water bowl and went to the kitchen to refill it.

"Listen," I began. I knew I was butting in, but I was not able to stop myself. It had been bugging me since I'd arrived. "The door was open earlier. Now that you're out here alone, it might be a good idea to keep it locked."

Marin looked startled. "Oh. I didn't realize. Of course, I will, thank you."

I nodded and smiled. "Okay. I'll be back around 6 AM. I have an early shift tomorrow, but I'll be quiet, so I won't wake you. You won't even know I'm here." I walked toward the door. "Bye, little bit." I bent to pet the dog's head one last time.

"Thank you, Ben. I'm so grateful for all your help."

Even all rumpled with messy hair she stole my breath away. "No problem. Take care." Her gratitude was genuine, and it made my heart swell a bit.

"You, too."

I sucked in a big breath of the clear night air on my way to the truck, reluctant to leave. This was a small town, but as such, everyone in town knew she was out here by herself after her boyfriend had perished in the fire. She shouldn't be out here alone, especially when she was still incapacitated from her injuries. I felt very uneasy leaving, which was the last thing I should be feeling. Marin was a victim of one of my fires. I'd rescued a lot of others like her in the past, so why was this woman tugging at my emotions?

I got into my truck and glanced at the house as I turned on the engine and made the turn needed to drive back out of the lane. The entire time I kept glancing in the rearview for any sign that she was moving inside the house. The porch light turned off as I neared the white mailbox perched on a wooden post where the lane met with the county road that would take me back to Jackson. The full moon that shone bright overhead illuminated the black letters; LANDRY written on the side.

One thing I was sure about; I needed to speak to the chief about changing my workdays around. Normally, I liked the twenty-four hours on, forty-eight off schedule, but that would be a problem when I needed to be out at the ranch every morning and evening to care for the horses. For the time being, at least, I'd need twelve-hour days. I was pretty sure the chief would accommodate with a four-day-on and then four-day-off schedule, but because the roster was made a month ahead, I'd have to get some of my coworkers to swap for the next couple of weeks. If I wanted them to help me out, it would leave a lot of the guys asking questions that I wouldn't be able to avoid.

Especially, Davis.

everything
HAPPENS FOR
a reason

Chapter 4

Marin

Two days later, I was getting used to Ben's stealthy visits to care for the horses and peeked out the window whenever I heard his truck in the lane. He took care of the horses in the early morning without any contact but knocked on the door to check on me last night, though just took off his cap and stood on the porch for a couple of minutes conversing about the horses, asked how I was doing and then left. He was a complete gentleman.

I felt a huge wave of guilt because I felt lucky to have met Ben and Gina and I wouldn't have done if not for the fire. I felt safer around Ben in the three days I'd known him, than I ever did around Carter. I found myself wanting to be in his company even though it seemed way too soon after Carter's death.

Gina volunteered to help track down Carter's family and called me with some information the first night after Ben had left. She found a woman with the last name who turned out to be Carter's mother. After an awkward and painful phone call, his mom had taken over the funeral arrangements and insisted on returning the body back to Minnesota for burial next to his father. I was surprised we found anyone, given Carter hadn't painted a great picture of his family, but I was grateful that I didn't have to make the arrangements. I doubted lying in the family plot for eternity would be what he would have wanted, but I had no reason, or right, to object.

I didn't really want to travel, yet, if I didn't want to look like a murderous bitch, I'd have to go to Minneapolis for the service and play the role of grieving girlfriend. The thought left me nauseous. I had only two more days until the service, so I was packing up a small bag. I still had the black dress I'd worn to Uncle Leonard's funeral and I carefully folded it into the suitcase.

I wondered if maybe Uncle Leonard was watching over me from Heaven as a guardian angel and had a hand in putting Gina and Ben in my path.

Gem was laying in the center of my bed looking at me with adoring eyes and my heart filled with love. She was so sweet; snuggled into the fluffy comforter, so at home and safe. I couldn't take her with me to Minnesota and I hated to leave her behind. I had no choice but to fly to Minneapolis if I wanted to make it in time for the funeral.

My plan was to ask Ben if he could watch her for the two days I'd be gone, and I planned on doing so when he came over to take care of the horses later. I was unsettled, but I vowed to get my shit together as soon as this funeral was behind me.

I'd made a simple supper of chili and cornbread and hoped Ben would decide to stay. Anxious, I kept looking out the window so I wouldn't miss him drive in. I hadn't had much of an appetite since the accident, but it was the least I could do when I was going to ask him to take care of my puppy again.

I finished packing by placing two pair of shoes, a blazer, a pair of dark jeans and my favorite casual blouse inside the open suitcase. It was navy blue flowy material dotted with an orange and white floral-patterned sheer fabric over a solid navy chemise. I grabbed a pair of old exercise shorts and baggy T-shirt to sleep in and I'd just done into the bathroom down the hall to grab the needed toiletry and make-up items and shoved them into a smaller bag when I heard Ben's old black truck pull up in front of the barn. Hurriedly, I rushed back into my room and tossed the make-up bag on the top of the suitcase.

"Come on, Gem!"

The puppy woke up and started wagging her tail as she walked, with some difficulty, across the comforter toward me. She was still too little, and afraid, to jump from the bed so I picked her up and put her on the floor so she could follow me downstairs. Gemmy still had some difficulty with the stairs, too, but I coaxed her down and made sure she didn't tumble down headfirst. "Come on, girl. You can do it. That's it! You're getting so big!" I encouraged.

At the bottom of the stairs, the pup followed me to the back door in the kitchen where I shoved my feet into my old Vans. They were my work shoes and quite worn out. I was dressed in frayed jean shorts and a purple V-neck T-shirt. My hair was in a loose knot on the top of my head, and I was sure it showed that I didn't give a damn about how I looked. I didn't have one bit of make-up on, and so I hesitated a second to consider my appearance. I'd just lost my boyfriend and I shouldn't be worried how another man would see me. My heart started to beat a little faster as I pondered my predicament.

I sighed and bent to pick up the puppy. "Come on, baby. It is, what it is." I shrugged as I pushed open the screen door and walked out into the balmy evening air. When I placed her on the grass, she wagged her tail excitedly. She barked happily as she took off toward the barn.

The sun was low on the horizon and casting beautiful hues of orange and pink that reflected off of the fluffy cumulous clouds and radiated behind the mountains. I loved the ranch at dusk when the stars just started to peak out into the lavender sky. It was a beautiful sight.

I walked past the dust covered truck, which had both windows down, then headed through the open barn door and into the huge building. The familiar smell of hay and manure had already assaulted my senses before I was fifty feet from the entrance but intensified once inside. The horses were neighing and stomping in their stalls awaiting their evening meal. There was no sign of the man I was looking for and I reasoned he'd be back inside the feed stall or out refilling the water troughs.

"Ben?" My voice echoed through the tall and empty space.

"Oh, hey!" he called just before he emerged with a pitchfork full of alfalfa and put it in the first stall. His face lit up when he saw me, and I thought his blue eyes would melt my insides as they smoldered over me. His broad shoulders and solid biceps made light work of the job. "How are you feeling?"

Ben was dressed in the firehouse uniform of blue pants and T-shirt with the St. Florian Cross on the upper left chest in gold, red and white. His sandy blond hair flopped onto his forehead boyishly and he unconsciously pushed it out of the way with one of his gloved hands. I couldn't help but smile as the action deposited a long strand of the alfalfa into his hair.

"I'm doing a little better." I walked over and patted Siri's nose as she waited for her turn to get fed. She nuzzled my palm and snorted. "Hey, girl." I scratched her forehead and behind her ears.

Ben rested the pitchfork against one of the stalls so that he could bend down and pick up the rambunctious puppy clamoring for his attention. "Little bit! I missed you!" His laughter rang out at the enthusiastic greeting.

My smile widened at his interaction with Gem. She didn't much care for Carter, but she seemed to adore Ben. My uncle always said that animals, especially dogs, could tell a person's character immediately, and this was obvious proof.

Ben's laughter continued to echo through the barn as Gem licked at his stubbled chin. Seeing the two of them together, and how gentle he was with her warmed my heart. The two of them playing made me feel a little bit better about the favor I was about to ask.

"Do you have plans for supper? I made homemade chili and cornbread. I know it's not gourmet, but—"

Ben's eyes met mine and he nodded slowly. "That sounds great. Thank you, though you don't have to put yourself out."

"I'm not. I figure if I can't help out here, the least I can do is feed you." I continued to pat my favorite horse, setting my forehead against hers. I felt slightly embarrassed that I felt such an easy attraction with the handsome fireman who had volunteered to help me, and I didn't want him to see the blush of heat I knew was gracing my cheeks.

"Well, it sounds good. I love homemade cornbread and I haven't had any for at least a year."

Ben gently set Gem on the concrete aisle between the stalls that led to the big equine exercise arena at one end of the building and resumed distributing feed to the rest of the animals. I found myself watching him through hooded eyes, mesmerized at his strength and how his lean, but muscled, body moved. It left me feeling a little flustered.

I had to keep reminding myself that Carter had barely been gone seventy-two hours, and I shouldn't even be interested in another man. But then, Carter was a mean bastard and Ben was kind and gentle, even though he had the goods to crush most other men. My hormones were in overdrive even though my mind resisted my body's reaction. Carter's treatment of me dictated that I guard my heart and my physical well-being. It could be a long while before I could let another man get close to me, though I hoped that Ben would want to be my friend.

I moved away from Siri when she was happily munching away on her dinner and walked to the feed stall where Ben was getting another pitchfork full for the black stallion.

"I wish I could help," I murmured, leaning on the side of the doorway. The pain in my ribcage was still screaming, but I did my best to ignore it.

"You don't need to help," Ben brushed me off. "You just need to heal."

"Well, I feel stupid and indebted to you. I don't like being helpless."

He huffed as he emptied the laden pitchfork into another of the horse's stalls. He looked like he'd been born for this kind of work, though I imagined fighting fires and saving lives was more rewarding.

"Pfft," he said, with a small grin. "Everyone is helpless sometimes, and you certainly have good reason. You need to take care of yourself right now. You've been through a lot." I could sense an unspoken question as his eyes raked over my face. He had such gentle eyes that I found myself drowning in their blue depths.

I decided to watch in silence, gathering my composure until he was almost finished, when I would have him come inside the house to eat. "I'll go inside and set the table. Just come on in when you're ready."

"Are you sure?" He wiped perspiration from his brow with his shoulder. "I'll be really sweaty when I'm done. I probably smell worse than these horses."

"That's okay. I'm used to smelly men—" I stopped myself in horror. I could literally feel my eyes widen. "Um, I mean," my eyes slammed shut and I shook my head abruptly. "Uncle Leonard always used to work with the horses, and the guys always smelled of grease from the shop."

Ben laughed lightly, walking away to get more feed. "I knew what you meant."

"And anyway, if you want to clean up…" It wasn't proper to offer to let him shower since we barely knew each other, so I stopped myself again. "Wash up… there is a sink in the mudroom off the back door. I'll lay out soap and a clean towel."

"Sure, thanks."

Ben had finished with the hay and was now dumping scoops of oats into each of the feed bins. "I'll just be a few minutes more."

I made a move toward the house and looked over my shoulder. "Come on, Gem. Time to eat!" I paused to watch her cock her head and look at me before sitting her little butt down on the concrete floor near the feed stall. "Come on," I said again and patted my thigh. "Gem, come."

She looked at me and whined a little before laying down and putting her head on her front paws.

"Apparently, my dog is a traitor," I said wryly.

"She just wants to be where the action is, I guess." Ben's lips slid into a genuine smile. "I'll bring her in with me when I'm finished."

I nodded and went into the house smiling to myself. It felt good that my puppy trusted Ben and so I felt a little easier in allowing myself to follow my instinct and do so myself. I'd just finishing laying out the fresh towel I'd promised on the sink in the mud room and set the table before lifting the lid on the crock pot to stir the simmering chili when there was a light tap on the screen door.

"Come in, Ben," I called. "The towel and soap are right there. Do you see them?"

"Yep, I got it! Thanks!"

Gem came scurrying around the corner as I took the shredded cheddar cheese and sour cream from the refrigerator and placed them on the table. "So now you expect to eat, do you?" I asked accusingly. She was so sweet, wagging her tail eagerly. I wanted to pick her up for a quick snuggle.

The dog food was kept in the laundry room in a big Rubbermaid tub. I took out a cereal bowl from the cupboard and went to put a small scoop of the kibble inside. The water turned off in the other room signaling Ben was finished washing up, as I put a little dab of chili on top of Gem's food and proceeded to blow on it to cool it off.

I used my finger to mix the chili in with Gem's food and took note it was cool enough for the puppy to enjoy. I set it on the kitchen floor and Gem came over and started eating.

"Looks like she's spoiled." Ben walked into the room still drying his hands, then laid the towel over the back of one of the chairs.

My left shoulder lifted in a shrug as I rinsed the chili off of my fingers. "Well, I guess it's in my nature to spoil those I care about. Besides, a little people food won't hurt her, and she'll have a much happier life." I turned from the sink and indicated the man standing opposite me should take a seat. "Besides, how boring would it be to eat the same thing over and over, day in and day out?"

"The horses don't seem to mind," he said with amusement, pulling out the chair with the draped towel and taking his seat.

"Do you think they don't get the occasional apple, carrot or sugar cube?"

"Ahhh. I should have known." Ben chuckled, shaking his head.

"How about a beer this time?" I asked retrieving two from the refrigerator and setting them on the table before he had time to answer.

"Sure." Ben picked up first one, then the other, and twisted the caps off placing one by my place at the table and took a long swig from the other.

Soon, I had two large pieces of steaming cornbread on a small plate and a bowl of chili sitting in front of him, then went to dish up smaller portions for myself. I took my seat across from him.

"This looks delicious." His words caused a flush of pleasure and I couldn't hold back my smile.

"Dig in," I encouraged. "I wasn't sure if you liked your chili with all of the fixings or not, so help yourself."

"Don't mind if I do." He was smiling from ear to ear as he loaded up his soup with cheese, sour cream, green onions and a big squirt of sriracha. There was butter and honey for the cornbread. "It smells amazing. Thank you for inviting me, Marin."

"It's my pleasure. The least I can do for all you're doing for me. I want you to know I'll try to get back to it as soon as I can."

We both began to eat after I'd added a bit of cheese and sour cream to my bowl as well. The enjoyment on his face as he took his first few bites filled me with satisfaction.

"There is no rush. Truly." His stunning blue eyes studied my face. I could almost see the wheels turning in his mind. He knew the black eye was an old bruise and wasn't from the fire. It was all I could do not to reach up and touch it. "Give yourself time to heal. Are you planning on rebuilding the shop?"

"I probably will, but first I have to find out if I have anyone who would want to work for me. Most of the mechanics left after my uncle passed. They are most likely already employed elsewhere."

Ben's brow dropped in a frown. "That has to be tough, but Jackson is a small town and people are loyal, from what I've seen so far."

"Maybe. What do you mean, so far?"

"I haven't been here even a year yet. I moved from Billings some months back."

"Oh, I thought you were from Tallahassee?"

"Sure, but I moved to Billings for a while, then my best friend, Davis, moved here, and I had no family in Montana, so the rest is history."

Maybe he was in as much need of friends as I was, except he was new to town and I was just a loner.

"Do you like it here in Jackson?"

"I love it. The cost of living is a bit pricey, but the country is beautiful, and I like smaller towns. People are less imposing and it's easier to make friends. I mean, I hope you and I can be friends, if it's not too painful for you, considering how we met." He paused eating and contemplated his words. I could see the conflict on his features. "I'm sorry—"

"No, it's okay. I'd like to be friends." I nodded, trying to blink away the tears suddenly filling my eyes at his compassion.

"I know this is a bad time for you and I just hope I can help out in some way."

He was showing a level of compassion that I didn't receive from a man who professed to love me…. At least, after he didn't have to pretend anymore.

"Thank you, Ben. It means a lot to me. You already are my friend. I'm feeling a bit guilty because I'm grateful for you and Gina; two people I would have never met if Carter hadn't died.

Am I an awful person?" My voice cracked a little as two tears finally tumbled from my eyes and I wiped at them quickly.

"Good God, no," he answered emphatically. "You didn't choose this to happen. Marin. There is nothing you could have done, and it's for best to find something positive to hold on to."

Ben seemed to know what he was talking about; as if he'd suffered a loss in his past. He reached a hand across the table and held it there waiting for my response. I placed my smaller one into it without thinking and his fingers closed around mine. I could feel the callouses of a hard-working man, but his heart was so soft that it made me cry even harder.

Ben's fingers squeezed mine. "I'm so very sorry. I don't know, because I've never lost anyone close to me, but I've seen some horrific things in my line of work. It has to be awful to lose the man you loved like that. I'm an idiot for bringing it up."

I couldn't even remember if Ben was the one to begin talking about the fire or if it were me, but I knew for sure that no love was lost on Carter. Ben's expression looked pained, and I could see how sincerely he empathized. After all, he was the one to pull Carter's charred body out of the rubble of the shop.

I guiltily pulled my hand back, picked up the paper napkin on my lap and dabbed at my eyes and nose. I longed to tell him the entire story about Carter, but now wasn't the right time.

"No, it's okay, but speaking of Carter, I have to fly to Minneapolis for the funeral tomorrow morning. I'll be gone for two days." I could hear the tremble in my own voice. "I hate to ask, but can you watch Gem for me?"

He didn't hesitate. "Of course, I'd love to! I'll take her with me to the station when I'm on shift and if we have a call, I'm sure Shannon or Dave would be happy to take care of her. Shannon is our administrative assistant and Dave's the fleet mechanic, so even if I'm away on a call she wouldn't be alone."

"Okay." I wasn't sure if I'd be ready to face the Stanton family if I was worried about my puppy. "I really appreciate it, Ben. Gina works long shifts so I couldn't ask her. I barely know either one of you, so I feel like crap asking, but since Gem is so taken with you…"

Ben stopped me. "I'm glad to do it. But…. can I ask, what part of the city you're staying in? I've heard there is a pretty high crime rate there. Will you be staying with Carter's family?"

It was an uncomfortable conversation. How would it look to a man like Ben Brady that I'd never met my boyfriend's family, and only spoken to his mother for about a minute on the phone?

"Um, Gina made reservations for me at a hotel near the mortuary. I'm not sure the name of the suburb. I've never actually met any of his family."

"What?" He looked uneasy. "I know it's not my place, but I don't feel good about you going to a strange city alone, especially since you're not staying with them."

His concern was sweet, but I absolutely had to go to the funeral, and I had no one to make the trip with me.

"I have no choice. I have to go. I want to." I hoped I sounded convincing.

"Okay, but will you at least text me to let me know where you are?"

I shook my head. "You're already doing so much. You don't need to worry about me."

"But I will, anyway. As your friend."

I blinked, surprised how that word, friend, hurt. "Okay, I'll text."

My answer seemed to satisfy him. "Good. What time is your flight? Do you have a ride to the airport?"

The Jackson airport was located in Grand Teton National Park and was a good thirty-five, or forty-minute drive from the ranch. "It's very early. Just after 6 AM. I have a long layover in

72

Denver, so the total travel time is about eight hours. I was just going to drive Uncle Leonard's truck and park it at the long-term parking."

"Is there anyone who could go with you?" My heart beat a little faster at the concern that laced his tone. His spoon was hovering over his bowl, and he set it down.

"No. I was always a home-body, and most of my high school friends went off to college and didn't come back. The lure of city life, you know. I wouldn't feel right about asking any of Uncle Leonard's friends."

"I guess," he agreed. "Though, I've tasted the big city and I prefer the slower pace and closer-knit community here. Didn't you want to go to college?"

"I did. I attended Denver University. I have a degree in Business Administration. I'd always planned to come back and help Uncle Leonard run the business and the ranch. He has boarded horses since I came to live here, and I've done the books and payroll since I was sixteen. It almost feels like college was a waste of money and time. Lately, anyway."

"Wow. That's impressive." He smiled again, and it eased the awkward tension of talking over the turn of the conversation. "I bet your uncle was really proud of you."

I nodded, as a melancholy emotion flooded through me. "He was my best friend. I never imagined I'd lose him this soon. After he died, I've been planning on getting some sort of job because the shop wasn't doing as well in the past months."

"Is that what you want to do? Have a new start with something different?"

I hadn't really thought about it, I'd been so overwhelmed. The insurance from my uncle's life insurance was still sitting in the bank, and I'd have property insurance on the shop which should let me rebuild.

"Not really. I kind of want to get the shop up and running again, because it's Uncle Leonard's legacy, but I can do something in addition after it's up and going. I can't work on cars, and the books only take me one day a week. I just wanted to get out of the house and do something. I applied at the diner and a few other places, but after Carter's death, I'm not sure."

"It sounds like you've always wanted to continue your uncle's legacy. Why change it?"

"I don't know, I guess…. It just seems so overwhelming. So much has changed in such a short time."

"I understand. You'll have your hands full with everything involved in rebuilding it and hiring everyone. Plus, it might give you the time you need to feel better. There is plenty of time to work your life away, later. Trust me. And, you'll have help, if you need." His white teeth flashed in a brilliant smile. My heart flip-flopped inside of my chest. He was so down-to-earth and genuine.

Something about this man put me at ease. He settled me. His words and presence seemed to make it seem possible to rebuild the business and resume the life I'd had. I sucked in a deep breath, filling my lungs to capacity, then nodded. "You're right. Thanks for giving me some perspective."

Ben winked. "What are friends for?" He picked up the honey jar and squeezed a large amount of the thick amber liquid onto his buttered cornbread, lifted it and took a huge, exaggerated bite. His eyes got wide in a blissful expression. "Oh my God!" he said with his mouth full. "Are you kidding me with this?"

I couldn't help but smile. "The secret is to use all whole cream, not just milk." I was teeming with pleasure at his response. "It's terribly fattening," I admitted.

He rolled his eyes as he chewed the delicate quick bread. "Who cares? It's the best I've ever had. Come here, Gemmy! You gotta have some of this!"

The puppy went scampering to Ben's side of the table. He broke off a piece of his cornbread and bent to give it to her. Her little pink tongue lapped some extra honey from his finger and thumb after she'd devoured the offering.

"You said I spoiled her, before," Marin pointed out.

"Well, I take my job seriously. You're her mom, and you say she gets spoiled! I'm all in."

My heart leapt painfully inside my chest. I wished I could run over and hug him.

This was the sort of man dreams were made of... I wished with all my being that we'd met under different circumstances and that he really was "all in".

With *me*.

everything
HAPPENS FOR
a reason

Chapter 5

Marin

My stomach was in knots. I was overly anxious about meeting Carter's family. It was going to be painfully awkward. I was a terrible liar, and this would be all an act for me.

Ben helped me put my suitcase into Uncle Leonard's blue truck and took Gem with him when he left the night before, so I could just get up, shower and leave for the near hour drive to the airport. The Jackson airport was relatively small, so I didn't need the three-hour lead time of the busier airports around the country, but it was still before dawn.

I sighed as I drove along Highway 191 in my uncle's old beater Ford truck, I regretted the loss of my little Cooper Mini that Uncle Leonard had gotten me as a graduation gift. It gone up in flames when the building exploded shortly after I'd started running away from the scene. At least, I would have been able to plug in my iPhone and listen to my playlists. Its burned-out shell was still sitting in front of the ruins of the shop. I wasn't allowed to clean things up until the fire commissioner was finished with his investigation, and I wasn't sure if I needed to file that loss as part of the building claim or with my car insurance.

This truck had been Uncle Leonard's favorite ever since I could remember, but this was the first time I'd ever driven it myself. It had to be at least fifteen years older than I was and was so much bigger than I was used to. My Uncle rebuilt the engine once and completely replaced the block when it broke from an accident where he ended up taking a deep dive into a ditch. The thing was vintage, dusty and dented, sort of like my uncle.

As I got closer to the airport the lights from planes taking off and landing dotted the sky. The sun was just starting to give a small golden glow on the eastern horizon. I sucked in my breath, my mind racing with awful memories of the fire, Carter's screams as the lantern fell and the guilt brought on by the relief that I felt that he was out of my life. How could I look his mother in the eye and lie? My stomach ached and got worse as I parked the truck in long-term parking and took the shuttle to the terminal.

As they handed me the boarding pass, the pain in my stomach intensified and my head began to throb as I took my carry-on with me to the gate.

"Just breathe," I told myself. "It's only two days. Two days."

I spent the first leg of the flight in misery; wishing the trip were finished and I was on my way back home instead of away from it. I spent the time wandering around looking at families and couples of all ages, wondering what their lives were like.

After I boarded the second plane bound for my final destination, I tried to close my eyes, but the rotund man in the seat next to me overflowed into my space and snored obnoxiously. I wished I'd brought my laptop so I could have played games or watched a movie during the flight. They were selling headphones to watch the inflight movie when I first got on board and I berated myself for not purchasing some. It was the longest leg, just over three hours, and it felt like forever.

Finally, we were on the descent into Minneapolis and the flight attendant made his last pass for the trash and empty glasses. My heart felt tight with apprehension as I contemplated the next two days. Gina made reservations for me at a Holiday Inn Express near the funeral home and texted me the address so that I could get a cab from the airport. I only had the one bag so I could bypass the lines at the baggage claims.

My heartbeat seemed to get louder in my ears as the plane got closer to the ground. I closed my eyes until the wheels made a slight squeal as they touched down on the runway.

The snoring man next to me finally woke up with a snort and hit me in the chest with his elbow. "Ow," I blurted, moving a hand under my arm to cover the offended part of my anatomy. This entire experience was from hell.

After we taxied in and were finally allowed to disembark from the plane, people poured into the busy terminal. It was a fairly long walk from the gates through the terminal and I thought it would never end. I was wearing jean shorts, a white T-shirt, black zipper hoodie and new Vans, and my hair was pulled back into a ponytail. The picture I made was nothing out of the ordinary, yet I felt as if everyone was staring at the country bumpkin from Wyoming. Each step seemed as if it were one closer to the gallows. I knew it was ridiculous to feel that way, yet I couldn't make it go away.

I watched the signs to the main terminal and when I passed the security checkpoint there were a few people with signs waiting for passengers coming up from the various flights. I inhaled deeply and found the escalator down to street level.

As I started to walk toward it, I heard a man say my name. My heart dropped into my stomach and I stopped then turned toward the voice.

A man, maybe a few years older than Carter stood before me. He was wearing slouched jeans and a dirty wife beater, his dark hair was slicked back with some sort of hair grease, and his face was covered with a beard and mustache. His dark eyes were the only part of him that seemed a little familiar and hinted at his relationship to Carter. Maybe this was a relation, but looking at him, I was scared shitless.

"Ye—yes?" I said, self-consciously putting a hand to the base of my throat.

"I'm Carter's older brother, Apollo. I'm here to get you."

I swallowed as fear ran through me. I had no reason to fear this man, except his appearance was menacing and his name seemed extreme. I tried hard to keep a shocked expression off of my face.

"Thank you, but I have a reservation at a hotel…"

He took my bag from my hands and shook his head. "Nope. Ma said you should stay at our house."

"But…" I stood there watching him walk off with my bag.

"Come on." He paused impatiently and glared at me before resuming his stride.

I started to walk in his direction, though not quickly enough to catch up, unsure that I was doing the right thing. I'd hoped I'd just stay in the hotel, show up for the funeral, and then be on my way back to Wyoming to the entire unpleasant experience behind me. "Um…"

Carter's brother stopped and scowled at me again, more annoyed. "Look, woman, I ain't gonna bite you."

"I know, I'm just in shock, I guess." What I was, was frightened.

"We all are. We didn't hear from that little bitch for years and now, we're mopping up another of his messes. Fuck me," he huffed.

Apparently, there was no love lost between them. I began walking again, and when I reached him, Apollo fell into step with me. We didn't speak until we reached the curb outside the terminal. There was a souped-up vintage Oldsmobile waiting, though I didn't know the year, but I guessed the seventies or early eighties. It was shiny black with chrome trim.

He threw my bag in the back seat after he'd walked around. "What are you waitin' on, Christmas? Get in," he commanded.

I scrambled to open the door and slid inside. The inside of the car was not kept as well as the outside. The leather bench seat stretched across the entire car and was torn in several places and the ripped edges scraped against the sensitive skin on the back of my thighs. The old-time ashtray was pulled out and was overflowing with cigarette butts and ashes that spilled onto the floor.

I couldn't help coughing from the offensive stench and lingering smoke. Apollo reached through the open window, grabbed the ticket that had been left on his front window for parking in a no-parking zone, crumpled it up, and then threw it over his shoulder into the back seat.

"Fuckers," he muttered.

I wondered what other crimes Apollo committed, sure that he had. I sat like a stone on the passenger side of the vehicle, afraid to even speak, but felt I needed to offer my condolences. "I'm so sorry about your brother."

The engine roared to life and the car jerked away from the curb into the traffic in front of the terminal. Someone honked and Carter's brother lifted an arm out of the open window to flip whoever it was the bird.

"Why? Did you kill him?" he asked with a laugh, grabbing a pack of Camels from the dash and hitting it on the smooth steering wheel to knock one forward until he could get his lips around it.

I shook my head in fear. "No."

"Okay, then, don't be sorry."

I was shocked at his callousness. Apollo pushed in the cigarette lighter until the element inside glowed red and it popped out to signal it was hot. He pulled it out and put it to the end of the cigarette already hanging from between his lips and sucked until it was lit.

I tried not to cough and held it in, but my eyes began to burn despite his window being rolled down. There was nothing electrical in this car, from the manual windows to the analog radio. My eyes began to water when he blew out smoke from his lungs and the cough I'd been holding in burst from my chest. I coughed hard until tears ran down my cheeks.

"Ah, a little princess, eh?"

Apollo flipped the cigarette out of the car onto the street.

"I'm sorry, I'm allergic to smoke." I tried to explain. "I didn't mean to offend you."

My phone pinged in my purse. I hadn't texted Gina or Ben, and there was no one else to check on me, so it had to be one of them.

"Not a problem, though my old lady smokes like a chimney, so you might want to watch what you say in front of her."

"Maybe it would be best if I stay at the hotel? It's really no problem."

"I got my orders. I'm to deliver you to the house, then you can talk to my ma and figure it out."

By now, Apollo had turned off of the interstate and into the streets of an older neighborhood. "What is the neighborhood called?"

"My brother didn't tell you shit about us, did he?"

"I'm sorry, he never mentioned his family much, no."

"Stop apologizing for shit you can't control," he barked. It was obvious that he was angry at Carter. "He disappeared years ago. Fucker thought he was better than the rest of us, and he broke my ma's heart."

I wondered what Carter's background was. Was his family involved in some sort of serious criminal activity that made him leave? Of course, there was no way to know. Apollo's appearance was rough, but that might not be anything to judge by. Maybe his family was poor, or maybe there were into something illegal, but there had to be a reason that Carter left and didn't speak of them.

The further we got away from the highway, the poorer and more dilapidated the houses became. There were people on the street, loitering by an old-fashioned drug store. Clearly, this was an older part of town, the houses were probably built in the thirties or forties. Some of them were kept up well, but most were plagued by rotting siding, damaged roofs and crumbling sidewalks. Many of the yards were filled with trash and old, incapacitated automobiles.

My unease grew. I pulled out my phone and saw the text was from Ben. I quickly scrolled to revisit Gina's text. "The hotel is the Holiday Inn Express downtown. My friend booked it for me. She said it was the closet to the funeral home."

"Well, that's pretty ritzy, and definitely not the closest."

Pretty ritzy? The price was reasonable, and I'd stayed at the chain of hotels and motels before, so I knew it was nice, but in no way ritzy. I called it up on Google maps.

"It says here it's three miles away. If it's too much trouble, I can get a cab in the morning."

I prayed to God that he'd agree, but the dread inside me said that was asking for too much. I shouldn't have come. "Look, princess, I told ya. If my ma says you can go, you can go. She has some questions for ya about how my little brother died and you're gonna answer 'em."

My heart immediately fell into my stomach. The woman I'd spoken to on the phone had been abrupt with a raspy voice, but I was starting to become terrified of the confrontation.

"Okay, I can. I just thought that it might be awkward having a stranger around during this difficult time."

"Why ain't you crying or something? Shouldn't you be bawling your eyes out? After all you were Carter's woman, right?"

He pulled up in front of an older house with greyish siding that had seen better days. I guessed it had been white at one time. It was a small, two-story house with three concrete stairs leading up to a porch lined with metal floral motif columns and railings. It was rusted in many places, the rust stains trailing down the front of the porch to the dirt patch that served as a lawn. There were many motorcycles and old cars parked in front and up and down the narrow street.

"I have been, but I guess I'm all cried out," I answered carefully. "I'm going to miss your brother, very much."

He shoved the transmission into park and leaned toward me, so close I could smell rancid liquor and smoke on his breath. "Why don't I believe you?" His teeth were crooked and stained yellow from years of smoking.

"I don't know." Obviously, I wouldn't miss him. Guilt was the only emotion I felt in regard to Carter.

Apollo laughed. "Listen, I say good riddance to that little prick, so you won't hurt my feelings, either way. My ma; that's another story."

He climbed out of the car and slammed the door hard. The doors were heavy and needed grease, so I struggled to push mine open as the man grabbed my small roller bag from the backseat. I was out of the car and he pushed it shut with a loud bang.

There were weeds growing unchecked around the chain-link fence; the gate directly on the broken sidewalk leading up to the house. "Is this where you and Carter grew up?" I asked.

"Home sweet home," Apollo answered with disgust. He held the gate open and ushered me in. This could explain why Carter never wanted to come back, but surely, he loved his family, even if the place where they lived was poor and unkempt.

When we went inside it was full of people, talking, eating and drinking. The room was foggy with smoke which caused me to instantly start coughing. I put a hand up and covered my mouth with the back of my wrist.

Some children were held in the arms of adults and others were running around screaming, playing games, or fighting. It was the definition of chaos. Other than the children who didn't notice me, silence settled upon the room as many pairs of eyes turned in my direction.

"Bring her here," the gruff voice I recognized from the brief phone conversation commanded from the back of the room.

Apollo nodded in her direction, and ushered me forward, dropping my bag at the door.

"Ma, Princess. Princess, Ma."

The woman didn't look well. Her grey hair was uncombed, and her skin was a sallow yellow shade, her eyes bloodshot and watery. She was super skinny, and her clothes were rumpled, mismatched and large for her.

"Hello, Mrs. Stanton. I'm so sorry about your…Carter. My name is Marin," I corrected Apollo's sarcastic introduction.

The dark eyes that the woman shared with Carter and Apollo, studied me. The other people crammed into the room were a mixture of ages, young and old, but they all stared at me expectantly. The inside of the house was just as junky as the outside and I felt sorry for Carter for the first time, ever. "I'm so sorry for your loss," I said, to everyone in the room.

"You want something to eat?" Mrs. Stanton asked. My upbringing demanded I address her in a formal way until such a time she instructed otherwise. I didn't think that would happen; ever.

"No, thank you; I'm okay." The trip was long, and I hadn't had anything other than nuts on the plane, but I had no appetite. I yearned for a hot bath and the bed at the hotel.

"Come over here. Sit beside me." The old woman's eyes followed me as I moved closer, and the dark-haired young woman sitting next to her moved to let me take her chair. She seemed much older than I'd imagined that she'd be. He was only twenty-eight, but this woman seemed to be close to seventy. Maybe it was the effects of a very hard life that had aged her beyond her years. Her teeth were black, some of them missing. Her hair looked like it hadn't been washed in quite some time.

I swallowed hard at the lump of distaste forming in my throat. "Thank you," I said in acknowledgement, moving cautiously through the room. She only nodded, wide-eyed.

As I sat down next to Carter's mother; a sour, sweaty smell assaulted my nostrils. I felt sorry for the woman, and for the entire family. The house was a mess, and it reeked.

"Tell me how my son died."

I closed my eyes and my face fell. This was the last thing I wanted to recount. She reached for my hand and I let her take it. I could see the pain behind her watery eyes, even as she exuded a hardened demeanor.

"It was an accident at my Uncle's mechanic shop where he was working. A lantern was accidentally knocked over and the grease and oil caught on fire."

"Why was he using a lantern? Are things so backwoods out there that you have no lights?"

"We do, but there was a thunderstorm. The electricity was out."

"Did you see it happen?"

My heart felt like it would explode. Surely, the woman must feel my pulse raging in the hand she held. Tears filled my eyes at the memory, I wanted to spare her that vision. "I did. I'm so sorry."

"The mortician wouldn't let me see my son's body. Said he was fried to a crisp." The woman didn't seem as emotional as me.

I cleared my throat in an attempt to void the emotion. "I didn't see him after. I'm so sorry."

Her eyes narrowed menacingly. "How did you manage to get out without a scratch?"

I wanted to tell her I wasn't unscathed, but the fading bruises on my face and my cracked ribs weren't from the fire. Only the bandaged knees. "I was hurt, but I managed to get out. I was closer to the door than Carter was. The bays were all closed because he was working after hours."

"You didn't try to save him?" Her hand squeezed mine painfully, and I pulled it back with a jerk.

I could feel my skin start to burn on my face and neck. I was sure I was turning bright red. I shook my head. "Unfortunately, his clothes caught on fire right away. I ran to get help, but my car was close to the flame. I had to run—" Like I wanted to run, right now. Tears started in my eyes, more because I feared for my safety than any sadness over Carter. He'd been a monster to me those last months.

"What was the—?"

"Ma, leave her alone," Apollo stated from across the room. "What's done is done."

The woman's head snapped around in the direction of his voice, then a few seconds later she turned her attention back to me.

"It was your uncle's shop, eh?" she wanted to know.

"Yes, ma'am."

"Well," Her disposition suddenly shifted, and she pushed out of the old, upholstered chair she'd been sitting in. It was an old style and appeared to be a faded cream and red floral pattern, but now was yellowed and filthy. "I need a new dress for tomorrow as do Apollo's girlfriend and my daughters. My son needs a new suit, too, so we're going to the mall, and you're buying."

I gasped, completely taken by surprise. "Mrs. Stanton, I'm not rich. I don't have a lot of money."

"Bullshit. You have that business, don't cha?"

"It hasn't been doing well the past few months since my uncle passed," I replied honestly.

"Well, don't tell me there isn't insurance money from the fire, and you know… maybe we oughta get it." Her eyes narrowed menacingly. "My son died!"

Didn't her son mean anything to her? Was his death and my presence here, only about getting a pay day?

"I-I don't have any of the insurance money yet," I stammered. "The fire department is still investigating the cause of the fire, but I'm sure if there is a payout, there could be something for Carter. I can call them on Monday to ask, but I'm sure nothing will be paid until the investigation is completed. I don't have any money right now." I could literally feal the waver in my voice.

This was new for me, too, but my business degree and experience with it in the past dictated that insurance policies typically had some sort of liability coverage on accident victims. The issue would be that the blaze was Carter's fault. He was the one drinking; it was his asinine decision to keep working by lantern in a greasy shop.

"My daughter Googled you, and the fire my son died in. You have all that land."

I felt sick that I was being subjected to this interrogation, surrounded by what seemed to me to be a bunch of delinquents and criminals. "It's not liquid."

"What the hell is that supposed to mean?" The woman scowled and sucked on her cigarette. Surely her voice and leathery skin had been destroyed from years of smoking.

"Having land is not the same as having cash," I tried to explain without giving too much away. Did she or her daughter know how to look up the land value from the Teton County Assessor? I'd have to borrow against the land, wait for the insurance settlement, or sell it in order to get money for her now, which will still take weeks or months.

She seemed to consider this for a minute. "I lost my son! I deserve to be paid!"

I felt they could kill me, and I was positive that there was someone in this room that would be capable of doing just that. I sucked in my breath. I had to get the hell out of here and fast. All thoughts of attending the funeral vanished. I just had to get home.

"I agree, but I beg for your patience. I can't get anything significant right away." I glanced at Apollo who was leaning up against the wall with his beefy, tattooed arms crossed over his chest, a stoic expression plastered on his face.

"Give Sierra your credit card," Carter's mother demanded. I didn't know what to call her, even in my mind. My mouth fell open in astonishment. This was bad. I was in serious trouble.

"Hey, Ma," Apollo said, moving closer. He put his head down and whispered something in her ear. When he moved away, he kept speaking. "Know what I mean? Stolen plastic will only draw attention to the family. We need to be patient. The insurance payout is where the big money is. She wasn't married to Carter, so it will come to you. Chill out for now."

"Right. I can make sure the investigation goes as planned and then follow-up with my insurance company." I could hear the tremor in my voice and tried to quell it.

"How much do you think it will be?" Apollo demanded.

My sheltered life in Wyoming had not prepared me to deal with any of this, but I had to keep my wits about me, or I could end up dead, or worse. "A hundred thousand, maybe. I'm not sure. It depends on the policy, but I'll look into it."

My response seemed to placate her, and the old woman nodded. "Right," she agreed. "But I still need a new dress for Carter's service, and you're gonna buy it for me."

I nodded, scared out of my wits. "Okay, I can probably afford a few dresses for you and Sierra and, I'm sorry, I don't know Apollo's girlfriend's name." I was careful not to say something to set him or his mother off.

"Greta," a voluptuous woman, sitting on the arm of the shabby sofa, spoke up.

"Greta," I nodded. "I'd love to get to know all of you better and it will be fun to all go shopping together. I'd like a new outfit, too," I lied. A public place was the safest place to be and maybe I could find a police officer or a mall security guard who could help me.

"What about Apollo's suit? And my grandkids? They need something cute for their uncle's service."

"What about us?" one of the other men asked.

"You, too," the old lady agreed.

I tried to remember how much open credit I had on my one credit card, but hopefully I wouldn't need it. "I think I can do that." Another lie, but anything to get out of this house. "Then later, maybe the kids can come and swim at the hotel pool." I tried to smile, but the attempt was pathetic. "Sound good?" I could almost feel the lie screaming from my face. I knew I had to look terrified.

"Come on, girls. You and the kids ride with the other guys and me and Carter's girl will go with Apollo". The women and two of the men rose to do as the old woman requested, but as they gathered the kids and left the house, many nasty looks were cast in my direction. This was a nightmare.

When Mrs. Stanton came out of her bedroom, she had put on a pair of sandals on her bare feet, though little else had changed. She was drunk and probably high.

"Come on," she grumbled, moving slowly with a slight limp on her right leg. I stood to follow her, glancing at my bag sitting by the door. When I got close to it, I bent to pick it up, when Apollo grabbed my arm. "Don't do anything stupid," Apollo stated. "We'll be watching your every move. You better not run or call the cops."

I met his eyes steadily. My bravado was all an act, but I was scared for my life. "How is this going to work with the insurance money if you keep threatening me? I agree your family deserves some compensation, but stealing my credit card, or hurting me will only put your family under suspicion. If something happens to me, do you think they won't look here first? If I don't make it home in two days as planned, my friends will call the police. How does that help you get the insurance? I just wanted to get my bag. I thought we were going to take the kids swimming after shopping."

He glared at me warily and grabbed my arm painfully as I passed. "We have a way of getting what we want, princess," he threatened. "See all these dudes?" He pointed around the room to the men who were staying behind. "They and my bro-in-laws are my crew. They got my back. Understand?"

"Yes. I'm trying to buy your mom a dress and help you get the money you're after."

Everything inside me was quaking. Once they had the insurance money what would they want then? Would they keep threatening me until I sold the ranch and handed over the proceeds? I was more scared and vulnerable than I'd ever been in my life... My heart cried for my Uncle Leonard. My heart cried for... Ben.

Chapter 6

Marin

The Mall of America was huge.

I'd never seen anything like it in my life. It was crawling with people, especially in the center courtyard where there was a full-blown amusement park in the center atrium.

"Ma, the kids want to play on the rides." The woman who had been pointed out as Sierra was speaking.

I knew I looked out of place among Carter's family. The women all wore tight clothes full of spandex and had unusually long, fake fingernails. They had the figures to carry it off, and clearly, this was the look their men liked judging by the way they were hovering over them and touching them in what seemed very inappropriate for a public place.

My eyes were scanning the mall for the uniform of someone in authority.

"Sure, baby," her mother answered her daughter than looked at me. "Got any cash for my grandkids?"

Given the events of the day I shouldn't have been shocked by the woman's request. "Sure," I pulled out my wallet and handed over the only cash I had. A one-hundred-dollar bill, which was promptly conveyed from her to one of the men.

"Come on, kids," one of them mumbled and then the group of them turned away to disappear into the crowd in the direction of the ticket booth.

The kids were all rambunctious until the other man barked at them, loud enough to carry through the throng. "Quiet! If you don't behave, you'll get nothing but my hand on your ass!"

Nice way to speak to children, I thought. I shouldn't be surprised, given what I'd already witnessed. They were all out of control, adults included.

"Apollo, you come with us. We don't want our princess getting any ideas."

I decided if Carter's mother didn't trust me, I'd never get the hell away from her, or Apollo, who was the real threat. "Look, Mrs. Stanton, can we please make the best of this? I lost Carter, too. Can't we just shop and try to respect each other? You don't need anyone to watch me every second."

She looked a little taken aback that I would challenge her, but I needed them to relax so I could get away and was trying to be as convincing as I could be. The look on her weathered face said she was leery, but I had to get her to relax.

"What is your favorite store?" I asked with a lift of my eyebrows. I saw the big box stores in the background. There was a Macy's and Nordstrom's, plus an Express and Marshalls. I prayed they'd pick something less expensive.

"Sears," she answered. "They usually got stuff I like."

"Ma," Sierra moaned. "I wanna go to Express!"

I nodded. "Why don't you and Greta go look there and when we have your mom taken care of, I can meet you there in time to pay? I'd like to look there, too." I smiled in the hope she was buying my act.

"Yeah, Ma," Greta chimed in. "I can't stand that old lady store."

"Great!" Sierra said, beginning to tug her sister by the arm away from us. "Greta, come on!"

"I guess that's the plan, Ma," Apollo said.

We found Sears on the directory and located it on the Northeast side of the food court, and I knew this was my chance. I quickly shoved my phone into the back pocket of my shorts and turned to Apollo. "I'd like to use the bathroom, please. I didn't get a chance to go at the airport. I can meet you in Sears when I'm finished."

Luckily the Sears' ladies' department was on that level and Carter's mother had walked just inside and was already looking through one of the racks.

"Nope, ain't gonna happen." He shook his head.

"Should I just pee my pants, then?" I gave him my best impression of being pissed off. I couldn't let him know I was terrified.

I was starting to think of him as a modern gangster. He was a bully and undoubtedly a violent criminal. He wore gold chains and big chunky rings, while the family lived in squalor and, from the looks of it, didn't have a lot of money. His girlfriend and sister dressed sort of sleazy, both of their bodies were poured into atrocious, overly tight clothes, their flesh spilling out of their low-cut shirts and above their waistbands of their micro-shorts.

"I'll come with you." He turned to his mother. "Ma, I'm going with her to the john." His words got louder so his mother inside the store could hear.

"Son," the woman said, as she rummaged through some dresses on a rack. "Get her purse and give it here."

95

He nodded. "Good idea." He held out his hand and motioned for me to hand it over. Reluctantly, I placed the small black leather handbag in his palm and watched in horror as he handed it to his mother.

"Even Carter let me pee by myself," I protested. Apollo grabbed my arm painfully and turned me away from his mother. I yanked my arm away then stormed off in the direction he'd indicated.

My suitcase was still in Apollo's car so it, and its contents, would have to be a loss if I had the opportunity to run away. I had to think this through, though. If I ran or called the police, would Carter's family show up at the ranch or burn it down in my sleep a week from now? These people were sinister, and it would be in my best interest to try to get an insurance payout and be rid of them. My blood ran cold, I had a sick feeling inside, and my heart was thumping uncomfortably hard inside my chest. What was I going to do? My ribs were still painful from Carter's last round of abuse, and it wasn't likely I'd be able to outrun Apollo.

"I'll be here, Princess! Don't keep me waiting too long." Apollo called after me as I disappeared into the bathroom. There was no door, but rather a short hallway, that led into the facilities that would ensure privacy of those inside, yet still allow for an easy flow of patrons. I longed for a door. "There ain't no back door to the john, so don't get any big ideas."

"Jesus, please help me," I said softly under my breath, grateful I'd had the foresight to keep my phone out of my purse and in the back pocket of my shorts. I went into a stall and locked the door. In seconds I had my phone out and was holding it in my shaking hands. There was a text from Gina asking if I'd arrived safely, and one from Ben showing up on the screen in the moment.

I quickly opened his message. There was a video clip that I could tell from the still was of Gem, but I didn't have time to watch it. I felt like hell reaching out to him again, but who else did I have? He was too far away to help me himself, but would this band of goons show up in Jackson? If I got them arrested, it might only cause them to retaliate harder. I sat down on the toilet and pondered my next move, knowing I had little time to decide. I considered that money might get them to leave me alone, but my uncle's voice in my head convinced me otherwise. *"You can't reason with a bully."*

I needed advice, and I hoped Ben would be off of his shift by now. Sucking in a deep breath, I began to type out a text.

Ben, I'm in trouble. Carter's family is like the mafia and I can't get away from them. His brother is waiting for me outside the bathroom in the food court of the Mall of America. I thought about calling the police, but I'm afraid if I don't play along, they'll show up in

Wyoming and do something horrible to me, the ranch, or the horses.

Maybe it's best to go to the funeral as planned and try to leave tomorrow? I'm sorry to bother you with this, but I really don't have anyone else I trust.

Within seconds my phone rang, and my nervous hands fumbled to answer. I almost dropped the phone but thankfully caught it just before it hit the hard tile floor.

"Ben!"

"You need to call the police, right now, Marin!" he barked.

"Carter's family is terrifying! They took my purse and my cash!" I knew the pitch in my voice was elevated and it was starting to break as I whispered frantically into the phone. "Even if the police get me out of here, there are more who could come after me. The police can't protect me all night."

"I know you're scared, but you need to call the police. When they arrive ask them if you can stay at the station, or if they will escort you to a hotel; one with the doors to the rooms inside the building. I'll come get you."

"Can they just take me to the airport? I can catch the first flight back." As scared as I was, my heart seized a little at how he was so willing to drive twelve hundred miles to help me. Was this guy for real?

"How, without your purse or credit cards?" Ben asked shortly; anger lacing his voice.

"That's true, but it will be the same story for the hotel. I have no money."

"Don't argue. I'll leave now. Call me from the hotel lobby —"

My mouth fell open in shock at Ben's willingness to do so much for me. "But it's so far…"

"Marin, stop fucking around and call the police!" He commanded. "Please." His voice changed to more coaxing and comforting. "When you're safe, call me back, and we'll figure out the hotel."

Blood and adrenaline were rushing like thunder through my veins; the sound thundering in my ears. "Okay."

"Call them, right when you hang up. I mean it!" He ended the call without waiting for a reply, and instantly I dialed 9-1-1.

"9-1-1. What is your emergency?"

"Someone is holding me against my will."

"Are you saying you've been kidnapped?"

"Yes. I mean, I guess. I'm in town for a funeral and the family of the deceased took me to Mall of America to buy them new clothes. They won't let me leave and I'm frightened. They've stolen my purse."

"How many suspects are there?"

"Three men, three women, and five kids."

"Kids?"

It sounded ludicrous, even to my own ears.

"Yes. They split up, but the plan was to make me buy them all a new outfit for the funeral. Two of the men took the kids to the rides, two women went shopping on their own, and one woman and one man remained with me… until I went to the bathroom."

"Ma'am are you sure this is an emergency?"

"Yes! Please! He's waiting outside. I can't get away."

"Calm down, Ma'am. Who is the deceased?"

"My boyfriend, Carter Stanton. He died in a fire."

"Who is detaining you?"

"His brother, Apollo. He followed me to the bathroom and is waiting outside! His name is Apollo, I think his last name is Stanton, too. Maybe not, I'm not sure. The others are close by, too. The mother has my purse with her."

"Can you give me a description of the man and woman?"

As quickly as I could, I described Apollo and his mother, trying to remember details about their clothing, tattoos and hair.

"Stay where you are until the officers arrive. Do you know what side of the food court you're on?"

"By Sears. That's where Carter's mother is shopping. I think they said it was the Northeast side."

"What's your name, ma'am?"

"Marin Landry. I'm from Jackson, Wyoming."

"The officers are on their way. Please stay on the line with me."

"Thank you."

"A female officer will come into the bathroom to get you."

"Will it take long? I've been in here too long. Someone might come in to get me."

"Are you locked inside a stall?"

"Yes."

"Just hold on. There are officers on the property."

As I sat there shaking on the toilet, the seconds felt like minutes, but was I startled when I heard Apollo bellow my name.

"Marin! Do I have to come in there? What's taking so fucking long! You better not be playing me!" Apollo's voice echoed off of the tiled walls. Clearly, he was either hovering in the doorway or had already come into the restroom.

I didn't answer, and in under thirty seconds I could hear the deep voice of a police officer demanding he move away from the door and put his hands behind his back.

"Oh, thank God," I said, pressing a hand to my chest. Relieved tears rushed to my eyes and rolled down my cheeks.

"Marin?" A strong female voice rang out. "I'm Officer Mills with the MPD. You can come out now, ma'am. You're safe."

I sniffed and used the back of my hand to wipe at my tears. "Thank you," I said, unlocking the door to the stall I had been hiding in. The door opened slowly, and I peeked outside into the main part of the bathroom. A woman, maybe ten years older than me, wearing a blue police uniform was standing there.

Relief flooded through me, manifesting as a torrent of tears. I should never have come. I should have stayed safe in Jackson on my ranch.

The police officer put her arm around me. "Can you come outside so we can take your statement? It will be okay, now. You're safe."

"Do I have to see him?" I asked, hesitating to leave the room.

"We ran his name and pulled his rap sheet. We have mug shots, so we knew exactly who we were looking for, but we need an ID. Also, on the others."

A new wave of terror flooded through me at the thought of identifying them. Surely, they'd come after me.

In the food court, a crowd was starting to gather around another policeman who had Apollo up against a wall and was putting handcuffs on him.

"The rest of you, move along. There's nothing for you to see." The command was delivered in a clam, but direct voice. "Go about your business."

He read Apollo his Miranda rights, then pulled him around and off of the wall to start walking him out of the area.

Sheer hatred radiated from Apollo's eyes. I was surprised he wasn't resisting arrest. His expression looked so evil; his eyes locked on my face. "Come on, honey. Is this really necessary?" Apollo crooned, then pursed his lips in a mock kiss. "What did she tell you? Officers, this is just a family issue." His tone was level and steady. "We're all on edge. My little brother just got killed. Her boyfriend. She agreed to come with us."

"Is that true?" The woman officer said unnecessarily.

"He his brother did die, and I'm here for the funerals. Yes, technically, I came with them, but I felt threatened. There were so many of them." I felt like it was all getting turned around on me and fear clutched at my insides. I found it difficult to breathe.

"Take him downtown," she instructed.

"Let's go," her partner said, beginning to move Apollo out of the area, and then toward the outer doors that would lead to a parking lot or garage. "I didn't find any credit cards or the purse."

"His mother has my purse, and her daughters have a hundred-dollar bill. It was all the cash I had with me."

"I'll have someone pick up the woman. We'll take your statement at the precinct."

* * *

Later that night, I was sitting alone in a hotel room unsure what to do with myself. It wasn't the Holiday Inn that Gina reserved because I'd told Apollo which one that was.

I'd texted Ben to let him know he shouldn't drive all this way, explaining that the officers were able to recover my purse, so I had my credit card. I'd be able to take a cab to the airport and catch a flight home tomorrow. Except, he didn't answer, so I wasn't sure what to do.

It was strange being rescued from several strangers by a man I hardly knew. I mean, Ben was almost a stranger, at least he should feel like one, but somehow, he didn't. I'd only known him four days, but instinctively, I trusted him completely. Even though it didn't make sense for him to drive this far, I was happy about it. Ten minutes later, I typed in the name and address of the hotel and hit *send*. I already knew it wouldn't work to argue with him.

I was thankful to have my purse back. The police found Carter's mother in the checkout line at Sears and got to her before she was able to charge her purchase. They kept me separate from Carter's brother and mother, taking us to the police station in different squad cars.

My suitcase was still in Carter's car and I considered it a loss.

I had been taken to the police station to give my accounting of what happened. Apparently, it was their word against mine. The women, children and the other man were released because they came in a separate vehicle and weren't directly involved, and they all backed up Apollo's story. I felt sick at the thought. These people were professional thugs, and they knew how to work the system.

Ben was still ten hours away and when he arrived, he'd be exhausted. Still, I could not believe that a man I barely knew had become so involved in my life so quickly. He was easily the most amazing man I'd ever met.

I used a delivery app to deliver my dinner to the hotel, but still had to go down to the desk to get it. I had no cash to tip and so didn't feel right about asking one of the desk personnel to bring it up to the room.

I ate some of the salad and half of the cold roast beef sandwich I'd ordered and put the rest in the small refrigerator under the television. The thought of putting my dirty clothes back on was repulsive, yet I longed for a bath. I was tired, and just wanted to relax.

The deadbolt on the door securely in place, I took my phone into the bathroom and ran a bath. I was thankful that this hotel room didn't have one of those godawful bathtubs without a sloping backrest. I picked up one of the small shampoo bottles and sighed, longing for the full-size bottles of toiletries in my suitcase.

"Oh, well," I murmured. "This will have to do." My uncle would chastise me for complaining. "At least I have a tub and hot water."

After adjusting the water temperature, I poured a small vial of body wash under the running water, rinsing it out to get all of the soap out and under the running water. I decided to save the shampoo and conditioner for the morning. I used the Relax Melodies app to conjure a rushing wave sound, mixed with a crackling fire then shed my clothes and underwear. The light from the phone would be enough to see what I was doing, so I switched off the light before climbing into the deliciously hot water and sliding down until it covered me up to my shoulders.

Once I shut off the water, I was able to concentrate on the soothing sounds coming from the phone. Slowly the anxiety that had built up during the day was starting to ebb. Ben was coming to get me, and I had a deadbolt and one of those flippy locks securing the room. I might still be afraid, but the hotel, though more expensive than I had planned on for this trip, had lobby security and no other way to get up to the rooms.

I inhaled and closed my eyes enjoying the warmth that was slowly seeping into my muscles. My eyes started to droop, and the bliss of the plateau between drowsiness and deep sleep settled over me.

As I lay there, my head lolled to one side suddenly, quickly jerking me awake. I wasn't sure how long I'd slept in the bathtub, but the water was tepid and the skin on my fingers and toes was wrinkled.

"Oh," I said, blinking, and began to push from the tub, carefully wrapping one of the fluffy white towels around me as the low light from the phone illuminated the room in a soft glow. I was so tired and ended up under the covers in one of the two double beds closest to the bathroom, still wrapped in the damp towel, barely aware of how I got there. I couldn't have opened my eyes if my life depended on it, and the damp heat permeating around me made my body go limp and my muscles relax. I realized I didn't know what time it was, but surely it would be several hours yet until Ben arrived. "Uhhh," I sighed. I'd left my phone on the counter in the bathroom but didn't have the desire or ability to get out of my warm cocoon to retrieve it.

I'll wake up in plenty of time, I thought then slipped into a deep, exhausted sleep.

* * *

I was startled awake by the hotel phone ringing shrilly beside the bed. I sat up, then scrambled across the bed toward the phone with an outstretched hand. What if it was Apollo? I tried to fortify my thinking, but I was still rattled from the events of the day before, and still afraid.

The thought was insane. There were thousands of hotels in Minneapolis and there was no way he'd be able to find me. I lifted the receiver with one hand, rubbing the sleep out of my eyes with the other. I inhaled my first deep breath of the day.

"Hello?"

"Miss Landry? This is Lisa from reception," an unfamiliar female voice asked. "I'm sorry to disturb you ma'am, but you have a visitor. I can't let him up to the room without your approval."

The curtains were securely drawn, and I had no idea what time it was. The red digital numbers of the alarm clock on the bedside table blinked 0:00.

"What time is it?" I asked.

"3 AM."

Ben couldn't possibly have driven all this way already. It had already been close to dinner time when the police rescued me from the mall, and it had been after nine when they'd delivered me to the hotel. I'd texted Ben from the mall bathroom around seven. There was no way he'd be here yet. My heart started pounding painfully inside my chest as panic seized me. "What does he look like?"

"Um…" The woman sounded hesitant. "Tall, sandy blonde hair, blue eyes."

"Marin, it's Ben." I heard his voice in the background. "May I just speak to her?"

Relief flooded through me. "It's okay, Lisa," I agreed. "I know him."

"Hey, are you okay?" I could hear the exhaustion in his husky voice; that beautiful voice that I was starting to rely on. "I've been worried."

"Hi. Yes, I'm fine. What are you doing here so soon?"

"I decided to fly. I rented a car at the airport and we can drive back tomorrow. I'm going to get a room and get some sleep. I had an early shift today. I guess it's yesterday, now. I'm wiped out."

My mind was filled with questions. I'd wondered why I hadn't had another text from him, but now I knew it's because he'd spent three hours on a plane. I had a hard time placing the feeling that filled me, but it was a mixture of gratitude, jubilation and something deeper. "Um, it doesn't make sense for you to pay for a room. There are two beds in here and I can deal if you can."

There was a moment's hesitation. "Are you sure?"

"Yes. If you'd come all this way to help me, I think I can trust you with my virtue." It was the truth. "I trust you, Ben. Plus... I feel safer with you here. I'm in room 406."

"Okay, I'll be right up. Thank you."

A small smile graced my mouth as I replaced the phone into its cradle. Why was Ben thanking me after he'd done so much for me? He was truly amazing.

I pushed back the covers and started to stand up, realizing that the towel I'd wrapped around me after the bath had fallen off and was still laying between the sheets. I pulled it out and wrapped it back around me. It was still warmly damp.

I rushed into the bathroom and quickly began to redress. I didn't quite make it before there was a soft rap on the door.

"I'm coming, Ben!" I said. I didn't have time to put on my bra, and so shoved it and my panties, into the pocket of my shorts. I couldn't look at my reflection, but I knew I had bed head like crazy and probably a pillow imprint on my face.

I hurried to the door and quickly opened the double lock. When the door opened, his tall broad-shouldered frame filled the doorway. He stood there with a big duffle slung over his shoulder and an angry look on his face.

My instinct was to hug him, but his expression stopped me cold.

"Don't you ever open a door without the safety on again!" he commanded.

I stared at him at a loss for words. He was right, of course, but I was so happy to see him, I was hurt by his disposition, and it must have shown on my face.

"But... I knew you were coming up..." I offered.

Instantly, his features softened. "Look, I'm sorry, but I've been worried sick."

I nodded and stepped back from the door as a new sort of rush overtook me. "Come in. I took the bed by the bathroom. Is the other one okay?" For the first time I felt awkward in his presence.

"Sure."

The minute Ben entered the room it felt about half the size. He was tall and his lean, muscular body seemed to tower over me. The smallness of the space emphasizing that this was the closest I'd ever stood to him.

He moved past me and threw his bag on the bed before turning toward me. "Are you okay?" he asked again, his expression concerned.

"Yes, though I don't have my suitcase, so I just have this one set of clothes."

His eyes skated over me standing in the low light. "Did you know this family was like this?"

I shook my head. "No. Carter didn't mention them much. In fact, hardly at all."

Ben nodded. "Maybe because they were so shady. He probably was ashamed of them and didn't want you to know."

Or he was one of them, my mind protested. "Probably," I agreed.

"I'd just like to get a quick shower and then get some sleep," he said, unzipping his bag and rummaging through it.

"Of course. There are plenty of clean towels."

"Great." He pulled out a small pile of clothes and handed me a white T-shirt. "You'll probably swim in this, but at least it's clean. You can use it for sleep."

Gratefully, I took the soft cotton shirt, and folded my arms around it. "Thank you," I said softly. "For everything." I meant it. "I didn't expect you to do all of this. I'll pay you back for the plane ticket."

"Nah, don't worry about it. What are friends for? You'd do the same for me, right?"

The corners of my lips lifted in a faint smile. "You know what? I would."

Ben's white teeth flashed, and he nodded. "I know."

I didn't want to seem ungrateful, but I needed to know about Gem and my horses. "What about Gem?"

"Davis is taking care of the horses and the pup went home with him. I was going to bring her with me, but then…" he hesitated briefly, seeming to struggle with the admission. "I just… needed to get here sooner than driving would allow. You were in trouble, and even the flight took too long."

I nodded. Heat rose beneath the surface of the skin on my face. "I understand."

"I trust Davis. I promise."

"Okay."

"Okay." Ben said, then headed toward the bathroom.

I felt embarrassed. The tub was still full of the cold bathwater. "Oh, Ben, I'm sorry, I forgot to drain the tub. I sort of fell asleep as soon as I got out."

"No worries. I'll drain it. I have a sister. She did crap like this all the time." He laughed, then disappeared into the bathroom.

As soon as I heard the door lock, I slipped out of my shorts and shirt and slid into the soft white T-shirt Ben had provided. He was right, it was huge on my smaller frame, but it felt like a big hug from him. I wrapped it around me and crawled under the covers of my bed.

As soon as the warmth of the covers started to permeate my body, my eyelids drooped. I was so sleepy, and now with Ben here, I knew that I could rest easy; I was safe.

everything
HAPPENS FOR
a reason

Chapter 7

BEN

I slept like a log. Once I saw that Marin was safe it was as if my entire body physically uncoiled.

She was sound asleep when I'd come out of the shower and I'd fallen, exhausted, into the second bed after I'd thrown on a clean T-shirt and a pair of loose-fitting knit shorts. I used them for working out, and I figured I could sleep, then drive back to Jackson, in the same set of clothes. I'd barely had time to gather anything before I drove to the airport.

I wasn't sure if Marin would want to drive the entire twelve hundred miles home in one day or take a slower pace. We could do it, but it would be more than sixteen hours in the car. I had spoken to my chief after I was already on the way to the airport. I wasn't sure what I was going to do if he denied my request for an extra day off, so I'd already met up with Davis to drop off Gem and he'd agreed to swap one of his days off to cover for me. I already had today off, so it was only tomorrow I had to worry about and thanks to my friend, it was taken care of.

Adrenaline had flooded my veins and I'd launched into action the minute Marin's frantic text hit my phone. I chastised myself for letting her go alone, then realized I had no right to *let* her do anything. She wasn't my girlfriend so she didn't have to take my advice, but for reasons I didn't fully understand, I felt extremely protective over her.

I rolled over and reached for the phone I'd left on the bedside table checking the time. It was just after 8 AM and if we were going to drive the full distance today, we probably should get going. My head fell down to rest on my arm as my eyes fell on the sleeping woman in the bed opposite me.

She was curled onto her side, her body folded into a fetal position with one hand curled up by her face. She was beautiful; her features relaxed and her skin barely showing the shadow of the old bruise and the glorious mane of blonde hair flowed loose over the pillow. I wished we'd met under different circumstances and her heart wasn't broken. Fury rose up inside my chest. How could she love a bastard who abused her? I knew the signs of abuse and she clearly had them; I'd seen similar marks on my sister, Missy. Thank God she'd finally been able to flee her abusive situation.

Obviously, Marin was helpless without her uncle around to help her. I wondered how she could be so isolated with so few friends, but then remembered how Derrick had isolated Missy. That's how abusive men controlled their victims.

Well, she had me now, whether she liked it or not. I'd be damned if I'd let anything happen to her and who knew if Carter's family would leave her alone. It was safer to plan on them being persistent.

I sighed and rolled onto my back. The room was shadowed by the drawn shades, the white walls appearing a lilac color and the furniture and carpeting cast in darker, though equally faux, shades of purple. I ran an open palm over my face, noting the scruff on my jawline. It felt a bit itchy in its longer state, but realized I'd failed to pack a razor in my haste to get to Minneapolis.

I wondered if I should wake Marin. "Hey," I said softly. "Marin." She didn't move so I tried again, a little louder. "Marin."

She stirred this time and her light grey eyes fluttered open, then closed again. "Hmmm?" She settled back into her pillow briefly before her eyes flew open and she sat up, leaning on one of her arms. "Oh," she said blinking. "I forgot where I was for a minute."

"No worries. I just wondered if you wanted to get going? It's early, so we can make the entire trip today if you want, or we can stop halfway. I have today and tomorrow off, so it's up to you."

"Oh, I wouldn't want to take too much of your time, but it's a long drive." Marin seemed undecided. "I mean, either way it's asking a lot of you, so you can decide which works better for you. If you want, I can pay for a plane ticket for you. I still have mine, but it doesn't leave until tomorrow."

"I figured you'd want to get out of here right away, considering," I said, throwing back the covers and pushing off of the bed. "Unless the police need more from you?"

"The officer said the DA would decide if they were going to prosecute the case and if so, then I might need to come back to testify, but she said she didn't think it would come to that. She said I wasn't hurt, and the kidnapping would be hard to prove because Carter's entire family would say I was there willingly, and it's their word against mine."

I could see a visible shiver run through her and every instinct told me to fold her into my arms. She was afraid. When I lived in Billings, a lot of my friends were cops, and the DA rarely took a case they didn't believe was a definite win. "Bastards. It sucks, but yeah, I've seen it several times before. Bigger cases make careers and so many criminals skate."

Marin nodded, ruefully. "That's me, small potatoes."

I paused and looked at her. "I didn't mean it that way. I just know it is mostly politics. It's not right, but it often happens."

Marin's eyes welled with tears. "I understand. I'll just be glad to get out of here." She stood up and my T-shirt, hung down to her mid-thigh. "I'm going to change."

I nodded. "Okay. I'll call the front desk and let them know we're checking out."

I could see a deeper fear behind her luminous eyes, and I wanted to know what was worrying her. Maybe I'd be able to find out more on the drive.

By the time she came out of the bathroom I'd already thrown the clothes and shoes I'd worn the day before into my duffle and moved past her into the bathroom to quickly dampen my hair. I ran a quick comb through it, then brushed my teeth and shoved everything into my Dopp kit.

"Are you ready to go?" I asked, picking up the T-shirt she'd laid on top of my bag, then quickly put it into the bag, and then the toiletries before zipping it. I put on the pair of Nikes I'd brought for the drive.

"Yeah, I don't have a suitcase."

"In that case, maybe we should drive the whole way today," I suggested. "I'm sure you'll be anxious to get home." I paused, remembering her boyfriend's funeral was this morning. "Unless you want to go to the funeral first? We can, if you'd like. Or I can go get your suitcase."

Marin shook her head adamantly. "No. I don't want to antagonize Carter's family. The stuff in the suitcase is replaceable."

"Okay. Probably a good idea," I agreed. I didn't even want to suggest it, knowing it wouldn't be good to confront them again, especially with me in tow, so I was grateful for her answer.

It wasn't long before we were both seated in the white Toyota Camry I'd rented and headed west out of the city. I was already on the interstate with the rising sun behind us. "Are you hungry? We can run through a drive thru."

"It's early to eat for me, but if you are, please get something." She smiled, clearly hearing the signs of my plight.

My stomach was growling obnoxiously, and I grinned. "I'm starving," I admitted. It was normal for me to get up with the sun for work, and earlier lately because of the horses.

I found a McDonald's right off of I-394 and within a few minutes I was ordering breakfast sandwiches and two coffees. Marin said she wasn't hungry, but I ordered extra, thinking she'd feel better about eating when the city was behind us.

"Wow, you must be hungry," she laughed at the half a dozen sandwiches I ordered.

I was a big guy, who worked out a lot and I could put down three of these sandwiches easily. "Firemen eat a lot," I said, good-naturedly, handing her the bag and putting the coffees in the console between us. "It's your job to feed me." I found myself looking forward to this time alone with her and I hoped she'd feel at ease.

She pulled one of the sandwiches out of the bag and handed it to me. I had it devoured in four bites and held my hand out for another.

She laughed and obliged as I zoomed toward the exit for Highway 169. "Want me to use maps?" Marin asked holding up her phone.

"Nah, I can read the road signs," I winked, unwrapping the second sandwich. "You know, you can eat one or two of those. I got extras."

"Good to know you're not a hog." She smiled.

I patted the flat, solid wall of muscle of my abdomen. "I'm a growing boy."

Marin picked up her coffee and took a sip. "Thanks for coming to get me, Ben. I felt safer just knowing you were on your way."

Warmth spread through me. I didn't want to put her off by getting all heavy, but I couldn't help how her words made me feel. There was nothing I wanted more than for her to need me. I deliberately took a bite of my sandwich, chewed and swallowed before speaking. "I don't know what the situation was with Carter, Marin, and you don't need to tell me, but just know that I can be your friend and you can count on me."

She shifted in her seat toward me, still holding her coffee. I could feel her eyes on my profile as I drove. I could sense the conflict raging inside her. "I appreciate that, but... why?"

I lifted my right shoulder in a half shrug. The last thing I wanted to say was that her situation reminded me of Missy's, for two reasons; I didn't want her to think I looked on her as a sister, and secondly, she hadn't confided in me that Carter had abused her.

"I can't really say...I guess, I feel very protective of you. I know you just lost someone you loved, and you and I just met under the most terrible circumstances. As horrible as that was, I do think that I was working that night for a reason. Call it fate, I don't know. I don't want you to think I'm trying to take his place. I just think we could both use a friend. For now."

Marin swallowed and looked out the passenger window. I could see her struggling to keep tears at bay. "I agree. I'm very happy about meeting you and Gina. I've felt blessed to know both of you in the past days. You're both so kind."

I wasn't sure how I felt that she'd lumped me in with the nurse, but I had to remind myself that her man just died, and she wasn't ready for anything other than friendship and probably wouldn't be for a long time, even if he was abusive. It would be difficult not to show my attraction toward her, but I vowed that I'd keep it to myself.

"So, tell me about growing up on the ranch." I wanted to distract her and also stop myself from blurting out several questions about her relationship with Carter.

I listened intently as I drove, and soon we were approaching the South Dakota boarder. Marin told me of her life in Denver before moving to Jackson when she was nine. The love she had for her uncle was clear, though she said the first few months were difficult because her uncle didn't have a clue about raising a kid, but then they found a mutual interest in the horses.

She told me how he taught her to ride and how she learned his business long before she went off to college. She was animated and happy when talking about her uncle, and so I hesitated to ask about her boyfriend, though after the text last night about how she feared the family would follow her to Wyoming, I felt I had to know. I needed to know what she was dealing with so I could protect her.

It was around 11:30 AM the next time I looked at the clock on the dashboard. We didn't need gas yet, but I knew that between Sioux Falls and Rapid City, towns were few and far between.

"It's too bad we can't just have a straight line to Jackson. All this jagging increases the drive by at least two hours," I said absently. "Do you want to stop? Who knows how far it is until the next gas station or rest area?"

"Okay, sure. I'd love a cold drink, then when we get back on the road, I want to hear your story. I've been talking about me for two hours. Do you want something?"

"Root beer sounds good." I took that last exit into Sioux Falls and the car smoothly slid into the closest convenience store.

Marin went into the store while I topped off the gas tank and hit the bathroom. I found her waiting in line to pay for the drinks and a bag of Fiery Cheetos. I smiled as I pulled my wallet from the side pocket of my shorts and took out some bills.

"No, Ben, I got this," Marin began.

I frowned wryly and shook my head. "Pfft! I got it. You paid for the hotel." I didn't tell her that I'd told the desk attendant to put the room on my card and not hers, but she wouldn't find out until she got her credit card statement.

"Yeah, but you paid for your plane ticket to get me out of this mess."

I handed the bills to the older woman at the cash wrap. "Here you go, ma'am," I said, insisting she take the cash from my hand.

"Ben!" Marin said, exasperated.

"Don't argue or I'll make you listen to elevator music all the way to the Wyoming boarder," I teased, then grabbed the bag of Cheetos, pulled them open and started to walk toward the door.

"Let your boyfriend take care of you, dear." I heard the employee speaking to Marin as I popped the first few Cheetos into my mouth. "You two make a beautiful couple."

"Oh, we're not—" Marin started to explain.

"Come on, honey," I called with a smirk, pulling my Ray bans from the neck of my T-shirt to put them back on. I was being cheeky, but it felt good that the woman would assume we were together. My response made Marin shut her mouth and smile. She looked so young and wholesome without any makeup on. "We gotta haul ass." I winked at the clerk for good measure.

"Bye, now. Be safe!" the woman said as I held the door open for Marin, who walked through under my arm.

Back in the car, she reached inside to grab both of the mostly empty coffee cups, tossed them in the trash by the gas pump and placed the two soda bottles in their place.

Being with her felt as natural as breathing, I thought as I watched her slide into the passenger seat next to me and buckle up. I handed her the open bag of Cheetos and started the engine.

"So?" she asked within seconds.

"So, what?" I glanced in her direction as we pulled onto the ramp back onto the highway.

"So, what's your story?"

"I told you a lot of it already."

"No, you didn't!" Marin admonished. "Only that your mom and dad divorced when you

were young, and you moved to Tallahassee and you moved here from Billings with Davis."

"That's pretty much it," I said languidly. "My life isn't very interesting."

"I think it is," she answered. "At least you've lived in different places all over the country. I've only lived within the same two states all of my life."

The road stretched out over eastern South Dakota miles of farmland on both sides of the highway in front of us, the brilliant blue sky dotted with white cumulous clouds. I was relaxed, enjoying getting to know her. "I've only lived in three or four. I have to admit, Jackson is my favorite. I loved Billings too. Florida is too hot and humid for my taste, though I loved the Gulf coast."

"What do you love about Jackson?" she wanted to know.

"I like that Yellowstone is close. I love the Teton Mountains. I love nature. I promised to take my nephew camping later this summer if I can get the family to come up here. They've all got big-time jobs and their schedules are busy."

"I was always sad that I didn't have any siblings. I picture my life when I'm older, sort of lonely."

I wanted to tell her that whoever she ended up with could have a family and include her, but after losing Carter, I knew it would be insensitive.

"Do you just have one sister, then?"

"Yep, and she has a young son. Dylan. He's awesome."

"I can see that you miss them. Is he your only nephew? No nieces?"

"I think she and Jensen will have more kids. I know Missy wants a girl."

"I think that sounds amazing."

"My brother-in-law has a stepdaughter and I think they'll probably bring her with them if they came up to camp. I'm not sure if Chase and Teagan, Remi's parents, will join or not because their youngest, Mace, is only a toddler. Chase's schedule is jammed in the summer. too. He plays on the National Men's Soccer Team."

"That sounds impressive, but I'm not much into soccer."

I laughed. "Jensen and Missy both work for ESPN, as well. It's all sports, all the time for that family."

"Wow!" Marin exclaimed. "But… so I'm confused." Her pretty features wore a perplexed expression. "Your sister's husband's ex might travel with them?"

"So was I, believe me." I picked up my bottle of root beer and took a swallow. "This is the abbreviated version; Chase and Teagan were college sweethearts. Chase moved to London to play for Arsenal, and Teagan found out she was pregnant so, Jensen, Chase's best friend, married Teagan. Then, years later,

Jensen and Teagan divorced, and she got back together with Chase, but for Remi's sake they all co-parent. I know it seems weird, but it works."

"That sounds amazing if they all get along." Marin's expression was astonished.

"They more than get along, and it's great for all of us. I think you'd like Missy, a lot."

"I'm sure I would. I'd love to meet them."

"Dylan was hyped when I told him I was helping with your horses. Maybe you could give the kids a riding lesson? I've invited them to Jackson for the camping trip this summer."

"I'd be happy, too! I'm sure Siri's foal will be here by the time they visit."

"Now that would be incredible! I know Dylan and Remi would absolutely love that! I might even be able to compete with the superstar for a minute or two."

Marin smiled. "You're a superstar in my eyes. You save people every day. That's way more impressive than kicking a dumb ball around."

I laughed out loud, as pleasure ran through me. I glanced in Marin's direction, taking my eyes off of the road for a brief couple of seconds. Her bruises were healing, and she seemed more at ease than I'd ever seen her. Almost serene. She was gorgeous.

My heart contracted inside my chest and I sucked in my breath as my eyes returned to the road. I could already feel myself falling in love with her, but the last thing she needed was some dude she barely knew trying to get romantic. I'd have to bide my time… but it would be worth it.

everything HAPPENS FOR *a reason*

Chapter 8

Marin

My heart had been flopping inside my chest all day.

Ben was amazing. His smile was electric, and he was so beautiful. He was incredible, and I couldn't understand how he didn't have a wife or girlfriend. Watching him drive turned into an erotic experience. He was so strong, and it exuded from him. Even his strong forearms flexing when his hands gripped the wheel, or when he put the car into gear was enough to get me going.

It was dark and we were getting close to the airport. I was sad that soon, we'd have to part company.

"Are you too tired to drive your car home from the airport?" Ben's voice was low and he was bathed in the blue light from the dashboard. It was like he read my mind.

I shifted in the seat, pulling myself more into a sitting position and ran a hand through my hair. "No, I'm okay."

"Are you sure?" he asked gently. "I can take the car back to Jackson tonight, and then drive you back to the airport to pick up yours tomorrow."

"I'm sure. Why don't we just return this one at the rental return at the airport and then get mine? I'll drop you off at your place."

"It's so late and it will take time to return the rental and then grab the shuttle to the long-term parking."

"It's okay. I couldn't be so ungrateful to make you drive all the way back tomorrow. I've already taken way too much advantage of you."

"No, you didn't." He shook his head wearily and smiled. He looked as tired as I felt. "I volunteered. It's not the same thing."

"Yes, but still. I don't know what I would have done without you. I can't thank you enough."

"Sure, you can. You can share your pup." He could have been teasing, but it felt like he was serious. "At least, let me borrow her when you need to work or something. I've grown rather attached."

My eyebrows shot up in surprise. "Really?"

Ben laughed. "Yes! I don't think Siri will fit into my apartment, or I'd ask to share her, too."

Delight raced through every cell in my body. "You love Siri, too?"

"Yes, she's sweet and I feel for the poor thing. She looks so uncomfortable."

"She's due to foal soon. It's her first baby. Uncle Leonard knew she was my favorite, so he had her bred for my birthday present. If he was going to leave me one last gift, this was a good one. I'll have this baby a long time... Unless I have to sell the ranch."

"The way you talk about your uncle, it's clear he meant a lot to you."

"Yes. He was a little rough around the edges, but he had the best heart. I miss him."

Ben glanced my way, his lips pressed together in a small smile, his right hand reaching out to touch my arm, but he stopped himself, abruptly putting his hand on his thigh and rubbing it across his jeans. "It sounds like it."

My heart sped up. He was going to touch me, and I wanted him to. It was wrong. Carter wasn't even cold in the ground, and I was hoping another man would put his hands on me.

Oh, God, I thought.

Embarrassed, I turned and faced forward again, settling myself back into the seat. I could sense Ben had something else to say but didn't want to say it. Maybe he needed a little prodding.

"What is it?"

"Oh," he began, looking surprised that I'd picked up on his discomfort. "It's just... you don't speak about your boyfriend the way you do about your uncle. I mean, I get it, it's painful to lose someone you love, but I thought you'd be talking about him more. I probably shouldn't even bring it up. Maybe you're still in shock over the whole ordeal."

I pulled in a deep breath, completely filling my lungs, my head cocking to one side as I considered what to say. It had been an ordeal, but the last week after Carter's death had been so much more peaceful and less of one. "Yes, it has been."

"And now, with this kidnapping thing. It's rough. I'm sorry."

"You don't have to be. You've been so wonderful to me... the last thing you have to be is sorry, Ben." I swallowed at the painful thickening beginning in my throat and blinked at the sting of tears began in my eyes. "I'm just not ready to talk about Carter. Is that okay?"

His hand shifted position on the steering wheel and ran the other through his mop of thick sandy hair with the other. I wanted to study him, memorize him because he was that beautiful His soul was that beautiful.

"Of course, it's okay. I'm sorry I'm an insensitive jerk."

Now it was my turn to want to reach out and touch, but I didn't. "You're not. Please don't think so."

"I guess, I'm just curious about him. I saw the bruises. They were too old to come from the accident, or a fall on your run to the ranch during the fire."

I shook my head. Of course, he knew. First responders saw abuse victims a lot. I guess, I didn't think there would be a lot of abusers in Jackson Hole.

"You're right… but I still don't want to talk about it." I wanted to tell him everything, but I was afraid he'd realize Carter was dead because of me, that maybe I was actually responsible for killing him. I trusted Ben more than I'd trusted anyone since my uncle, but I just couldn't open up about this right now. Maybe someday, I could. "Not yet. It's nothing to do with you, it's all me."

Ben nodded. "Okay, but when you're ready, I'm here. I've seen this before. You can trust me."

As Ben navigated his way off of the interstate at the airport exit, I struggled. So, if it wasn't from seeing abuse victims at his job, did he have a girlfriend who had been abused? A spark of jealousy burst inside my heart. I wanted to ask questions, but then I'd have to share the whole sordid ordeal and I didn't think I could do it without breaking down.

"I know. That's the hard part." My voice held a bit of a crack, so I cleared my throat. "I want to, but I'm just not ready."

Ben followed the rental return signs into one of the lower levels of the parking garage and was guided along by one of the attendants, finding a parking space inside.

"Okay, no more pressure, but just know you can talk to me without judgement, as a friend."

Wow.

Why did one word hurt so much? I reminded myself again that it was ridiculous to think of Ben as anything more than a friend. I could feel myself flush with embarrassment at the direction of my thoughts. Thank God it was dark, and he couldn't see it well.

"Right. So, do you have to do anything about the car? Sign something?" I asked awkwardly.

"I think I just have to hand over the keys and let them look over the car." He reached in front of me to open the glove compartment to retrieve the paperwork. "Excuse me."

"Sure," I acknowledged. The hair on my arms rose his nearness; goosebumps covering every inch of my skin and shiver running through me. I quickly reached for the door handle when he was done.

I stepped out, followed closely by Ben.

"Good evening, sir." The male attendant in the rental car jumpsuit took the keys while Ben grabbed his bag from the back seat. I felt like an idiot that I'd lost my carry-on to Carter's family. The sisters had probably doled out all of my clothes and shoes like a Goodwill store.

Ugh, I thought. The entire thing was messed up. I was so dumb to fall in love with someone like Carter. I wouldn't be in this mess if I wasn't moved by a pretty face and a pile of lies. Well, I wouldn't be that susceptible again.

I stood in silence, watching the attendant look over the car haphazardly and nodding at Ben, who looked tired and rumpled.

"You're good to go. I hope you both had a nice trip, and that you'll consider using Enterprise again."

Ben smiled good-naturedly. "Sure will. Thanks." He hoisted his blue duffle bag over his shoulder and walked around the back of the car toward me. "Ready?"

"Yes."

We walked out of the garage to the curb and got in the shuttle line. An older couple with a lot of bags was struggling on the sidewalk, both of them carrying small bags and dragging larger ones. Ben slid his bag off of his shoulder to set at his feet. "Be right back," he said under his breath and walked quickly in their direction. "Hello! My name is Ben. Looks like you've got your hands full. Do you need some help?"

I smiled as I watched the older couple's faces light up in gratitude. "Thank you, my boy," the gentleman said as Ben took the woman's shoulder bag and lifted the man's small roller bag up to attach it to the larger one.

"You're a blessing," the woman said. "We've been struggling since the baggage claim. Goodness, I'm out of breath!"

"You're very welcome. Just a second and I'll be back for the rest, Ma'am. Just leave that large bag."

I had a huge smile on my face as Ben approached, loaded down with the couple's baggage. He really *was* perfect. An adorable dimple appeared in his cheek as his mouth split into a grin. "What?" he asked innocently.

"You got a glass slipper hidden in your pocket?" I asked, amused.

"Wouldn't you like to know?" he said happily, setting the bags on the sidewalk next to his own. I almost giggled, as a laugh burst forth.

"I would, actually."

Ben winked as he straightened up, starting to head back to get the other bags. "I have to keep some secrets to myself, sweetheart."

My heart jolted at the endearment as I stared after him. I had to snap out of this. I barely knew him.

Soon, he was on his way back, pacing himself this time because he was having a conversation with the older couple. They were all talking, joyous expressions on their faces.

"My goodness!" The lady beamed. "What a beautiful girl, you have here," she said to Ben then turned to me. "And you! What a lucky young lady to have such a thoughtful and handsome young man."

"Well…" I started to let her know that we weren't a couple, but I caught Ben's amused eye, and his brow wrinkled wryly as he shook his head, signaling to let the lady think what she wanted. "I agree. He's quite something."

"My dear, he's a keeper."

Coyly, my eyes drifted up to Ben's, hoping to get an unobserved look at him and maybe figure out what he was thinking. He was still smiling, listening to something the old man was telling him.

The woman's hand wrapped around my forearm, leaning in to speak more softly. "I haven't seen that kind of chivalry in years. He looks so strong and virile, too… I bet he keeps you busy in the bedroom."

My mouth dropped open. "Um…" My eyebrows arched and my eyes widened in shock "He's… uh, certainly… red-blooded."

It wasn't as if the thought hadn't occurred to me. At least a hundred times. I couldn't even think about him without feeling an attraction, but any woman would want him. Ben was perfect. I'd have to be missing my ovaries to not notice how masculine he was, and it wasn't as if I didn't have the fantasy of more happening between us, but I was still reeling from the events of the past week and I felt guilty that I wasn't more of a sobbing mess. Instead, I blamed myself, and now, I was worried about the retaliation of Carter's family and maybe they'd try to hurt Ben if he was around me.

Thankfully, the shuttle arrived and stopped further contemplation. The elderly couple preceded us onto the bus and Ben helped the driver load all of the luggage and popped his head back in. The lights on the interior of the bus showed the tired lines on his face. "Can you wait just a second?" he asked the driver, then directed his blue gaze straight at me. "My car is in short term parking, here. Do you want me to go with you to get your truck and then you can drop me off at the main terminal again?" He seemed a little anxious and I wanted to soothe him.

"Oh, you're so tired. I'm not scared here. I'll be fine."

He paused, looking at me. "Yeah, I know, but it's late and I'd feel better if I knew you were safe. If you don't want to, I understand."

Once again, he caused fireworks to explode inside me. I smiled gently. "Okay."

"Great," he smiled then raced up the stairs. "Sorry, mister," he said to the bus driver.

"No worries. We don't get many passengers at this time of night."

Ben took a seat across from me and the woman next to me leaned in. "I predict lots of babies."

"Oh," my hand came up to rest on my chest. "We... well, we're... uh..."

I met Ben's gaze and he was grinning from ear to ear. He shrugged slightly, with a wry cock of his head and an arch to one eyebrow.

"No need to get flustered, dear. I just wish you the best!"

Her brown eyes were so kind that I wanted to wrap my arms around her and hug her tight. I could see years of life and experience reflected there; they were satisfied and wise.

"Bev, leave the girl alone," her husband admonished. "You're embarrassing her."

I remembered Ben's look at the airport and how he thought it was easier to let the couple believe we were together, and so I played along.

"I'm not embarrassed. We're… trying."

The woman's hands clasped together as a bright smile graced her weathered face. "How wonderful!"

Thankfully, we were pulling into the parking lot, and said our goodbyes to the sweet elderly couple as the driver searched for their car. I watched as they disembarked from the shuttle and walked a few steps away, waiting for the driver to help with their luggage. True to form, Ben followed the couple, stopping to address the driver, who was slowly getting up out of his seat to assist them. He looked like he was in pain with maybe a back problem.

"No, that's okay, sir, I'll help them. That large one is easily seventy pounds. Take a rest."

The driver seemed surprised by his offer. "Really?" he asked, hopefully sitting back into his seat.

"Sure thing. Be right back"

The man and his wife settled into their new burgundy SUV thanking Ben profusely after he stowed their mountain of luggage into the back. He hopped back onto the shuttle through the open door, which the driver quickly closed behind him, then sat down across from me as we continued his slow journey through the large lot.

"Thank you. I hurt my back last weekend when I slipped on the dang stairs. They are steep and my wife's little dog was in the way. I didn't hurt the pooch, but I'm still very stiff."

Ben smiled and nodded. "No problem. I could see that you were suffering some sort of injury back at the terminal."

"Well, I appreciate your help. Believe me, if I didn't need to have this extra job, I wouldn't, but we're on a fixed income and my wife has a bunch of medical bills."

"That was nice," I mouthed without sound, and was rewarded with one of Ben's crooked grins and half shrugs. He was so humble, and this action was just part of him; shrugging off his kindness as if everyone possessed it in equal measures when that was far from true.

A pothole in the pavement caused the bus to jolt and drew me out of my thoughts, abruptly.

"Oh! There's my truck," I told the driver, pointing to it. "In the back row. That old blue one," I told the driver. He was a kind-looking older gentleman, and I felt sorry for his plight. Unfortunately, the only cash I had was stolen by Carter's family, so I was unable to follow my heart and give him a hefty tip.

As we neared my truck, the driver stopped and opened the door and Ben and I rose to exit the vehicle. "Here you go kids."

"Thank you for the ride," I murmured. "I hope you feel better soon and that your wife does, too. You've been so nice."

The man's face lit up with genuine pleasure and he nodded. "My pleasure." He stopped the shuttle and we rose to leave.

Apparently, Ben shared my thoughts because he grabbed his bag and flung it over his shoulder then paused on the shuttle stairs reaching into his front pocket and pulling out a messy wad of bills. He quickly straightened them out and handed the pile of money over to the driver, who seemed astonished and just looked from the money and then to Ben's face.

I couldn't tell if the money consisted of a lot of ones or if they were larger bills, and I realized, it didn't matter. It was just the enormity of the gesture that moved me. Ben was handing over every cent he had on him to a man he knew nothing about but believed was less fortunate… and he did so without a second thought. The contrast between Ben and Carter screamed once again. Carter wouldn't have even tipped the driver, and I doubted he would have helped the old couple.

"Oh, I can't take that," the driver began.

"Yes, you can. Please?" Ben asked graciously.

I stood frozen on the gravel pavement of the parking lot looking on at the scene playing out in front of me.

"You'll need money to get out of the lot," the man offered.

"Debit card," Ben replied. "Please take it," he insisted, presenting the money closer this time.

The driver reluctantly took the cash. "Thank you," he said quietly. I could see he was as touched as I was.

"You're welcome. Have a great rest of your night," Ben told the driver, coming down the stairs toward me and then past me onto the passenger side of the truck.

Once inside and finding my way out of the parking lot, my hands trembled on the old steering wheel.

Ben yawned; putting his hand up to cover his mouth. "Sorry."

"No need to say you're sorry. I'm the one who should be sorry… I'm sorry that I had to call you."

Ben sighed. "Marin." He paused; contemplation clear on his handsome face which was highlighted in the darkness by the dashboard light. "I'm glad you did." Without missing a beat, he changed the subject. "So, we'll get my truck and I'll follow you back to the ranch."

"You don't need to follow me all the way. It's outside of town on the opposite side." I already felt so guilty. We'd just driven seventeen hours and weariness settled on him like a cloak.

"I know where the ranch is," he said simply; quietly. "I'll make sure you get home, safely. We'll get some sleep, but if it's okay, I'll get Gem from Davis tomorrow morning and bring her out early when I come to take care of the horses."

"That's right, you don't have to work tomorrow," I murmured hesitantly, inwardly cursing my still unhealed injuries. I wish I didn't have to impose on Ben any further. I was just pulling up to the parking booth. It was automated and I was able to feed the parking ticket into a machine and then swipe my credit card. Ben had offered me his, but I turned it down. "I got this."

The machine processed the card and the arm lifted allowing me to leave the parking lot.

"Nope." He nodded and leaned back into the seat of my uncle's old truck. "I was able to get the day off. I wasn't sure if I'd be back from Minneapolis. I'm all yours for the day if you want me."

I swallowed and concentrated on the road.

If I wanted him...

I knew that wasn't how Ben meant the words. He'd been nothing but a gentleman, but my traitor mind and heart couldn't help wishing.

If only it wasn't so soon after Carter died. If only I wasn't certain it was my fault. If only I could tell Ben the entire truth. I wanted to give in to my feelings, but were they real or was I just enamored with this beautiful, perfect man because he had treated me so well? I couldn't ignore the contrast between the two men and the effect that might have on my emotions. Plus... would he blame me and see me as a killer? My stomach sank. I thought of myself as one, so why wouldn't he?

I glanced in his direction and his eyes were closed, his arms crossed over his chest. It was only a few minutes ride until

I'd have him back at the airport to get his car, but I decided to let him rest his eyes during the short drive.

The real truth was that I was scared and confused. If I thought Carter hurt me with his fists, what could Ben do to my heart?

I swallowed hard and licked my lips as I wrapped my head around it.

What if this strong, gentle man's opinion of me changed? I couldn't stand it. Ben could absolutely destroy my heart and leave it in shambles.

everything
HAPPENS FOR
a reason

Chapter 9

BEN

I didn't know what the hell I was doing. I knew I was headed in dangerous territory. I shook my head in disbelief at how much this woman affected me, and in such a short time.

The red taillights of Marin's old blue truck were a hundred yards in front of me and as she turned off of the highway onto the gravel road that led the two or three miles to the ranch and ruins of the shop.

I was following her back to her ranch but had serious trepidation about leaving her there alone. There was a tightness in my chest and a knot in my gut at the thought alone. It was ridiculous to be feeling this way after knowing her for only a week, but there it was. Maybe it was because she seemed so fragile, maybe it was because she was alone, or maybe the psychopathic family her dead boyfriend left behind...maybe it was because I knew that she'd been abused. More likely, it was how beautiful and mesmerizing she was. My mind and heart were racing.

I'd felt bad for her boyfriend at first; lighting up like a roman candle as he did and the unspeakable suffering that he must have gone through, but if his relatives' actions and Marin's bruises were anything to judge the situation by, then maybe he'd gotten what he deserved.

One thing I did know, I wanted answers. These feelings eating away at my insides needed to know. I felt frustrated as fuck trying to be sensitive to her situation, when I didn't understand why a woman, *any woman*, stayed with an abusive man.

Marin hadn't admitted he was abusive, but I knew it as sure as I knew my own name. Why didn't she want to talk about it or share her experiences? What if she was one of those battered women who still thought she was in love with the bastard doing the beating? Anger flared and my jaw tightened. Missy was like that at first, always making excuses for Derrick, until Dylan became the subject of some of the abuse. Then she woke up.

I sucked in a heavy breath and let it out, my fingers tightening on the steering wheel of the old Chevy truck as it lumbered down the dirt road, bouncing obnoxiously with every bump I had the misfortune to hit in the dark.

When she pulled into the driveway and stopped the truck in front of the house, I rolled to a stop behind her. The single light on top of a high pole that stood between the farmhouse and the barn cast a soft yellow glow across the yard, while the full moon shone in the inky black sky; the stars brilliance muted by the illumination of both.

I was already out of my truck when she opened the door to hers and slid the short distance from the seat until her feet touched the ground. I put my hand on the open door ready to close it for her and looked down into her eyes. They sparkled in the moonlight as she looked up at me, but she didn't move. It was if the warm night air wrapped us up together and desire stirred as my eyes roamed over her face, then dropped to her luscious, moist mouth. It would be luscious... it could be nothing less. I wanted to find out more than anything... ever.

Marin's skin, illuminated by the low light, glowed. I could see she was tired, but to me at least, she looked vulnerable and so incredibly beautiful. Her loose bun of blonde hair was messy from all day in the car and soft tendrils moved in the slight breeze. Instinctively, my hand raised to brush her hair back, but I realized what I was doing before my fingers touched her jaw, and I dropped my arm to my side.

"Marin, I..." I began.

"Thank you, Ben." She reached out and lightly touched the front of my shirt. Her fingers burned me through the thin material caused the muscles there to contract. Her eyes expression soft and unknowingly alluring. I felt the ache that I'd been fighting all day begin anew and with increased fervor.

"Will you be okay?" I stood two feet from her, longing to lean in and kiss her sweet mouth. I could almost taste it and my body responded involuntarily, though I willed it to stop. I wanted to reach out and brush her hair back again, my fingers tingled with it. "I can stay," I suggested softly, caught up in the moment, my gaze locked with hers.

"What?" she asked, stiffening a bit.

When I realized how she'd interpreted my words, I rushed to explain and took two steps back. "I didn't mean like that. I'm worried about those goons showing up, and I'd just rather not leave you alone in the middle of the night." It was true, but I knew I'd let the attraction I felt for her get the better of me and she could see it. I had to get it under control. At least for now.

"Oh," she said, flustered. "I see. Um, sorry I didn't mean to suggest—"

"Don't worry about it. We've both had a long day, and we're both exhausted. I'll just look in on the horses and then I'll get out of here."

I was embarrassed at my own weakness and that Marin had immediately jumped to the conclusion that I was suggesting we have sex. It wasn't as if I wasn't aroused by her nearness, and her fragility screamed at the protector inside me, but if we ever made love it wouldn't be because she was grateful or feeling needy. Something inside me suffered that she might think so little of me.

"No, Ben…" she called after me as I turned and headed in the direction of the barn. "I'm sorry!"

I turned back but didn't close the distance; just stood drinking in the site of her. "I don't know what happened to you, and maybe one day you'll be able to tell me, but you can trust me. I'm not *that* guy. You don't have to be afraid of me. I promise. I'd never take advantage of a vulnerable woman."

"I know that," she said softly, regretfully. "I'm just… cautious. I'm not used to someone being so unselfish and kind and wanting nothing in return. The last time I trusted someone it didn't turn out well."

A plethora of emotions ran through me. A flash of anger surged at the thought of anyone expecting sex from her… for any reason, and I was ashamed that I desired her myself. It should be the last thing on my mind considering her situation. It was difficult not to want her, but I'd be damned if I'd make her think less of me by acting on it.

"I was trying to be a good friend… and I feel protective of you. If something happened to you, I'd never forgive myself. I won't lie, Marin… I feel a strong attraction between us, but I know you're not ready for another man in your life. I was only offering to stay on the sofa; to be here in case you needed me."

"Okay," she answered. "Like I said, I'm sorry for the misunderstanding. I'm just a little punchy after Carter dying and all of the stuff this weekend."

"I understand." I nodded starting again in the direction of the barn, hoping the hurt I felt wasn't showing on my face or at least the shadows of light and dark were hiding it. It was insane that I was feeling so rejected when I should understand it was too soon. I *did* understand but knowing it didn't soften the turmoil I was feeling.

Davis had left both entrances to the barn open, so the interior of the building was flooded with moonlight. The horses were mostly silent, though a few snorted and one of them moved around, stomping the stall floor as I passed. I walked through, pausing by each stall and touching any nose that was within reach.

"I missed you babies. Were you good for Davis? Did he take good care of you?" Davis would have had to feed and water them three times in my absence and I went to the feed stall to check the supply of alfalfa. It looked like the right amount had been used.

Knowing Siri was Marin's favorite mare and that she was due to foal in the next couple of weeks, I paid extra attention to her as was my habit over the past week.

"Hey, Siri… how is the pretty mommy?"

A soft whinny from the back of the stall was preceded by the horse moving forward to the stall door where I stood. She nudged my shoulder with her nose, and I leaned into her neck, rubbing her mane and behind her ears. She bobbed her large head a couple of times and neighed loudly causing some of the other horses to stir and offer answering calls.

I noticed her feed was as empty as the others, but she was walking around her stall, and nudging at the bin and empty oat bag still hanging on the wall next to it. Marin hadn't said exactly when the mare would foal, but maybe the restlessness was a precursor. I decided to text Davis the next morning to see if he'd noticed anything amiss while we were gone.

Undoubtedly, Marin would already be in the house, but I needed to let her know how Siri was doing before I left.

I finished my check of the second half of the horses and satisfied all was well, except I added a bit of oats to Siri's feed bin. I left the barn and moved passed the trucks toward the house. The lamp in the living room was on and I could see Marin making up the coach through the window. She smoothed down the sheet and then unfurled a red blanket. I'd have to talk to her about keeping the blinds drawn when she was home alone. I didn't feel she was safe out here all alone. Sure, Jackson was relatively safe, but it was a small community, and it wouldn't be long before it was well known she was out here without Carter.

I used the back of my knuckles to lightly knock on the screen door, then pulled it open and popped my head inside. "Hey."

"Hey," she answered, straightening up. "I decided you're right. I would feel better having you here." She hesitated for a second. "Unless you've changed your mind."

I shook my head then pointed over my shoulder. "No, but maybe you want to take a look at Siri? She seems restless. I think she's hungry or something. I wasn't sure if it's a sign of foaling?"

"Maybe," she said, walking toward me and out onto the porch. "It's probably nothing to worry about. I've seen a lot of mares eat more during the last days. Did she seem off, otherwise?"

"Just restless. Swishing her tail and walking, snorting a little, but maybe you still want to check on her." I asked. "Just to be safe?"

Within a minute, we were at the barn entrance and just inside Marin began rooting around for something on the work bench. Turning, she produced a high beam flashlight and switched it on, pointing the light at the floor. "Let's go." She turned and headed down to the other end of the barn toward Siri's stall.

"Hey, baby. I missed you, Siri." she cooed, sliding one arm around the horse's large neck to hug the animal and shone the flashlight into the stall and around the floor and walls, then the feed bin. "Yeah, she's probably getting close. She's due in a week, but it's her first pregnancy so the vet said it could go long or short since the foal is so big. It's kinda hard to tell."

Marin continued to speak softly to the horse, her tone a little worried. "Back up, Siri," she urged, opening the stall door and I followed her inside. There were four huge piles of manure on the floor and I made a mental note to clean out the stalls when the sun came up. She used the flashlight to look at the mare's teats. The mammary glands were swollen with beads of a dark yellow substance at the end of each one. "She's waxing," Marin said.

"What's that?" I asked, curious.

"It's colostrum. She'll foal soon."

I felt happy that I would get to witness something so miraculous. At least, I hoped I would and found myself wishing I could take the next week off so I wouldn't miss it. "How soon?"

"Not sure. Waxing is usually between twelve to thirty-six hours out, but since I've been gone about that long, I can't say. Can you hold this, please?" She handed me the flashlight.

I took it without answering and watched as she ran a practiced hand over the mare's flank and bulging stomach.

"Should we get her to lie down or something?"

Marin laughed shortly. "You can't make a horse lie down. She will if she needs to."

"What do we do, then?" I felt anxious, unsure what was coming.

"She doesn't seem like she's in pain and I haven't felt any contractions. She's not in labor but will be soon, probably by morning."

"So, what do we do?" I asked again. Marin's eyebrow shot up and she laughed again. "I'm sorry. I'm a moron about this."

"Well, you can't be perfect at everything," she teased, moving to switch on the stall light. "I need to clean out this crap."

I chuckled at her veiled compliment. "I was planning on cleaning all of the stalls tomorrow."

"It can't wait. She's not in active labor yet, but if she foals tonight, I don't want manure around when she's birthing so I'll have to keep checking every couple of hours. I should also put down some new hay for bedding. Can you grab a shovel? Not the one used for the oats; the big scoop near the door?"

"Okay." I switched off the flashlight and took large, hurried steps to the opposite end of the barn. I set the light down on the bench where Marin took it from moments before and then found a big aluminum scoop with remnants of manure on it. Apparently, this was the correct shovel.

I hurried back and went into inside. Instead of handing it to Marin, I bent and scooped up one of the large piles. Marin was stroking the horse's neck and cooing comforting words. I stood there with the full scoop not really knowing what to do with it. "I never thought I'd be wondering to do with a load of horse shit. I probably should have gotten something to put this in, huh?"

Marin burst out laughing. "It would be easier than carrying it out into the pasture to dump each one of those piles. Did you see the wheel barrel by where you found the shovel?"

"Yeah." I answered, setting the full shovel down carefully on the floor along one wall so the contents wouldn't fall out. "Be right back."

Within the next five minutes I'd returned with the wheel barrel, scooped up all of the poop, removed it from the stall and emptied the wheel barrel in the pasture.

It wasn't that exerting but the speed in which I'd rushed to do Marin's bidding caused me to break out in a sweat. I wiped my face with the neck of my T-shirt.

I watched Marin move around the back of the horse and inspect what I could only assume was her vagina. The small woman disappeared behind the huge horse's flank. "I think I read somewhere you shouldn't get behind a horse or they might kick the crap out of you," I murmured.

"That's true, but I raised her from a baby. She's used to me."

"I'll get some hay for new bedding while you do that."

Soon, the stall was lined with clean hay and we were both on the outside of the closed stall door observing the horse. Marin was standing with her feet on the lower cross board of the stall door in order to see inside, her arms hanging over the edge while I stood behind her.

"It will be several hours until she goes into active labor, at least. Why don't you go get some sleep on the couch? You must be tired from the drive."

"I should be, but I'm not at all. I was before, but not now. Must be the excitement of all of this."

Marin's brows lifted as she looked at me with wry amusement. "It might be a while. I'm just going to stay for a bit to make sure she's okay, then I'll check on her in the morning."

"I'd like to stay with you. If it's okay."

Marin was still standing on the first rung of the gate. In that position she was just a smidge shorter than me. She reached around and flipped the light switch and the stall was once again shrouded in darkness, lit only by the moon.

"She'll settle down faster in the dark."

"Will she lay down?" I grew up in the city and no previous knowledge of horses or other livestock.

"Horses can sleep standing up. If she starts having pains, she may lay down," she said softly. Her voice held a pleasing, comforting quality that I found soothing.

"I wish I could do that," I mused.

Marin's head tilted to one side as she glanced up at me. "Ben, go lay down on the couch. I'll be in shortly."

I shook my head.

"Boy, are you stubborn. You drove for sixteen hours."

She was pointing out the obvious. The truth was, I was dead tired, and my eyelids were getting heavy. "I don't want to leave you out here alone."

"What do you think will happen? I might get a mosquito bite?" She huffed out a laugh.

I leaned over the gate beside her; our shoulders were just a few inches apart. It was a warm, sultry night, but I could still feel the heat radiating between us. My lips turned up in a half smile. "Funny. No, those criminals could show up. Your uncle's shop was well known and all they have to do is Google to find the address."

"But the shop has a different address than the house."

I ran a hand through my hair and sucked in a sigh, then let it out slowly. "Marin, you're a young woman out here in the boonies alone. Do you think they can't find your home address the same way?"

"Yeah, gotta love the Internet. The funeral was today, so I don't think they'd follow yet."

"Oh, great. So, tomorrow, then," I reasoned with mock sarcasm. "That makes me feel so much better."

"I have to call the insurance company to file a claim about the shop. There should be something in there for death or bodily injury. If there is, I'll just give the money to Carter's mother. Money seems to be what mattered to her… more than her son."

"You don't think they'd just keep blackmailing you? You can't reason with terrorists or criminals, Marin."

She stepped down off of the gate. "Probably not, but what else can I do? Sell the land and the ranch? I grew up here. I don't want to leave. Coming?" she asked as she pointed toward the barn door.

She started walking and I followed a few steps behind, enjoying watching her silhouette walk down the corridor between the two rows of stalls the moonlight framing her.

"I wouldn't want to leave either, but I wouldn't pay them a damn dime." I couldn't understand her reticence. "Why aren't you angrier over what happened? They kidnapped you and who knows what else could have happened. Get a restraining order, at least."

She shrugged and shoved her hands into the front pockets of her shorts as she waited for me to close the distance between us. We were outside now, and our shoes crunched on the gravel as we walked toward the house.

"Would that really stop them if they wanted to hurt me? If you could only have seen Apollo. He was menacing. I'm sure kidnapping is only the last offense on a very long rap sheet."

I reached out and wrapped my fingers around her arm at the elbow, my goal to stop her and have her look at me while we spoke about it. "Right. You're making my point. You're vulnerable out here. Why are you willing to take the chance?"

"They can't kidnap me. There is no one to pay the ransom," she said a bit more flippantly than I could stomach.

"This isn't a joke."

Her slim shoulders lifted in a shrug. "What am I supposed to do, Ben? At least with the horses boarded here, there is some money coming in. Even if they show up, I already told them I didn't have much cash. There is still a mortgage on the house because my uncle took out a loan to upgrade the fencing and make repairs to the barn."

"Until you get the insurance money, Marin. Even if you hand over any allocated for Carter's death, they may still demand more. Even if you lied to them about your situation before, they can figure out there will be other money for the rebuild coming in."

"I don't even know what kind of insurance my uncle kept on the place. There might not be anything at all." She was getting annoyed. "You know, this really isn't any of your business."

I stopped short of the porch while she went up the steps. Anger exploded inside me. "The minute you texted me from that bathroom in the mall and brought me into it, you made it my goddamn business!" I wasn't exactly yelling, but the timber and volume to my voice had changed enough to make her flinch and back away from me.

Instantly, I regretted my outburst. If she had suffered abuse at Carter's hands, this would make her afraid of me. I put up my hands, spreading the fingers wide, consciously lowering my voice. "Look, I'm sorry, Marin. I didn't mean to shout. I'm just worried about you."

"No, you're right. I shouldn't have called you. I just… thought… I thought…" I could hear the tears and tremble to her voice. I felt like a total and utter asshole.

"You thought right. You were right to call me. I told you that I'd be here for you and I meant it. I just…"

I wanted desperately to move closer to her, to somehow make her understand. Instead, I turned away and locked my fingers on top of my head, unsure what to say next. After a few seconds I started speaking, but still keeping my back to her. "I don't know what your situation with Carter was, and I'm not asking you to tell me about it right now, but my sister was beaten by her first husband and I've seen the yellow bruises and heard the excuses before. Maybe you loved the guy, but the thought of someone hurting you like that just makes me want to kill something." I spoke softly, hoping it would put her at ease.

I turned, then, to see her still standing on the porch with her head down and her hands covering her face. She was sobbing, softly. I couldn't help moving toward her, then. I wanted to comfort her, to pull her close and hold her while she cried it out.

"The last thing I want is for you to be afraid of me. I was out of line and it won't happen again. I promise."

I moved closer still and reached out to touch her shoulder. "I'm so sorry. Please forgive me, Marin."

Her head nodded but she cried harder. I wasn't sure if I pulled her close or if she slid her arms around my waist but suddenly, Marin was wrapped in my arms with her head resting on my chest. I rubbed her back gently. "I'm sorry." I pressed my lips to the top of her head. It felt so good to hold her. Her hair smelled of shampoo and she fit so perfectly inside the circle of my embrace. "I'll leave if you want, but I'll be worried."

"Don't leave." The softly uttered words made me relax and hold her tighter. I felt her fingers curl into the material of shirt at the back of my waist. Nothing had ever felt so right. Maybe I hadn't ruined our fragile friendship. At least, I prayed I hadn't because I knew one thing; I wanted to be part of this woman's life.

Chapter 10

Marin

After our embrace, Ben and I separated and entered the farmhouse.

I'd gone to my room upstairs and Ben stayed in the living room on the couch I'd made up for him. I showered and was wearing a clean pair of pajama shorts and T-shirt.

Having Ben in the house made me feel better, but my unease was due to something else altogether. His nearness, while comforting, was unnerving. How could I be feeling all of this pent-up desire and emotion when I should be pre-occupied with deciding what I wanted to do about the shop and the ranch, not to mention the terror over the past few days?

I'd been blind about Carter's true nature in the beginning and the experience should make me more cautious. My head was telling me that I could be making the same mistake with Ben, but my heart wanted desperately to believe he was everything he seemed. I was probably already in love with him, but that would be stupid and irrational. The last thing I needed was a new relationship when my life was so uncertain. And in a small town, it would look like I was easy, and people would gossip.

My body was buzzing. Somehow, I'd managed to keep from begging Ben to come upstairs to my room and make love to me. God knew, I wanted him to, but I also knew that my life was a mess, and it would be asking too much for him to take it all on. At least, until I had everything sorted out.

On the trip to Minneapolis, I'd considered my options. I could sell the ranch, take the insurance money and start over somewhere else. Or, I could stay and rebuild the shop, or stay and just run the horse boarding and get a job in town to supplement the income.

After the trip home with Ben, I found myself wanting to stay in Jackson. I felt drawn to him in a way I never was with Carter. Carter was good looking and was the first man to really pay attention to me, but Ben was different. I felt like a flower opening whenever I was near him. I sighed and rolled over for the tenth time; my sheet tangled in my bare legs and I kicked at it.

It was dark in my room, and I'd left the window open so that I could hear the crickets chirping and also anything coming from the barn just in case Siri needed me. A decent breeze was drifting through the room, making the lightweight curtains furl.

I was exhausted, but part of me was afraid to sleep. I pushed into a sitting position and reached for the scrunchie on my bed stand to twist my damp hair back into a bun on the top of my head. I sucked in a deep breath. I was thirsty, but I didn't want to wake Ben by going down to the kitchen. He deserved a good night's sleep.

Despite my reasoning, I found myself walking softly across the room and into the hallway. The upstairs railing opened over the living room and I crept to the top step to quietly sit down. Peering through the rungs of the bannister, I could see Ben on the couch. He was bare-chested, the sheet low in his waist, but his muscular legs were visible as it tangled between them, as mine had done. His right arm was slung over his eyes and his left hand rested on his stomach. My breath caught. Even in the darkness, his body's outline, combined with my overactive imagination had my blood racing in my veins. He was magnificent. I would have been happy just sitting there watching him sleep.

Suddenly, Ben sat up, moving with the stealth of a wild animal to the window to look outside. I jumped at his unexpected movement and the old stairs creaked.

He pivoted in less than a second. "Marin?" he called, scanning the room.

I stood up so he wouldn't catch me lurking. "I'm here."

Ben visibly relaxed when he saw me at the top of the stairs. "Are you okay?"

"I was thirsty, but I was trying to be quiet so as not to wake you."

"Oh, yeah. I was just dozing."

The wooden stairs felt cool to the bottom of my bare feet as I walked down and took a left into the kitchen. "Do you want something to drink? I have white wine in the refrigerator. It might help us both get some sleep."

"Maybe just one glass," he answered. His voice, softer now, held a husky tone.

He was wearing the gym shorts he'd had on during the drive and it occurred to me, I should have offered him a shower. "Hey, it was rude of me not to offer you a shower. It might help, too."

He laughed out a huff as I removed the bottle of wine from the refrigerator and leaving it open so I could use the light from it to move to the cupboard to take out two glasses.

"Like it helped you?" Ben asked.

"Touché," I said, setting the glasses down with one hand, then pouring the wine into the glasses. "But still, it was rude."

"It's okay. I was thinking, or maybe hoping, I was going to get to help with Siri and a shower might be moot."

"I'm not sure it will be tonight. I don't think so."

"Too bad. Do you want me to turn on a light?" he asked as I handed him one of the glasses.

Electricity ran over every surface of my skin when his fingers briefly brushed mine when taking the glass. I took a small sip from my own glass. "Not really... I mean, we're already having trouble sleeping and a bright light won't help." Heat began to seep up from my neck and under the skin of my face toward my cheeks in a flush. I was grateful for the grey shadows that cloaked the room.

We stood in the middle of the kitchen, both of us unsure of what to do next.

"Are you hungry?"

"Not especially. You should try to get some sleep. Do you feel unsafe with me in the house, Marin? Is that why you can't sleep?" He took a long pull on his wine, nearly emptying his glass.

My mouth fell open in astonishment. "No. I'm glad you're here. I feel like I've known you forever."

He nodded, then set his glass on the table. "That's how I feel, too. Do you think you can sleep now?"

I took another swallow of the wine. "I do."

"Okay, and you can sleep in. I'll check on Siri and feed the horses in the morning."

"You should be the one to sleep in. You did all of the driving."

"I can see you're going to argue about everything." He smiled and took a couple of steps closer. His white teeth flashed in the darkness.

"Not everything. I only argue when I know I'm right." I laughed.

"Oh, is that it?" Ben was close enough so that I could see the dimples in his cheeks when he grinned.

I cocked my head to one side. "Yeah."

"We'll see." He took my free hand and bent to kiss me on the forehead, sending a shiver right through me. I couldn't help wishing he'd kissed me on the mouth. This first kiss would be life changing. I was so hungry for him, though I knew I shouldn't be. "Night, Marin. I'll put the wine away."

"Night." I took my half full glass and moved away toward the stairs, feeling Ben's eyes on me the entire way until I disappeared into my room.

* * *

"Marin!"

Ben's voice broke through the haze of sleep.

"Marin, wake up! Siri's in labor. At least… she's laying on the ground, then getting up, and then down over and over. She's sweating and looks miserable. There is a white sack starting to come out. I don't know how to help her." Ben's words were frantic.

My eyes opened and I blinked to see Ben looming over me. When his words sank in, I was instantly awake and pushing out of the bed and going over to my dresser. "Okay, give me a minute to throw on some shorts and I'll be right out. She's up and down to get the foal into position. It'll be okay." I'd seen foaling at least twenty times and all that stuff he described was normal. It was sort of cute that he was acting like an anxious father.

"I'm going back out there. Poor thing," Ben said and rushed from the room.

It was barely dawn. The sun had not yet risen, but the sky glowed orange and purple through my still open window. I threw on some old shorts and quickly pulled my arms from the sleeves of my T-shirt to quickly throw on a bra and then shoved them back through as I ran down the stairs and shoved my feet into my old work shoes that waited by the backdoor. Soon I was running at full speed across the yard toward the barn.

Ben was inside the stall, softly speaking to Siri and patting her flank.

"It doesn't look like her water has broken. You might want to step out or run the risk of getting a warm shower."

He looked at me with a look of horror on his face, his eyes wide and his brow crinkled. "Really?"

I burst out laughing. It was hilarious. This man, who ran fearlessly into raging fires, was cringing at a little amniotic fluid. "Yes!"

"Oh, gross," he said, moving with lightning speed on his tiptoes to get out of the stall.

I couldn't stop laughing. "Are you sure you're the superhero who runs into burning buildings? There isn't anything on the floor yet, Ben."

"That's because I already took out two huge piles of shit before I woke you up," he said emphatically. He looked like a little boy with his flushed cheeks and exuberant grin.

"I see," I said, smiling. I felt myself drowning in his blue eyes. He really was striking. "Well, Siri and I thank you." I held open the stall gate that Ben had just come through and went inside. The mare was clearly in distress. I put a hand on her neck and moved it over her shoulder toward her stomach. I could see the foal moving inside her, as well as her side heave with the effort of her contractions. Siri stomped and snorted "There we go, baby," I cooed to her. "You're going to be okay."

"Is she? She looks miserable," Ben noted.

"Labor is no fun, that's for sure. I imagine it's akin to passing a watermelon." I continued to drag my hand over the Siri's side. I wanted to get a good look at her vulva and the white sack starting to extrude. I hoped to see a hoof and nose of the foal soon.

"Holy shit!" Ben exclaimed. "I'm glad I'm not a girl."

I smiled to myself. I was glad, too.

Siri moved away from me and laid down on her side. It was painful watching her drop to her knees in front. That alone had to hurt. Thank goodness for the thick layer of bedding Ben had laid down early this morning when we'd arrived back at the ranch. Siri kicked her back legs out stiff behind her. It was clear she was pushing.

"What can I do?" Ben asked anxiously.

"Go to that old cupboard where I got the flashlight last night and grab the stack of clean towels, the squeegee thing, and those long rubber gloves and tall rubber boots. There are two sets. My uncle's should fit you. The squeegee looks like one of those things used to clean out a baby's nose, only much bigger."

"Got it." He disappeared from the stall and I crouched near Siri's haunches. "Come on, baby. You're okay, Siri. I'm right here. I'll help as soon as your little one makes an appearance."

I had to be sure the foal was face first. Two weeks earlier, I'd wrapped the first twelve inches of Siri's tail in a bandage to keep it away from the birthing foal; it could contain bacteria that might cause infection. It also helped me see what was going on with the baby.

"I found two pairs of gloves and boots. I have them."

I glanced up at Ben who was still outside the stall. "Okay." I stood up and walked the few feet across the smallish stall toward him. The birthing stalls were a little smaller than the others with heat lamps hanging from the ceiling. I wouldn't turn them on until right before the foal was born. "Thank you for getting them." I reached out to take the stack of towels from him.

"Aren't you worried about getting doused?" Ben asked.

"Not really."

"Here are the boots." Ben handed them over and I stepped into them.

"As soon as I see the foal's foot, I'll help Siri by breaking her water. Then it's controlled and the baby will come faster. Since she's laying on her side it will help."

"Will she stay lying down? I Googled it last week during a slow shift and horses get up and down."

"They can. I just hope she doesn't." I set the towels down on the floor near the opposite wall.

"Pbrrrrbbbbb," Siri snorted, her legs stiffening again as she strained to push her foal out.

The white sack of fluid at her vagina got larger and a small hoof appeared. "Oh, thank God," I said with a relieved sigh.

"What?" Ben asked. "What happened?"

I pointed toward the obvious. "Do you see that? It's a hoof."

"This is amazing." Ben was astonished as he watched. "Thank you for letting me be here, Marin."

"You've earned it; besides, I might need your help." I smiled brightly; happy he was with me.

"Gladly." He winked.

After a few more hard pushes, the leg and nose started to show outside Siri's body, but encapsulated in the milky white amniotic sack that was ballooning with fluid.

I put on the gloves Ben had retrieved from the cabinet. The rubber went up my forearms and just over my elbows. "Ouch," I complained as I crouched down. The spikey hay jabbed my knees and thighs when I knelt behind Siri, reminding me that should have put on long pants, but now it was too late. The rubber boots covered my calves, at least, but made bending down more difficult.

"Can I come closer?" Ben asked.

"Sure, just put on those gloves. And this hay is painful on the knees," I warned.

"Wait. I'll be back." He ran out of the barn and was back within a minute with an empty box from a 24 pack of soda that I'd placed in the recycle bin in the kitchen. He was pulling at the ends and opening it up until it was a flat piece of cardboard. "Here. You can keel on this?" He opened the gate. "Stand up, please."

I was amazed at his thoughtfulness, but I did as I was told. He placed it on the floor on top of the hay where I'd been kneeling, then bent to brush the stray strands of hay stuck to the skin of my knees. "There you, go."

"Thank you." I smiled up him as he towered over me. "What about you?"

"I'm tough," he said blankly, and proceeded to crouch down next to me after he'd donned the gloves and was holding the squeegee. "Do you need this thing?"

"I will. Can you see the nose of the foal there, just inside the liquid bubble? I'm going to break the water then hopefully both feet and then the nose will come out. Then it will be born soon."

I reached out and used my index finger and thumb to break the membrane. Water gushed out at first, then ran out in a steady stream.

"Wow, that is a lot. Should I get the towels?" Ben wanted to know.

"No, let's save those for the foal after birth. We can change the bedding later today."

We both watched Siri as she strained another push. One of the hooves showed and the black nose. "I need to get the other foot out," I said. "May I have the squeegee please?" I used it to suction out the foal's nostrils, then handed it back to Ben. "Thanks."

Inside I was panicking. I'd seen this done by my uncle... I'd seen him up to his shoulder inside a mare trying to turn a foal, so this should be easy in comparison, but I was still nervous.

Sitting down onto my butt I gently put my hand inside Siri on the other side of the foal's nose, searching for the other foot. Thankfully, it wasn't too far up inside her, and I wrapped my hand around it and applied gentle pressure trying to gently pull it outside with the nose and other foot. "Both feet should have presented before the nose. I just have to get it out or it might get caught and it could injure one of both of them." I pulled with a bit more strength. "Ugggggh!" I grunted.

"Can I help?" Ben asked.

He was stronger than I was, clearly, but it was a balance between helping and hurting. I waited, with my hand still inside, until Siri had another contraction. I grunted and pulled, but still no result. Ben threw off his gloves and got behind me, sliding his hand down my arm and just inside the horse. His fingers closed around my forearm. "So, we should pull when she pushes, right?"

I nodded. His body was close against mine as he added his strength to mine. "Don't let go and tell me if I hurt you, Marin."

His grip was firm but gentle and when Siri strained with her next push, we were able to get the foal's second hoof to present and the head almost to the ears. "Oh, thank God."

I let go and fell back against Ben's body. He was kneeling behind me, so my butt was effectively on his groin, his hand still wrapped around me arm, and the other placed around me waist.

"Whoa," he laughed and then stood up, lifting me as if I weighed nothing to set me on my feet in front of him.

If I didn't have so much going on with Siri, I would have sworn my ovaries exploded. Feeling his hard body against mine caused shivers all over me. He was all man. I found myself comparing the way Ben felt against me to the softer, less fit body of Carter. If I weren't eaten alive with guilt over his death, I'd be letting myself revel in the sensations Ben created inside me.

"Will she be okay, now?" His words broke me out of my daze.

"Oh, I think so, but I want to be here, just in case." I bent to lift the white fetal sack away from the foal's face. "Ben, can you hand me one of those towels?" I took off my gloves before kneeling again to wipe the face clean. The red bag, as the sack was called, had some blood seeping out. Ben saw it.

"Marin, she's bleeding!" he exclaimed.

"A little blood is normal. It's okay, Ben." I loved how invested he was with Siri and her foal. His love of animals mirrored my own and that was just another thing to love about him. I paused and sucked in a breath. Could I already be in love with him?

"When will he be out? How long will it take?"

"Are you so sure it's a boy?"

"It's a gut feeling," Ben answered easily.

I sat next to my horse and wrapped a hand around both forelegs. I pulled until the head was completely free, careful not to injure the foal. Siri snorted as her stomach heaved again. I pulled in concert with her contractions. "It will just be a few minutes and the little one will be out."

Ben was sitting on the floor a few feet away, leaning up against the wall. He had a bird's eye view of what was happening. "Well, this is truly incredible. I'm already in love."

Again, my heart stopped. I knew he was speaking about the foal, but still, it affected me. "Me, too. How about if it is a boy, I'll let you name him?"

His face lit up, as I glanced over my shoulder. "That would be fantastic. Thank you, Marin. It means a lot to me."

"It's the least I can do." I turned back to the foal, now halfway out of his mother. I pushed the sack further back and dried off the foal's shoulders and front legs. He was black as night with no markings on his face. Now that Ben said he was a boy, I started thinking of the little thing that way. I patted Siri on her rear flank. "Rest a little, Siri. My sweet girl."

"Why don't you just pull him out of her?"

"I don't want to injure the placenta or umbilical cord. If it separates too soon it might affect the foal's oxygen or it could cause internal bleeding for Siri. It has to come out on its own after the birth."

"I see. Is this the first foal that's been born since your uncle died?"

I fell back onto my butt with my legs crossed in front of me. "Yes. I'm glad you're here, so I'm not alone. I would have been sad. This foal was a birthday gift last year."

"Yes, you told me. That means your birthday is coming up or just passed?"

"In a couple of months. Unfortunately, Siri's heat cycle didn't cooperate with my exact birthday. I had to take what I could get." I laughed softly.

Siri's four legs all tensed as she started pushing again. "Oh, here we go." I helped the foal a bit, but he slid out of his mother with her last push. I got rid of the sack and started to briskly rub him dry. His eyes blinked at me, so he was obviously breathing. "He's out."

"He?" Ben teased.

The truth was, I hadn't checked, but as I rubbed his back legs, I looked to determine the sex. "Yes. Hello, little man," I said softly. "Aren't you just the most handsome little guy, ever?"

"He is jet black."

"Like his sire," I gathered up the damp towels. "In about twenty minutes the placenta should be delivered."

Siri's head came up and she sniffed and licked at her foal.

"Doesn't the horse eat it?"

My face crinkled. "Ugh! No, thank God."

Ben laughed. "Some animals do. Like dogs. To get the milk flowing."

"Not horses. She'll lick him a little, but no, she doesn't eat it. I do have to save it to show the veterinarian, though."

Ben's handsome face showed surprise as he balked. "What the hell for? Remind me to be glad I didn't become a vet."

I laughed again as I got up and walked out of the stall to dispose of the towels, my intention also to go into the kitchen to get a large bowl for the placenta. "To make sure it all came out, silly. If some is left inside, she could get an infection and the vet would have to come out and manually extract any remnants."

"How would he do that?" Ben called after me.

He was just so funny. "He's got a much longer glove."

"Sorry I asked," he said dryly.

I chuckled all the way into the house.

everything
HAPPENS FOR
a reason

Chapter 11

BEN

The shower felt great as it washed away the sweat, slime, and grime of delivering the foal. After that we both went to sleep for a couple of hours, but now the delicious smell of bacon wafted in the air as I walked into the kitchen.

Marin glanced over her shoulder as she worked at the stove. She had also cleaned up and had on fresh clothes. My eyes couldn't help but roam over her slim back and rounded bottom now encased in clean, but frayed, sexy jean shorts. Her hair was still in the knot on the top of her head and the gracious column of her neck was revealed. My mouth almost watered at the sight.

"Are you hungry?" Marin asked over her shoulder as she cooked.

"Starving, actually."

She was beautiful, even in this easy, casual setting. It suited her and she had an ease about her that I found extremely attractive. She didn't have make-up on; she didn't need it. "Breakfast is almost ready."

I snapped my fingers and placed my closed fist with the flat of my hand. "It smells mouth-watering, but do I have time to run into town to pick up Gem first?"

She turned around to look at me, setting the fork she was using to turn the bacon frying in a cast iron skillet down. "Yes, that would be great! I miss her!" Her face broke out in a wide smile that only added to her fresh-faced gorgeousness.

"Me, too. I've been thinking about her since we started home from Minneapolis." I pulled the keys to my truck out of the front pocket of my jeans. I was wearing a white tank so the tattoo on my upper arm was visible. I had a few, but this was the biggest; a fireman's helmet and gas mask with an American Flag reflected in the face shield. The flames surrounding it and the flag were in full color. Marin's eyes lingered on it.

"Cool tattoo."

I shrugged. "It's what I do. I got it after I'd been doing it a year and knew I would always be a firefighter."

"Well, I like it. I'm making waffles, so don't take too long."

"I see, but I also have to feed the horses."

"Oh, I already did."

She was amazing, but I wasn't sure how I felt about her not needing help with it. Especially since I knew she was still nursing her sore ribs. "I could have done it."

"I know, but I wanted to let you sleep in. I'm surprised I was able to sneak out of the house with you on the couch, but you were sleeping hard."

I studied her for a moment wanting to admonish her for doing too much too soon, but I couldn't help but smile. "Are the waffles homemade or box?"

"Please." Her face wrinkled wryly, and she shook her head.

I noticed the waffle iron setting on the counter next to the stove. I couldn't remember the last time I had homemade waffles. This woman was too good to be true.

"Good to know," I said, heading out the door. The screen door banged behind me and I walked to my truck parked in front of the house. I could get used to this. What guy wouldn't want a beautiful woman cooking him breakfast after a night delivering a foal?

I was smiling from ear to ear as I decide to check on the baby. I wanted to get some pictures or a video to send to Dylan and Remi. I went to Siri's stall to find the foal was nursing with gusto. He was healthy and his mother seemed fine. She snorted when she saw me.

"Hello, girl. You did a good job on your baby. He's a fine one." I reached out and laid the flat of my hand on her forehead. "You're a beauty, Siri. I bet Gem will love this little guy."

I patted her again, and then hurried to the truck and was soon driving into town and to Davis' apartment.

I climbed the stairs two at a time. The air was cool, reminding me that fall wasn't that far away. Though it would get warmer later in the day, the morning breeze felt nice.

Wrap! Wrap! Wrap! I knocked on Davis' door, anxious to see the little puppy.

Davis opened the door holding Gem, who started to wiggle and wag her tail when she saw me. She whined and wiggled some more until I reached out to take her from my friend.

"I thought you'd be back last night, man." Davis' hair was sticking up from sleep and he rubbed his left eye with his first two fingers. "That's what your text said."

"Sorry, we got in late, as in early morning and I figured you'd be sleeping."

"Yeah, I gotta get going. I have to be at the station in an hour. How'd it go? Did you rescue your damsel in distress?"

I ruffled the fur on Gem's head as I held her against my chest with the other hand. Her coat was so silky soft. "I didn't need to rescue her. The police had her situated. I just brought her home."

"Yeah, whatever." Davis' eyebrow lifted knowingly. "I haven't seen you so googly-eyed over a woman before. Like ever."

My face twisted wryly, and I gave him an eye roll. "Uh huh. Whatevs, Davis. She just needs help right now. Later." I put up a hand in a make-shift wave then turned and retraced my steps to my truck. I lifted Gem up to look in her little face. "Come on, sweet face. Let's go see mommy."

The pup was still wagging her tail happily, and I let her stay on my lap as I drove the five miles back to Marin's ranch. No, it wasn't the safest thing, but she sat there calmly during the short drive. As we got closer to the ranch it was as if she knew we were close to her home. She stood up and moved to put her front paws on the door below the window so she could look outside. "Yes, we're almost home, sweets. Wait until you see the new baby. He's the same color as you."

When I drove into the yard, Marin was waiting, sitting on the porch and she got up and walked briskly toward the truck. There was something super-hot about frayed shorts and cowboy boots, her firm body and shapely legs. I couldn't help but notice how the V-neck T-shirt she was wearing molded around her shapely breasts.

I pulled the pup to my chest with one hand and opened the door with another. *"Man, you gotta stop,"* I told myself silently. *"The girl is off-limits."*

For now, my mind protested.

168

The pup squirmed in my arms, so I set her on the ground, and she took off like a rocket toward Marin on her short puppy legs.

"Hey, baby face!" The smile on Marin's face was stunning as she crouched down

so that the running dog could race into her embrace. She picked her up and held her to her face so she could kiss her head and cheeks over and over. It was clear the pair was equally excited for their reunion. "I missed you, so much!" Marin kissed Gem a few more times in quick succession as the pup tried to lick her face furiously. "I could just eat you up." She hugged her close. "Did she pee?" she asked, glancing in my direction, but still hugging the puppy close.

"Nope?" I shook my head.

"Okay." Marin turned and walked the short distance to the lawn portion of the large yard. She bent to release the dog in the grass, but the pup jumped up on her leg, clearly wanting to be snuggled for a longer period of time. "Go potty, Gem. Be a good girl for Mommy."

It was only a couple of minutes until the dog complied and we were all in the kitchen; Marin lifting the top of the Belgian waffle iron and ladling some batter into it. The table had been set with silverware and napkins and there was a bowl of fresh berries and a small, but old, yellow ceramic pitcher holding maple syrup. It was steaming hot and positioned next to a platter full of bacon.

"Do you want a couple of eggs?" Marin asked.

"If it's not too much trouble? I need the protein."

"You certainly, do," she murmured, then flustered, said, "I mean, sure thing. How do you take them?"

"Over medium. I never could stand runny whites."

Soon the eggs were frying, and the second waffle was in the iron. I sat at the table watching her in silence, the puppy lying at my feet. Within five minutes she laid a feast before me. The waffle with the berries over top, fresh maple syrup, steaming coffee, orange juice. I wasn't sure if I should start eating without her.

"Help yourself to the bacon. Do you think you'll want another waffle?"

"Sure, but I'd like to wait for you to begin eating."

"I'll just be a couple of minutes until this gets finished. You go ahead and start before it gets cold." She took one finished waffle out of the iron with a fork and placed it on a plate before ladling more batter into the iron.

"Okay, but my mother would kill me for such horrible manners," I murmured, reaching for the syrup to pour the steaming liquid over the waffle and fresh fruit, then I added salt and pepper to the fried eggs. "This looks amazing, Marin. Thank you." My stomach growled hungrily.

Her brow crinkled and she snorted a little. "Thank *you*. You've done so much for me there is nothing I can do to make it up to you. The least I can do is make you a decent breakfast, Ben."

"Well, I appreciate it. It's been a long time since anyone has cooked for me like this."

She placed her plate across from me just before she took the last waffle out of the iron, put it on a plate and covered it with a skillet lid to keep it warm while I finished the first one. I was more and more curious about her.

"It's my pleasure. This was Uncle Leonard's favorite breakfast. I added the berries because I thought he needed something organic and not just a pile of carbs and fat." She smiled, pouring a scant amount of syrup over the waffle and fruit on her plate.

Her eyes were curious, and I nodded, then forked up the first bite of waffle. The real maple syrup and fruit made it extra delicious. "Oh, my God," I managed after the first bite. "*So good!*"

Her smile brightened. "Ben, can I ask you something?"

I nodded. "Of course."

"Why aren't you… with someone? I mean, you're so… like the perfect guy, so well… you came to get me, and you're here now… I can only assume if there was someone special in your life, she wouldn't approve."

Pleasure burst inside me at the question. If she was asking, then it meant she had an interest in me as a man. I looked at her through hooded eyes. There was a faint blush to her cheeks. "I'm not with anyone. Since I moved here, I've been working a lot and pulling as much overtime as I'm allowed. I'm saving up to build a new house," I explained.

"That sounds like a great plan."

"It is." The corner of my mouth lifted in a half smile. "Too bad I have no life in the meantime."

"You're incredible at your job. I can see how dedicated you are."

Our eyes connected and locked. "I didn't do so well at your place."

"It was too far gone when you got there. I just know you're the best," she said, simply. "You all did all you could."

I was enjoying the feeling her confidence caused, but I still felt like I'd failed her.

We continued eating but there was a nagging need inside of me to ask about her relationship with Carter. Could she really love a man who raised a hand to her in anger? "Forgive me for asking this, Marin… it might be too soon, but was Carter… good to you?"

She hesitated, rubbing the back of her neck nervously. "What makes you ask?"

"The bruises. Did he beat you?"

She set her fork down and shrugged her slim shoulders, her eyes getting glassy. "Not until after Uncle Leonard died. He was sweet and attentive before that, but it was like a light switch was flipped. He became very different. He drank a lot and got angry if I did or said the smallest thing he didn't like. He yelled a lot. I thought if I changed, maybe he'd go back to how he was before, but even though I was careful, he didn't. He got worse when I wouldn't marry him."

"Why did you stay with him at all?" My heart ached for her, but I was also angry that she'd stay with someone who would abuse her.

She shrugged again. "Carter was all I had, and I just didn't have the strength to be alone right then. He tried to spend the money I got from the life insurance, but I wanted to use it to pay off the mortgage on the house. That's what Uncle Leonard would want me to do. I think Carter expected me to put the check into the business account. He was running the business and had access. That was the first mistake, but I was so sad after my uncle's death, and I trusted him. When the money wasn't there, he basically ran off all of the other mechanics who had been at The Shop for years, and then, the customers stopped coming. Two months later, we had only a fraction of the jobs we had before, and he was hitting me daily and drinking heavily. I didn't go into town as much because I didn't want people to notice."

"If Carter were here right now, I'd literally beat the shit out of him," I growled. Marin's eyes widened in surprise. "I mean, I'm sorry he's dead, but maybe he got what he deserved." I wished I was sitting next to her and not across the table. I wanted to touch her, to hold her, to take away the pain I saw behind her eyes. "Remember, I told you about Missy."

"I remember." A tear tumbled from her beautiful eye and she quickly brushed it from her cheek. "I don't wish him dead, but I do wish I'd never met him. I was stupid. I believed him when he said he loved me. He was good looking and he swept me away. All he wanted was the money and the business, and I realized that the man he was at the start, was just a charade. He played both me and my uncle."

Did Carter kill her uncle? I couldn't keep it from crossing my mind after what she'd told me. As delicious as the food was, the conversation was taking away my appetite. "Well, he can't hurt you anymore."

"You're right, but his family..." Fear laced her voice. "They blame me for Carter's death since it happened at my business."

"I'll ask Davis if he knows a good lawyer to help figure it out, but I think you need to file a restraining order."

"Would it work? I mean, I know Apollo's name and his mother, but there were many others. I can't get a restraining order on someone when I don't know who they are."

She was right, it could be complicated, but I was grasping at straws. I couldn't stay with her twenty-four-seven because of my job, but the thought of them hurting her filled me with terror.

"All of the files from the business burned up in the fire, but I'll call the insurance company on Monday. I think it best to just pay his family off."

I ran a hand down my face and over my jaw, feeling the growing scruff on it. I was frustrated and angry. "Marin, you can't reason with criminals. They won't stop."

Something haunting crossed her face and another tear fell. "My uncle said something just like that. About reasoning with bullies, I mean."

"He sounds like an amazing man, but I think he'd agree you can't pay those bastards off because they'll just keep coming," I insisted.

"I don't know what else to do," she said simply. "I think there is an injury or death clause in the insurance, and we carried workmen's comp insurance, too."

"It was an accident, right? What happened, Marin?" It was direct of me to ask, but I wanted to help her, but I couldn't do it without the full story. "What were you doing there?"

I could see her visibly stiffen and the color drained from her face. She hesitated a moment too long.

"I'm just trying to help."

"I know." She nodded. "I went to The Shop to talk to Carter. He - he was drunk, and he got upset. He came at me and knocked over a lantern and it started burning some spilled oil on the floor. There was grease everywhere and it flashed. He was standing too close."

Tears flooded her eyes by the time she finished. It was a short explanation, but it was clearly an accident. I wondered if the coroner had taken a blood sample as part of the autopsy. Even though the poor bastard was burnt to a crisp, it was usual for any victims who succumb during fires to be taken to the coroner and an autopsy done.

"Was there an autopsy report?" I didn't know why I even asked. The poor bastard burned to death and had been obvious by the condition of the body.

"I'm not sure, but I think it would have been sent to his family."

"As business owner, you have a right to know, too. I'll check it out. If it's okay."

"Okay." She wiped at her face with both hands but ended up burying her face in her hands and crying.

I felt like crap. I should have just shut my damn mouth and just enjoyed breakfast. I got up and walked to her side of the table, crouching down so my face was level with hers.

"I'm sorry. Marin. I shouldn't have brought it up and ruined this amazing meal. I just... I want to take care of you." My voice was soft, but she only started crying harder. I couldn't help myself, I reached out and pulled her into a tight embrace. Her forehead landed on my shoulder, her face turning into the cord of my neck as she cried. I stroked the back of her head with one hand and held her close to my chest with my other arm. Her arms curled against me.

"Ben, what am I going to do?"

I inhaled a big breath and filled my lungs completely while I continued to comfort her. "It will work out. I think you need security cameras on the house, though."

She pulled back to look up into my face with sad eyes, then nodded. "Okay."

"I'll handle it, if you'll let me." I reached up and pushed a stray tendril behind her ear and placed a long, gentle kiss on Marin's opposite temple. Our bodies were still close, and her hand came up to circle my wrist and her chin lifted, silently begging for my kiss.

Electricity shot through me at the innocent touch of my mouth against her skin and went straight to my dick. I wanted to kiss her mouth so fucking bad. I was shaking, yet I resisted, telling myself that she was still too vulnerable. I wanted her so much it hurt, but I wanted more than sex once. She was fragile and she needed more than an orgasm and I realized... so did I. I wanted more and that would take time.

"Ben..." she sighed my name and her hot breath rushed deliciously over my mouth. I swallowed as our mouths hovered together. Her fingers drifted up to lightly touch my jaw. I was struggling in a big way.

"Marin," I returned, knowing I was losing the battle. The puppy whined and I pulled back, regaining my sense of logic, my hand running down her arm to squeeze her hand. I bent to pick

175

up the pup and hand her to the young woman in front of me. "You'll be okay. You have Gem and me to take care of you. I think she wants a bite of that delicious waffle."

Marin sat back in chair, as if suddenly aware of what almost happened. She blinked, tears still clinging to her eyelashes as Gem licked at her face. Her hand ran down over the puppy and she reached forward onto her plate and broke off a small piece of the waffle, holding it while the dog gobbled it up greedily.

I moved back to my chair and started eating the now cold waffle. It was still delicious, and I had another one to down. That was close. If the dog hadn't intervened, I was certain I would have been making love to her on the kitchen floor, and that wasn't what I wanted for Marin. I wanted her, but when I made her mine, it would be in a bed with candlelight, and soft music. She deserved no less. I knew it would happen; the attraction between us was a tangible thing, but it would take more time. I had to be more aware so this "almost sex" didn't happen again.

"After breakfast, let's go see the foal. I told Gem about her new brother." I winked at Marin, trying to lighten the mood, hoping she wouldn't see my reticence as rejection.

I relaxed when Marin reached forward to pick up another small piece of waffle for Gem who happily gobbled it down licking her fingers. "Have you thought of a name yet?"

"Not yet," I shook my head, pouring the now barely warm syrup on the second waffle Marin had made for me. "All good things come to those who wait."

"Well, don't be too long. I can't keep calling him little colt."

"That would be bad. I thought I'd speak to my nephew about it. Would that be okay?"

She smirked. "How old is he, again?"

"Eight," I replied.

"As long as it's not something dumb like Happy, Lucky, or Blacky." Her nose crinkled in disdain and I burst out laughing.

"Hey don't make fun! Lucky was my first dog's name."

"I rest my case. This little colt needs a dignified name. I can tell by looking at him he's going to be magnificent."

"You would know," I said, taking a bite.

"I've seen a few foals over the years on the ranch, and he is just about perfect."

"I got a few pictures to send to Dylan. I'll talk to him later."

As if on cue, my phone rang from my back pocket. I pulled it out and checked the screen. It was the station calling me in.

"Yeah?"

It was my chief. "Ben, we have flames on the west range of the Tetons and it's windy. We have to get in front of it and we need all the help we can get. Sorry to pull you in on your day off, but we need you. It's three-alarm already."

"Not a problem. I'll be there as soon as I can." I shut off my phone and stood up from the table. "Marin, I'm sorry, I have to go. There is a forest fire in the Tetons. They're calling me in."

"Oh no!" Marin stood up anxiously. "Is there anything I can do?"

"Just pray we get it under control. It's on the west range so Jackson is safe for now, but I have to move. I'm sorry."

Marin rushed forward and grabbed both of my forearms. "Ben… please be careful!"

My hands closed around her elbows as she looked up at me with worried eyes. "I will. Promise. I'll call you later."

She nodded and I rushed from the house and to my truck. Adrenaline was already kicking in as I tore out of the driveway of the ranch and I raced into town.

everything
HAPPENS FOR
a reason

Chapter 12

Marin

I spent the day with Siri and her new foal in between watching the news for information about the fire. I was scared for Ben but tried to calm myself down by telling myself he was excellent at his job and keeping myself busy.

Gem followed me out to the barn, and curiously peered into the stall as we waited for the vet to arrive to give Siri and her foal a check-up. She was too small to crawl over the first board to get into the stalls but stood on her hind feet with her front paws holding onto it to peer in curiously between the slats. Her tail wagged furiously, and she barked a couple of times.

Yap! Yap! Yap! Yap! Booowwwww!

Her little bark reminded me that she was just a baby, too. "Come here, sweetie." I picked her up and held her in my arms. "Soon you can go in and meet the new foal, but even though he's a baby like you, he's much bigger. I don't want my little sweet face getting hurt," I cooed, kissing her once on the cheek and the top of her smooth black head. When I set the puppy down again, she scampered around the barn as had become her custom, running up and down the main corridor; sniffing and exploring everywhere she went.

I pulled out my phone to call Dr. Porter; the large animal vet that Uncle Leonard had always used. I wanted to check on his arrival time, so I scrolled through my contacts to find the number.

"Marin?" I heard Gina's voice from the outside in the yard.

I quickly moved toward the entrance to the barn. "Gina! I'm in here!"

It was nice to have a new friend. She smiled tiredly when she saw me. "Hey!" Gina was dressed in her hospital uniform and must have finished an overnight shift. "I just stopped to see how you were doing."

I'd texted her from the hotel in Minneapolis, letting her know I'd be coming home early but without a full explanation. "What happened?"

"Oh," I answered, mentally forcing myself to refrain from cringing. "Carter's family was a bit more colorful than I'd bargained for."

She came forward and hugged me lightly. "Why didn't you text me the details? I've been curious about what happened."

"I just wanted to get home as quickly as possible. His brother and mom… well, suffice it to say they were sort of thuggish. They basically…" I wondered if I should spill my guts and tell my new friend the entire truth. Who knew what they'd do to anyone who knew the truth and the last thing I wanted was to put her in danger. "Well, they only wanted me to come for the funeral because they wanted to talk to me about an insurance settlement."

Gina's expression changed to one of disgust. "His mother did that? That's hard to believe she'd be thinking of money at a time like this."

I nodded once. "Yes, I was stunned, as well. Maybe that's why Carter didn't have much of a relationship with his family. There were several of his relatives there. They reminded me more of a gang than a family. I just decided to get back to Jackson and figure it all out as quickly as possible."

"Wow. That sucks. I'm sorry. It must have been weird being surrounded by a bunch of people you'd never met."

"It was, but I'll sort it out." I decided to change the subject. "My mare had a new foal early this morning. Wanna see him? He's so precious."

"I'd love to!" Gina agreed, and walked with me into the barn. "You have a lot of horses!"

"Not all of them are mine. We board them for other people who don't have the land or facilities needed to maintain them. My uncle started doing it for a friend and it's grown into a little business. I'm at maxed-out capacity now, though."

Gina looked in a number of the stalls as we made our way toward Siri's stall. "They're so pretty."

"The little guy is in the last stall on the left." Within a minute we were both standing on the lower rung of the stall with our arms folded over the top one.

"Oh my gosh! He's gorgeous, but he doesn't look like his mom, does he?" Gina exclaimed.

I laughed softly. "Nope. He's all his sire."

"He's so sweet."

I agreed with a nod, watching the little foal laying in the hay. Siri was standing, finally munching away at her alfalfa. "He is. He's a tired little man. Being born wore him out."

"All babies sleep a lot. I mean, human babies do, so animals must, too." I couldn't argue with her logic and after all, she was a nurse.

"Did you get to watch the birth?"

"Yes. Siri needed a little help, but not much. I was worried because this is her first foal. If you come back in a couple of days, he'll be running around all over the place by then."

"It's incredible how quickly little animals can walk."

"Yep. He was up and nursing within a couple of hours."

The little colt struggled to his feet and pranced around the small stall the best he could, his short, brush-like tail swishing behind him.

"What's his name?"

"Not sure, yet. I told Ben that he could name him." Gina's head snapped around to look at me, her expression surprised. "Since he's been so nice to me," I explained guiltily.

"Really? I mean, I knew he helped take care of your dog overnight, that once."

"Yes, and he's helped with the horses and with Gem when I went to the funeral. And…" I bit my lip, hesitating. "He was here when Siri gave birth."

Oh, crap, I silently chastised myself. Now I'd have to explain why Ben was here so early in the morning.

"Was he staying here while you were gone?"

I didn't want to lie to my new friend, but I wasn't up to explaining every detail of the past few days, either. I vowed to come clean and tell Gina the entire truth when I had a chance to come to terms with it all myself. "Um… he was here when I got home this morning." It wasn't exactly a lie, though I was teetering right on the line.

"What a welcome. Ben is so hot," she murmured, almost to herself. "So… virile. I just want to lick him from head to toe."

My eyes widened in surprise at Gina's boldness. I felt uncomfortable and I wasn't sure why. "He is attractive."

"Understatement of the century!" Gina's expression became more animated. "Oh, my God, I wonder if he's seeing anyone."

"I don't think so."

Her smile brightened. "Wow. That's sort of unbelievable."

"Isn't it?" I agreed miserably.

"Is he coming out here later? For the horses, I mean?"

I put my hand out and patted Siri's nose, then rested my forehead against hers. I didn't want Gina to see how red my face was. It must be, if the heat flushing my cheeks was any indication. I closed my eyes and sucked in a shaky breath.

"Yes. He insists that I can't care for them yet." I wasn't sure that Ben would be back because it was uncertain if the fire he was fighting was getting under control.

"Well, he's right. You shouldn't be lifting anything yet. Cracked ribs take time to heal."

"I know, but I feel guilty asking him to continue to help out." I couldn't deny the pain and stiffness I still felt, but I wanted to get back to normal as quickly as possible.

"So? He seems like the type to enjoy hard work. What time is he coming over?" Her question held more than surface curiosity and it stung.

"I'm not sure. He usually comes out around five or six, I think? Except he's fighting a big blaze on the northern range." I ran a nervous hand through my long hair, pushing it back off of my face in the process.

Gina turned to lean her shoulder on the stall gate. "Oh, yeah. I heard about that on the radio on my way out here. It's a pretty big one."

I'd planned on listening to the news after I'd checked on the foal and dealt with the vet. "Yeah. He told me."

"He did? What's going on with you two?" Gina's coy curiosity was crystal clear.

"Nothing." I shook my head uncomfortably, moving away to the feed stall to get a handful of alfalfa and offered it to Siri when I came back. "He's just been helping out and naturally, I'm concerned for his safety. It's dangerous work."

Her questioning eyes left me unsettled. Deep down, I hoped Ben was more than a friend, but how could I know for sure? I was feeling fragile, and he was used to rescuing people. I didn't want that to be the reason for the start of something to develop between us.

"Does it make you feel uncomfortable? I mean, having any man around this much right after Carter's death? It must remind you."

"Everything reminds me, Gina, but I'm thankful for Ben's help," I said stiffly. "He's been a perfect gentleman."

She looked surprised. "Oh, I wasn't suggesting otherwise. I just meant Ben being one of the firemen on the scene could be weird."

"Well, it's not. Ben has become a friend, just as you have. You've both been wonderful."

She must have sensed my trepidation at the direction of the conversation. "Awww! That's sweet of you to say." Gina's smile was genuine. "Do you need anything at the house? I can drive you into town if you need to get groceries or anything."

Instantly, I felt ashamed at my brief moment of annoyance. If I were honest with myself, it was more Gina's interest in Ben than her bringing up Carter's death that bothered me. But why shouldn't she be interested in him? He was single, she was single, both attractive as hell… why shouldn't they hook up, especially since it was way too soon for me to want him? My heart fell sickeningly into my stomach. She had no way of knowing that I was attracted to him.

"The vet should be here any minute, so I should wait for him. But thank you."

"Oh, is something wrong?"

"I don't think so. Just a check-up after foaling."

"Oh, that makes sense." Her eyes lit up excitedly. "But maybe we can grab lunch later?" When I hesitated, her face fell a bit and she continued. "Or I can bring out anything you need if you'd rather not go into town."

"I have to make some phone calls to the insurance companies to file the claims after the accident, and I have no idea how long that will take. My car was a total loss as well as the business."

"How is it going with Mama and her new baby, Marin?" Dr. Porter's voice echoed through the barn as he made his way toward us. I couldn't believe how relieved I was when he made his appearance at that moment. He was similar in age to my Uncle Leonard, and they were life-long friends. He was almost like another uncle to me.

"Oh, hey, Doc! They both seem okay. I don't think any of the placenta is missing."

"That's wonderful!" the doctor exclaimed. "Has Siri allowed him to nurse yet?"

Gina and I stepped back to allow him into the stall with Siri and her foal. He was carrying a very large duffle bag, which he set down just inside the stall and unzipped it.

"Yes. I think it's all good."

He moved forward and slid a hand down Siri's flank. "Do you have the afterbirth? I'd like to take a look at it after I check out this fine young man."

"Yep. I'll be right back." I'd put it in a plastic bag inside the old refrigerator that resided at the other end of the barn and I rushed to get it.

"You keep it?" Gina asked, horrified. "Oh my God! That's gross!"

Dr. Porter laughed heartily. "Only until I check it for missing pieces."

I smiled as I listened to Gina groan. I hurried and retrieved the bag, then ran back to the stall. Gina was still talking with Dr. Porter when I set the bag on the concrete by his duffle bag.

"Then what happens to it?" she asked.

"I can take it back to my office and put it with other medical waste. I have a service that disposes of it," Dr. Porter explained.

"Uncle Leonard would sometimes burn it in a barrel out back," I added upon my return to the pair.

"Ewww!" Gina moaned. "I didn't think it could get any nastier."

I laughed as Dr. Porter shot me an amused look as he chuckled.

He had finished his examination of Siri and her foal and had moved on to the contents of the bag, bending to untie the knot I'd placed in the white plastic bag. "You might want to leave for this, miss" he suggested.

"Oh!" I exclaimed, realizing I hadn't introduced them. "Dr. Porter, this is my friend, Gina."

"Nice to meet you, Doctor. Marin, can we step away?" Gina asked with a cringe. "Before he gets to that?"

I couldn't help my amusement. "You're a nurse. What's a little afterbirth?" I teased.

"Ugh. God, it looks like it's a lot."

"About twenty pounds," I confirmed, with a short laugh.

"Yuk!" Gina started moving toward the exit without waiting for me. "Let's talk out by my car. Please?"

"I'll be right behind you! Dr. Porter, so they're both okay?"

He continued his work, examining the contents of the bag by pulling it out and holding it up, searching for rips or holes. When he was finished his examination, he returned the afterbirth to the bag, tied it shut, and shot me a wink. "A nurse, huh? Surly this can't be any worse than emptying dirty bed pans, but maybe that's just me." He laughed gruffly.

Dr. Porter made me giggle. "I think the nurse's aides to the dirty work, Doc."

"That explains it" He chuckled again. "They're both fit as a fiddle."

"Awesome." A big smile split spread across my face.

"You did a good job. Run along with your friend, Marin. I'll finish up." he insisted. He had known me since I first arrived to live with Uncle Leonard, and he still treated me like a young girl.

"Okay, but don't forget to send me a bill." I knew he wouldn't. He hadn't since Uncle Leonard died.

"Okay, sure."

"I mean it!"

"Uh huh," he used a gloved hand to shoo me away. I'd learned over the years that it was no use arguing with the old man who was like family. He was sometimes grumpy and surly, but with a heart of gold.

I found Gina waiting by her car, and Gem waddled along at my side as we emerged into the bright light of day. It was warm, but not hot, and the breeze made for a comfortable morning. "So? Do you want to go into town? My day is all yours! You can catch me up on the details of your trip to Minnesota."

I had no reason to hide anything from Gina. She'd been so nice. No reason, except I didn't want to tell her that Ben had come to get me, or the details about the road trip home. I was worried if I shared too many details about Carter's family and the attempted kidnapping, then the rest would follow, or I'd have to make something up and I was a terrible liar. I knew this about myself.

"I'd love to shop with you sometime, Gina, but I just got back and spent all night up with Siri. I'm tired and Gem missed me. I want to spend some time playing with her and getting those calls to the insurance companies made. Maybe I'll get a nap later, too."

"Oh, okay. I understand, but listen, when you feel better, I'd love to hang out."

"Sure." I bent to pick up my puppy, holding her against my chest and kissing the top of her head as I petted her silky black coat. "Me, too. I was just telling Ben that I was feeling guilty because Carter's death brought the two of you into my life and you're both so wonderful. I mean, I'm truly blessed to know the two of you."

Gina offered a genuine smile and covered her heart with both hands. "Well, I'm glad we've become friends, Marin, but I knew what you meant."

"Thank you."

"Maybe we can all hang out sometime, too," she suggested happily. She was so pretty. Her vibrant red hair the perfect foil for her green eyes. "Ben, too?" she asked hopefully.

"Sure, I can ask him."

"How are your other injuries healing?" Gina asked as we hovered around her car. "That's the real reason I stopped out."

"Oh, nothing hurts except a twinge in the ribs here and there."

"It is probably best if you rest, but if decide you need anything I can bring dinner later, if you're too tired to cook." She paused and met my eyes. "If Ben will be here working, I can bring enough for him, too," she said coyly.

"I don't know how long he'll be here. He may just feed the horses and leave. At this point I don't even know what time because of the fire." I wished Gina would just come out and say she wanted to me to hook them up instead of dancing around it. I was probably being overly sensitive, but something akin to pain took root in my chest. I had no claim to Ben, and it would be weird and unseemly to get into another relationship this soon after Carter's death. Especially, when I felt responsible for it. Ben and Gina were both good people and I shouldn't stand in their way.

"That's okay. I'll still bring you something, either way. I don't have any other plans and I'd love to find out what Ben names that little guy."

I forced a smile. "Sure. That's nice of you. Gina."

"Okay! See you later, then! I'm off!" She hopped into her car and backed up to head out of the driveway.

I kissed the top of Gem's head again as I watched her leave. Why did I feel so awful?

"Come on, baby. Let's get this call out of the way."

I took the puppy inside and up to my room, then set her on my bed. She found a cozy spot near my pillows to curl up and was asleep in seconds. I took my cell phone from the back pocket of my shorts before sitting down on the bed's edge for the tedious task of determining exactly what our liability coverage was for the business. An hour and a half later, the claims with the business and car insurance companies were filed, and I could finally relax. I had explained the situation with Carter and was told that they would need to access the police and fire commissioners' reports, as well as the coroner's, but the woman was nice and offered her condolences, telling me she'd reach out as soon as she had approval.

I rolled over to curl around the pup and thought about Gina and Ben. "Ughhhhhh!" I moaned miserably.

"What am I going to do, Gem?" My throat got thick just thinking about it. I couldn't help my feelings for Ben, though I'd probably be labeled the floozy of Jackson if we started dating this soon after Carter's death, and it might raise suspicion that I didn't want raised. Deep down, I felt responsible for Carter's accident, so maybe I didn't deserve someone as wonderful as Ben. I had no right to tell Gina I wanted him.

I swallowed hard and wiped an errant tear that had slipped from my eye away. I sucked in a shaky breath. "Ben," I murmured his name with a tangible ache in my voice. He was out there somewhere being a hero. *Again.*

Gem was still sleeping soundly at my side as I stroked her little body. My eyes were sleepy, but the turmoil inside was preventing me from getting in the nap I needed. As the hours passed, I'd become more and more worried about Ben. His job was so dangerous.

I reached for my phone to see if I could get any new updates on the fire, but it still wasn't contained. After a few more seconds, I started typing out a text to Ben. I was sure he wouldn't see it until his work was finished, but I hoped he'd ease my worry more quickly than the news and text me when he was finished.

Afterward, I finally laid back on my pillows and closed my eyes, still holding my phone.

Chapter 13

BEN

Finally, we got the fire under control, but it was just after midnight. I was so sticky and sweaty; it felt as if the night air had glued my clothes to my skin.

Each of the stations responding had taken a section and worked in unison until we'd snuffed the entire thing out. The fire covered over a ten thousand acres of forest and we were all spent. My arms and legs felt like wet noodles. We used the combined methods of air drops and fire breaks to get it under control. The muscles in my neck, back, and shoulders ached from the fifteen hours of chopping and sawing down trees to deprive the fire of fuel.

I was exhausted and covered in soot. I hadn't had a moment to check my phone until the trip back to Jackson and was hoping Marin had been in touch. Though I'd normally shower before I went home, it was the middle of the night and I had to be back at the station early in the morning.

I was pleased to see there were two messages from her. One telling me not to worry about the horses and another sent a little later checking up on me. I smiled as I read it. It made me so damn happy that she was worried. I found myself smiling like a giddy schoolboy.

Hey, just checking in to make sure you're safe. When you're able, let me know, no matter how late it is.

My heart sped up at her words. Maybe I wasn't crazy. Maybe there *was* something happening between us and I hadn't imagined the incredible pull I felt every time I was near her. She would be sleeping by now, but I tapped out a response anyway.

I'm done for the night. The fire is finally contained, and we're headed back. I have to work my regular shift later, but I'll stop out and feed the horses, early morning. Thanks for checking up on me. I'm sorry I wasn't there to help you tonight.

It wasn't long until my phone pinged in response. Again, my lips slid into a huge grin and Davis noticed.

"It's kind of early to get involved with that woman, isn't it, Ben?" he asked knowingly. "You warned me off of her and now you're trying to hit it?"

I scowled at my friend, my brow furrowing beneath my helmet. "I'm not trying to *hit it*, dickhead," I retorted angrily. "She needs help right now. Not that it's any of your damned business."

Davis smiled slyly, the white of his teeth flashing against his dirty face and the cover of night. "Uh huh," was all he said. "Well, the fire commissioner ruled the fire at her business was an accident. The report came down while you were away, and I didn't have time to tell you before this job."

My expression softened. At least that was some good news. I wasn't aware that they even spoke to Marin yet. At least, she hadn't mentioned it. "Good. That's something at least."

"Is she going to rebuild? If it were me, I'd just take the cash. I mean, she doesn't have any shop experience, right?"

I wasn't sure what she was going to do because, again, it wasn't something we'd discussed in detail. It dawned on me that if she didn't rebuild, she might sell the ranch and move out of Wyoming. She didn't have any other family in Jackson and running the ranch alone might get overwhelming. More than anything, if she moved and Carter's family didn't know where she lived, those slimy bastards from Minneapolis couldn't harm her. I sucked in a breath. If I looked at the situation objectively, that would probably be the best thing for her, so why did my gut get so tight when I thought about it. I mean, it literally ached.

"She has done the administrative work for years, but I'm not sure of her plans. I think she's still in shock over the whole thing and may mull it over for a bit. She's been through a lot, Davis. Her uncle passed away a few months ago, too."

"I remember," Davis answered. "If that forlorn look on your face means anything, I'd say you better make sure she stays around here… because I'll kick your ass if you follow her. I'm not helping you move again."

Davis and I were facing each other in the left rear passenger compartment of the engine as we drove back to Jackson. I leaned back in my seat and stared at him. "We're friends. Am I attracted to her? Yes. I'd have to be dead not to be, Davis."

His eyes widened. As we got into town and we passed under a streetlight, I could see his expression despite the smoke stains and soot around his eyes and mouth, and the line where his mask had been. "True, that," he agreed emphatically. "What about the guy who died? Her boyfriend, right? It's got to be too soon for her."

Davis was my closest friend and I felt comfortable sharing.

"Exactly, but the prick was abusive. She had a few cracked ribs and some bruises after the fire, but some of the bruises were yellow and green so obviously from before. She fell running back to her ranch, but she wasn't thrown from the blast, so the ribs were from before, too."

"Oh, shit," Davis said. "That's bad."

We had to speak loudly due to the open cab and the roaring of the engine, though the roads were relatively empty due to the hour.

"Yeah, if that bastard wasn't already dead, I swear to God, I'd kill him."

Davis studied me. I knew what he was thinking; I was screwed. "What did you find when you got to Minneapolis? I guess he wasn't much different from his family, huh?" Davis asked astutely. "Is that situation sorted out?"

If only I knew. "I'm thinking no. That's another reason I need to stay close."

"You can't be out there on the ranch the nights you have to overnight at the station, so how is that going to work?"

I shrugged, though the heavy turnout coat I wore hid the movement. "I don't know, yet."

"How many of them were there?"

I shook my head. "I didn't get to see any of them. Marin was already away from them by the time I got to her and she didn't want to go get her suitcase that was still in the brother's car. She said there were a few men and a few women there, and it appeared they all lived under one roof."

"A regular commune…" Davis said.

"Marin said it seemed more like a gang than a family."

"Scary shit. Well, if you need any help, just let me know."

"Thanks." I nodded and looked out the window. Davis was a good man and better friend, but I hoped it wouldn't come to that.

I had a twelve-hour shift ahead of me and the gravity of the fire we'd just fought meant all of us that were coming on duty at 6 AM were already on duty coming up on 1 AM. Our asses would be dragging, but maybe we could stagger in a couple of hours of sleep. We had to clean up the engine, gear and equipment to ready it for the next fire, as well as the other duties that occupied us during the day. Thankfully, it wasn't my day for banging pots. Cooking wasn't something I loved doing and half asleep, no way.

My phone pinged again.

I figured you'd be tired and hungry, so I made up the couch and left a sandwich and some cookies on the table. I know you have to work tomorrow, and I thought it might be easier than going home. Your choice.

I was elated. My heart soaring. She was so thoughtful, and this would mean I could sleep another hour. Maybe she was scared to be alone but afraid to tell me. Either way, I was happy to stay over. She was an angel.

That sounds good. Thank you.

You remember where the spare key is?

There are drinks in the refrigerator, and you know where the shower and towels are.

Help yourself.

195

You're awesome. Get some sleep. I'll be quiet when I come in.

I was sure my heart would burst with satisfaction. This didn't mean we had a relationship, but it sure as hell meant Marin trusted me. Now if only I could make her see how amazing she was. I wanted to wipe all of the self-doubt and pain out of her life. I wanted it as if my own life depended on it. In the meantime, I knew what I had to do.

Marin

My life fell into an easy routine and I felt as if a huge weight had lifted because Carter was no longer in my life. I never realized how he had dragged me down, how awful he made me feel about myself, or how scared I was every moment in his presence.

The time I spent with Ben had made it all so crystal clear. Being with Ben was the best part of my day. I looked forward to seeing him, but I knew he wouldn't be keeping up the twice daily visits and staying for dinner now that I was feeling better. After I was healed and I could take care of the horses myself, he'd no longer have an excuse to come out to the ranch, though he was growing close to Siri's foal.

He and his nephew, Dylan, had settled on the name, Dark, for the new colt. It couldn't be more appropriate for our almost black baby, and I simply adored it. It was perfect for the frisky little horse, and my heart melted every time I saw how tender Ben was with the little colt, and how Dark would always snort, neigh and trot toward Ben whenever he saw him coming. It was definitely a mutual affection, and it was special. I melted every time.

I hoped with all my heart that the camping trip Ben mentioned before would come to fruition very soon. There was still a good portion of the summer left but the first snowfall was unpredictable, and it would be better to plan the camping trip for no later than October first.

I'd decided not to rebuild the shop, for now at least; happy when the local diner owner, Arlene Reynolds, called me and offered me a job from 6 AM – 3 PM five days a week. I would be starting in ten days. I barely remembered applying because it was the day Carter died, and I'd been so focused on getting away from him. I was a bit surprised by her call, but I knew I would enjoy a low stress job that I could leave behind at quitting time. Even if it made little use of my education, I felt it would give me a chance to figure out what I really wanted to do while making enough money to pay for utilities and groceries.

After the fire commissioner's report came in and the claim was filed, the insurance company soon approved it. I was waiting on a pretty sizable settlement, but I thought it best to bank it until I made some more tangible decisions about my future. I'd given them Carter's mother's phone number so they could contact the family directly about the accidental death claim, though I wasn't sure of the status. The sooner I was able to distance from that family, the better.

Today, on my follow-up appointment, the doctor had cleared me to do light lifting; the cracks in my ribs were knitted and healing nicely, and the ugly green and purple bruises had finally disappeared. Maybe now, Ben wouldn't be reminded of the abuse every time he looked at me, but it would also mean I wouldn't need him to help at the ranch. I exhaled sadly at the thought. I would miss him more than I wanted to admit and hoped we'd still keep in touch afterward.

Gina continued to pester me about Ben and so far, I'd managed to skirt the issue, but it was beginning to wear on me.

She made me promise to schedule a casual run-in at the Mangy Moose, one of the more popular local hangouts, so she could talk to him without being conspicuous, and it would be better to take myself out as intermediary. My heart wasn't in it, but tonight was the night we had all settled on. Gina was picking me up and we were meeting Ben and a couple of his friends at the Moose.

Ben worked four twelve-hour shifts per week but had tomorrow off, so I felt better about asking him to meet us out knowing he could sleep in in the morning.

Oh, who was I kidding? I felt sick to my stomach. I knew exactly what was going to happen and I wasn't sure I could stand watching Gina cozy up to Ben… which, I admitted to myself, wasn't my business. He wasn't my boyfriend… I was just lucky to call him my friend.

"Ugh!" I moaned as I picked out a floral chemise to wear over my favorite jean shorts.

It was a warm night and I'd chosen to wear my long hair pulled up into a messy bun and had put on only light make-up; mascara and a light pink lip gloss. The only jewelry I wore were the simple half-carat diamond stud earrings that Uncle Leonard had given me for my eighteenth birthday.

I went downstairs and was in the middle of straightening up the kitchen, more to settle my nerves than because it needed it, when Gina arrived. She was all smiles and looked gorgeous in a lime green dress and heels that perfectly complimented her deep red hair and emerald eyes, showing off her long legs and perky, voluptuous breasts. I suddenly regretted my casual wardrobe choices.

"Hey, girl! Are you ready?" Gina beamed. The smile on her face made her even more beautiful. "I'm so excited!" She laughed nervously. "Nervous, though." She walked into the kitchen where I was adding a boiled egg to Gem's dry kibble.

I glanced at her with a brief smile before placing the puppy's dish on the kitchen floor in front of her. Gem immediately dove into it with relish.

"You don't need to be nervous," I said. "It's not as if it's a first date." I cringed inwardly. My words almost sounded bitchy, and I instantly regretted them. "I mean, it's just a casual night out with friends."

She didn't seem to notice the slip. "I know, but this is the first time I'll really be able to talk to Ben. I invited some colleagues, from the hospital, to meet us at the bar. I thought the more the merrier and, even better, I invited my super handsome doctor-friend, Ross, to meet you. I think you and he would be great together!" she gusted. "He's so gorgeous."

I tried to muster some enthusiasm, but wondered why, if this Ross was so amazing, why wasn't Gina interested herself? "Awesome. Thank you." My lips lifted in a half smile.

Gina walked forward and grabbed both of my hands in hers. "Cheer up, Marin. This will be fun. You look so pretty."

My eyebrows raised skeptically, but I offered a nod. "Thanks."

Gem was finished with her dinner and I bent to pick her up and give her a snuggle. "Be a good girl for mommy, Gemmy." I kissed her on the top of her head and gave her little body a squeeze. "I feel guilty leaving her alone in this big house, especially after the sun goes down."

"She's a dog. They sleep all the time, right?" Gina put in. "Leave the radio on for her or something."

"Yeah, that's a good idea." I turned on the television in the living room, hoping the noise and the light would comfort the little pup.

After I'd locked the house, we were on our way to the infamous Mangy Moose. It was a combination saloon and restaurant with a huge dance floor. Gina spent the entire fifteen-minute drive chatting away, speaking aloud her hopes for the evening.

As much as I was looking forward to seeing Ben, I wished it were just the two of us.

"I should have asked you to drive, Marin. You never know what will happen over the course of the evening."

"You mean, you're planning on going home with Ben?" I asked cautiously, my heart beginning to beat in a heavy, grotesque thump.

It shouldn't have surprised me that this was her goal. I mean, he was super sexy. I had to admit, even I had my fantasies in the weeks since we met. I had dreams about his muscled body taking command of mine more than once. Thinking of him with anyone else made me feel sick inside. I stared out the window.

I could see Gina's happy face glance in my direction through my peripheral vision before she looked back at the road. She shrugged. "Well, I mean, if it goes well. I don't usually hook up with guys right away, but he's so yummy. Oh, my God, Marin... I'm so excited!" she gushed.

I swallowed hard as my heart fell into my stomach. She was very pretty with the confidence to tempt any red-blooded male. "Yeah," I answered shortly as she parked in the crowded parking lot on the west side of the bar. "I can tell."

"Yeah? Can I get a hell-yeah?" she asked enthusiastically. "I've been waiting for this ever since I saw him in your hospital room!"

She made it sound like it had been years, when it was just a few weeks. "It hasn't been that long, Gina," I said caustically, pulling open the door and hopping out, my cowboy boots clacking on the pavement of the parking lot as I landed.

"Well, Ross will keep you occupied. He's super cool."

We started walking toward the entrance, passing several others leaving the restaurant and following a new crowd into the bar. "Why aren't you dating him, then?" I couldn't help but ask.

"Oh, he's great, but I think because we work together, it's just not in the cards."

There were a couple of bouncers checking ID's and taking the small cover charge. I handed both over and the burly man checking mine nodded. "Have a great time."

The other bouncer had checked Gina's driver's license and collected her money. Inside was loud and filled with modern country music. There was a golden glow from the low lights and people   everywhere.

My eyes searched for Ben, but it was impossible to see beyond the few tables in front of the dance floor, the long lines at the bar, and the couples dancing. There was no way to find him without texting or just wandering around in search of him.

"Do you want to get a drink, Marin? I'm parched!" Gina said loudly over the music playing.

"Sure!" I answered. Standing in line waiting our turn, I texted Ben.

We're here. In line at that bar.

I'll come find you. We have a table in the corner.

"What'll you have?" The good-looking bartender almost shouted at us. We were crammed with a crowd, body-to-body, at the mahogany bar. The floors were hardwood and there were wonderful smells of grilled steak and bar-b-que permeating from the connected restaurant.

Gina ordered a light beer and I asked for a glass of white wine. After we received our drinks we turned, ready to push our way through the crowd and away from the bar. My eyes connected with a pair of smiling cornflower blue ones a few rows back as he towered over those in front of him. Somehow, he'd honed right in on us. I smiled at the sight of him, and Ben winked.

"Excuse me," he said to a few others who blocked our way. "Please let the ladies through." He used his hands to motion for the crowd to part so Gina and I could pass.

It wasn't hard to see the appreciative glances on a few of the women's faces fall to disappointment at Ben's request.

He was dressed in a nice light blue button down, untucked over dark jeans and black boots. The shirt was tailored and tapered from his broad shoulders to the trim waist on his tall frame. His hair was combed, held in place with a light gel, and the scruff on his strong jaw just making for a very masculine shadow.

"Wow," Gina breathed behind me as we approached him.

"Ladies," he flashed a brilliant smile showing the dimples in both cheeks. "You both look amazing!" As I approached, Ben slid a hand down my bare arm, and it sent shivers rocketing straight through me. "We're over here," he nodded to the far corner, near the edge of the dance floor. His hand slid around to rest on the back of my waist.

"Hi, Ben. Nice to see you again," Gina said as she beamed up into his face.

"You, too," he answered politely.

Three men occupied the round six-top table, but there were three empty chairs, two together and one between the two of the men already occupying the space. I'd told Ben Gina was coming with me and asked him to bring a friend or two with him, though I didn't think the table would accommodate Ross and more of Gina's friends.

A beer sat on the table in front of one of the empty chairs, which I assumed was where Ben had been seated. The other three men stood as we approached. I recognized Ben's friend, Davis, but couldn't remember the names of the other two.

"Gina, Marin, these are my friends, Davis, Marcus, and Jake." Ben made the introductions. "We work together."

"Are all firefighters this handsome?" Gina asked, openly flirting. "My goodness!"

I couldn't believe she'd say something so sickeningly sweet and obvious. I crossed my arms and willed myself not to roll my eyes. Maybe she was just nervous, but... *gag*. I was a little surprised that she would be so bold.

They were certainly all very attractive and were the epitome of chivalry; remaining on their feet until Gina and I were both seated, each in one of the empty chairs. Gina was quick to take the one between Davis and Ben, leaving Marcus to offer me one between him and Jake.

Ben opened his mouth to say something, then promptly stopped himself, meeting my eyes apologetically. At least, I knew he'd planned on sitting next to me and it afforded a little comfort, and a lot of regret, as I resigned myself to make the best of the evening. It was certain that all of Ben's friends must be affable or they wouldn't be Ben's friends.

I smiled as I sat down and the two of them started to speak to me at once. They were both engaging and sweet, but I was painfully aware of what was going on across from me, even as I tried to interact with them. Gina was leaning in toward Ben as the two of them spoke, and Davis looked on with an exasperated expression on his face, while nursing his drink.

Ben's eyes shot to me across the table, but I quickly looked away diverting my attention to Jake as he asked me some of the questions people ask when trying to get to know someone new.

I didn't want to be rude to Jake or Marcus, plus I didn't want Ben to be able to sense how uncomfortable I felt. I did my best to smile and keep my focus on the charming men closest to me. I was painfully tenacious to make sure my face didn't show how upset and unnerved I was at not being near Ben, not being able to speak to him, or not being able to make sure that he didn't take Gina home.

"So? Are you planning on rebuilding The Shop? My best friend, Dave Granger, used to be one of the mechanics."

I dragged my eyes away from Gina who just bust out laughing at something Ben said and then the two of them got up and moved away from the table toward the dance floor. I shifted in my chair and leaned my elbows on the tables, running my hands up and down my bare arms. "Um…" I ripped my eyes back to Jake's face. "Doesn't he already have another job?"

"Oh, sure," Jake replied, "but I'm sure he'd want to come back if it were an option. He worked there for ten years and he really respected your uncle."

"He was a good guy. My uncle really liked him."

"Listen, I'm really sorry about your boyfriend."

"Thank you." I reached for my almost empty glass of wine and took a sip. "I'm pretty sure Dave hated Carter… with good reason."

"Well, he did at the end, anyway, but I wasn't going to mention it."

"Understandable. Don't worry. I know a lot of people didn't like Carter."

Jake's brow dropped and he looked like he was searching for the right thing to say in an awkward situation.

"Listen, it's okay. It doesn't really matter."

"I'm still sorry. I feel like an ass bringing it up," he admitted.

I couldn't really say *Hey, no worries, he was a first-class bastard and I ended up hating him, too,* so I did the best that I could. "No, really, it's fine," I assured him.

"I'm going to the bar for another beer. Anyone else?" Marcus asked.

"Why don't you just get another pitcher?" Jake asked. "I'll buy the next one."

"Sure thing. Would you like another glass of wine, Marin?"

I smiled up at the blond man who was a lot shyer than his two counterparts. "Thank you, Marcus."

He looked pleased but hovered near my chair before walking toward the bar. "You can call me Mark, and would it be okay if…. I mean…. can I have a dance when I get back with the drinks? I'm not too good at two stepping, but I'll sure try." His face was flushed with excitement. He was clearly younger than me or the rest of his crew. He seemed barely twenty-one.

"Of course. I'd be honored." I offered a small smile.

"That's so awesome! I'll be right back."

"Shit. I was going to ask you while he was getting drinks," Jake said.

I laughed softly, trying not to let my eyes drift toward the dance floor. Gina's dress was bright enough that it would be easily be ascertainable, even from across a room and through the crowd of couples and cowboy hats, but there was no sense torturing myself.

It wasn't long before Mark was back with a fresh pitcher and my glass of wine and wasted no time in holding out his hand when a new song started playing. It was a new one that I particularly liked by Dan & Shay and the tempo wasn't too fast, so if Mark was new to the two step it would be a good one.

I placed my hand in his and stood to go with him.

"Remember, Marin, I'm next," Jake put in with a wink.

I smiled with a nod. The attention was just what I needed.

"I might as well put my request in, too," Davis added.

"Of course! I love dancing much more than drinking, so I'd be happy to dance all night!"

As Mark and I were leaving the table, Gina and Ben were returning and we passed them on the way. Ben nodded to us while Gina still clung to his arm.

I was thankful for the way my old cowboy boots slid across the worn wooden dance floor. Mark's style of dancing had him place his arm on my shoulder and the other hand holding mine. I would have preferred his arm around my waist, because his arm felt heavy as we shuffled across the floor in the classic two-step rhythm.

I let myself get lost in the song except for the two times Mark stepped on my foot.

"I'm so sorry," he said, embarrassed.

I just grinned. "Don't worry. I walk on them, too."

He laughed. "That's funny, but I still feel shitty. I'm sorry I'm so bad at dancing."

"Well, you're doing fine," I reassured.

"Maybe we can practice a few more times?" he asked gingerly.

I laughed. "Sure, but I promised I'd dance with your friends, too. Maybe we can all do a line dance."

"Oh, no! Those are way too hard for me," Mark protested.

I was a bit disappointed because my uncle would sneak me into the Mangy Moose when I was young just so I could dance, and line dancing used to be huge. It was so much fun.

"They're just a series of patterns. You'll see."

The music changed to a much slower song and I was hoping we'd go back to the table, when I heard the huskiness of a familiar voice.

"Hey, kid. Mind if I cut in?" Ben was towering over both of us. My head had to fall back to look up into his face and our eyes met. "That's if the lady will have me."

My heart started thumping hard inside my chest. So hard, I was afraid he'd be able to hear it, or feel it, if he held me close enough.

"Sure," Mark said. "See you back at the table."

I didn't have to say a word. There was something unspoken between Ben and me. He took me into his arms easily; one hand slid behind my back and the other closed around my right hand and pulled it to his chest. I felt completely engulfed as we started moving together like we were made to do it. He smelled like clean soap and cologne; the solid wall of his chest beckoned for my cheek to rest upon it. The song was a new one, but it fit. It fit the situation and it suited Ben, too. The lyrics were impactful... a tough guy, but a gentle man. It couldn't be more perfect, and I knew I'd never forget this first song or the magic of being in this man's arms for the first time.

"Are you cold?" Ben bent his head to murmur in my ear.

I shook my head. "No." I knew I was shaking and that's why he asked.

"Well, don't worry... I got you."

"Do you?" I lifted my eyes to his face.

Ben nodded. "If you'll let me."

I swallowed, my fingers clasping into his shirt, bunching it up where my hand laid on his shoulder. My heart was ready to explode. How could I already be in love with him? Not the stupid, youthful love you feel with a first crush or some cute guy you meet who flatters you, but the deep, soul-shaking kind.

"What about Gina?"

We continued to dance, not missing a beat of the song as he easily guided me around the dance floor, our bodies plastered together.

He frowned down at me. "What about her?"

"She likes you—" I began.

"So what? I just met the woman. I like *you*."

I closed my eyes, losing myself in his embrace, letting his incredible words sink in. In this amazing moment, I should have been two steps below heaven, but fear and guilt washed over me. "What if they see us?"

He looked perplexed. We were body to body and my head tilted to look up into his face.

"What are you afraid of?" His deep voice and hot breath washed over the skin of my temple.

That everyone close to me has died and I can't risk that with you. That when you know the truth about Carter's death, you'll think I'm a killer. That I won't be good enough for someone as perfect as you. Afraid of loving too much and losing. Afraid of hurting. A plethora of answers flooded my brain. I could tell him I wasn't afraid, but I didn't want to lie to Ben.

"Maybe it's just too soon… and I can't expect you to wait around."

Suddenly, Ben twirled me around quickly in time to an acceleration in the music. I was taken by surprise and laughed out loud. It was so fun… so incredible dancing with him. I felt like I was standing on the precipice of the most exciting jump I'd ever been faced with, yet afraid of the depth of it.

"Look, Marin, I feel something between us, and we can take it slow. If you're not ready, that's okay, too. The last thing I want is to pressure you. I just want to spend time with you."

"Me, too. But… Ben, Gina's a friend and I just don't want to explain this to her, or anyone else, tonight." The fingers under his hand spread flat on the solid wall of his chest. "Please?"

"I'm fairly certain one of us will have to explain something to her tonight, Marin," Ben said matter-of-factly. "She wants me to take her home with me."

"Did she say that?"

"I can just tell." The song ended, and Ben reluctantly released me.

"I don't want to hurt her. She's been so excited to get to know you." I felt stupid, rambling on like this. I didn't want to hurt Gina, but I didn't want Ben to think I was passing him off to my friend.

"What are you saying?" he demanded, gently, his eyes intent on mine.

I shook my head and shrugged, conscious of how conspicuous we were becoming standing in the middle of an active dance floor. "Nothing. I just... I'm so screwed up about everything."

"Come on." Ben grabbed my hand and pulled me along behind him toward the table. "We'll just hang loose tonight. We can talk more when we're alone. Let's just have fun."

When we got back to the table, he walked me to my chair then took the seat he had vacated next to an eager Gina.

"You two looked very in sync," Davis said pointedly. "In step, I meant," he corrected when Ben shot him a look.

"Well, Marin is a great dancer. She's been holding out on me." He picked up his glass and downed the rest of the beer inside, then reached for the pitcher and refilled it.

"It was fun. Maybe on the next line dance we can all go out there together?"

The next two hours were spent with a lot of dancing, drinking and awkward glances from across the table. Gina's friends showed up and we pulled more chairs up to crowd around our table. Ross was as handsome as Gina had said, and he was clearly interested in me. I could see that Ben's feelings were bruised. He'd put himself out there earlier and I'd choked. I huffed to myself, chugging down the last half of my fourth glass of wine.

The DJ announced the Watermelon Crawl line dance, and it was pure reaction to jump up. It was one of my favorite line dances from my youth. "Come on! Everyone, come on! It's so fun!" I motioned with my arms that they should all come with me. "Hurry, or we'll miss too much of it!"

"I'm game!" Mark jumped up to follow me. Jake was out dancing with a woman he'd met earlier in the evening. Gina, Davis and Ben looked at each other, skeptically. Ross got up from the table, indicating he was willing.

"Let's go," Ross nodded. "I'm much better one-on-one," he said suggestively, "but I'll give this a try."

"I'd prefer to watch," Davis said, crankily. "This song is old."

The song *was* older, but I wasn't even sure how old it was. It was one that my Uncle Leonard taught me when I was only ten years old, but who knew how old it was by then.

"Party pooper," I said to Davis.

"Come on, Ben. It will be fun," Gina insisted, but I was already on my way out to the dance floor to find a spot in line. There were easily twenty dancers in each line and ten or twelve lines. After I'd taken my place and waited for the song to begin. I saw Gina dragging Ben out to the floor.

Soon all of the dancers were moving to the song, some of us better than others. It wasn't the easiest line dance to master, especially on the fly, but that was what I loved about it. The steps were fairly easy, but they were fast moving. Mark had a harder time, bumping into me a few times because he got his grapevine step going in the wrong direction, but I just put my hand on his should and pulled him in the right direction smiling the entire time. Ross was a much better dancer and took a position close to me. He smiled and flirted with his eyes. I couldn't help but smile. It felt good getting out, dancing, and forgetting my problems knowing a deeper conversation was coming with Ben.

When I turned around, I was able to see him dancing next to Gina. He was pretty good at it, while Gina was watching her feet and laughing outrageously each time that she made a mistake, tripping purposefully into Ben.

I loved the song and knew the dance by heart so that, and the several drinks I'd had since my slow dance with Ben, made me a little more carefree. I was having a blast and we were all laughing our asses off.

When the song ended, we all ended up seated back at the table.

"Marin, I have to use the ladies' room," Gina said.

"Okay," I nodded. "Go ahead."

My friend's eyes got big, and her head cocked to one side, clearly indicating she wanted me to accompany her. "Oh, okay. Me, too."

The bathrooms were at the back of the bar and she let me lead the way, weaving through the crowd of patrons.

Once inside, Gina turned to face me. "Well? I've been dying all night to ask you what Ben said about me when you guys were dancing. He's so charming and... *so* sexy!"

I figured she was going to ask me what I thought of Ross, but not so. I had to be careful what I said. I was still feeling lightheaded from all of the alcohol. "He said you're nice and pretty."

"Nice and pretty?" She seemed disappointed. "That's so generic."

I wasn't lying. Ben did say she was nice, and he'd told us both we looked great when we arrived at the Moose.

"No, it's not. Gina, I need to pee," I said, walking past her into a stall. "Ross is gorg," I tried to change the subject away from Ben.

There were other women inside the bathroom, one puking in the far stall and several of them talking or re-applying make-up.

"Nice and pretty," she moaned again. "Jesus, my boobs are almost hanging out of this dress and all he's got for me is nice and pretty?"

"Don't sweat it, sweetheart," another woman's voice said. "Look around, there are hundreds of men here. I'm sure you'll be able to find someone else who could muster a little more enthusiasm for your boobs."

I almost laughed out loud as I finished up inside the stall. "Yeah? Thanks for nothing," Gina retorted.

Obviously, Gina didn't have to use the toilet as she'd said. She just wanted to grill me about Ben.

"We're all a little drunk, Gina," I said, washing my hands as she pouted, leaning one shoulder on the wall by the dryer. "Why don't you try to talk to him another time?"

"Talking is great, but I wanted to do the no-pants dance with him tonight."

I moaned miserably. "Now, that's soooo romantic, Gina."

"Marin! Ben is all that sinew and muscle, and I want him. I can't help it! I've been salivating all night."

I put a hand to my head. It was starting to pound. Maybe the wine was getting to me. "There's more to him than his body, Gina."

"Now I've heard everything," the rude woman said, before leaving the bathroom.

"I want to learn all about his mind, and family and work, too. I really want to get to know him, but he's just so damn hot."

Didn't I know it? It wasn't as if I didn't want to be with Ben, too, and I knew what she meant about the yearning he caused, but I couldn't tell her to back off. Once again, I found myself relying on Ben to fix the situation.

"Yeah, he is. Let's go back to the table. It's getting late and I want to go home. Gem has been alone long enough."

"Marin!" Gina protested, reluctantly following. "I need more time with Ben."

I led the way out of the bathroom, eager to get out of Gina's scrutiny. If I didn't get out of there, I'd be blurting out that he was mine and to back off and the Gina would think I didn't care about Carter at all. *God, what a mess*, I thought.

The bathrooms were down a long hallway off of the central bar area and I began to walk through and back into the main room but stopped cold. Terror ran through me as my worst fears became reality.

"Hiya, princess. Miss me?" Apollo sneered. He was all decked out in leather and chains, leaning casually against the opposite wall. "I thought I'd have to wait all night to talk to you." He flashed a knife, but discretely, so only I saw it under his jacket. My breath caught in fear.

He'd been waiting for me to emerge from the ladies' room. Clearly, he'd been watching me all night, biding his time until he could get me away from the table full of others.

"Who is this, Marin?" Gina asked cautiously. Apollo's demeanor and appearance were menacing and enough to make my friend pause.

I half turned toward her, suddenly sober. "Um," I put up a hand and patted the air a couple of times hoping she'd understand what I needed her to do. "This is Carter's brother, Apollo."

I hadn't told Gina the awful details of the kidnapping, but now I wished I had.

"From Minneapolis?" Clearly, she was confused by his sudden appearance in Jackson.

"Has the princess been talking about me?" Apollo pushed off the wall and took a step toward me, looming over me, and much too close to me. Gina stepped back, amid the other women and men coming and going in the tight space of the hallway. "I'm flattered."

Truth be told, I was terrified, and I wanted to get as far away from Apollo as possible but making a scene wouldn't end well.

"I'll meet you at the table, Marin," Gina said, caustically. Instinctually, Gina was anxious to leave, and was in effect, abandoning me to this bastard. I could only hope she'd tell Ben and the others that I was talking to some mean looking dude by the bathroom and he'd come back here. At least, I hoped so.

"Good idea," I agreed with a short nod. I knew my fear showed on my face.

"But what should I tell—?"

"Um… just—" I interrupted, hoping she'd tell Ben I needed him, but not wanting Apollo to know, though if he'd been watching me all night, he knew we were with a group of guys. However, I didn't know what he'd do, and I didn't want anyone to get hurt. "Let them know, er…" My eyes shot up to Apollo's face. His stare was intense. "I'll join you in a couple of minutes."

She didn't wait to turn and walk back into the main bar area.

Hopefully, Ben wouldn't take too long until he would come looking for me.

Chapter 14

BEN

I'd been watching for the girls to return to the table, hoping I wasn't being too conspicuous.

"Man, you got it bad," Davis muttered, before chugging the rest of the beer in his glass.

It didn't make sense to argue; not with my best friend. Gina appeared before Marin and took her seat next to me before I could respond.

"Ben, some bad looking guy stopped us outside the bathroom. Apollo something or other."

Instantly, my muscles coiled, and I was ready to jump up from my chair. "Where?"

"He's talking to Marin in the hallway by the bathrooms."

"Is he alone?"

"I think so, but I'm not sure," Gina answered. "He looked so scary. What's his deal?"

I didn't answer but was on my feet and on my way to find Marin within the span of a second. "Davis." I nodded in the direction of the bathrooms. "If we're not back in a couple of minutes, follow me."

"What's going on?" Ross asked and I just shook my head at him.

Davis stood up instantly. "Why don't I just come with you now?"

I nodded and we were both striding toward the bathroom, leaving the rest of the people at our table wondering what was happening. As I preceded Davis down the hall off the bar, I looked for Marin, my eyes scanning back and forth. Apollo was within inches of Marin's body, his face close enough to breathe on her skin, leaning in to say something in her ear. Her expression was terrified, and her back was plastered against the wooden paneling of the wall.

Another surge of adrenaline pumped through my veins and it was as if a red bomb exploded in front of my eyes. "Son of a bitch!" I said under my breath, more to myself than my friend. "He's got her cornered!"

My hand was already reaching out to grab his shoulder and pull him away from her. "I suggest you get away from her, now! Did he hurt you?" I asked in with the same breath. Marin shook her head.

The man turned and I got a good look at him, as much as I could in the darkened bar. He looked like a sleazy thug both in dress and mannerism. His hair greasy and overly long, his dark eyes were hooded as they narrowed on me. "I'm just talking to the lady, man. What's your problem?"

"You're my problem," I growled, positioning myself between him and Marin. "If you hurt her, I'll kill you." I sincerely believed the venomous words spewing from my lips. I didn't care what the consequences would be. I didn't care that I could lose my job, or even go to prison. As long as Marin was safe.

"Who the fuck are you, anyway? She was my brother's old lady until just a few weeks ago. Are you telling me you're already boning her? Maybe his death wasn't an accident after all, eh?"

"Or maybe he was a drunk asshole who didn't watch what the hell he was doing," I hissed.

Davis stood shoulder to shoulder with me between Apollo and Marin. I could feel Marin curled into my back behind me.

"I suggest we take this outside, fellas," Davis put in, stepping between us, sensing I was about to let loose on the guy, his hand coming up with splayed fingers. "Ben, come on. Not inside the bar. This prick isn't worth it."

My hand flattened on the side of Marin's hip to reassure her that I would protect her. I felt her hand curl into the back of my shirt. She was still up against the wall, but now it was my body, and not Apollo's that was against hers. I knew she was scared shitless, and that fact made me furious. Despite the loud din of the music and people talking inside the building, I could almost hear the blood rushing in my ears. Who did this bastard think he was that he could show up in Jackson and harass her? It was something we'd both considered and here it was.

"Says you," Apollo retorted. "I'd say if you're doing her, you got a vested interest in the outcome here... maybe you oughta make sure I get my money."

I nodded with a sneer. "Oh, I'm vested, all right. Maybe you should get the fuck out of here while you can still walk."

"I told ya; I just want to talk, dude." The other man put up both hands in front of him, as if to ward m off.

"Yeah. It's real brave to ambush a couple of women outside of a bathroom," I spat sarcastically. I wanted to rip this bastard's head off. "You're a real saint."

"She owes my family money!"

I could literally feel the air rushing in and out of my nostrils as my chest rose and fell. "Bullshit. Your brother was working drunk in a greasy shop during a power outage. Not very smart of him, so if you don't want to get your face smashed in, I think we should do as my friend said and go outside," I suggested sternly. I couldn't remember a time in my life when I was this angry. Not even when that bastard Derrick had beat up my sister, though it was close.

People coming and going from the bathrooms were casting curious glances our way.

Apollo put his hands up in acquiescence. "Whoa. Down boy. Princess, put your dog on a leash."

I couldn't wait to beat the shit out of this fucker, and I'd do it out in the parking lot, but he moved closer, getting up into my face, leaving literally only inches between us poking me hard in the chest with his index finger. It hurt and I'd probably have a bruise, but nothing I couldn't handle. I stood my ground.

"Man, her pussy must be really fucking amazing. Maybe I should try it."

Marin's forehead dropped onto my back between my shoulders. I couldn't see her face, I couldn't know what she was thinking, but I hoped she wasn't letting this prick humiliate her. He wasn't worth it.

"You must have a death wish," I breathed as I looked down my nose at him. Fury was like a living thing inside my chest. Despite Davis's warnings, I didn't care about the repercussions. Both hands made contact with his chest as I shoved him forcefully onto the opposite wall, but he resisted and pushed back. I planted my legs for leverage, and I had a height and weight advantage.

"Ben! He has a knife!" Marin screamed too late.

It would explain the searing burn I felt in my side. I touched my left oblique and felt the warm ooze of blood soaking the cotton of my shirt.

I pulled back my fist and let it fly as hard as I could, hitting the man hard in the jaw causing him to sprawl on the floor, his knife sent flying. Several women screamed and scattered... leaving only a few men to look on.

"Marin, go back to the table with Mark and Jake." I spoke over my shoulder.

"But you're hurt!" she protested.

"I'm okay. Go!" I commanded, taking a step forward to give her room to slide out from behind me and walk away. She didn't hesitate and quickly took her leave as Apollo scrambled for his knife, but I put my boot on his hand effectively breaking several of the bones. He squealed like a pig.

Davis reached down and grabbed the back of Apollo's jacket with both hands. I moved back, holding my side as Davis pulled him to his feet and ushered him out of the hallway. I was bleeding more than was safe.

"I'm gonna kill you, you mother fucker! Do you hear me? You're dead!" The other man screamed out as Davis hoisted him to his feet.

"I'll make sure to tell the cops you said that, you dumb ass," Davis said, disgust dripping from his words as he hauled the injured man out. "Come on, Ben. We gotta go."

I didn't argue. Blood was starting to soak the material of my shirt as I pressed my hand to my side. I inhaled sharply.

Davis disappeared with Apollo through the bar to the front entrance, where a couple of bouncers took over, and I made my way back to the table where Gina, Marin and the other two guys were sitting and waiting with Gina's friends looking on. Marin stood and ran to my side, sliding an arm around my waist and instantly, my free arm went around her shoulders.

"Marin told us about what was going on, but we figured you and Davis had it handled, but you're bleeding, man!" Jake stood up and rushed toward us.

"That looks bad, Ben," Ross interjected. "You need to keep pressure on it and get to the ER."

I shook my head. "It's nothing. I'm taking Marin home."

"But... should we all come?" Gina asked. "You should see a doctor! Ross can help."

"You can do what you want. Stay or go, but I think it's best if I take Marin home. A broken hand won't keep that fucker at bay."

"But Gina and Ross are right; you need the hospital, Ben" Marin protested.

I was more concerned with making sure she and her ranch were safe.

"Nah, I'll be okay," I insisted

We started walking out of the bar and one of the bouncers who knew me stopped me. "Ben, should I call an ambulance?"

I rolled my eyes. "Nah. I'm okay Jimmy. It's just a scratch." Truth be told, I was starting to feel a little lightheaded.

Jake, Mark, Ross, and Gina followed us out.

"I'll drive your truck, Ben. Mark can follow to pick me up," Jake offered.

"We'll follow, too! If you're too stubborn to go to the ER, we can stop by the hospital and grab some sutures and meet you at Marin's ranch," Gina added. "Ross can stitch him up."

"I can, but it's best to take him to the ER. He might need a transfusion," Ross protested.

Soon the group of my friends were shuffling me out and I had handed over the keys.

"Take off your shirt, Ben," Marin ordered. "I need to fold it up to press against the wound."

Blood was now dripping down the left leg of my jeans. I hesitated long enough for Marin's fingers to fly into action, unbuttoning my shirt and pushing it from my shoulders.

220

"Somehow I saw this scenario differently in my head." I tried to laugh, making an attempt to tease to take the focus off of my gaping wound. It was much worse than I'd originally thought. It was a slice about seven inches long and at least two inches deep. Jake laughed and Marin's eyes flashed up to mine. Her face looked pained and full of concern.

Marin quickly folded my shirt and pressed it to my side. "Can you hold it? Just until we get into the truck, then I'll take over." I nodded, then Marin climbed into the cab ahead of me. "Jake, we gotta take him to the hospital."

"Roger that," Jake said.

"Ahhhh," I winced as I got into the truck as gingerly as I could and slammed the door behind me. The truck wasn't as old as Marin's uncle's, but it had seen better days and the door squeaked. "No, just go to Marin's ranch."

"Jake, no," she insisted. "He's losing way too much blood."

"Yes, Ma'am!"

I leaned back and closed my eyes. Shirtless, Marin held my ruined shirt to my side. After holding her earlier on the dance floor, I'd had different hopes for the end of this evening than me bleeding all over the front seat of my truck and the beautiful woman beside me.

"Hurry, Jake," Marin pleaded. I could hear the crack in her voice. My eyes opened and my head turned toward her. The streetlights, shining in as we passed, were reflected by the tears in her eyes.

My hand reached out to rest on her leg. "Hey… I'm gonna be fine."

"This is all my fault."

In pain as I was, my brow still rose wryly. "Like how? Did you know that dick nozzle was going to be at the Moose tonight?"

"No," she sniffed, "but it's still my fault."

I shook my head as Jake pulled into the ER drive-up. "No, it isn't."

"I'll be back," Jake said, hopping out of the truck and disappearing through the doors.

Marin slid out the driver's side and came around to open the passenger door. Her right side, even the bare skin of her leg was covered in my blood. There was blood on her forehead where she'd run her hand through her hair, but she still looked like an angel to me.

"Come on. I'll help you. Lean on me."

I slid off the seat, still holding onto the now completely soaked shirt when Jake and an orderly appeared with a wheelchair.

"My legs aren't broken," I complained.

"You're still bleeding, Ben. Will you just get in the damn chair?" Marin demanded. Her words were worried and weary and there was a crinkle in between her brows.

I met her eyes knowing she was right. I wasn't sure I could walk on my own. "Okay."

She nodded. "Good."

I eased myself down into the chair, handing her the ruined shirt.

Gina, who had obviously stopped by the hospital as she has mentioned, appeared as she rushed from the double sliding doors of the ER. "I'm so glad you just came here."

The orderly was already turning the chair away from the truck and wheeling me inside when I heard the two women talking as they followed.

"Should I just throw this away?" Marin asked. "It's ruined."

"Keep it for now. The doctors might want to see it to see how much blood was lost. He might need a transfusion," the orderly answered.

"The hell I will," I muttered, though if I were honest, I was feeling woozy, though it could be the alcohol I'd consumed over the course of the evening.

I felt Marin's hand on my bare shoulder. I wasn't sure how I knew it was her and not Gina, but I just did. "Stop being a tough guy."

Despite the gaping wound in my side, the corner of my mouth lifted I a smile. "I can't help it. It's my job."

"Yeah, yeah," she said.

They wheeled me into a room; the orderly telling Marin and Gina to go to the waiting room. Ross was conspicuously missing from the group, but I was glad.

"Really?" Gina protested. "I'm a nurse at this hospital."

"You're not on duty," the orderly answered. "You can wait in the waiting room."

She huffed, but it was Marin I was concerned with. I didn't want her out of my sight. We didn't know if Carter's brother was alone in town or he had more of his gang with him, and I didn't have time to ask before the big blue double doors that led to the examination rooms closed behind me.   It wasn't long before another nurse came into the room. I was waiting on a bed and the woman from admitting came in and asked for my insurance card. The ER nurse followed and started cleaning the wound with iodine swabs and I winced. A doctor, who I knew from a couple of times I'd been in with the rescue squad, soon followed.

"How did this happen?" Dr. Burton asked stoically.

"Bar fight." It was a simple answer to a complicated question.

The older man's white eyebrows arched. "Hmmm, how did the other guy fair?"

"Did you get anyone in here with a broken hand?" My tone was bland.

"I can't discuss it, Ben. Looks like you lost a good amount of blood."

"Not that much," I argued. "Ugh," I winced as the gash burned as he poked and prodded.

"This is pretty deep. Let's get it stitched up. Are you lightheaded?"

The nurse had the supplies ready on a tray and the doctor reached for one of the instruments.

My impatience was growing. "No," I lied. "How long will this take?"

"It's a long, deep cut. He sliced you good."

"Ah, so he is here, then. He sliced me before I broke his hand. In case you're wondering."

The doctor rolled his eyes but didn't bother addressing my comment. I could only hope that I'd totally maimed him for life. "You'll need some subcutaneous stitches that will dissolve and then another layer to close the skin. How do you feel? We might need to start an IV to replace some of the fluid you lost. We don't want you going into shock."

"How long will this take?" I asked, again.

"Unless you want a nasty scar or to bleed out later, it will take as long as it takes."

"That prick who knifed me was really after someone else, and I have no way of knowing if he was alone. I can't leave her out in the waiting room." My eyes implored him.

"Is she family?"

"No, but she's… a friend."

"What's her name?"

"Marin. She's in the waiting room. The pretty blonde with blood all over her."

"Bring her back," Dr. Burton said to the nurse, blotting the wound before injecting my side with Novocain.

It stung like a bitch, so I sucked in my breath and gritted my teeth. "Thank you."

The doctor started stitching as soon as the wound was numb and at the same time another nurse started the IV Dr. Burton mentioned. I tried to relax but couldn't until the glass door to the room slid open the curtain was pulled back. Marin entered with the returning nurse.

"Ben! Are you okay?" Her eyes were wild as she rushed to my side, taking in the IV.

She reached out and wrapped her fingers around the hand lying beside my right hip and squeezed.

"I am now. Did you see anyone lurking in the waiting room?" I flipped my hand over to enfold hers.

"No? What do you mean?"

"Any of Apollo's thugs?"

She shook her head. "Just Davis, Mark, Jake and Gina, but they all left when the nurse came to get me. Jake asked me to give you your keys."

"Oh, this young man can't drive tonight," Dr. Burton noted. 'He's lost way too much blood."

"I'll drive," Marin said. "I don't want him to be alone tonight."

"That's probably a good idea," the doctor agreed.

everything
HAPPENS FOR
a reason

Chapter 15

Marin

Ben fell asleep on the way out to the ranch and his head had fallen back and sideways to lean awkwardly against the window of the passenger door. He looked so uncomfortable, yet he was completely out.

I wanted to touch him, but he was too far away. His bloody button-down shirt had been replaced by an old grey T-shirt Jake had found behind the seat of the truck.

His medical treatment had taken two hours at the hospital, and so now it was close to three in the morning. Gem would probably be miserable and need to go out as soon as we got home. I didn't think Apollo would bother me this morning; considering his own injury, but that didn't stop Ben from insisting he sleep over, just in case. Even if he hadn't been so adamant, I would have asked him to stay so I could take care of him.

Ben was a tough guy and refused to stay in the hospital. He wouldn't admit his weakened state, but it would take time to replace the blood he'd lost, despite the IV he'd received. Dr. Burton had given Ben a tetanus shot and some antibiotics to be safe.

The truck rolled to a stop in front of the house, and I turned off the engine, pulling Ben's keys out of the ignition. I sat there for a moment because I hesitated to wake him, though he'd be better off if I got him into the house.

"Ben," I called softly, hoping to stir him awake with a gentle voice rather than the loud opening of the door. I leaned closer. "Ben."

He sucked in his breath and sat up in one quick motion, reaching out his left arm to find me nearby. "Marin! Are you okay?" His head snapped in my direction; his surprised eyes wide until he finally registered that he'd been asleep.

My hand closed around his forearm to calm him down. "I'm okay. We're just home. Don't move so fast. You'll hurt yourself."

Ben leaned back in the seat and ran both hands through his hair, sucking in another deep breath. "What a night," he murmured.

"Stay there. I'll come around to help you." I opened the truck door and slid out and down to the gravel driveway, but he had gotten out before I could walk around the front of the vehicle. "You should be careful. I don't want you to start bleeding again and it has to hurt."

"I've had worse," he insisted with a crooked grin. The moon was glowing in the starlit sky and the evening had gotten cooler. The slight breeze caused goosebumps to break out on my arms and legs and I couldn't help but shiver.

When I reached his side, his strong arm slid around me.

"Come on, let's get you inside." I wasn't sure if it was a thrill that ricocheted through me at his touch, rather than the brisk night air. My arm found its way around his waist in an attempt to take some of his weight, but Ben only laughed.

"I'm not complaining, but I'm really fine, Marin."

Outside of a stiffness to his gait, I couldn't tell if he was being completely honest. "You don't always have to be a invulnerable, you know," I insisted, handing him the truck keys.

"Sure, I do." He chuckled wryly. "How else am I supposed to impress the girls?"

We got to the stairs and I noticed a tightness around his mouth indicating his pain. "I know it hurts."

"Hell, yeah, it hurts, but I'd do it again."

I didn't speak again as I opened the front door and flipped on the inside light, but his words warmed me. My throat was tight and there was a suspicious burning at the back of my eyes. I blinked rapidly.

Gem barked repeatedly as she scurried around our feet and jumped up on her hind feet against my legs. I bent to pick her up and I was rewarded with loads of puppy kisses as she showered me with affection. "Why don't you go on in while I take her out?"

Ben shot me a look. "I'll take her." He held his hands out, silently asking me to hand Gem over.

"Are you sure? You're—" I began, knowing he'd do what he wanted no matter my protests.

"Yeah, and I have no way of knowing if Apollo is lurking outside."

I huffed in astonishment. "His hand is broken, Ben. He can hardly fight or handle a weapon after that."

"Why tempt fate? He might simply be more pissed off, or he might not be alone." Ben turned and walked back out the door with the puppy. He held her up so he could kiss her head.

As injured as he was, he wouldn't let me even take my own dog outside to pee and that worried me. I followed him outside and noted how he drew his breath in with a hiss as he bent to set the dog down on the ground, and how slow he was to straighten up. I could only imagine how sore he was, and how any movement must surely put strain on the wound.

"How effective would you be in your weak state, anyway?" I argued.

He shot me an annoyed look. "Trust me, I'm strong enough to kick his ass."

I shook my head in exasperation. "I've already called the insurance company and they said after they received the fire commissioner's report, the claim could be paid fairly soon," I said calmly.

We both watched Gem walk around and quickly squat to relieve herself. Ben glanced at my face. "Did you tell him that?"

"I—tried. But you showed up in the hallway before I could."

His eyes narrowed. "Did you expect me to just take my chances with your safety that he would accept what you had to say? I doubt it would have even mattered."

Ben seemed angry.

"No." I frowned and shook my head. "I knew you'd come, so I shouldn't have panicked. It was a public place and there were hundreds of people there. What could he have done?" I seemed to be cursed. Carter died and now Ben was injured.

"Oh, I don't know… remember he kidnapped you before. He might have done so again or knifed you then left you there to bleed out."

I shook my head. "That wouldn't have happened, and even if it did, there were many people walking through that hall. Someone would have gotten help."

Ben called Gem and walked up the wooden steps to hold open the door for the puppy and for me. He nodded me inside. "Yeah? You're awfully brave all of a sudden," he countered.

"Bastards like Apollo don't play! Or didn't you learn that lesson from Carter?"

Having Carter thrown in my face stung. He stood there holding the open door while tears flooded my eyes and my throat thickened painfully. Maybe I seemed ungrateful for his help and I didn't want that either. "I shouldn't have told you."

"I've known since I first laid eyes on you."

"How?" I wondered, embarrassed.

"I told you. My sister, remember? Gemmy, come on," Ben called to the dog.

"You're hurt!" I exclaimed, seeing him wince as he moved.

"I'm fine. Come on, sweet face," he called again. "Let's go night-night."

He was such a big, strong man and he was talking so sweetly to my puppy. How could I hold his protective nature against him? What woman wouldn't swoon over such a handsome, compelling man standing up for them? Embarrassed heat flooded my cheeks at the thought.

I watched Ben take Gem inside, and I followed closely behind. He gave her some water and as she lapped at it, he turned back to me. "Maybe I should go," he said shortly.

I sighed; a deep breath that filled my lungs to the hilt as I stood there gazing up at him. We were standing close enough for me to reach out and touch him, and I did; letting my fingers graze his arm tentatively. "I'd like you to stay."

Ben's head cocked a fraction as he digested my words. He grabbed my arm and yanked me closer still. His eyes closed and his head bent so that his forehead rested against mine.

"Marin," he breathed. "I don't know what the fuck is happening. I know it's too soon after Carter, but I…" His warm breath bathed the skin of my cheek and mouth deliciously.

"You, what?" I whispered, aroused at his nearness. My eyes closed and I could feel myself sway toward him, as if we were magnets fighting an impossible pull. He was so sexy, and I trusted him implicitly.

"I want you more than any woman I've ever seen, but more than that... I want to take care of you." The words dragged out of him. "When I walked into that hallway and saw you with Apollo, I saw red. I didn't even know if it was him for sure, and it didn't matter. I wanted to fucking kill him. I know it's too soon to expect that you'd—"

The sound of his voice was like magic and I felt myself giving in, my body was craving his, and my heart began to race. It wasn't as if I hadn't wanted him, too. It wasn't as if I didn't lie in bed at night fantasizing about him. I knew he was too weak to make love, but maybe...

"Ben," I sighed, my chin lifting in silent beckoning for him to put me out of my misery and kiss me. Somehow, I ended up in his arms and my hands rested against the sides of his waist. The bandage reminded me of his wound, but Ben didn't seem to notice.

He hauled me closer in the dim light, turning me around until my back was up against the wall in the hallway; his hard body pressing blissfully into mine leaving no doubt to his desire, as his mouth hovered over mine. God, it was blissful torture. "I'm sorry. I can't help... this."

"Ben," I whispered again, my voice aching. My lower lip nudged his upper one, eliciting a guttural groan from deep in his chest.

His hand flattened on the wall beside my head, and he lifted me enough to part my legs and press his hips hard into the cradle of mine. It was bliss.

"It's like you're this gorgeous demon that haunts me, Marin. Day and night, you're all I think about. I know I shouldn't want you, but I've lost my free will."

He started kissing me gently, taking the lips I offered, and worshiping them, but I was hungry, and I wanted to devour and be devoured. It was like no first kiss I'd ever experienced, and I'd known it would be. My thighs tightened against his hips and he thrust against me in a heavenly rhythm that was echoed in the giving and taking of his mouth and tongue against mine. His hands slid around my thighs under my bottom, and he pulled my groin closer against his. I could feel the outline of his hardness pressing into me, teasing; a delicious hint of what being with him would feel like.

Soon we were out of control, our kisses deepening, our breathing increasing in perfect unison. My hands slid up his arms, over his shoulders and into his soft hair. I wanted him to devour me, and I communicated it with him by sucking his tongue deeper into my mouth.

When the kiss broke, Ben was breathing hard, his face turned into my neck to drag his mouth down until it opened hotly over my collarbone, then he sucked lightly. I was dying, my body open and hungry, screaming for his to fill me.

I tried to surge my hips against his, but his hands stopped me, his forehead falling onto my shoulder. "Marin, are you trying to kill me?" His voice was low and deep.

Instantly, I stilled. "I'm sorry! Did I hurt you?" My eyes searched his in the shadowy darkness, then he pulled me close again while he surged toward me. I could feel his erection through my shorts and now damp panties, hard and throbbing against me.

"In a good way," he said before taking my mouth in a slow, deep kiss, his tongue parting my lips and laving mine. He sucked in his breath as the kiss ended. "Having you in my arms, finally… it's incredible. I say finally, because these few weeks have felt like years."

I could tell he was struggling; fighting to stop, but I wanted more, though I was worried about his stitches breaking open. Clearly, the Novocain injection hadn't worn off, but I was betting that when it did, he would be in a lot of pain. "Ben… let's go upstairs to my room. I'm worried you'll start bleeding again. You need to rest."

I drew in a shaky breath as he lowered me to the floor yet slid his hand under the curtain of my hair to cradle the back of my head and tangle in the loose curls. My fingers curled into the fabric of the T-shirt as he kissed me again. His lips teased mine open, and our mouths were once again engaged in a series of hard, then soft kisses, his arm hooked around my waist and pulling me close, and off the floor to leave me feet dangling. I resisted the urge to wrap my legs around his waist.

"Ben," I said, my hand flattening on the hard muscles of his perfect chest. God, this man was perfect. "I'll get Gem settled, but why don't you go up to my room and crawl into bed? It's the last door on the left. The bathroom is the door before it."

The farmhouse was built long before ensuite bathrooms became fashionable, but it was next to my room.

"Will you lay with me, at least?" he asked with a slight smile, the back of his knuckles grazing my jaw. He was so hot yet had such boyish charm. My heart stopped inside of my chest.

"As long as it doesn't hurt you," I acknowledged under my breath as I gently tore myself away.

"It will hurt more if you don't." His voice was low; intense, but hesitant. "I mean, I'd sleep better if you were next to me."

I needed to collect myself, so I moved out of his arms, and he released me reluctantly. Despite the passionate kissing and dry humping that we'd just engaged in, and as thrilling as it was, I forced myself to remember his injury. My body was throbbing with unresolved desire and judging from the big bulge in his blood-stained jeans, Ben was suffering, too. It was unlike anything I'd ever felt, and I wanted to feel every inch of him inside me. I shuddered just thinking about it.

I cleared my throat; acknowledging to myself that he needed to get cleaned up, and he needed rest. "Do you want some water?"

"I wish I could take a cold shower," he groaned, reaching for me but then dropped his hand.

"I'm sorry. You know I want to, but I'm worried."

"I understand."

"So? The water?"

"Sure. Thank you."

I nodded, then went to the kitchen to get two glasses filled with ice and water. Ben stood at the foot of the stairs waiting for me to join him rather than going up like I'd asked.

"Come on, Gem. Let's go to mommy's room." She knew the nightly routine, but she was still quite small, so it took her sometime to climb the stairs.

Ben took the glass I offered, and took a long, thirsty drink, then ushered me to follow the puppy in front of him. I was extremely cognizant of his presence behind me as I made my way into my room. I turned on the small lamp next to the bed and the room was bathed in the low golden glow.

It was late so Gem went into her crate and laid down without prompting. "She's so good about getting in her kennel," Ben commented, hovering and uncertain if he should sit on the bed or wait.

"I think she's pretty perfect," I agreed. "She sleeps with me sometimes, though."

I felt nervous, as I sat my glass on the nightstand and began pulling the extra decorative pillows from the bed and tossing them on the floor next to it, then pulled down the covers on one side.

"You can't sleep in those soiled clothes. You must be so uncomfortable." The dried blood had made the denim of his jeans crusty and stiff, and the shirt was dirty from being stuffed behind his seat in the truck. "I'll be right back. I'll find a clean T-shirt and pajama pants from Uncle Leonard's room. I haven't given his things away, yet." I rushed down the hall and soon found what I was looking for. I held them to my chest and inhaled a deep breath to steady myself. I waited a beat before making my way back to my room.

Ben was seated on the edge of the bed, on the side I had turned down, but he'd managed to remove the T-shirt, kicked off his black boots and had unbuckled his belt and unzipped his jeans but had stopped there. The white bandage was stark against his skin in the low light, but the muscles in his arms, shoulders, chest and abs were clearly defined. My breath caught, but I quickly gathered myself and held out the clothing to Ben.

"I know you're not supposed to get the wound wet so you can't take that shower you wanted, but I can get you some warm water and a washcloth." I was rambling and we both knew it.

He reached for my hand and rubbed his thumb over the top of my hand.

"Marin, relax. Nothing will happen that you don't want to happen."

His face was level with mine, sitting down as he was. "I know, and I want it to, but I just don't want to hurt you. You lost a lot of blood and you need to recuperate."

His mouth curved into a slow smile as he studied my face and continued to rub my hand, lifting it to his mouth to kiss it softly. "You're probably right, but I'm not sure if that won't hurt more in the long run."

236

I lifted my hand and pushed back his hair. I just wanted to touch and be touched by him. I felt like being connected to Ben would mean the difference between life and death, happiness and sorrow, turmoil or solace, togetherness or solitude. "We've got time," I murmured.

Ben tugged me closer, then ran the tip of his nose up the side of my neck, inhaling deeply. I was content to just be like this; close to him, his face nestled against mine, his hand softly moving up my back, gently kneading. "Do we?"

"Yes." It felt like a promise. I could lose myself, but I needed to think of him, first. "I'll go get the washcloth."

"That's okay. I have to use the bathroom anyway. I'll just clean up in there, if it's alright."

My heart felt bereft at the thought of him not touching me, even for the brief moment that would separate us. He kissed my temple and then stood up, holding the clothes I'd given him bunched up in one fist he disappeared into the hall.

Should I leave him to sleep in here without me? I started to second guess myself, second guess how he made me feel, second guess that this closeness was even real.

I turned toward my own dresser and pulled the drawers open, frantically searching for something to sleep in. I didn't want him to think I was a prude, yet I didn't want him to think I was trying to jump his bones when I'd just said he needed sleep. *Oh, God*, I thought as my hands rummaged around inside first one drawer, then another further down. I finally settled on an old fleece sweatshirt and a pair of pajama shorts. I changed my clothes as quickly as possible, so Ben wouldn't walk in in the middle of it, registering that my own skin was caked with his blood. I'd also need to wash off.

I quickly shoved the shorts and top I'd worn to the bar into the hamper in my closet and just in time, because Ben appeared in the doorway.

"I rinsed out the washcloth and hung it over the edge of the bathtub. I hope that's okay?"

I turned and folded my arms across my chest, suddenly self-conscious. I didn't know why I felt naked; I was wearing more than I had been for our evening out, but this situation was more intimate even if Ben was too incapacitated for sex. "Of course. Was it bad? I should probably soak your jeans in cold water, or the blood will stain." I was rambling again.

"Nah, they're toast anyway."

He moved slowly, yet within seconds he was in front of me; his large hands sliding down my arms from my shoulders to my elbows. "Ah-are you sure?" I stammered, looking up into his face. I bit my lip as my eyes closed. "They looked new."

"Yes. Where do you want me?"

I couldn't tell if the fluttering inside of me was desire, or fear of getting hurt. My luck with men wasn't good, but I was well aware it was already too late. "You take this side and I'll go around. Maybe I should sleep in my uncle's room."

Ben paused just before he was set to crawl into bed, his eyes locking with mine. "Marin, if you're not sure about this, I can sleep downstairs or be the one to go to your uncle's room."

I shook my head in the dim light. "No. I did promise I'd sleep with you."

"That's right, you did, but I won't hold you to it." He was suddenly serious.

I touched his shoulder, letting my fingers slide over it and up toward his neck. I brushed my knuckles against the strong column of muscle, and then against the stubble on his cheek. "No, I should be close... in case something happens."

"No argument from me." Ben pushed back the covers and got beneath them.

I left him briefly to use the bathroom and used another washcloth to clean the skin of my right leg, arm and side, then went back into my room and walked around and got into the opposite side of the bed. I reached up to switch off the lamp.

Ben reached for my hand under the covers.

"You don't know how hard it is for me not to make love to you right now."

I drew in a shuttering breath. "That's not helping, Ben."

His fingers squeezed mine. "I know. I could if you'd help me."

I turned on my pillow to face him, still holding his hand. It was imperative that he lie on his back to minimize the pain and not irritate his wound. My fingers threaded through his, my body aching to be as close to him as I could, wishing I could curl next to his body, my head on his chest and his arm around me. Warmth started to creep around us, the blankets heating up from our bodies. I listened for his breathing to even out.

"I want to, but I know what it's like to have sex when—"

I stopped, realizing what I was confessing. Ben's muscles coiled, his entire demeanor hardening.

"When you were injured," he finished for me.

"Yes," I admitted reluctantly. Carter was dead and he couldn't hurt me. The last thing I wanted was any feelings Ben had for me to be based on sympathy.

Ben sighed heavily. His face was in shadows; a combination of the dark room and the blue moonlight coming in through the half open blinds. "I can't stand the thought of anyone hurting you."

"How did you know he hurt me?" I asked softly.

"Your bruises didn't come from the accident. I've seen the signs before."

My eyebrow arched in question. I vaguely recalled him mentioning it once before. "On Missy?"

"Her first husband used to beat her badly."

That explained it, for sure. "I see. What stopped him?"

"She took my nephew and ran away."

"I see. I didn't have anywhere to run to, and I had to take care of the horses and the business."

"What really happened the night of the fire, Marin?" His fingers continued to stroke mine, coaxing out a response that I wasn't sure I was ready to give.

"We had a fight. He'd been drinking and knocked over a lantern."

"Was he coming for you?" he asked knowingly? "To hurt you?"

I lifted one shoulder in a half shrug, still reluctant to share the entire truth. Would it change the way Ben thought of me? I couldn't bare it. "I shouldn't have provoked him. I should have left him alone when I saw that he'd been drinking. It's my fault he died."

Ben turned toward me, and I could see by the slowness of his movements that the pain meds were starting to wear off. "No, it isn't. No matter what happened, he had no right to raise a hand to you in anger." He reached out and cupped my cheek. "Not in anger."

Tears flooded my eyes. "It feels like it. His family blames me."

"They're trash. You don't need to be afraid of them, either. I'll protect you."

An ache started in my throat as emotions welled and a tear dropped out of each eye to fall across the bridge of my nose and onto my pillow. I was speechless and I said the only thing I could say, thankful he was next to me. "You need sleep. We can talk more in the morning.

"I still want you, Marin." The admission was ripped from him and my heart swelled.

"I don't want the first time to be when you've just been sliced open." It would be better to wait, though it would be difficult.

"Can I at least hold you?" His voice was like velvet in the darkness. He lifted his arm up so I could come into his embrace.

Just as I'd wished for; his arm pulled me close, and my head came to rest on his chest as I snuggled in close, careful not to disturb the bandaged side.

"This feels perfect," Ben sighed as I felt his lips press to my temple, and I closed my eyes, breathing in his scent. "I don't want you to be here alone until I'm sure Apollo will leave you alone for good. I think I should stay here with you until we're sure there is no danger."

Contentment settled over me for the first time since my uncle died. "Okay."

"Good," he sighed and soon, the trauma of the evening and his injury made him succumb to sleep.

As I lay with Ben, his arms wrapped securely around me, his heartbeat beneath my ear, I relished in the feel of him close to me. I felt safe, and my heart was full.

everything
HAPPENS FOR
a reason

Chapter 16

BEN

I awoke to the smell of bacon frying and Gem barking happily from downstairs.

My arm snaked out to the empty side of the bed that Marin had vacated as my eyes snapped open and I sat up. Pain and a feeling of tightness grabbed my side as the prior evening's events came flooding back.

I wondered where that prick, Apollo, was but something inside me knew we hadn't seen the last of him. I reached for my phone where I'd left it on the bedside table by the lamp, glancing at the time. It was almost time for me to be at the station and I frantically dialed the number.

"Shit!"

I needed to let them know I'd probably be running late, and I was pleasantly surprised to know that Davis had filled in Captain Connors about my injury. He wasn't too hard on me considering I'd gotten into a fight in a public bar and told me to take a couple of days off so my wound could heal properly. I was sure it wouldn't take long until I was feeling back to normal. The wound was deep, so the main concern was breaking the stitches open; which would only delay healing.

"Just take it easy, Ben," the captain said.

I had a couple of weeks of vacation time racked up so I could afford a day or two to relax.

"Listen, Cap, I don't think I want more than a day off. I've been saving my vacation to take my nephew on a camping trip, but I have to get it all lined up."

"We just had that new class of recruits finish training and they start on Monday, so if you want, you can take some of it now."

"I'm not sure my sister could make it happen on such short notice," I answered.

"How old is your nephew?"

"He just turned eight. I owe him this trip for his birthday, but they live in Atlanta, so the logistics need to be worked out."

"That sounds like fun. Why don't you give your sister a call and ask her?"

"She might not be able to get off work this fast. She travels for her job."

"Oh, that's right. She's on ESPN."

"Right. Both she and my brother-in-law."

"Well, if you can swing it, let me know," the captain said.

He was much more amiable than I expected, considering the reason I was calling in. I'd have to buy Davis a six pack for helping me out.

"I will." I decided to talk to Missy as soon as I hung up the phone. It would also give me time with Marin to make sure she had the situation with the Minneapolis thugs taken care of. "Thanks, again."

As soon as I ended the call, I found Missy's number and she answered on the second ring.

"Hey, stranger," she said happily. "I was just thinking about you! Dylan has been bugging me about that camping trip and coming to see the new colt before he gets too big. He won't stop yapping about it." She chuckled softly into the phone. I could picture her all smiles and it was one of the benefits to her new life with Jensen. She was finally happy, with someone who deserved her and treated my nephew like his own.

I laughed. "That's funny because that's why I'm calling. I thought it would be good to do soon, before school starts."

"Great minds think alike, but I didn't think you'd be able to get the time off. Jensen and I already have time off together next week. Would that work or is it too soon?"

"It would. Something happened that has freed me up. This is perfect timing!"

"Oh? What?" Missy sounded concerned.

"It's sort of a long story, but I've got a new friend who has a lot in common with you so this will be good for a few reasons."

"Really? What's her name?" she asked, knowingly.

"Marin," Her name rolled easily off of my tongue. I smiled to myself, surprised at how giddy I felt. The feelings Marin stirred inside of me were new and exciting.

"Well, it's about time! How long have you been seeing her?"

"We're not exactly seeing each other." I paused, considering my next words. We'd almost made love last night and if I had my druthers, we would have, but we had yet to define what we were.

"What's that supposed to mean?" Missy was incredulous. "You sound like it's a done deal."

"As far as I'm concerned, yeah. But it's only been a few weeks."

"How did you meet her?" My sister never was one for subtly when it came to me. We were close. Our father bailed when we were kids and our mother worked two jobs, so we had to take care of each other while we were growing up.

"On the job. She was a victim at one of the scenes."

"Oh no! I hope she wasn't hurt!"

"Not bad," I said. I decided to let Marin share the rest of the story when they met, thinking it would create a sort of camaraderie.

"Well, you have a week to seal the deal. Dylan will probably want to share a tent with you"

"I'll work on it." I rubbed the back of my neck as I sat on the side of the bed. "I'll see what kind of equipment I can borrow. Davis has a bunch of that stuff."

"Maybe we can go to Yellowstone, too?"

"It will depend. We can pack quite a bit in, but maybe the kids would be happy with horseback lessons and a camping trip this time." I was hoping Marin would join us on the trip, but she would be concerned about the horses. Gem could come with us, but the horses would need feed and water.

"I'm sure they'll be over the moon, no matter what! I'll see what flights we can get, but maybe Friday night or Saturday?"

"Okay, cool. Do you think Chase and Teagan will be able to make it? I wasn't sure if they'd feel comfortable bringing little Mace into the wilderness. If not, can you bring Remi with you?"

"Pfft! I think Teagan for sure and she'd bring Mace with her. She's due again in November. Her baby bump is barely showing. I hate her!" Missy said, but I knew she was kidding. Teagan was like a sister to her, which, considering she was also Jensen's ex-wife, was a major miracle. The two got on like a house afire.

"That's right. I forgot that she's pregnant again."

"Her due date is still far enough out, but Chase still has a few games on his schedule. I'll have to call them to ask if he can join."

"Well, even if he can't, I look forward to seeing Remi and Teagan."

"It will be fun," Missy responded. "Remi will be excited for sure. Dylan has her so worked up about the pony, and the two of them are inseparable."

"Miss… It's a colt, not a pony," I corrected.

"Well, either way, it will be fun!" She laughed through the phone.

"It will be great! I can't wait to see you guys."

"We've missed you, too. Ben."

"You sound, happy, sis."

"I really am! Life is a whirlwind. Now we just have to get *you* married off!"

"Whoa, let's not get carried away," I argued. "Like I said… this is new, and I don't want to scare her away. She's getting over some stuff."

"I understand, but once she meets us all, she'll fit right in," Missy mused.

"Oh, yeah? Like I'm not enough?" I suddenly felt elated; encouraged by the make-out session last night and now the prospect of seeing my family was the cherry on top.

"Of course, silly, but I remember when Jensen and I first met; Teagan, Chase, and Remi made us feel so welcome, and I'm sure we can make Marin feel included, too."

"Ben?" Marin called from the base of the stairs. "Are you up? Breakfast is ready!"

"Hmmm," Missy mocked cheerfully. "It's new, is it? What's for breakfast? Or is it brunch?"

"Enough out of you!" I was grinning from ear to ear and heading out of Marin's bedroom. "Text me when you have your flight information and I'll pick you up in Jackson."

"I will! I love you!"

"You, too."

My face was starting to hurt from the permanent smile I'd worn throughout the conversation with Missy, and it only grew wider when I walked into the kitchen and Marin came into view. My heart almost stopped.

She looked gorgeous; there was a pink glow to her face that was freshly scrubbed and free of makeup. Her grey eyes were sparkling, and she was dressed in frayed jean shorts and a scooped neck top in dark purple. It made her eyes pop inside their dark fringe of lashes, and the color was the perfect contrast to her flowing blonde hair. I had an uncontrollable urge to kiss her and given her receptiveness last night, I didn't see why I should deny myself.

She was dishing up cheese omelets onto two plates. The toaster popped up on cue and she threw a smile over her shoulder. I walked up behind her and slid my arms around her waist, leaning down to place my open mouth on the curve where her neck and shoulder met.

"You're going to make me drop these plates," she pretended to complain. My arms only tightened, pulling her back and flush against me. It would be easy to get excited, but it felt good just being in her kitchen with her, waking up and knowing she'd be the first thing I'd see… and being able to touch her like I wanted.

"Sorry, I couldn't help myself." I wanted to kiss her mouth, but she did need to put the food on the table or she'd drop it, so, reluctantly, I released her. "You look beautiful."

Her face twisted wryly then she smiled. "What? I look a mess. I just fed the horses, and I probably have straw in my hair." Marin set the food down and went back to pull the toast from the toaster.

"I could have fed them for you." I said, unable to tear my eyes from her face. I pulled out a chair and sat down. She had everything laid out. The coffee steaming, orange juice poured into two small glasses and the omelets with hash browned potatoes now set at each of our place settings.

"I wanted to let you sleep," she said, her white teeth flashing into a broad smile. "You needed it."

"Want some help buttering the toast?" My heart swelled inside my chest. I realized she was the reason that fate had brought me to Jackson. I'd had girlfriends, and friends with benefits before, but for the first time, I could see my future with a woman in it. This woman.

"Sure!" She pushed a crystal butter dish toward me and set the small plate stacked with six slices of toast near me.

After it was finished and the butter was melting, I placed two slices on my plate and offered the side plate back so Marin could help herself. "This looks amazing." The food did look tempting, but not more than the young woman in front of me. I picked up my fork, but it hovered over my plate.

Marin took a bite of the buttered toast, then stopped. "What are you thinking?"

"You look happy."

She nodded, with a slow smile. "Yeah. I am. This feels good."

"So… last night… it was okay? I thought it might be too soon."

I used the fork to cut off a piece of the delicious looking egg concoction and lifted it to my mouth.

"Too soon after Carter's death?" she finished my thought.

"No." After finding out he hit her all sense of propriety or consideration for him was distinguished. "Too soon after meeting me." I chewed my food, then swallowed.

"Well, Carter is the only man…" Her eyes flew to mine, and then widened in shock. Clearly, she'd exposed something she hadn't meant to. "Um…"

She seemed embarrassed by the fact that Carter was the only guy she'd ever been with, and I didn't want her to be. I deliberately made it appear that I misunderstood to spare her. "He wasn't a man at all if he could hurt a woman." I was disgusted by guys who could only felt like a man by hitting women. "Was he always that way?"

Marin shook her head. "No. Not always."

I felt regret at my words. "Listen, I'm sorry. I didn't mean to imply anything bad about you. It's all on him."

"I know you didn't, Ben. He was a completely different person at first. He changed. Obviously, he only using me to get the business and money."

She seemed a bit melancholy and I could have kicked myself for letting bad memories ruin what was shaping up as a stellar day. It was doubtful he had changed at all, but rather put on an act to get close to her. I made a silent promise I'd never disappoint her the way Carter had, but I decided to change the subject rather than tell her what I'd decided.

"What should we do today?" I smiled and took another bite of my breakfast.

"Don't you have to go to work?" She looked at me hopefully.

"It just so happens… I have the day off." I winked, hoping it would get her back to her happy place. "Davis told the captain about the little scuffle at the Moose and so when I called in, he told me to stay out today."

"Well, I was planning on working with Dark. I need to get him used to people so I can get a bridle on him pretty soon. Maybe exercising some of the others."

"So, we're hanging with the horses! Cool!" I grinned at her. "Dylan was happy you used the name that he thought of. He was beside himself when I told him."

"It suits the little guy," Marin agreed. "It's cute when he's small but will seem much more majestic when he grows up."

"I can't wait for Dylan and Remi to get out here to meet him."

"That's another reason to get him used to people, soon."

"So, remember how I mentioned that I wanted to take Dylan and Remi on a camping trip?"

She nodded. We both had continued to enjoy our breakfast. "Yes. Is that happening?"

"Missy wants to come out next week. I know it's short notice, but I'll be able to take vacation and then my side will heal up."

Marin's eyebrow shot up. "Will it? You might over do it."

"You can keep me honest," I said, reassuringly. I was watching her reaction, trying to gauge her mood.

"Can I?" Her gorgeous lips lifted in a smile.

"You know you can."

"The sooner the better. I'm supposed to start working at the diner soon."

I remembered she'd mentioned that she'd applied for a job there. "Really? You still think you need a job outside of the ranch? You've got a lot of horses boarding, maybe you should take it easy for a while."

Marin shrugged slightly. "I just thought it would get me out of the house, and around people."

A twinge of selfishness reared. "I can see that," I said, wishing it could wait a few weeks. I was almost finished with my breakfast and was looking forward to the day ahead. "This was incredible."

"I'm glad you liked it."

My demeanor changed and I became deadly serious. "Are we going to talk about last night?" I reached across the table for her hand, waiting until she placed it in mine. My fingers closed around hers. I loved touching her in any way possible. "I told you that we didn't have to do anything you didn't feel comfortable with."

"I know. I trust you."

"I wanted to make sure you were okay with what happened." How much should I tell her? I didn't want to freak her out by blurting out that I was falling in love with her. "Or, if anything else were to happen between us." I watched her cautiously.

"I'm…" Marin's eyes were filled with fear. "Ben, I'm… I'm… a little scared."

Panic made me pause. "Of me? I know, I got a little crazy last night, but that's only because—"

Marin raised her hand in front of her, effectively stopping me mid-sentence. "I love being with you," she admitted. I could see her visibly swallow as if the words hurt. "But… I feel like I'm cursed. Everyone who has gotten close to me, everyone I've loved, has… died." Her eyes glassed over, and she blinked a few times to rid herself of them. "I'm not sure I want to risk it, again."

Wow. I hadn't considered it could be anything like this. I thought she might not be ready to trust me, though logic argued that a man who hurt her, could possibly be in love with her.

"Don't you think that's a little superstitious?" She didn't strike me as the type. She seemed so grounded.

Marin's shoulders lifted in a little shrug, and she shook her head. "It's not superstition if it's reality."

I paused for a few seconds, gauging my next words. "I'm happy to just spend time with you." After I'd said it, I realized how true it was. I was extremely aroused in her presence, but I took a lot of joy from just being near her. "We can take it slow." It would be hard as hell, and it might even kill me, but I knew I had to be sensitive to her needs. "No one knows what will happen tomorrow, next year, or ever, but I don't want to miss out on what's possible between us."

Our eyes locked, and I could feel her pain in the air around me.

"I know that. I do like spending time with you... I do. I'm just... I'm terrified something will happen to you. I'm sorry, Ben."

Abruptly, I stood and moved around the table, taking her hand and pulling her quickly up and into my arms. I held the back of her head with one hand and let my other arm slide around her waist to hold her close to my body. I wanted to comfort her, to absorb any and all of her pain.

My lips pressed to the top of her head, the sweet fragrance of her hair filling my nostrils. "Nothing is going to happen to me."

"How can you be so sure?"

My arm tightened. "I can't," I spoke the words against her temple. "But I just have to have faith. I believe God put us together for a reason and he won't separate us. It will be okay. I'm invincible." I tried to put some amusement into my words to take away her fear.

"I want to believe that," she said softly, looking up into my face. I wiped away an errant tear with gentle fingers.

My heart ached with love for this fragile, beautiful woman. I acknowledged that I was, indeed, falling in love with her. Maybe I was already gone. It was all I could do not to blurt it out, there and then. My lips lifted in an easy smile. "That works out well, then."

I hugged her close again, inhaling deeply and silently praying everything would work out. I couldn't promise nothing would happen to me because of my job. It was dangerous, but with everything I had inside, I wanted to ease her fear, even as hope bloomed in my heart. She cared if it was affecting her this much.

"Come on, let's go play with Dark," I coaxed. I bent and placed my mouth on hers in a soft, gentle kiss that left me wanting more. Maybe I shouldn't have done it, but my heart was so full of Marin that I couldn't hold back my feelings completely. I hoped the restraint of the kiss would communicate that I was willing to take it slowly, but also, the direction I wanted our relationship to go. My body protested my self-control, and I knew that I'd probably have a lot of self-love in my future, but I was willing to suffer if, in the long term, I could call her mine.

"Did you have enough to eat?" Marin asked, almost tearfully. I could sense, in the way her fingers had curled into my flesh, and the way she had responded that she'd been struggling to hold back, too.

My heart lurched, and blood rushed into my groin at the thought. "I did. It was very delicious, thank you."

"I laid out some other clothes in the bathroom. Just some old jeans and a worn-out cotton shirt. Sorry they aren't nicer." Marin watched my expression carefully. "I've got your others soaking. I think I can save them."

"I don't need anything fancy to sit in a barn all day." I pulled back, releasing her slowly; regretfully, but not wanting to call attention to my newly erect dick. "First, I'll help you clean up." Thankfully, she didn't seem to notice the obvious bulge in the flannel pajama pants as I turned away toward the sink to hide it.

"I got it. You go ahead and get dressed." She started clearing the dishes from the table. Gem whined at Marin's feet who then bent to give the pup a few bites of her leftover omelet. "You want to play with Dark, too, Gem?" she cooed at the little dog. Gem had already grown a lot in the weeks since we met, entering into the gawky stage where her legs were long and disproportionate to the rest of her body. I couldn't help pausing to watch their interaction. "Gemmy and I will meet you in the barn."

Marin looked up and caught my gaze again. Her eyes were sad as she nodded toward the stairs and I wanted nothing more than to ease that sadness.

"I'm going," I lamented, but with a smile. I was looking forward to the day in front of us.

everything
HAPPENS FOR
a reason

Chapter 17

Marin

My haert was flying, even as I tried to stop feelings for Ben from staking claim on my heart.

The previous night when he held me in his arms and pressed his body into mine, and then, the caring embrace after breakfast, I was in sheer bliss. The only thing that could make it any better was if he'd made love to me.

I was struggling between what I wanted to happen and being afraid of the outcome. I was ultra-aware of him; as if my skin vibrated whenever he was around, and my heart swelled to bursting. I was so aroused; it was all I could do not to jump his bones or kiss him silly.

The attraction to him was different than it had been to Carter, and beyond that, I had no experience. Ben was so masculine I was certain he had a lot more experience. He oozed confidence. At the bar on the dance floor, I had melted into him. I almost forgot that Carter ever existed, until Apollo showed up.

Last night, I knew Ben should rest, but if he would have given one hint that he wanted me, I would have been all over him. This morning, I couldn't completely push away the nagging concern that seized control of my heart and mind. My parents had died, Uncle Leonard had died, and just months later, Carter, too. I couldn't risk anything happening to Ben. He could have died when Apollo stabbed him, and I couldn't tempt fate. He was such a good man, and I wanted to give in to what we both obviously wanted, but I'd rather stay friends than lose him. I didn't think my heart could stand it.

When I'd first met Carter, I was young and infatuated with the first man to pay any attention to me, but this felt incredibly different. Being in Ben's arms felt like somehow, whatever was missing, wasn't anymore. I sucked in a deep breath, filling my lungs to capacity, trying to steady myself and keep my head clear.

I opened the door to the house, then Gem and I headed for the barn. It was a warm summer morning and the air smelled clean and fresh. I made up my mind that the laundry I would do later would be hung on the clothesline outside to dry so it would smell nice.

The horses were out in the two pastures. I'd let them all out after their morning feed, except Siri and Dark. But I planned on doing so after an hour or so in the stall. Newborn horses were naturally skittish around people and he needed to get used to us without being able to run away. I smiled when I realized I'd used the word "us" in my mind.

"Hey, Siri," I murmured softly coming up to her stall. She answered with a snort and walked over to the side near the gate so I could pet her. I held up my hand and she pushed her velvety soft nose into it. "You're a good girl, aren't you? How is your baby?"

I continued to rub her nose and ears, peering into the stall. Dark was lurking behind his mother's flank, cautiously eyeing me. "It's okay, Dark," I cooed. "See? Your mommy trusts me. We're going to be great friends. We have to work fast, though, because there are some young kids coming to see you."

Gem was exploring around the barn, as was her habit, so I opened the gate; slowly lifting the latch slowly. I moved in quietly and sat in one corner on a half bale of hay that remained there. Siri moved toward me, wanting more attention. I wouldn't make any sudden moves toward the colt and just let him get used to my presence and my voice. He would soon learn that I meant him no harm and he'd get curious enough to come closer.

"Good girl, Siri," I continued to soothe. "You did such a good job bringing your beautiful boy into the world, didn't you?" The horse snorted as if she understood what I said.

"Mind if I join you?" Ben asked from just outside the stall. I hadn't heard him come into the barn.

I smiled. "Of course."

Ben brought in one of the empty oat bags from the feed stall.

"I never realized oats came in bags like dog food," he said. "I brought this for you to sit on. The hay must be poking you."

I smiled at his thoughtfulness. Huffing out a sigh as just looking at him.

"What?" he asked quizzically.

"They have supplements added," I explained. "That's why the bags."

"Oh. Makes sense. Are you gonna just sit there? Do you like getting poked in the ass?" He joked, then his expression twisted in horror when he realized how that sounded. "I mean… you know what I meant." His face turned a slight shade of red.

I burst out laughing and stood. I took the bag and put it on top of the hay before sitting down on top of it. "I do! That's sweet of you. Thank you for thinking of it." I patted the bag beside me. "Take a seat with me. I'm letting Dark get used to me."

Ben sat next to me. Close. The oats came in fifty-pound bags and probably wouldn't accommodate both of us, but Ben had jeans on while I just had on shorts.

"So, we just sit here?" he asked. His arm fell behind me and I leaned into him, but only slightly. I was on his good side, so it wouldn't hurt him. The barn was several degrees cooler than the outside, and I could feel his body heat seeping into me.

My head snapped back to look into his face, and I nodded. "Pretty much. At least, for a while."

"I had hoped I could pet the little guy."

"He'll warm up in his own time."

It was easy to lean on Ben. Easy to let my head rest against his shoulder and jaw. He reached out and patted Siri. We sat in silence for a while. I was enjoying the time together, watching Dark nurse. When he was finished his ears perked and his little dark eyes studied us.

I put out my hand toward him, moving it slowly closer. "It's okay, baby. Come on," I coaxed. "Remember me? I helped you be born."

Siri snorted. "Phrrrrbbbbbb!" and bobbed her head up and down, then stomped one of her front hooves on the floor.

Ben reached into his pocket and pulled out a carrot, offering it to her. "Sorry, I raided your fridge," he explained with an easy grin and I let out a soft laugh. The dimples in his cheeks were adorable.

Siri took Ben's offering all at once; pulling it into her mouth and began munching happily. "Do you bribe all of your girlfriends?" I teased.

"Want to find out?" Our eyes locked. I felt his hand cup the side of my face and my eyes closed of their own volition. I felt his breath on my face about one second before his mouth descended deliciously onto mine. My hand closed around his wrist as his lips teased and coaxed mine. My breath left my body as the kiss deepened.

We were hungry, kissing over and over again. I didn't know how it happened, but somehow, I was straddling his lap; my knees resting on the empty bag. His arms were strong around my body, one hooking the back of my hips and pulling my groin tight against his. I could feel his erection straining against me, through both layers of denim and silk. Desire grew as our mouths ebbed and flowed, my hands slid up and into his hair, pulling his mouth tighter against mine at the same time my hips thrust forward.

Ben groaned and stood up without breaking the kiss. My back was pressed against the wooden gate and I could feel him fumbling for the latch. I pulled my mouth from his, both of us panting.

Ben stopped, gazing up into my face with love drunk eyes. "No?" he asked.

"Only if it won't hurt you."

Ben opened the gate and closed it after he moved through it, still carrying me as if I weighed nothing. "Ben don't rip your stitches out. Please." I wasn't sure if I was begging for him to take me then and there or to stop so he wouldn't hurt himself. "Maybe you should put me down."

He shook his head. "I'm fine. Better than fine. I'd promised myself this wouldn't happen if not in a bedroom, but we're both wound so tight."

He carried me into the feed stall at the end of the barn, setting me on top of the stacked bags of oats. They were purchased in bulk and stacked chest-high on one side of the stall with the bales of alfalfa stacked up on the other side. He rested his arms beside my hips his hands clasped behind my bottom. My arms naturally fell around his shoulders. I bent and nuzzled Ben's neck just below his ear. He sucked in his breath and turned his head into my neck. The way he kissed my neck with his open mouth and tongue made me hungry for other things.

"Ben," I sighed out his name just before his mouth found mine. He kissed me hard and deep. His tongue laving with mine until finally he broke free from me, turning he peeled off the shirt he was wearing.

I could do nothing but watch him, muscles rippling. The white bandage was a stark reminder. "Ben," I began again.

"Shhh!" He stopped me. He pulled a generous amount of the alfalfa free of the open bale and made a large pile on the floor. He laid his shirt down on it then turned back to me. He reached out, his hand fisting around the front waistband of my shorts, then pulled me forward. I slid to the edge of the full bag I was sitting on. He unbuckled my belt and undid the front of my shorts. "Last chance," he murmured, his deep blue eyes looking deeply into mine.

I wasn't even sure if he saw the slight shake of my head, because he bent to remove my boots, tossing them to the side. He lifted me down until my feet landed on his shirt. Within seconds Ben was on his knees in front of me and slid my shorts down my legs. He kissed my stomach just above the top of my string bikini panties. "God, I've wanted this," he breathed against my skin. It was a good thing his arm hooked behind my waist steadied me or I would have fallen as he pulled the white silk and lace down and I stepped free.

My eyes were closed, and I bit my lip, completely lost in the sensations building, putting my complete trust in Ben as he lifted one of my legs by closing his hand around the back of my left knee and hoisting it up onto his shoulder. I knew he wouldn't let me fall, though it felt like I was floating. My insides tensed, knowing what came next. My body was singing even before it happened. I'd never been this turned on.

Ben pushed my shirt up and drew down one cup of my matching bra. He traced his tongue across the nipple, taking it between his teeth and sensually tugging. It was as if I were floating. Long, sure fingers, ghosted over my abdomen and lower, to softly part my flesh, teasing my arousal, finally dipping inside me when I moaned aloud. I felt desperate. I wanted more. Just the thought of him inside me made me clench around his fingers. I was aching.

"Uhhhh," I breathed. I wanted to touch him, but he was out of reach. My fingers wound in his hair. "Ben…"

"Jesus, Marin," he groaned when he was finished torturing my breast. It left his mouth with a pop and he laid me down, careful to keep his shirt under my bare bottom and hips. With gentle hands he pushed my knees apart and at first, I resisted, my hands falling to cover myself. I was embarrassed by the vulnerability of it. Ben clasped my hand in his and lifted it off of my body, lacing his fingers through mine. "Stop. You're so beautiful. Just relax" His other hand continued to make small circles on the tender flesh. It felt amazing. I closed my eyes as my breathing deepened and my back arched. "Let me take care of you."

I felt myself getting close, sensations building to the point of exploding, but then he would lessen the pressure. I could do little else but moan his name. I writhed and struggled, wanting the climax yet never wanting this moment to end. He slid one, then two fingers inside me, thrusting them in and out of me as his thumb continued its blissful teasing. I thought I'd die. A desperate moan erupted from somewhere deep inside me. I'd never felt anything like it. Carter made me come once or twice, but not like this explosion ready to split me open.

"Ben…. Ben…. Ben…." I begged.

Suddenly his fingers were removed, and he was kissing me, his body looming over me. My knees dropped open; both feet hooking behind his legs. I wanted him inside me. He left me wanting and it was killing me.

I could hear the buckle of his belt working and the rip of a foil packet as he put on a condom, and soon the tip of his cock was pressing against my clit over and over, his hardness sliding up and down in my wetness. My hands slid down his bare back, and over his hard glutes. My fingers clutched and pulled, silently begging for him to put me out of my misery. I lifted my hips toward his.

"Marin. Relax… it will happen," he murmured softly against my mouth. The kisses gentled, as Ben licked and nipped at my lips, pulling the lower one into his mouth and sucking on it.

My body clenched, aching for him to fill me. "Ben… please."

My words elicited a deep groan from Ben. I felt his erection, hard and thick, sliding up and down my folds, bumping against my clit then lower, in a slow purposeful quest to gain entrance. I arched again, allowing him to find purchase.

Our eyes met as he slid inside, gently he pushed in, stretching me wide until he was deep inside. My mouth dropped open and my head fell back as sensations exploded inside me.

He stilled for a moment as my muscles spasmed around him. One of our hands were still entwined and he reached for the other one. He pulled both of them over my head as he began to thrust, slowly in and out.

"You feel so good. So good," he said into the curve of my neck, then pulled back, watching my face as he pulled out then thrust forward again. I closed my eyes as he bent to kiss me. We kissed and moved together, our bodies sweaty and sliding together for several minutes. Ben's breathing got shallow and his grip on my hands tightened. He was close.

He changed the angle of his thrusts, using his pubic bone

to push into me just right, pushing me over the edge with him. "Oh, Ben," I cried.

"That's perfect. Come on… Marin," he moaned. "Oh God."

We clung together, even as our orgasms overtook us. He kept kissing me, the kisses still deep and worshiping, his hips kept thrusting gently until the last shudder was milked from me.

As our breathing softened, he let go of my hands and raised up on his elbows, staring down at me. Both of his hands stroked my hair back off of both sides of my face.

He was still inside me and I never wanted to let him go. My arms and legs caged him in. Emotions overcame me and tears stung at the back of my eyes. He bent to place one languid kiss on my open mouth, then another softer one at the corner of my lips.

"That was amazing," he said softly. "You are perfect."

I reached up and laid a hand against his cheek. My throat hurt preventing me from speaking. I wanted to tell him how wonderful I thought he was. I wanted to tell him that I never wanted to spend another day without him. I wanted to tell him that I'd never felt like this… that I loved him.

Gem began barking in the distance. Her little voice far away.

"Oh shit," Ben exclaimed, pulling out of me and quickly getting to his feet.

He found my panties and handed them to me. He removed the condom and looked at a loss with what to do with it. It was almost funny. He dropped it on the floor, then buckled up his pants. "I'll get that later." He grinned. "Wait here. I'll see what she's barking at."

I scurried into my panties and shorts after rolling off his shirt and tossing it to him. I hoped it wasn't too wrinkled or full of hay.

"Who is it?" I whispered. "Is someone here?"

Gem continued to bark.

"It's okay, Gem," a female voice said.

"Oh, crap," I squeaked in a whisper. "It's Gina!"

"Stay here," he whispered. "I'll handle it."

"Marin?" Gina called from the other end of the barn.

Ben threw on his shirt in a mad haste. "Hey, Gina!" he called, leaving the stall in a rush.

I crawled to the corner so she wouldn't see me. I didn't know why we were hiding, except that I'd told Ben I didn't want to hurt her.

"Ben! What are you doing here?"

"I'm helping Marin muck out the stalls."

"Should you be doing that? With your injury?"

"I'm fine. Marin's taking a nap in the house."

"Well, you're just the person I wanted to see, anyway. I realized that I didn't get a chance to give you my number last night, so this must be fate."

I held my breath, straining to hear the conversation taking place down at the other end of the barn. Whatever he said next would be telling.

"Yeah. Listen... about that. I'm really a dick because I'm kind of into someone else and I wasn't sure where that was going. I thought since it was up in the air, I could be open to other things, but the truth is... I'm just not."

I couldn't help being thrilled by his words, yet I knew how they must have devastated Gina. A silence of several seconds ensued.

"Oh," Gina answered finally. "Marin?"

"Yes."

"But... her boyfriend just died. The other night... she set the evening up for me to meet you."

"I know. She doesn't know how I feel about her, but I'm just... I just have to give her some time and then I can see if we have a shot."

"Boy, do I feel dumb." I could hear the embarrassment strain her voice. Clearly, she was hurt. "Well... don't tell Marin I stopped by, okay?"

"Sure. I'm really sorry about this."

I sat as still as a stone until a couple of minutes later Ben's head popped over the top of the stall. "She left."

He disappeared again, then Gem's little black face appeared in his stead. He was obviously holding her up. "Hey, mommy!" Ben took on a falsetto voice, pretending to be the puppy. "Mommy! Come out and play! I missed you!"

I rose and took her from Ben, cuddling her close, but I felt withdrawn from the closeness we'd just shared. Gemmy licked my face a hundred miles an hour. Ben opened the stall door so I could walk out and join him in the corridor, closing it behind me. "Are you sure Gina is gone?" I asked.

"Why are you so worried about it? We didn't do anything wrong. You didn't cheat on anyone, and neither did I. Just tell her the truth."

"What's the truth?" I asked, stoically.

"You tell me," he said, irritated, and began to walk out of the barn. "You tell me."

"Ben! Where are you going?" I called after him, my voice echoing in the empty space. How stupid I was to let my insecurities belittle what had happened between us. I groaned.

He turned and stopped. "I'm going to let Siri and the little man into the pasture, after that... I don't know what I'm doing. I thought I was spending the day with you, but not if you're ashamed of us."

Gem wiggled in my arms, anxious to get down. I put her on the floor, and she ran after Ben.

"That's not it at all! Please, come back." I hated to see him upset and it hurt something deep inside of me. "I don't know what I'm afraid of. I'm sorry."

He was angry and I understood why. If only Gina hadn't shown up when she did then the day would have been perfect.

"I care about you, Marin. Did you think that after we had sex it would change anything? Did you think I wouldn't want you anymore or that I'd stop coming around?"

"Of course, not." I started walking toward him as quickly as I could.

"Good, because it's just the opposite. I only want you more."

I flushed at his words. The truth was, I was concerned that people would be suspicious of Carter's death if I moved on too soon and the ink was barely dry on the fire commissioner's report. That, and the people who knew me or knew my uncle might think I was too easy... "I – I..." I began, struggling to explain.

"Because I'm not him, Marin. Get that through your head, right now." He bent and picked up Gemmy, clearly exasperated. "Come on, girl." Ben stopped to face me. "I'm taking the dog with me into town," he stated, a disgruntled expression souring his face.

I sucked in a deep breath and walking out of the barn determined to make things better, hoping to stop Ben from walking away. I had a bad feeling inside my chest watching him go, but he was already striding across the yard and into the pasture to yank open the door to Siri's stall with his free hand. Siri and Dark emerged and trotted happily off across the pasture, Dark kicking his back legs behind him and prancing around in the sunshine.

Ben then proceeded to open all of the outside doors to the stalls on the west side of the barn before disappearing around the back to repeat the action on the east side. The horses all came out into the pastures.

He was still carrying Gem as he emerged then walked toward his truck, not even glancing in my direction. He opened the passenger door and put her inside before going around and getting behind the wheel. The truck rumbled to life and he backed out and started down the lane as I stood frozen in place.

An emptiness settled into my chest and a sadness engulfed my heart as I watched his truck disappear from my property. I sighed shakily and dropped my head, putting my fingers to my temple, contemplating my next move.

I'd make a delicious meal, and tonight, show him what he meant to me, then try to explain. I needed to convince Ben that he was the farthest thing from Carter, but also to understand. Would I have to tell him everything? Would he think I killed Carter on purpose? I suddenly realized that Ben's opinion of me was truly the most important thing.

everything
HAPPENS FOR
a reason

Chapter 18

BEN

Missy left a message on my cell phone indicating her family would be coming next Friday, though Chase who had a game on Saturday, would join afterward.

I should be excited, but the weird fight with Marin left me unsettled. I felt like shit all morning and thought I wanted to call my sister back, but I needed to get things straight with Marin first. I wanted my family to visit either way, but it would be a big disappointment to the kids if horseback riding was off the table. If I didn't make it right with her, I'd be distracted.

Frustration gripped my chest which made me inhale deeply. I filled my lungs to capacity in an effort to rid myself of the restriction. If only Gina wouldn't have shown up when she did. The interruption only pointed out that Marin seemed ashamed of what happened between us when I was floating on air. Was she worried about how things would look if she started seeing a new man so soon after the last one died, or worse, was she still dealing with softer feelings for that bastard? Her reticence would have been expected if it weren't for the abuse, but it still pissed me off. I should have been more understanding, but I'd never felt this way about a woman. It was new and exciting, and I didn't want to hold back.

Somehow, I'd managed to shower, shave, change, and throw a few things into a bag. I wasn't sure if I'd be staying over again, but I threw it in the back of my truck just in case. Gemmy was oblivious to the turmoil of my emotions, sitting on the passenger seat and trying to look out the window as best she could. She was just tall enough where her chin was at the window's bottom edge. I kept it closed because I didn't want her to fall out and was blasting the A/C instead, adjusting the blowers to land on her. She seemed to be enjoying the cool breeze that it created and was a good little rider. Gem was just another thing I'd lose if Marin told me to take a hike.

"Damn it," I muttered under my breath, glancing in her direction. "You're my little baby, now, aren't you, honey? Yeah."

If this was what being in love felt like, then it sucked. Sure, that rush of intense passion and emotion felt amazing, but this… the sudden pain over a small disagreement and this awful fear over losing the relationship was debilitating and unexpected.

I didn't want to come off like an asshole, so could I smooth things over without looking like a jerk? I could suck it up and blow it off, but I needed to know if she still loved Carter, or we couldn't move forward. I needed to have that conversation with her no matter what happened.

Maybe I was howling at the moon. Maybe Marin just needed someone… anyone, and I just happened to be the one in front of her. The thought only made me feel worse.

"Ugggghhhhhh!" I yelled, startling the pup. "Oh, sorry, baby." I reached over and ruffled her little head. Gem answered with a furious wag of her tail and an attempt to crawl onto my lap. I lifted her and plopped her on top of my thighs, holding her loosely with one hand and steering with the other. "It won't be long until you won't fit here, so don't get used to this, little bit."

Fifteen minutes later, I'd made my way out of Jackson and my truck was lumbering down the gravel lane on my way back to the ranch. It was still late morning, but it was beginning to get hot outside.

When I got out of the truck, I let Gem down to the ground and decided to top off the water in both of the outside horse toughs. When I rounded the corner of the building, I saw Marin in the paddock with Siri and Dark. I slowed my approach to observe. It occurred to me that Gem might start barking and startle them both. I wondered how she'd managed to separate the mare and her foal from the other horses in the pasture.

"Come on, Dark," she murmured, reaching out her hand slowly. "Tkk tkk tkk," she made a sound by clicking her tongue on her teeth. Marin started to run her hand softly over the tiny horse's neck. "There we are," Marin said. "I won't hurt you, see? You can trust me."

She continued to work with him, and I stood mesmerized as she gained his trust and on the third attempt was able to get the halter over his nose and then buckle it behind his ears, scratching with a couple of fingers to distract him. She spoke so softly that I couldn't hear what she said but Dark's ears perked and turned toward her.

"There!" Marin said happily, petting his back and scratching his neck with her fingernails. He appeared to really enjoy her ministrations. "Now you have a bridle just like your mommy! That wasn't so bad, was it?"

Marin had a knack with the horses. Siri neighed behind her and the stunning young woman turned toward the mare. The big red and black horse came forward and rested her chin on Marin's shoulder in what appeared to be a short of hug. Marin's arms flew up around her neck to return the embrace. "I love you, too, Siri. You don't have to be jealous of your baby. You're still my girl." Marin kissed the large horse's head on the cheek, then her eyes landed on me.

"Sorry, I didn't mean to sneak up on you," I said calmly.

"No, that's okay. Did you see?" Her beautiful face lit up and my heart literally stopped inside my chest. "I got Dark's bridle on! Now I'll be able to work with him because I can attach a lead." Her face lit up with her excitement. "Isn't that incredible?"

"Yes," I nodded, pleased that Marin apparently put our disagreement on the back burner so we could enjoy the moment. "Can I touch him?" I asked hopefully.

Nodding, she reached out and took hold of Dark's bridle, holding it lightly. "Sure," she held up a hand and motioned for me to come closer. "Just approach slowly."

Gem was wagging her tail furiously and started to whine as she scampered around at my feet, so I glanced at Marin. "Will Gemmy be okay if I leave her out here? She can run under the fence easy enough."

"I'll hold her, if she barks then Dark will get spooked. Give her to me then take the bridle."

I bent to lift Gem as Marin showed me the part of the leather to hold under Dark's chin. We made the transition without a hitch; me passing Gem over and taking hold of Dark's bridle in one motion. "Just pet him lightly and keep your voice low. Sweettalk him. He has no reason to fear humans and will soon learn we aren't going to hurt him."

I smiled as I nodded. "Hey, little man. Remember me?" I said softly near his ear. I had to bend down a little because the horse was so small, and I was tall. Siri snorted her approval from behind me.

At first, Dark pulled away and gave a strong nod to try to jerk free, but my fingers tightened around the thin strap preventing him from moving away, as I stroked down his neck with the other hand. "Shhhh… You're okay. You're okay. I'm not going to hurt you, Dark."

The black coat was soft and shiny, his mane short, and his tail was like a bushy hairbrush. I smiled happily as I started to pet him, and he relaxed little by little. Siri neighed and moved a few feet away. Marin had walked in the opposite direction, toward the fence and stepped outside the paddock, finally letting the squirming puppy down.

"Stay out here, Gem," she commanded. "Mommy doesn't want you to get kicked in the head." Marin took a seat, sitting legs crossed in the grass near the gate and Gem pranced over and crawled onto her lap, laying down in a small round ball that fit perfectly in the cradle Marin's bent legs created.

I glanced up from the colt to where Marin sat watching through the spaces in the fence and gate. "Now what do I do?" I asked, perplexed with a soft chuckle.

Marin laughed out loud. "Nothing! Let him go and see if he hangs out close by. Just give him some time to get used to you. It won't take long and then he'll come when we call him. Just like Siri does."

I dropped my hand from the bridle but kept petting him, sliding a hand up to scratch behind his ears. He took a step closer and butted my arm with his nose. "This is so great!" A bright smile split my face and I almost didn't notice the blistering sun beating down on me. "He's adorable."

"He's beautiful," Marin beamed.

After about fifteen minutes of my hanging out with the horses Marin called out to me.

"Before you arrived, I was going to set up a sprinkler in one of the pastures for the horses. Wanna help me? It's getting hot so I thought they'd like to walk around under the spray. They loved it last time I did it. That's unless you're still mad at me?"

she asked sheepishly. I could see the regret in her face and instantly I felt like an ass for getting upset before.

"No, I'm not mad and I'd love to help!" I agreed happily, pleased the unease that had clouded my morning faded away. Once more Marin surprised me. Who else would think to consider how uncomfortable horses were in the hottest part of the day? "Should we use the hose near the trough?"

"Yeah, it's long enough. I'll go get the sprinkler from the barn and be right back." She scooted the puppy off of her lap before she stood and disappeared around the front of the barn. I went toward the spigot and started to gather up the hose and pulling it away from the trough and further into the pasture.

Marin reappeared with the sprinkler and handed it to me over the top rung of the fence. It didn't take long before I attached it and set it down as far into the pasture as the hose would allow.

"Move if you don't wanna get wet!" Marin shouted from her place near the spigot. Her hand was on the lever and she pulled. Instantly, water shot up from the sprinkler, catching me in its spray.

"Hey!" I protested at the same time I dodged the spray, running quickly toward her, though I still got squirted with enough water to drench the back of my shirt. Gem barked and tried to run toward the rotating sprinkler when I opened the gate, but I bent to catch her and scoop her up. "Sorry, sweet face. You'll get stomped and I can't have that!"

I rushed to the fence and climbed over despite the pain in my midsection. Already the horses were neighing and trotting toward the spray, rallying for their place under the water. Little Dark followed his mother and pranced around her. Clearly, they enjoyed the cool water splashing on their backs and bellies.

Standing beside Marin, I petted Gem as we watched the horses in the pasture. Some walked around trying to stay under the spray, and others happily chomped on the newly moist grass.

My free hand inched over, and my fingers reached for hers, clinging to them as hers answered. "I'm really sorry about before," I said continuing to concentrate my gaze on Siri and Dark as they played in the water, glancing only briefly in Marin's direction. I felt shy, which was strange to me. "I shouldn't have left in a huff."

Marin's fingers squeezed mine in return. "I shouldn't have been so pensive and scared."

I glanced at her and threaded my fingers fully through hers wishing she was close enough so that I could pull her hand up to my mouth for a kiss.

"Carter hasn't been dead two months, and already... I'm involved with you. What will people think?"

"If they know how Carter treated you, they'll think you finally have someone who will protect and cherish you," I stated simply.

Marin studied me for a few seconds, and I literally felt my face flush, realizing the gravity of my own admission.

"I mean," I tried to dig myself out of the proverbial hole I'd just jumped in to, "you deserved more."

A soft smile lifted the corner of her mouth. "The employees from the shop know how he was, but the rest of Jackson, doesn't. While Uncle Leonard was alive Carter was a good actor. Even I didn't know the real him. I'm afraid they'll blame me for his death."

I turned toward Marin, still holding Gem, and wanting to ease any lasting feeling of guilt she might have. I took her in my arms with the pup between us. It was hot, and I could feel a drop of sweat roll from my forehead down the side of my temple, but I didn't care. I wanted to be closer to her. "Look, the commissioner's report said it was an accident. Carter was a dumb ass for having a lantern in a sea of grease and oil. It was his fault." I rubbed her back gently. "End of story. Let's just move on from this." I bent to place a brief kiss on her lips. "Okay?"

Marin nodded with an easy smile. "Okay."

We turned and started to walk toward the house, our hands still entwined.

Marin stopped short and guiltily pulled her hand free as a juiced up old Oldsmobile pulled up the lane and came to a stop beside my truck.

"Do you recognize that car, Marin?" Her reaction, and the look of shock on her face certainly implied that she did.

"Yeah. It's Apollo. He picked me up at the airport in that car."

"That idiot from last night?" I asked, handing the Gemmy to Marin. She nodded, her expression turning to fear. "Take the dog in the house."

"No. I have to tell him about the insurance. Maybe then he'll leave me alone."

"Trust me, he'll leave you alone," I growled, glaring in the direction of the car.

Apollo and two other men emerged from it. The three of them looked menacing and out of place in Wyoming. Apollo's right hand was in a cast, but one of the other men used his fist to hit his palm, apparently trying to threaten us. I huffed in pissed off amusement.

"What do you want? Didn't you get a bad enough beating last night?" I asked.

"This doesn't involve you. It's between me and the lady," Apollo hissed.

"Well, I'm between you and her, so I'd say you have a major problem." Adrenaline surged in my veins. "You're trespassing," I said firmly. "State your business and then get the hell out of here."

"I want my money, that's all, man. I saw that charred piece of shit shop up the road. Total loss, so there should be lots of cash coming," Apollo said with a sneer. "And if this whore is already taking up with you, maybe the two of you murdered my little bro."

His companions were laughing and egging him on.

"You have *some* imagination," I chuckled offhandedly. "Your brother died because he was stupid. I guess it runs in the family."

"I gave the insurance company your mother's phone number, Apollo," Marin said from behind me and a few feet back. Her voice was weak and shaking. She was clearly terrified. "The payout goes directly to her."

"Well, I want some of the cash! This is a nice place. You're obviously rolling in it, so you can give me some money, now!"

"I don't have cash! I told you that already," Marin protested.

The ranch was nice, but it had seen better days, so I wasn't sure what the fuck he was talking about.

Apollo took a step in Marin's direction and I stepped forward in his path. "Stop. Get the hell away from her. Marin, get in the house." I nodded in its direction. Gem started barking wildly from Marin's arms. "Go." I turned my attention back to the three criminals as she took a few hesitant steps. I knew they were dangerous and probably guilty of all sorts of sordid crimes, but my back straightened, and my fists clenched at my side.

His friends moved closer. "You gonna beat up the three of us, tough guy?" Apollo goaded.

"Are you planning on punching me with your broken hand?" I asked sarcastically. "Ouch."

"I wasn't the one bleeding all over the fucking floor!" he seethed.

"Let's just beat his punk ass, Apollo," the bigger of his friends said, taking a step closer.

"Yeah, let's waste 'em!" the other said, his hand hovering behind his back, indicating he was armed. "Then we can take what we want. Ain't nobody around here."

"Oh, yeah, that's genius," I said, seething. "Do you think you can kill us and get away with it? Everyone knows us. The first place the cops will look is at Carter's family, there is a paper trail of Marin's trip to Minneapolis, and a police report of your little incident at the mall and last night at the bar, and now the insurance paper trail. Do you think you'll get to spend the payout from behind bars? Your IQ must be about the size of your dick."

"You're hilarious," Apollo shot back angrily. His eyes narrowed as he motioned to the other men to move in. I widened my stance and lifted my fists in preparation for whatever fight was coming.

Boom! A loud shot rang out behind me. Everyone was startled as we all looked behind me at the source of the noise.

Marin had emerged from the barn with her uncle's old hunting rifle. She'd fired the first round into the air, but now the gun was trained on the men as she walked forward, pumping another shell into the chamber. I was surprised, but proud of her. I felt almost aroused by her display of bravado, but I knew these men were dangerous.

"I realize a shot gun would have been a little messier, but this will do the job, and I know how to use it, so get the hell off my property!" Marin shouted. "Just leave!"

My eyebrows rose as she came closer. I was worried because I knew they were armed, but there was nothing to be done but stand with her. She kept walking forward holding the gun at the ready. My first instinct was to take it from her, but it would give the others the time to pull their weapons.

"You heard the lady. Get the hell out of here!" I added my stern warning to hers. I knew there was no way in hell I was going to leave her out here alone after this, and I had second thoughts about my family coming for the visit the following week. "And get out of town!"

"You'll get your money. I just want to be left alone," Marin added.

Apollo's eyes shifted from me then to Marin and back again. His two friends had their hands ready to pull out their weapons and I wanted to diffuse the situation.

"That money better get there in the next few days, or else." Apollo pointed a finger from his unbroken hand at her then moved it in my direction. I didn't know what the hell he was trying to prove.

"If we see you around here again, we'll shoot first and ask questions later. Now, be on your way."

My muscles were coiled and remained so as the three got back into their car and started to back out. I stayed put until they'd cleared the long driveway, then turned toward Marin. She might have put on a brave front, but I could see from her tear-filled eyes that she was terrified and frozen in place, both hands still clutching the gun so hard that her knuckles turned white.

"Hey," I murmured turning and walking toward her, my gaze never leaving her face. I reached out and wrapped a hand around the gun stock. "It's over. Let go, honey."

Marin's eyes shot up to mine and she started shaking. I gently lifted the gun away and holding it with the barrel pointed at the sky, my arm slid around her waist and pulled her to my side.

"Let's put this away," I suggested and all she could do was nod. Two tears slid down her cheeks. "You are pretty badass," I joked, using my arm to turn her around toward the barn. "Remind me never to get on your bad side. I'm proud of you," I said softly, kissing her temple.

Inside, I was shaking, too. Would Apollo and his goons be back? I couldn't take that chance.

"I didn't know what else to do," she said shakily. "I just asked myself what Uncle Leonard would do?"

"Well, it was damn awesome."

Inside the barn, I released her and put the gun back on the wall on the two hooks that had been used to hang it. Gem barked from one of the empty stalls. Apparently, Marin had put her in there to keep her out of the way and I was thankful she was still too small to get up and over the first rung of the gate.

Marin's hands covered her face, and I could visibly see her body inhale a deep breath. I went to her and wrapped both of my arms around her, pulling her close and sliding one hand up her back between her shoulder blades.

"Listen, I think I'm gonna need some protection from those assholes. They might come after me at my place. Think I can sleep here for a few nights?" I asked, turning my face into her hair and inhaling. I didn't care about the heat, I just needed to be close, and I hoped joking around would help ease her anxiety. And mine.

Marin's arms slid around me, and her hands curled into the wet material of my T-shirt. She nodded with a small laugh. "Yes," she said her voice muffled as her face buried into my chest. "Yes," she said again.

"Do I have to sleep in the barn with the horses?" I grinned down into her face as she finally looked up at me. All I wanted to do was protect her. My thumb traced the line of her jaw. "Because I think I'm allergic to hay."

"It didn't seem to bother you this morning," she said, with a grin.

"Well, that's because I was preoccupied," I kidded. I bent to kiss her gently on the mouth, then moved to the corner of her lips and up to her cheekbone.

"Uh huh," she sighed into me as my mouth took hers again as I gently cradled her head.

"Bat! Bat!" Gem barked loudly, reminding us she was still locked inside the empty stall.

Reluctantly, I pulled my lips from hers, softly caressing her cheek with the back of my knuckles after I released her from my embrace. "Get your baby, and let's go inside the house. I don't trust that they won't be back," I said, more seriously.

Marin nodded and opened the gate to the stall. "I'm glad you were here," Marin said softly as we started to walk out of the barn. I slid my arm back around her waist.

"Me, too," I agreed. "I'm not going anywhere anytime soon. At least until that check clears." I resolved to call the police and give them a description of Apollo's car and what had just happened. Maybe a friendly police reminder to leave town was in order.

A feeling of pure love settled over me when Marin's arm tightened around my waist, and her head came to rest on my shoulder. "At least," she returned with a smile.

I inhaled a deep, satisfying breath.

everything
HAPPENS FOR
a reason

Chapter 19

Marin

My chest seized in panic then I sat straight up in bed, disoriented.

I was sweating. My breathing was shallow, my heart pounding hard, and the wetness of tears dampened my cheeks. I pulled my knees up to my chest, resting my elbows on them as I struggled to catch my breath. I glanced at Ben, peacefully sleeping on the right side of my bed, and then at clock on the nightstand. It was 2 AM.

My face crumpled as the content of the dream came back to me in living color. It was so vivid, so real… so heartbreaking. A sob broke from my throat and I quickly covered my face with my hands trying to silence the pain, but my brow creased as the torrent of tears overwhelmed me. I prayed I wouldn't wake Ben, but I couldn't stop the pain from overwhelming me.

This was the second time in a week I'd had this nightmare. I was reliving the fire, except this time I was running through the flames trying to save the victim, my skin melting away in a scream of pain that didn't stop my progress to the man on fire. His face imprinted on my brain; his face morphing from Carter's into Ben's… his screams forever scared on my soul as Carter's voice turned into Ben's. My worst fears were coming to life in my sleep. It didn't matter that I was also dying in the fire… *Ben*. He was all that mattered. I gasped in another deep breath.

Oh, God, my mind railed as I cried, harder now. My head dropped and hung between my arms and bent knees, my body shaking with the effort of my sobs and keeping them from erupting so he wouldn't hear, but this time it was to no avail.

Ben had stayed at the ranch after Apollo's visit, and I was glad to have him with me. He made me feel safe, except Apollo and his goons weren't what scared me. Losing Ben was my worst horror. In such a short time he'd become so important to me. As the nightmare had materialized, he was more important than my own life. I'd let him convince me that I wasn't cursed, that nothing would happen, but now…

"Hey," Ben's voice called softly in the darkness which was only broken by the blue light of the digital numbers indicating the earliness of the hour. "What's wrong?"

His strong hand reached out and slid down my back over the T-shirt I was wearing as a nightgown. His touch was so comforting. I would have turned and melted into him if it wasn't for the awful dream and direction of my thoughts.

I sniffed, wiped my nose on the back of my hand then used both hands to wipe the tears away. Unable to resist the pull between us, I laid back on the pillows then turned toward Ben. His face was visible only in light blue and black shadows. I sniffed again as his arm slipped easily around my shoulders to pull me closer, still.

We were nose to nose, and I couldn't help reaching out and pushing the hair that had fallen forward on his forehead away. His hand came up to cover mine as it slid down his cheek, now bristled with almost a day's worth of beard growth. I liked the way it prickled my fingers; I liked the way it made him look so masculine and tough. Ben kissed the inside of my palm.

"I like your scruff," I said softly, hoping I could revert the conversation away from the nightmare. I didn't want to lie to Ben, and I didn't know if I'd be able to even if I tried. "It makes you look hot." I smiled gently.

Ben huffed out a short laugh. "Thanks, I think."

We lay in silence for a few seconds, both of us gently touching the other. The back of his fingers brushed up and down my arm beneath the covers.

"Why were you crying? Don't worry about Apollo. I won't let him hurt you."

I inhaled a shaky breath and nodded. "I know." I wanted to tell him about the dream, but I struggled with what to do about it. I wanted him in my life, but what if staying with me would mean something bad would happen to him?

"Okay, so don't sweat him," he brushed off casually. "We can follow-up with insurance on Monday, then when the old lady signs the release to get the check, you're free of him. If he comes back around, I'll take care of it. I think we should file a complaint with the sheriff so there is something on file. We'll do that on Monday. Just don't worry, babe. I'll take care of you."

Babe. My heart leapt and an aching lump formed in my throat.

It was the first time he'd called me that and it made my heartbeat faster and heat flush beneath my skin. He was staying with me, and we'd made-out every night, but we hadn't made love since the day in the barn. It was a sort of sensual torture that I couldn't get enough of.

"If I'm your 'babe' why haven't you made love to me again?"

Ben sighed heavily in the darkness, his warm breath washing over my face; his hand came up to cup my cheek. "I was wondering if you'd get around to that."

"Is that bad?"

It was dark in the room, but I was close, and my eyes had adjusted enough to see the corner of his mouth lift in a half smile. "No, I just don't want to rush you. I don't want you to think I just want sex with you, plus you're worried about what everyone will think."

I offered a half nod as my heart skipped a beat. "Having you stay here overnight is enough to get tongues wagging, so that part is moot."

He shook his head. "No, it isn't. We just tell them I'm here as protection. Personally, I don't give a rat's ass what anyone thinks, but I don't want you to stress about it. I want to take things one day at a time and to have fun this next week. You're going to love the little munchkins." His white teeth flashed in the darkness. "They'll get your mind off all of this. They're a trip."

I was all set to begin my new job the following Monday, but today was the day Ben's sister was arriving with her kids. I was excited for the weekend and it would be a good distraction from the awful dreams.

Ben had planned a couple of one day excursions into Yellowstone, but other than that we were just going to pitch some tents on the property, go horseback riding, and cook on an open campfire.

Ben's side was healing nicely, but still not fully. I had thoroughly enjoyed the last lazy week at home just taking care of each other. He was so perfect that, at times, I forgot to worry and tried to enjoy my time with him. Nothing ever felt so right as it did with Ben.

"I'm looking forward to spending time with them."

"They'll fall in love with Dark, and Remi really wants a puppy, so she'll adore Gem. They'll have so much fun. I wish you could push back starting at the diner," he said regretfully.

"I know. Me, too, but I don't see how I can. Arlene was so nice to offer, I can't can on her."

"I don't think you even need that job," Ben protested.

"Maybe not, but it will be good to get out. I can't just sit on the ranch all day. Especially now that I have to do the dirty work," I teased lightly.

"You think so, huh?"

It would be sad next week when I wouldn't see him as much, and I was thinking about what he said. I really didn't need the job at the diner. Taking care of the ranch would keep me busy enough and maybe I could solicit a few more horses to board, but it would help me meet people and get back to normal. "I do."

We continued holding each other in the middle of my bed, though I wanted more and sensed that Ben did, too.

"It's going to be a busy week. Try to get some sleep, honey." His hand slid up my arm and gave a little squeeze near my shoulder.

My heart fell. "Sleep?"

"Yes, and no more bad dreams. I command you," he said, amusement lacing his voice.

I drew in a frustrated breath, my hand sliding down his chest and lower, but his hand closed over my wrist, stopping me.

"Plenty of time for making love to come. If you still want to."

I wondered if he was joking as my body quickened and the air between us electrified. "I want to," I whispered.

Almost involuntarily, my hips arched toward his, and my chin lifted. Mouth open, I was silently begging him to kiss me. It was the truth. In that second, all of my fear of losing him melted away and all I wanted was to be in his arms, his body possessing mine, his mouth consuming me.

"Well, that's good, because if you didn't, I might not survive." His voice was low and hungry.

He was so chivalrous and romantic, it only made me want him more. I didn't want to come off as a wanton slut, but I wished with my entire being he wouldn't make us wait. "What about a quickie?" I teased.

He laughed and instantly, I was taken by surprise when Ben rolled on top of me, pinning me to the bed and parted my legs with his muscular ones. "Listen, woman, there will be no quickies. Not with you." His hand gently pushed my hair back. "Only long, slow, amazing, delicious nights together."

I could feel that he was already hard; my loose knit shorts barely providing a barrier between us. Suddenly, I wished I'd worn something sexier to bed.

I smiled softly; the promise made a thrill shoot through every cell in my being.

"Got it?" he pressed his erection into my tender flesh emphasizing the words, leaving me in no doubt of his desire. Ben laughed sexily, sending a jolt of lust straight through my core.

"Uhhh," I lamented. "Not yet, but I'm hoping to," I said, half joking and arching my hips in answer. Our eyes met, his sparkling in the darkness.

Ben groaned and dropped his head, burring his face in my neck and hair. "Marin, stop teasing me. I promised myself that I wouldn't push you. After the last time and your regret afterward, I decided you needed more time."

"You may be right, I probably do, but I don't want to wait, Ben. Here, right now, in your arms, I've never wanted anything more," I admitted honestly, hooking my legs around both of his, and digging a heel into the back of one of his thighs.

His face sobered as our eyes locked. "I want you so badly, but there will be no going back. The first time was giving into desire, now, tonight or whenever it happens again, is a conscious decision. I sense something is holding you back. Maybe not sexually, but emotionally, and when I make love to you again, I want you to be ready and all in. I want all of you."

I swallowed at the unspoken meaning behind the words. I reached up and slid my fingers down one side of his face. The most beautiful, handsome face would be burned into my memory forever. This moment would be burned into my memory forever. My heart was bursting inside my chest

"I love you, Ben," the words were out before I could stop them. I paused, afraid of the implications... and of my own fear. "I love you..." I whispered, again. I'd never meant anything more... though the strength of it terrified me. Would Ben be taken from me, would something bad happen to him? Instantly I regretted my words thinking I'd blighted us, but even left unsaid, it was the truth.

Ben's mouth lowered and he kissed me deeply, sweetly, and so lovingly, both hands cupping the sides of my face, his body still covering mine. My mouth opened to his and our tongues melded together in an incredible dance of love and desire. Slow and sensual; I melted into a puddle and I knew he loved me, too.

"I know it's crazy given that we've known each other only a few weeks, but I love you, too, Marin. So much, I can't breathe."

"Ben," I said breathlessly, ghosting my fingertips over his strong jaw, but he shook his head.

"You're scared of something. I don't know what it is, but I feel it hovering between us. We could make love tonight and it would be earth shattering, but *it will be everything* when you trust me completely and you're not afraid. I want you, but I want you forever, so I'm willing to wait until you can trust me. I will be here, and I'm not going anywhere." His mouth traced lightly over my lips and up to my cheekbone and temple as his words sank in. "I can wait. However long it takes for you to believe that."

Ben backed away and off of me but pulled me to him so that my head rested on his chest. His arms engulfed me in my stunned silence. My hand slid down his impressive chest to slip around his waist and I held on for dear life.

"You want me forever?" There was thunder inside my chest, my soul soaring. I'd never used that word with anyone before, never even thought about it. Not Carter even when he duped me into believing that he loved me.

Ben's arms tightened around me and his warm lips pressed a kiss on my temple. "I do," he said simply. "Now get to sleep. You'll need it. Dylan and Remi will run our asses off a few hours from now."

As much as I wanted Ben's hands and mouth on me, sleeping in his arms would have to be enough tonight. His strength and willingness to wait for me filled me with incredible love. Waiting would be difficult, but maybe time would ease some of my worry and help me to banish the bad dream. I couldn't bear to think of my life without Ben... not ever. I closed my eyes and pressed my forehead to the base of Ben's throat where his pulse assured me of his life-force. I inhaled his scent committing it to memory.

"Can't wait." I looked forward to completely immersing myself in Ben's life and that included his family. I couldn't wait to see him interact with the little kids, but I knew he'd be perfect in that, too.

* * *

Ben's tuck rambled up the drive followed closely behind by a shiny dark blue Toyota Avalon, obviously Missy's rental. His truck stopped next to mine on the gravel in front of the house as I waited anxiously on the front porch holding Gem in my arms. Ben got out and two rambunctious youngsters piled out of the passenger seat of the truck then rushed around to his side.

"Uncle Ben! Uncle Ben!"

"Can we go in the barn and see the pony, now?" They both spoke at once. A little girl with pink cheeks and shoulder-length dark hair was followed by a sandy-haired boy a little taller and both rushed up to Ben clamoring for his attention. His handsome face was filled with joy as the wind blew his hair off of his forehead.

My heart filled when he placed one large hand on the top of each of their heads. "Well, let's get your moms and Mace out of the car then go meet Marin first. It's her ranch, remember? I told you."

Two glamorous women in sunglasses climbed out of the front seat of the rental car. The brunette was visibly pregnant, and she opened the back door on her side and leaned in, soon emerging with a dark blonde toddler in her arms. The other woman had long lighter blonde hair, who I assumed was Dylan's mother, walked toward the youngsters and her brother.

"Hey kids, chill a little, will ya? We've got all week here. We don't need to bombard Uncle Ben the minute we step foot out of the car." She smiled and lifted a hand in a wave to me as I began my way toward them across the yard. "You must be Marin!" A genuine smile broke across her face and she opened her arms to welcome me into them. "Is this okay? I'm a hugger!"

I nodded and quickly set Gem on the ground at my feet. She immediately scampered off in the direction of Ben and the kids. "Of course! It's so nice to meet you!" I could see the resemblance, though her hair was lighter than Ben's which more resembled his young nephew's.

By now, the other woman who carried a sleepy little boy, came closer. "This is my friend, Teagan." The toddler hid his face in the curve of his mother's neck, turning to peek at me.

"Nice to meet you," I said.

"You, also," she agreed with a smile. "Thank you for having us. The kids have been looking forward to it for weeks."

"Mom! Don't forget us!" Dylan spouted off; coming forward and offering his little hand to me. "I'm Dylan, and this is Remi." He nodded to the beautiful green-eyed little girl standing next to him. "Thank you for inviting us on a real cowboy weekend!"

I shook his proffered hand, smiling from ear to ear.

Quite the little gentleman, I thought.

"Well, aren't you quite charming? It's nice to meet you, both!"

"Yeah! He's charming," Remi said with a grin, "and I'm his damsel."

"Oh, really?" I laughed, cocking one eyebrow. Ben told me the kids were being raised together, and it was cute the way Remi made the distinction. "And who is this little one?" I asked nodding to the shy little boy in Teagan's arms.

"That's just Mace. He's two!" Dylan piped up. Ben was smiling from ear to ear, happiness in every inch of his face. He must miss them very much.

"He's my little brother. May I hold your puppy, please?" Remi asked quietly, her eyes trained on Gem who was sniffing everyone's feet. She was growing rapidly and would soon be too large to carry and I wondered if Remi would be able to hold her, but her little arms were already reaching out for her. "This is

Gem," I answered with a nod. "I'm sure she'd love playing with you, Remi."

"Gem? Wow! This is the kind of doggy I want! My dad promised, but then we got Mace and now the new baby, so I have to wait. When I get one it's gonna be a girl and I'm gonna name her Jewel!"

"That's sorta the same as Gem! Isn't that cool?" Dylan observed.

"Yeah!" Remi answered.

I laughed out loud at their youthful exuberance. "It certainly is. Amazing coincidence." Gemmy started licking Remi's face profusely the minute the little girl picked her up in her arms. "She's getting heavy so you can set her down if you'd like. She'll stay with us."

"Is it okay to hold her for a while?" Remi asked. "I just love her so much, already!"

"Of course." I nodded.

"Remi don't sit down in the dirt until you get into your play clothes," Teagan reminded, gently.

"Aw, Mom!" she complained.

"Are you hungry? I happen to have some brownies and milk in the house." I tried to distract them. They would undoubtedly get filthy on the ranch if they were allowed to have any fun, but I could wash the Wyoming dirt out of their clothes, even manure if needed.

"Can we go to the barn instead?" Dylan asked boldly. "Can we, Uncle Ben? I want to see Dark! Can we?" he asked cheekily.

My eyes connected with Ben's and I nodded almost imperceptibly, silently telling him I didn't mind. We all chuckled at Dylan's precociousness.

"Sorry," Missy apologized for her son.

"Oh, no worries. We can get some tea and if little Mace needs a nap, you can put him down in one of the spare rooms."

"Thank you so much," Teagan said. "I think I'm as tired as he is. This pregnancy thing isn't all it's cracked up to be."

"Unclllleeee Beeeennnnn," Dylan insisted, yanking on the hem of Ben's light blue T-shirt. "Pleeeaasssee."

"Sure, sport. Remi, do you want to come with us? Gem can tag along if we make sure to keep her out of the stalls."

"Can I mom? I won't sit on anything!" she almost begged, her excitement making her bounce up and down. "Please."

"Okay." Teagan nodded with a smile.

"Yay!" Remi burst out. "Let's go!" She set Gemmy on the ground and patted her leg. "Come on, baby! Come on!" Clearly, she didn't want to be separated from the puppy. Gem yapped enthusiastically and started following her new friends.

"I got them," Ben assured the two women. "No worries." He strode off after the two children. "Hey kids, no screaming! You'll spook the horses!"

The trio hurried off toward the barn. "Be careful," Teagan called after them. "Mind Uncle Ben!"

"We will!" the kids said, once again in unison.

"We can get your bags later." I said with a huffed out laugh. "Come on in. You've got some beautiful kids."

"They're so excited," Missy put in as we climbed the few stairs of the porch to the front door. "They couldn't wait to get here."

"This is a great place. I love all of the fresh air," Teagan said. "And the views!"

"Yeah. I really love the mountains." I opened the door and ushered them inside. "The kitchen is to the right. It's not much, but it was my Uncle's house, and I haven't had time to remodel."

"I think it's perfect," Missy said. "Ben said you board horses and that you had an auto shop. I'm sorry that burned down. So sad."

I wondered if Ben had shared about Carter or just mentioned the fire. "Yes. But if that hadn't happened, I guess I wouldn't have met your brother, or now, any of you." When no mention was made of Carter, I guessed Ben had kept that part to himself.

"Are you planning on rebuilding?" Teagan asked, genuinely interested. "Because if not, this place would make a great bed and breakfast or how about a dude ranch? We've been looking at dude ranches to visit in the area for about a year, and they are in such high demand they're all fully booked."

"Hmm, that's a good idea, actually." I mused at the idea as I brought the plate of brownies to the table. "I'm not sure yet. A few mechanics were working for us and I thought I'd rebuild to bring back their jobs, but most of them had already moved on before the fire. So now, I'm not sure. If they want to come back, then I think I should rebuild."

"Maybe they could work for you on the dude ranch?" Missy asked.

I mulled it over for a minute. Some of them might. I'd definitely think it over and discuss it with Ben. "Maybe some might. Help yourself to the brownies. What would you like to drink? I have soda and iced tea, milk, juice or I can make coffee."

After I had the two of them situated, Missy with a Diet Pepsi and Teagan and I both a glass of green tea, I sat down at the kitchen table with them. Teagan held her adorable little boy on her lap as he munched on part of a brownie and sipped milk from his sippy cup. "Mace must resemble his daddy," I observed. Remi had her mother's coloring.

Teagan nodded and rolled her eyes with a grin. "Spitting image. Just as impetuous, too."

"I not *petuous*!" Mace insisted, making a chocolatey mess of his hands and face.

Teagan's eyebrow shot up wryly. "See what I mean?" she said with a smile, then kissed the top of her little boy's head. "Are you like Daddy?" Teagan asked.

He nodded profusely. "Yup!"

"See?" Teagan laughed.

"I hope Chase and Jensen will be joining us, too. I've heard so much about all of you." Ben had talked so much about them on the drive from Minnesota I felt like I knew them all.

"Oh, they wouldn't miss it! They're flying out tomorrow evening. Chase has a day game against Peru tomorrow," Teagan answered. "But it's at Mile High Stadium. So lucky."

"Wow. That's kind of a big deal," I said in awe.

Teagan laughed, happily. "You'll get used to it. Not a big deal," she said modestly.

"She says that, but trust me, Ace Forrester is, indeed, a big deal," Missy added wryly. "Fans all over the world. It's sort of insane."

I flushed guiltily. "Sorry, I don't really follow sports."

They both laughed. "That's refreshing! I need a vacation from sports," Ben's sister said. "I'm so sick of muscles and locker rooms, I can't stand it."

Soon, we were all giggling. "I can think of worse things than muscles and locker rooms," I said. I felt completely comfortable around these two and found myself excited for the rest of the weekend.

"Me, too," Teagan put in with a sly smile. "Jock straps."

We all burst into a tirade of giggles.

"Jensen is really looking forward to learning to ride horses with the kids," Missy stated.

"Chase, too. I wish I could," Teagan said. "But..." she said, laying a hand on her swollen belly, "I can't take any chances.

I'm going to have to satisfy myself with stuffing my face with s'mores."

I nodded, smiling. "Well, Ben has a lot planned for your kids. He's been like a kid himself; so excited for your visit, but s'mores over an open campfire are an excellent mollifier."

"Ben and Dylan have always been close," Missy added. "We lived with him in Billings during my divorce. He was a Godsend and a great role model."

"He misses you; all of you. Teagan, do you know what you're having?"

"We just had our twenty-week ultrasound and so yes. It's a girl."

"Oh my gosh! How amazing! Have you named her?"

"This is our last baby so we're taking our time deciding on her name. We keep harping on Jensen and Missy to get in gear, though. Dylan needs a sibling!" Teagan reached out and gave a gentle push to Missy's shoulder.

"Hmmm," Missy said, her cheeks turning a becoming shade of pink. "We're working on it." She reached for a brownie from the plate.

"Come on, Teagan!" I slide the plate closer to her. "You're eating for two and besides, no calories on a cowboy weekend!"

Fifteen minutes after I'd shown Teagan and Missy to their respective rooms, I met Missy back downstairs. She'd changed into some faded old blue jeans, sneakers and a baggy Denver Bronco's T-shirt.

"Your favorite team?" I asked as we walked outside. Teagan had chosen to lie down with her little boy and take a nap after their long trip. They'd been up early to catch a flight from Atlanta and had spent many hours on planes and in airports.

Missy waved it away. "Oh, this? Nah. I just get a ton of team shirts on my job. My wardrobe consists of suits and jerseys. I brought some for Ben. When I first got the ESPN job, I'd get shirts and signed balls for Dylan and he'd get all bent out of shape, so I brought him a suitcase full this time."

"That's so sweet of you. I'm sure he'll be surprised."

We walked across the yard and then over the dirt driveway toward the barn. We could hear Ben inside speaking to the kids as we approached the open door.

"He's so cute!" Remi's voice echoed through the high rafters.

"He's just two weeks old," Ben explained. "He's too little to eat hay or oats like his mom. Just like human babies, he needs milk."

"He's little, but he's big for baby and he can already run around?" Dylan asked.

"Yep. I was there when he was born. It was the most amazing thing I've ever seen. It was only a couple of hours before he was up on his feet."

"I wish we could have been here," Remi said.

Both kids were sitting on the top of the gate to Siri's stall. Ben was between them with an arm around each of them so they wouldn't fall off.

"Well, maybe if one of the other horses has a baby, or maybe if Siri has another one, we can arrange for you to be here," I said once inside the barn.

Both kid's heads snapped around with bright smiles on their faces.

"Really?" Remi said.

"Awesome!" Dylan replied at the same time. "This place is super cool!"

"Yeah! I wish we could move here!" Remi put in. "We could just play with Gemmy, and ride horses all day long. Every day!"

Missy was petting the nose of one of the other horses, and Siri came toward the gate once she saw me. She neighed loudly and snorted. I reached out my hand and she walked forward and butted her forehead against my open palm.

"Wow! Can I do that?" Dylan asked.

"Sure! Come over here and stand on this lower rail in front of me. Siri is a gentle horse. She won't hurt you."

"Me, too!" Remi exclaimed.

"Take it easy," Ben mentioned. "Remember what I said about moving too fast and spooking them." He lifted them down one at a time. They both climbed up and I stood right behind them with a hand around them.

"Okay, put your hand out like I did. It's okay Siri, girl," I said to my horse.

She snorted and moved her head from one to the other.

"She's so smart!" Missy proclaimed.

"Hi, Siri," Remi murmured, rubbing her head. "You're a good mommy, aren't you?" She bent and placed a kiss on Siri's face as Dylan rubbed her neck.

"Are they all this tame?" Missy asked.

"Most of them. Dark's daddy is more aggressive, but only in that he likes to run fast."

"You guys want to help me feed them? It's time," Ben asked.

"Cool!" Dylan said.

"Okay! I get to feed Siri!" Remi jumped down from the railing.

"Wow! Look at all the special help I have taking care of my horses! Thank you!"

Missy and I chatted while the kids hauled multiple buckets of oats to the horses. Ben had to lift them up in order to allow the children to dump them into the feed bins on the other side of the stall walls. It took a lot longer than normal, but it was a joy to watch his gentle interaction with the children. He was so patient and kind in every word and action. It only made me fall more in love with him.

"Ben seems to have a knack for this ranch life," Missy observed, knowingly. "It's about time," she murmured with a satisfied exhale.

After the horses were fed and Dark was happily nursing with both kids installed back on the top of Siri's stall gate, Ben walked over to us. "What do you think, sis?"

"I think it's great! I can't wait until Jensen and Chase show up and you make them muck out the stalls!"

"What?" Ben casually butted shoulders with his sister. "I was leaving that part for you."

"Hahaha! Um… nope," Missy protested.

Ben laughed and locked eyes with mine. "I'm starving!"

I offered a smile in return, my heart soaring. "Well, the chores aren't done, ranch hands! Don't you have a tent to pitch and a fire to build? I'll go rustle us up some grub to cook on the open fire! How do hotdogs and beans sound?"

"That's real cowboy food!" Dylan was so happy, and I could see the same joy reflected in Ben's features.

"Okay, come on crew!" Ben called. "You heard the boss! We have chores to finish. We can't eat without a fire."

Dylan jumped down from the gate with excitement and Remi waited beside Ben.

"Mom, this is the best vacation, ever!" Dylan shouted as he and Remi started after Ben.

"Yeah! I think we should come here every summer!" Remi announced.

I giggled happily. It was so amazing to see this excited reaction to the place I grew up.

"Wow," Missy said with raised eyebrows. "You even beat out Disney World. That's a major accomplishment."

"You ain't seen nothin' yet!" I said, proudly. Uncle Leonard would have loved these kids and their exuberance for his ranch. That dude ranch idea was looking better and better. Of course, I'd need a ranch hand or two. I couldn't wait to discuss it with Ben.

everything
HAPPENS FOR
a reason

Chapter 20

BEN

As I watched the firelight flicker across Marin's face, I knew there was nowhere on earth I'd rather be then right here beside her. I wanted to see that face every day for the rest of my life. I was thankful for Davis insisting I move to Wyoming, thankful for being a firefighter and even thankful for the awful blaze that brought us together. As far as I could tell, it was destiny and part of a bigger plan.

I used my pocketknife to carve points on a few limbs I'd taken from a live oak behind the house and passed them out for everyone to use for dinner by the campfire. They needed to be green so that they wouldn't burn while roasting the hotdogs and marshmallows over the fire.

Earlier, Dylan found some large rocks and made a circle while Remi's job had been to collect dead sticks for kindling, and later, they both helped me pitch one tent about twenty feet away. They struggled and it was a job, but we'd finally managed to get it up in the yard between the pasture and the farmhouse. It was still closer to camping out than either one of these kids had ever experienced and I was wary of taking a pregnant woman into the wilderness, at least until her husband showed up and came with us.

I was amazed at how well the kids got along, worked together, and shared food or their things. They were raised side by side, but in different households. They were best friends but didn't fight like brother and sister.

It was incredible how, even at this young age, Dylan was so protective of Remi. When her hotdog fell into the fire, he offered her the one he'd just finished roasting and then wiped off her stick with a napkin and asked Marin for another dog and began the roasting process all over again for himself. I was extremely proud of him and admired the job that my sister and her new husband were doing in rearing such a fine young man. I had an intense desire to be a father during my observation of his behavior. Maybe it was Dylan, Remi, and Mace's cuteness that got me thinking about it, or maybe it was meeting Marin that spurred the desire. I sighed at the intense emotion that overtook me.

Marin's face reflected how awed she was at the gesture of the little boy as she reached into the cooler and handed him another. As Dylan put the second hotdog on the stick and returned to sit on one of the six logs we'd placed in a circle, a safe distance from the fire, I winked at her. Her smile only got wider, the adorable dimples I'd grown to love making an appearance. I wanted to rush to her, pull her up into my arms and kiss her for all I was worth. My heart swelled inside my chest so much my lungs had no room to expand. I sucked in another life-saving breath and finished the hotdog in my hand.

Teagan held little Mace on her lap and helped him hold his hotdog over the fire, though he was quite impatient, and Missy sat on her own log to Dylan's left. It was an incredibly clear night and twilight was upon us, turning the sky lavender and purple as the stars began to appear… this was heaven on earth.

No words were spoken by the adults for a while as we enjoyed the evening, though Mace began to fuss until Teagan was able to hand him a finished hotdog and it wasn't long before Remi and Dylan both had another over the fire.

"This was a perfect set-up because Teagan and Mace can sleep in the house with Marin," Missy commented as she took a sip from her can of Diet Pepsi.

"Uncle Ben," Remi began, "Can Gem sleep in the tent with us?"

"Yeah, and can you sleep in the tent with us, Uncle Ben?" Dylan wanted to know.

"I wouldn't think of letting you sleep out here without me, buddy. It would be my pleasure. And of course, Gem can sleep with us. She'll be a good watch dog." We were right on the edge of Yellowstone and so coyotes and bears were possible, though rarely this far south and west of the mountain range.

"Remi, I think your hotdog is done," Missy said. "Marin has the buns, baby. Go get one."

Each of us had a plate with a scoop of pork and beans from a cast iron pot that was warming on the edge of the fire and Dylan had gobbled his down before he'd roasted his first hotdog.

Remi walked over to Marin, who put her plate down and reached in the top of the cooler to hand over an open bun so Remi could put her hotdog onto it. She then closed it around the hotdog.

"Now, pull on the stick, Remi," Dylan instructed. "Yeah, just like that."

The pretty little girl did as she was told. She looked a lot like her mother, except her vibrant green eyes were like her famous father's. I watched the interaction between the two, Remi making a funny face at Dylan's instructions and Teagan laughing under her breath, wondering what it was all about. Surely some secret, inside joke between the two.

"Hand me the stick, sweetheart," I said, then Marin handed her the completed meal.

Teagan shivered. "It's so cool here. I thought it would be warmer in July," Teagan said, hugging Mace, with a blanket wrapped around him, on her lap. He wiggled free and went over to sit next to Dylan and Remi unperturbed about the temperature. "Be careful, Mace. The fire is hot."

He glanced back at her "Spicy hot?" Mace asked, wide eyed.

"Temperature hot."

"Okay, Mommy."

"I'll help him, Aunt Teagan," Dylan assured.

Teagan smiled and nodded. "Perfect. It was in the eighties earlier, but now that the sun has set the evening air is so much cooler. I can't get over it."

"The mountain range in the west hides the sun much earlier than you're used to in Atlanta," Ben explained. "Plus, we're a lot further north."

"I wish I could sleep outside in the tent with you guys. It will be good sleeping weather," Teagan commented.

"Maybe you can when Daddy gets here, Mommy," Remi said wisely, walking over and sitting down on the log next to her mother. She was munching on her hotdog but leaned her head on Teagan's shoulder. It had been a long day traveling and they were clearly tired. They needed an early night so that they'd be refreshed tomorrow.

"Sure, you can," I offered. "One for you and Jensen, too, sis. We can pitch a couple more tomorrow."

"Marin, can you sleep outside with us tonight, too?" Remi asked.

My heart warmed at Remi's request and the delight that erupted on Marin's face. "I'd love too!"

"Goodie! Thank you!"

"Let's make s'mores and then turn in. It's been a big day. We can save the campfire songs for tomorrow night when your dad's show up. Deal?"

"Can we tell ghost stories in the tent, then?" Dylan asked.

"No!" Remi shook her head. "Cowboy stories! Ghost stories are scary."

"Duh. That's why they are called ghost stories! Girls are sissies," Dylan moaned.

"Well, I told ya, boys are dumb!" Remi retorted cheekily.

I almost laughed out loud, but managed to hold it in.

"Do ya think Uncle Ben is dumb?" Dylan goaded. "He's a boy!"

"No, he's not. He's a grown up man," she said matter-of-factly.

"Kids," Missy admonished. "That's enough."

"How about we roast some marshmallows before any stories, okay?" Marin suggested with a smile, and a knack for diverting their attention. "We don't want to miss dessert! I bought those fudgy covered graham crackers so we can just smash the marshmallows in between."

"Yeah!"

"Okay!"

The children answered in unison and Dylan, who was always keen on sweets was quick to get one roasting over the fire while Remi finished her hotdog but left a couple of bites on her plate. "Marin, can Gem have this please?"

Marin smiled. "Sure! She's been waiting so nicely just make sure to give her small bites and tell her to be gentle." Remi nodded and proceeded to offer the yummy remnants of her meal to the puppy who took it from her hand gently, but delightedly devoured it.

The stalls were left open and there were a few horses roaming in the pasture nearby, casually grazing. I decided that once we were finished eating, I'd get them settled inside their stalls but leave the top halves of the doors open so they wouldn't be over heated. Siri and Dark were already settled in for the night.

Dylan grabbed two marshmallows and shoved them onto his stick. "I'll make one for Macey, too!"

"Sounds good, buddy. Make sure you get them firmly on there and be careful, so they don't touch the flames, or they light up like a match."

"I will, Uncle Ben." Dylan sat down beside me and leaned forward so his marshmallows were hovering over the fire. I'd made the sticks long enough that their little hands would be far away to protect them, but I was still watching closely.

I helped Remi get her stick loaded and then watched as she took a seat next to Marin as she carefully held her marshmallow over the fire.

"Like this, Uncle Ben?" she asked, bright eyed. I nodded.

"Can we have s'mores every night, Marin? Can I call you Aunt Marin? Mace calls my mom aunt, even though she's not really his aunt," Dylan said.

"It's Auntie Marin, Dylan. And I call Uncle Ben, Uncle Ben even though he's just Dylan's uncle. I love him like my uncle, so he says it's okay," Remi corrected.

She rambled on and my lips pressed together as a closed-mouthed smile split my face. I met Marin's eyes as she put an arm around Remi and squeezed her shoulders, pulling her closer. She bit her lip, then beamed.

"That's perfect, actually. I'm an only child so I won't get to have any nieces or nephews of my own, so I'd love to think of you three as such. I'd love it if you'd call me Auntie Marin."

Boom! And just like that, Marin was one of the family. A short laugh broke from my chest.

Dylan got up and walked over to Marin. "'Cept, I'll call you *Aunt* Marin, since I'm a guy, and all. Kay?"

She laughed at the seriousness of my eight-year-old nephew. "Of course, I understand completely."

"Sorry, Marin," Missy said. "They get a little carried away."

"Not at all. I think they are incredible," Marin replied.

Teagan yawned. "Awwwww! If you don't mind, I'll head to bed as soon as Mace has his dessert. This little guy needs to sleep almost as much as his mama."

"Would you like a s'more, Teagan? I can make it," Marin offered. "I can do two like Dylan."

Teagan nodded. "Sure, thank you."

"I want s'more!" Mace demanded.

"You're getting one, Mace," Remi said. "Jeeze."

The rest of the evening wound down and Marin took Missy, Teagan and little Mace into the house to get settled, though Mace was upset he couldn't stay in the tent with us and cried all the way in as Teagan assured him that he could the following night when his daddy was at the ranch.

"What do we sleep in, Uncle Ben?" Dylan asked.

"Well, if we were out in the wilderness, we'd probably stay dressed, but you can put on your pajamas or sweatpants. Did you bring some?"

"I only have Jeans and leggings, but Mommy made me bring old ones."

"Leggings work, kiddo. Hurry in and change while I fill the canteen and lay out the sleeping bags. Brush your teeth."

"We will, Uncle Ben! Thank you for inviting us!" Remi came up and threw her arms around my waist and hugged me hard.

My hand settled on her little back and I patted her gently. "You're welcome, sweetheart." Remi had been through so much and even though I didn't know her when she had cancer, my heart still seized up knowing such a little child had to go through something so awful. Looking at her now, you'd never know she went through two rounds of chemotherapy and a bone marrow transplant. She was a vibrant and healthy child.

"I wish we lived closer," Dylan said sadly. "You're so lucky to live here."

"Every place has its good qualities. You can go swimming in the ocean where you live."

"So? The ocean all looks the same. I love the mountains. They're all different."

"Well, what about all of those soccer friends and the fun you have with Chase and your dad? Jensen and your mom wouldn't be able to get you all that cool sports gear I'm always hearing about if they didn't work at ESPN."

Dylan shrugged. "I guess."

"You guess? I'd love all that stuff!" I could see my nephew was still not convinced. "Listen, we have all week to play cowboy, and when we get in the tent, we can make plans for the week. Okay?"

"Yay! Come on, Gemmy," Remi called happily to the puppy and they both hurried toward the house.

Dylan stayed behind as I gathered the canteens and made my way toward the water spigot. He watched me fill the first one, then unscrewed the plastic lid off of the second one and held it under the water stream when I was finished. He struggled holding it steady with his smaller hands and the lid, attached by a short chain got caught up in it, and the water splashed everywhere.

I shut the water off when it was finally filled. "It's so cool on your ranch! You have your own campground water spigot, and everything!"

"It's Marin's ranch, sport." I reached out and ruffled his head. "Maybe next summer you can come spend more time with me and we can ask some of your friends from Billings to join for a week or so. Would you like that?"

"Oh, boy! Would I! Thanks, Uncle Ben!" His face lit up in a huge smile.

"Well, let's not get our cart before the horse. We have to clear it with your folks, first."

"They'll say yes! I know it!"

I couldn't help but chuckle as Dylan followed me back to the fire and I dumped the contents of the canteen in my hands over the now smoldering coals; the remnants of the campfire. "Go ahead and pour yours on there, too, but do it slowly so sparks don't start flying around. Then we need to poke around the embers with a stick and make sure all of the orange glow is out."

He did exactly as he'd seen me do and after another trip to fill the canteens again, the embers were out. We refilled them and stashed them in one corner of the tent. "I'll unroll the sleeping bags and you go get ready then come back out here with Remi, Gem and Marin. I'm gonna get the horses bedded down."

"Can't I help?" Dylan asked. "I'm good at getting my PJs on super-fast."

"It's getting dark, and you might get hurt out here. I just have to call them. These horses are more like dogs. I just offer them a snack and bang, they're in their stalls. You can help me tomorrow, buddy. Everyone is tired tonight."

"Awwww…" he complained.

I chuckled and ruffled his soft hair. "There is plenty of work to be done tomorrow. Get going. Hurry up."

After Dylan reluctantly did as I asked and he was on his way to the house, I grabbed a handful of alfalfa and started calling the horses, waving it in front of me. "Hup! Come on! Hup! Come on, horses! Let's go to bed! Hup!"

It wasn't long and they were trotting toward me and one by one, I got them in their stalls. It was a lot more work than I let on to my nephew, especially with my side still tight from the injury. The wound was healing nicely but most of the flexibility had disappeared from the skin around the fresh scar. When I shut the door to the last stall, Dylan, Marin and Remi were waiting for me outside of the tent. They were all fresh faced from baths in PJs and flip flops. Remi was holding Gem in her arms.

"Your turn to wash up. Your sister, Teagan and Mace are settled. I'll stay with the kids." Marin said.

"Are you sure?"

"Pfft. Of course. You need to change your dressing. Can you do it or do you need my help?"

My lips pressed together in a grin. I was scheduled for a follow-up appointment with my doctor on Wednesday to get the stitches out. "I can do it. I wish I could leave it off."

"You're not supposed to get the stitches wet, Ben," Marin admonished.

"Ah. Okay. I can manage." It was the first time since I'd been wounded that she wasn't going to help me. "The sleeping bags are laid out."

"Great!" She rewarded me with a smile. There was something in her eyes meant only for me.

I reached out and grabbed her hand as I passed her. She was herding the kids into the tent and I was leaving to go into the house and our fingers entwined fleetingly, but it was enough to send electricity through my body. I'd been wanting to touch her all night, but we'd been preoccupied with keeping the little ones entertained. Maybe I'd be able to sneak a kiss or two once they were sleeping. I glanced over my shoulder to find Marin watching me go. I couldn't help but smile at the rush it gave me. Her eyes on me, her hand in mine, the prospect of us... it was enough. It was everything.

Marin

I had Dylan all snuggled into his own sleeping bag, but Remi was reluctant to go to sleep and lingered, sitting on top of my bag with me.

"Honey, do you want to sleep in the house with your mom?" I asked. Maybe she was reluctant to be away. Earlier in the day and at the bonfire I'd witnessed how close she and Teagan seemed. I reached out and took a strand of her hair in my hand and tucked it behind her ear.

She shook her head. "No, but can I sleep in your sleeping bag with you?" she asked timidly. "Dylan said there are bears and stuff outside."

"There can be, but Uncle Ben will be with us, and they usually don't come up to the house. They're more in the mountains and in Yellowstone. They know to stay away from people. We don't bother them, so they don't bother us." *Mostly*, I thought.

"Have you seen any?" Remi asked.

"Sure, but not this close to the house." I unzipped the plush blue bag that my uncle had given me when I was eleven. It was faded blue color, but still warm. I hadn't wanted a new one, even when he offered. Dylan was using Uncle Leonard's and Ben

315

had a couple of his own but borrowed three more from his friends for the other adults to use tomorrow night.

Ben had laid the plush comforters I'd supplied from the house on the tent floor and underneath the sleeping bags, so we'd be quite comfortable.

I crawled inside and held it open for Remi to join me. "Grab your pillow and come on over here. I'm excited to sleep out here, aren't you? It's cozy."

"Yes," she said with a grin. The little girl did as she was told and was soon ensconced in the bag next to me, with my arms wrapped around her.

"Remi, I thought you wanted to sleep with the dog," Dylan chastised blandly, yawning and half asleep.

"I do, but I wanna talk to Auntie Marin, too. Gem can sleep on my pillow. Come here, Gemmy," she called to the pup and patted the pillow next to her head, but the dog laid down in on the edge of the sleeping bag. "I can pet her, like this." Her little hand reached out to smooth over Gemmy's glossy coat again and again. "See?"

"Your mouth works in your own sleeping bag," he said wryly. "Gosh, girls are lame sometimes." Dylan rolled onto his side but was facing Remi and me. His bag was closest to the wall of the tent and Ben's closest to the door.

"Well, boys are dumb," Remi shot back, and I decided to distract her before a squabble broke out.

"Whatever," Dylan shot back.

"You don't have to be afraid, Remi. Your Uncle Ben is quite protective of you. Mine was of me, too."

"You have an uncle?"

"Yup, but he died some months ago"

"That's sad," Remi said softly. "I'm sorry."

"It was very sad to lose him, but I'm still happy to have had him. I came to live with him on the ranch when I was a little older than you. He was my favorite person for a very long time."

"Uncle Ben's super cool," Dylan added. "I miss him a lot."

"I can see why. From what I've seen so far, he's an amazing uncle."

"You're Uncle Ben's damsel," Remi said out of the blue. "Right?"

My eyebrows shot up in surprise. "Um…" I began. "What?"

"Well, Mommy said he rescued you from a fire, didn't he?"

It wasn't exactly that way, but close enough. "He did, yes."

"So, then, you're his damsel. Did he do some other stuff to protect you, too?"

"Uhh, yes," I said slowly. He came to get me in Minneapolis, he stood up for me in the bar and he took the goons on in the yard. It hit me how many times. "Come to think of it, he has."

"So, see? You're his damsel, then." Remi was resolute in her logic. "If he does stuff over and over, then for sure, you're his damsel."

"Hmmmm…" I stalled, not sure what else to say.

Remi pulled the sleeping bag up to her chin with one hand, but her other arm was out and resting on the puppy snuggled next to her.

I reached across to pet my puppy, but her eyes were already closed, and she responded by doing that smacking thing dogs do before they go to sleep when they feel safe that always warmed my heart. Dogs and kids were so precious.

I was saved from further conversation about the damsel thing because the zipper on the outside flap of the tent unzipped and Gem's head popped up and she barked. "Hey, everyone comfy in here?" he asked as he unzipped the screen layer then bent to zip them both up again, after he came inside.

"Sure are, Uncle Ben," Dylan answered.

Ben surveyed the inside of the tent with a small flashlight, locating his sleeping bag and one of the pillows I'd brought out from the house. "I guess this is my spot?" he asked and then settled in.

"The biggest and strongest has to sleep by the door and save us from bears," Remi answered. "That's you, Uncle Ben."

I chuckled and Ben huffed out a laugh as he unzipped his bag and slid inside, arranging his pillow before he laid down and zipped up the bag from the inside. "Is that so? I guess that makes sense."

"Yup!" Remi was very enthusiastic.

"You *are* the biggest and strongest," I added cheekily.

"I am, huh?" Ben asked, amused.

"Oh, definitely," I teased. We both laughed under our breath. It was almost completely dark so I couldn't see his eyes, but I felt them on me, as he situated himself in his own sleeping bag on the other side of mine and zipped it up. Ben rolled onto his side and propped up his head with one arm.

"Okay, so what do you kids wanna do tomorrow? We can do anything you want."

"Ride the ponies!" Remi answered.

"Go fishing!" Dylan said.

"Fishing?" Remi said with disdain. "Yuk. Fishing is boring and stinky."

"Maybe we can do other things near the stream while the boys fish," I suggested. "We can go on a nature walk and treasure hunt or make something yummy to eat on the campfire. We can ride horses tomorrow and do another bonfire tomorrow night because both of your dads missed out tonight. Then plan a trip into the mountains on Sunday for fishing."

"That's sounds like a good plan, then we can take a drive into Yellowstone on Monday. I sure hope Jensen rents a big SUV."

My heart fell a little bit. I suddenly wished I didn't have to start my new job, but it was way too close to the start date to change my mind. I'd be leaving the diner owner in a lurch and I couldn't do that.

"I can text my dad and tell him!" Dylan said, then reached for the phone tucked under his pillow."

"Hey, no phones on a camp out! We're roughin' it! That's what Jensey said, remember Dylan?"

She was so adorable that I couldn't help squeezing her and kissing the top of her head. "This is semi-roughin' it. If we really went all in, you'd have to pee over a log."

A laugh burst from Ben's chest. "That would be just awful," he said wryly. My mind conjured him rolling his eyes.

"Not us guys, cuz we get to stand up." Pride rang through Dylan's voice.

"Not to poop!" Remi burst his bubble. "Didn't think about that, did ya?"

"Well, you have to do it for both, Remi! So there!"

I couldn't help but giggle out loud as an uproarious laugh from Ben split the night air, and the kids joined in.

"Seriously, logs aren't that bad. A little rough on the butt cheeks, maybe." I'd been on many camping trips with Uncle Leonard, and I was an expert at using nature for a bathroom. "I'll help you, Remi."

"What do you do with your poop, after?" Dylan had the innocent curiosity of a child of his age.

"You bury it," I explained. "We always take a shovel for that."

"Wow." Ben continued laughing, harder now and more like a chortle. "As much as I'm loving this conversation, I think we should get some sleep. We've got a big day ahead of us. Is everyone warm enough?"

"Yes, thank you, Uncle Ben." Remi sighed sleepily. "I'm tired."

"Heck, it's not even cold," Dylan exclaimed.

"It will get colder before morning, so hunker down, now."

Remi was pinned between my body inside the sleeping bag, and Gem's next to her and so we were toasty warm. I was anxious for the kids to fall asleep so that I could sneak a moment with Ben.

"But we didn't tell ghost stories yet," Dylan complained.

"Yeah, buddy, but you and Remi are tired, and we have lots to do tomorrow. Ghost stories tomorrow night around the campfire. Deal?" Ben asked.

"Oh, okay." His disappointment was clear, though he yawned again.

"You're here all week, kiddo. We've got lots of time. Besides, Marin is going to teach us all how to ride horses tomorrow."

"Can we go say goodnight to Dark?" Remi asked.

I hugged her close to me. "He's already sleeping, honey." I didn't think Ben, who was just getting settled and who had already said he'd bedded the horses down, would want to revisit the stable. "We can go see him first thing in the morning and you can help us feed the horses and watch Dark nurse. He's still just a newborn and needs lots of sleep." I kissed the side of her head. Her soft hair smelled like flowers.

"Okay, Auntie Marin."

Ben was closer now so I could see his face in planes of varying shadow. He caught my eye and winked. "Good idea, Auntie Marin," he said, reaching over and squeezed my shoulder. "You're kind of good at this."

My heart sped up at his touch. I wanted to feel his arms around me, his mouth on mine, if only for a goodnight kiss. I was lying on my side facing him, but my arms were around Remi who was lying beside me in my bag, so she and Gemmy were between us.

She solved my problem. "Aren't ya gonna kiss her goodnight, Uncle Ben?"

He chuckled and my face split into an embarrassed smile.

"Um..." he hesitated.

"She's your damsel, isn't she?" she asked innocently.

"Uhhh," Ben was as still as stone.

"Ugh!" Dylan lamented. "All dudes don't kiss girls. You keep saying you're my damsel and you don't see me slobbering all over you, do ya?"

Remi wasn't put out. "That's cuz you're just a kid, but someday you will."

"Gross! Will not!"

"You'll see," Remi insisted.

"Ugh!" Dylan said again and buried his head under his pillow.

Ben laughed out loud. "Not all guys slobber, Dylan."

A groan emitted from underneath Dylan's pillow. I laughed softly. This was too much fun.

"We aren't gonna sleep until you kiss her." Remi stood her ground.

"Oh, okay. If I must," Ben finally acquiesced. He leaned forward and placed a very soft, kiss on my mouth. It was still delicious the way his lips and the tip of his tongue teased mine in the brief contact. Ben cupped Remi's cheek and kissed the top of her head. "Satisfied?" he asked.

"Yes," Remi nodded. Her silky head moved beneath my chin as I held her close.

"Makes one of us," Ben muttered. "Goodnight."

I laughed softly. "Goodnight."

After everyone settled down, the zipper to my sleeping bag inched down and Ben's big hand wrapped around mine as the soft sounds of the night surrounded us.

BEN

I awoke to the sound of Marin crying.

I lifted my head. The soft light of dawn was peeking through the material of the tent to softly illuminate the inside. She was sitting up holding her face; Remi and Dylan were still fast asleep.

"Marin? What's the matter?" I kept my voice soft.

She shook her head and started to slide out of the sleeping bag, careful not to disturb the sleeping little girl. "Nothing," she whispered. "I just have to get up and get breakfast going."

I sat up, pushed out of my sleeping bag while Marin shoved her feet into her old Vans. Then she was unzipping the double layer of doors to the tent and rushing through. Gemmy got up and scampered after her owner. In a split second I was on my feet and following regardless of my lack of shoes.

The gravel, rocks and dried grass poked into my feet painfully. "Marin, wait!" I hissed the words in an urgent whisper. I didn't want to wake the kids before I got to the bottom of this. She must have had another bad dream. "Tell me what's going on!"

I caught up to her as she hit the lawn of the house and reached out to grab her arm. "Wait." When I turned her around, I could see the tears were still rolling down her face. "What happened, did you have a bad dream? I told you. I won't let Apollo—"

"That's not it," she interrupted. Marin hastily brushed the tears from her face with both hands, backing away from me. "This isn't going to work, Ben."

That was the last thing I expected her to say. "What?" was all I could get out. I was stunned.

"It's just too soon. You deserve someone who isn't screwed up like this."

I took two steps forward as a need to hold her engulfed me, but she backed up, just out of my grasp. "Well, I want you," I said. My heart was starting to ache inside my chest. "I'm willing to wait—"

"I don't want you to wait! It's just... nothing good will come from it." She was nervous, running her hands through her hair, pacing back in forth in front of me like she was possessed.

I felt the air leave my body; I felt like I'd been punched in the stomach. "I don't get this, Marin. You're doing this now when my family is here?" I was gutted.

"Carter died, Ben!"

"This again?" I sighed heavily as I stood there in front of this crazy person that used to be Marin. I reached for her again and she retreated. I ran a hand through my hair and then put my hand on my hip. This was too much. I wasn't sure if I was trying to reason with her or I was fighting for my life.

Her hands disappeared into her hair and she bent over in silent sobs. "I can't. Carter—"

I moved quickly. Too quickly for her to move away and scooped her up into my arms, pressing her head into my chest, my arms holding her so close, her sobs rocked through my own flesh. All I wanted to do was ease her pain. "You'll be alright, Marin. You have to let go of the past. I can't compete with a ghost, but I'm here and I want to take care of you. How can you still be in love with someone who beat you?" My voice was urgent and angry, though I kept the volume low so Remi and Dylan wouldn't hear.

"You don't understand," she cried into my chest, her tears wetting the front of my T-shirt.

Part of me was jealous of a dead man. How could she still love that bastard who abused her?

"You don't understand," she said again, but her arms suddenly wrapped around my waist to return my embrace.

My arms were still around her, but one hand came up to cup her face. "Look at me," I commanded. She did as I asked, and I used my thumb to wipe at the tears on one of her cheeks. "Make me understand, then. Are you still in love with Carter?"

The sunlight, just rising in the east, cast golden light across one side of her face and her light grey eyes sparkled with the remnant of tears. Marin shook her head. "No. I'm not in love with him. I feel guilty that he died." The words wrenched from her almost as if she didn't want to tell me. "I shouldn't have gone to the shop that night."

"Oh, Marin. You have to let that go. It wasn't your fault." I shook my head, a tenderness I'd never felt toward another woman sweeping through me.

"I'm trying."

I sucked in a relieved breath. "You have to, sweetheart." I bent to kiss her mouth, but she turned her head.

"What if I'm cursed?" she asked brokenly.

I sighed heavily. "I know you've lost a lot of people you cared about, but we can go slowly Marin. Please don't push me away. Who knows about tomorrow, but we have today. Please don't waste this time."

"I just love you so much. I don't think I could bare it if I lost you, too."

I almost didn't hear the last part of her words because my heart was flying. It was amazing how quickly emotions could

KAHLEN AYMES

turn on a dime. "Then don't lose me. Pushing me away is losing me, too, right?"

"I'd rather be without you than for you to die." It seemed like the admission was ripped from her.

I bent down, tightened my arms around her torso and lifted her off the ground until our faces were on the same level and her legs were dangling. "Well, I'd rather die than be without you," I said, with a smirk beginning to walk with her toward the house. "We are at an impasse, honey."

"I'm serious, Ben," Marin insisted.

"So am I. Stop being silly. You don't think I'd let a little thing like dying keep us apart, do ya?"

I walked up the wooden steps of the porch. "Ben—" she began.

"Keep practicing that name, babe. When my family leaves, I'm gonna love the shit out of you. Night after night I'll show you how alive I am."

I still held her close and realized the thoughts my words brought to mind. Just the thought of making love to her made my dick flood with blood. I set her down until her feet touched the floor of the porch and slid my hands down until they grasped her hips. I pulled her hard against me. "Feel that? That's all for you."

I bent my head to kiss her, my mouth taking hers in a hungry kiss. Her hands slid up my arms and wound around my shoulders. I had to lift her again so that I could kiss her as deeply as I wanted to.

"Good morning, you two," my sister called through the screen door.

Instantly, Marin pulled her mouth away in a startled flash, but I still held her close to me. I didn't care if Missy saw us kissing. I had to convince the woman in my arms that I wasn't going anywhere.

"Shit," I muttered, but smiled as I looked down at Marin. My erection would be tenting my flannel pajama pants the minute I pulled away. "Morning, Missy." Marin's forehead dropped to my shoulder as a small laugh burst forth.

"Um, I have a problem. This is not something my sister needs to see," I whispered in her ear.

Marin's head snapped up and she smiled as our eyes locked. "Okay. Go back to check on the kids and I'll get breakfast going."

"French toast?" I asked, hinting.

"Sure."

"Bacon and eggs?"

"Okay," she nodded.

"Hashbrowns?"

Marin's eyebrow shot up. "Pretty hungry, huh?"

"Starving." I backed up toward the steps and placed another hard kiss on Marin's mouth, then set her on her feet. "Love you," I whispered against her mouth. She hesitated. "Say it," I squeezed her to me. "You know you do."

"I love you, too."

I grinned, released her and hopped down the two steps in one stride. I pulled my T-shirt down and held it over the bulge in my pants.

Happily, I turned and jogged away from the house. I decided to check on Dark until my body was under control. "Come on, Gem!" I called to the puppy. "Come with daddy!"

Marin's tinkling laugh followed me. "It's gonna be a beautiful day!" I said to myself.

Chapter 21

Marin

How could my heart be soaring and heavy at the same time?

I loved Ben so much. I wanted to be with him so badly, but I was still scared there was something hanging over me that caused me to lose people I loved. I tried to push the apprehension down as I started breakfast. I smiled to myself remembering his cheeky grin as he hurried off to get Remi and Dylan up for chores. I told myself to trust him and steeled myself to trust the future. One day at a time, and today would be a wonder.

"Need any help?" Missy asked as I started the coffee.

"I'm good with this," I said, setting two frying pans on the stove and turning on the heat before I went to the refrigerator and pulled out the eggs and milk.

"You seem happy, this morning," Missy observed. "Ben has that effect on people. We really miss him."

I cracked some eggs into a bowl and used a whisk to break up the yolks and mix it with some milk. "He's great with the kids."

"Dylan adores him. Are you sure I can't do something? I'm not used to sitting around. Can I set the table?" Missy asked.

"Sure." I pointed to one of the cupboards as I added a splash of vanilla and a tablespoon of sugar to mixture for the French toast. "The plates are up there, and the silverware is in this drawer over here."

It wasn't long and Missy had the table set and was pouring us both a cup of steaming hot coffee. "Do you take anything in yours?"

"Never have. My uncle always said good, strong black coffee puts hair on your chest." I laughed.

"Ben mentioned you lost him a few months ago. I'm very sorry, Marin."

I laid several strips of bacon in one of the pans and it started to sizzle and fill the air with that wonderful smoky aroma. "I miss him, but it's getting easier."

"I'd say I'm sorry about your boyfriend, but if your situation was anything like mine, it was a blessing in disguise."

I paused for a beat, considering her words. "You know? I've never thought about it like that. What happened to you? I mean, if it's not prying. Ben told me your ex-husband was abusive."

"Yes. He would beat me whenever I had a thought of my own. If I defied him in any way or spent one dollar too much at the grocery store. When he started to direct his anger at Dylan as he got a little older, I took him and ran. It wasn't easy. It took a lot of planning. Derrick was charming to the outside world, but to me, he was the devil. It was like a prison."

"I'm glad you were able to get away." A shiver ran through me and I felt an even stronger kinship with her. "With Carter, it was whenever he got drunk that he turned violent."

"Maybe his death was your uncle's way of looking out for you from above."

I shook my head. "My uncle would never wish death on anyone, though he never liked Carter."

Missy set her cup on the table and came to stand beside me at the stove, picked up the fork I had laying on the counter and began to help turning the bacon as I worked on the thick slices of French toast. "Men can be awful, but most aren't. I'm so glad I was brave enough to try again with Jensen. My life has turned around a hundred and eighty degrees. We're so happy now." There was a glow to Ben's sister's face as she spoke about her husband.

I nodded as I flipped over a piece of egg coated bread. "Ben told me. That's wonderful."

"It wasn't easy, and I'm sure it isn't for you, but you can trust Ben, I promise. He's a keeper."

I felt a warm flush of pleasure run through me. "I'm seeing that. He's so protective. I've never had that before. Of course," I shrugged, "Carter was my only serious relationship, really."

Her shoulder touched mine in a gentle nudge as we stood there. "I know it's hard. Just give it a chance. Besides, if he hurts you, I'll just have to kick his ass," she said, with a small laugh.

We soon had a plate piled with fried bacon and another of French toast warming in the oven while Missy poured orange juice and I started the scrambled eggs.

"Do you have one of those triangles to ring for meals?" Missy asked. We both laughed out loud.

"No, but you know, that's a good idea," I replied.

"If you do start a dude ranch, you might need one. How big is your ranch?"

I'd have to consider it seriously. "Well, the ranch is only about five-hundred acres."

Missy's eyes widened. "Only about five-hundred acres? That's huge!"

"Some of those are hills, but there is a stream running through it, and a lot of trails." The more I thought about it, the more the vision of the property as a dude ranch materialized. Maybe cabins could be built instead of rebuilding the shop.

"Well, I think it's a great idea!" Teagan said as she came down the stairs with Mace in her arms. "Something smells amazing! You ladies have been busy!"

"We aim to please around here," I said. "Good morning, young man," I addressed the adorable little boy squirming in his mother's arms. "What do you like for breakfast?"

"Beckfust!" he piped up. "Beckfust!"

I couldn't help but giggle, just as the door burst open and Remi and Dylan rushed into the kitchen, followed closely behind by Ben.

"Mom! Dark is so cute! He came right up to me and I kissed his nose!" Remi's excitement was contagious as she went and stood by Teagan who put one arm around her little girl.

"Really? That's amazing! I can't wait to meet him!"

"Yeah, she canned on feeding the rest of them. Uncle Ben and I did it, though Aunt Marin. We gave them oats and alfalfa!"

"I see that!" I beamed at the little boy as I walked up to him and picked several pieces of the green stuff from his hair. "It looks like you rolled in it!"

"Nah," Ben said, shaking his head. "Come on kids. We have to wash up before breakfast. I'm starving!"

"Oh, boy! Me, too!" Dylan exclaimed.

"Yeah!" Remi said following Dylan. Ben waited for her to precede him back into the mud room to the sink in there.

"Maybe they should take a bath," Missy suggested.

"Why? They'll just get dirty again. There won't be any keeping them inside today," Teagan offered. "But they smell like they have horse manure on their pajamas."

"My uncle said it's the scent of money! I can throw them in the wash after breakfast." I chuckled as I removed the food from the oven and started to fill the plates that Missy had stacked on the counter near the cook top. She had purposely added a small bread plate on top and I knew that was for Mace.

"Beckfust!" Mace demanded again.

"It's coming, sweets," Teagan reassured her youngest.

The aura of family and joy that filled the house was so incredible. I knew Uncle Leonard would approve. My eyes met Ben's as he towered over the two little ones scampering in to take their place at the table. The corner of his mouth lifted in an adorable grin and he winked.

Just having him look at me like that set my heart and blood racing. He was so beautiful and experiencing the kids and seeing what could be for us, I wanted it. I couldn't wait to talk to him about the dude ranch idea to see what he thought about it. Maybe he could be my business partner and then he could stop putting his life in danger fighting fires.

Once the children had their plates and Dylan was pouring an obscene amount of warm maple syrup on his and Remi's French toast, Ben finally took his seat. "Do you think you made enough food?" he teased, pulling out the chair next to him and patting the seat suggestively. I nodded, silently communicating I'd sit next to him.

"Well, I got my marching orders in the yard."

"I'll eat it!" Dylan exclaimed. "I'm starving!"

Teagan was already helping Mace with his breakfast and he was chewing happily.

"Yes, thank you for making it, Auntie Marin," Remi said politely. "It looks so yummy! French toast is our favorite, right Dylan?"

"Hey! I helped!" Missy put in playfully.

"Thank you, Auntie Missy," Remi added.

Ben squeezed my hand underneath the table as the children regaled us of their adventure feeding the horses and playing with Dark. I was so excited for the day ahead I could hardly eat.

"Hey, eat up! Big day ahead," Ben reminded.

"Is French toast your favorite or just the kids?" I asked softly, already knowing the answer.

"Can't it be both?" He winked again.

BEN

The morning was amazing.

If it were possible, I only fell in love with Marin more and more. Her fear about losing me was unfounded but endearing and seeing her interact with my niece and nephews and my family, my heart swelled to bursting. Like Dylan, I found myself wishing that we all lived closer to each other.

Most of the horses were let out to graze in the pasture, but Marin and I saddled up three of them and they were tied to the fence waiting for us.

Marin was sitting inside the pasture with Dylan and Remi on either side as she called out to Siri and Dark. When they approached, Siri nudged Marin's shoulder and in an amazing show of trust, Dark, walked up close and threw his body into her lap. He was a newborn, but he was still huge, but laid down full body. She was giggling, but Dark knocked her over. Her arms wrapped around him as I moved forward. "Do you need help?"

She shook her head, and struggled to sit up, without trying to push the colt off of her. "I think this is incredible! I adore him!" Her arms tightened around his neck and she kissed his head. "He's perfect!"

332

Siri snorted at her baby yet seemed unperturbed.

"Look, Mommy!" Remi exclaimed. "Dark is like a dog! Can we get one?"

Teagan laughed. "I don't think your dad will be up for a dog that grows to two thousand pounds, Remi, but he is amazing."

"Awwww!" she lamented sadly.

"Come sit by me, Remi," Marin instructed, showing her to sit on my right on the side where Dark's head was and soon, she was close and it was as if she was also holding Dark in her lap, too. "How about I share Dark with you and Dylan? You can come visit anytime you want!" She put a hand up to stroke her dark hair. The silken strands slid through her fingers and Marin's arm went around her. Remi rested her head on Marin's shoulder.

"Really?" Dylan exclaimed. "That is awesome! Mom, can we move here?"

Missy was taken aback. "What? Uh, no honey, but we'll visit more often."

"Uncle Ben invited me back next summer and said I can invite some of the guys from Billings!"

"We'll talk about it with your dad."

"Can I come, too?" Remi asked, almost sadly.

"You don't think I'd have Dylan without you, did ya?" I bent and ruffled her little head. "You two are a pair!" Her frown quickly turned into a bright, but toothless smile.

Teagan and Missy were standing off to one side watching, Mace struggling to get down from his mother's arms, but she held tight so he wouldn't run behind the horses.

"Are you sure you're alright, sweetheart?" I asked Marin. "Isn't he crushing you?"

The little horse looked happy as hell, getting pets, pats and kisses from all sides. His tail was swishing happily.

Marin's mouth pressed together, and she shook her head. "He's only a couple of hundred pounds. I can handle it. I'm loving this. In a week he'll probably be too big, but I just love him so much. Isn't he the sweetest?"

"The best," Dylan agreed.

"I love him, too, Auntie Marin," Remi added.

"I know you do, honey."

Marin was radiant and completely in her element. I went to Teagan and reached for Mace. "Come on, Buddy. Let's get you closer." I walked the few steps back to the little group then went down on my haunches holding the two-year-old who reached out to touch Dark's main. "Be gentle. Don't pull his hair, just pet up and down, like this." I moved his little hand to show the proper way so neither would be hurt. The little boy laughed in delight.

I glanced in Teagan and Missy's direction. Their heads were huddled together, and they were giggling, and looking back at the picture we made. I knew what they were talking about and I couldn't have agreed more.

After a few minutes, Dark was ready to join his mother when Siri moved further away, and we decided to go on a trail ride. It wasn't easy when Teagan wanted to take little Mace in the house. He started crying. "Horsey! I want horsey!" he wailed.

"Mace," Teagan kissed his head and tried hard to hold on to him, but he was squirming hard. "We'll go read a book, baby,"

"Horsey! Horsey!" he cried harder.

"Listen, let's go on a short ride around the yard," Marin suggested, looking at me and sticking her lip out in an exaggerated pout. "Ben, you mount up and take Mace for a little bit, and we'll come back for the other two. That's cool with you guys, right?" she asked the kids. "We don't want Mace to cry."

"I think you should take him. You're more familiar with riding."

She huffed out a laugh. "These horses are gentle. Come on. Mount up on the big Buckskin, and I'll hand him to you." She took a few steps and held her arms open for Mace who went willingly into her embrace. "It's not fair if you don't get to ride a horsey, is it? Uncle Ben will take you, sweet pea."

Her eyebrow arched wryly when she turned around with the child in her arms and I was still hesitating.

I offered a half shrug knowing I wasn't going to win the argument and I gathered up the reins and placed my left foot into the left stirrup of the golden horse with the black mane. I chuckled as I swung my right leg over the saddle of the large gelding.

The horse was so tall I had to bend down to reach for Mace when Marin lifted him up toward me.

"Ben, be careful! He gets wiggly," Teagan warned.

"Don't worry, Teags. I'll keep him safe and sound. Mace, did you hear your mom? You have to sit still, okay?" I bent down to talk just above his little ear. His sandy hair was close to the same color as mine, though we were no relation, but I loved Remi and Mace as much as I did Dylan. I wrapped my left arm firmly, but gently, around his little waist as I settled him in the saddle.

Soon, Marin was clicking her tongue on the top of her mouth and patting the horse on the rump. "Giddy-up, Samson!"

The horse started a slow walk around the paddock. Mace giggled as we made our way around it three times. As we passed the women waved and shouted encouragements.

"Yay, Macey!" Remi said. She and Dylan were sitting on top of the metal gate, Missy and Teagan both had their arms steadying them on both sides.

"Mom, I'm cool! I won't fall," Dylan admonished Missy.

When we pulled up to the gate for the last time and I handed Mace down, he started fussing. "Nope, come on Mace,"

Teagan scolded. "The big kids get their turn. Daddy's coming tonight, remember?" She took her cranky child toward the house but called over her shoulder. "Have fun but be careful! We're taking a nap so take your time and don't worry about us."

"You take Dylan and I'll take Remi. Missy can ride the grey," Marin instructed, handing me a filled canteen. "Wrap the strap around the saddle horn. Dylan, come here." Soon, she had him securely on the saddle in front of me.

Missy was a bit uneasy, but Marin showed her how to mount up, then lifted Remi to sit in the saddle of another Sorrel. Siri couldn't go on a ride outside of the pasture as long as Dark was so small, so she chose another. "Missy, meet Star. Remi, this is Champ. He's tall, but he's very gentle. Don't be scared. Hold on to the saddle horn until I get us outside of the gate."

"I don't want to fall. Maybe I should wait here." Missy was apprehensive.

"Trust me. Star is one of the gentlest horses we have."

Missy still seemed reluctant but mounted up.

Marin draped Champ's reins over the fence then opened the gate and waited for Missy and me to ride through. My sister looked worried, but she repeated the sound Marin had made with her mouth and after a gentle nudge of her heel, the white horse she rode walked through and I followed. Siri was near and trotted closer.

Everyone was dressed in denim shorts and T-shirts, but Marin had a backpack strapped to her back and a rifle tucked into a holster in her saddle. It was just a precaution, and she knew how to wield a rifle, so I had no concerns.

I watched as Marin led Champ through the gate, then closed it behind us. She deftly mounted behind Remi, who didn't seem one bit scared.

"No, Siri. You can't come this time. Stay with your baby. I'm sorry, sweetie."

Siri and Dark lingered at the gate and Siri neighed her displeasure at being left behind as we walked the horses we were riding away. Marin and Remi took the lead as we left the yard.

"Let's go faster! Like real cowboys!" Dylan's voice was boisterous and maybe too loud.

"Hey, kiddo, don't spook the horses," I reminded.

"We'll see how we do with trotting after we get out of the yard. I always found trotting harder than an actual gallop. It feels like you can bounce right out of the saddle. Let's just walk for a while, okay?"

It was a wonderful afternoon. Marin led us through some wooded areas on some well-worn trails. We saw a lot of elk and deer as well as many species of birds, and then stopped for lunch near a section of a creek that was wider and faster moving. Marin produced a choice of roast beef or PB and J sandwiches, potato chips and a five-pound bag of apples from her backpack.

"Too bad we didn't bring our fishing poles!" Dylan observed.

"Ewww." Remi rolled her eyes.

"This is really nice, Marin," Missy commented. I really think you should consider what we talked about before breakfast."

My curiosity was piqued, but I decided to ask Marin about it later. I was pleased that my sister and my girl were getting along like gangbusters. My heart was full.

The sandwiches were delicious, and we passed around the canteen after we'd finished eating.

"Is this part of roughin' it?" Remi asked with the wonderful curiosity of her age.

"Yes. I think it's fabulous," I answered.

"Me, too!" Remi agreed.

"It's beautiful country." Missy was sitting on a large boulder near the edge of the water. "And the air smells so fresh."

"We oughta move here, Mom," Dylan reminded again.

"Dylan, you know we can't," Missy admonished, gently and her son's face fell.

"I wish you could, too, buddy," I said.

"Your family is great," Marin said softly, leaning her shoulder against mine. I thrilled in the familiarity of it. I glanced down at her beautiful face. It was serene and a far cry from the fear-filled terror that had shadowed it this morning. "I've already fallen in love with all three of the kids. I just love them to death."

"That was the plan," I grinned, putting the last bit of my second roast beef sandwich in my mouth.

"I should have known," she answered sardonically, with a huffed laugh.

"You sure brought a lotta apples, Aunt Marin," Dylan acknowledged.

"Well, the first rule of trail rides is to bring treats for the horses!"

Both of their little faces lit up and they scrambled to their feet.

"Yeah!"

"Yay!"

I moved to sit by my sister as we watched Marin open the bag of apples and show the children how to feed the horses with flat hands. "She's precious, Ben."

I nodded, not taking my eyes from Marin. "I know. I'm a goner."

"Well, I'm glad. You deserve it."

Missy squeezed my arm then slid her arm around my back. I hugged her back. "I'm happy you're here."

It wasn't long before every one of those apples was downed by the horses.

"Hey! You didn't save me any?" I teased the kids, holding my hands open in front of me. They both giggled.

"Uncle Ben!" Remi said.

"You didn't do the work, Uncle Ben." I could always count on my nephew to make a logical comment.

"Can't argue with that."

"Nope!"

We all burst into a chorus of happy laughter.

everything
HAPPENS FOR
a reason

Chapter 22

Marin

Our party had grown by two.

Chase Forrester, Teagan's husband, and Jensen Jeffers, Missy's husband, arrived right after dark to the delight of their wives and kids. They were just as beautiful as their wives and just as gracious. Remi and Dylan couldn't wait to drag them to the stables and pasture to introduce them to the horses while Teagan, Missy and I chopped a variety of vegetables in the kitchen.

Ben and the kids already had the bonfire going when the two others arrived, and I'd asked him to put some embers to one side so we could cook on them. It was pocket stew on the menu, tonight.

"The kids will love this," I explained as I piled the various veggies, raw hamburger and a big pat of butter into tin foil, salted and peppered everything and then closed the packets. "My uncle used to make this for me a lot as a child. I loved it!"

"It looks so easy." Teagan was sitting at the table watching me while Missy insisted on washing the few utensils we'd used.

"And so good." I smiled. "The kids were sure happy to see Chase and Jensen."

"I'm not sure who was more anxious to see whom. Those men adore those kids. Mace is always with Chase whenever he's around, and Jensen is great with both of my kids."

"We have a great little blended family," Missy commented from her place at the sink. "Dylan has a sort of hero worship of Chase. He loves sports. And Jensen is everything to Dylan."

"Yeah, Ben told me a little. It's wonderful the way things worked out. I'm not really sure how it all happened, but I'm not trying to pry."

"Pfft," Teagan dismissed. "It's not prying! You're probably going to be part of the family if the way Ben stares at you is any indication." She grinned, her smile going all the way into her blue eyes. "So, you should know."

I couldn't help but blush. I felt the heat flood my cheeks so much I wanted to cover them with my hands but resisted. "It's early, but we do care about each other very much."

Missy grunted in amusement. "Ben is head over heels. Seriously, the man is gone."

One of those smiles spread across my face. The kind that you can't help, the kind that literally hurts the muscles in your cheeks. I tried to hold it in, but simply couldn't. "I hope he is."

"He is, trust me!" Missy shut off the water and joined Teagan at the table while I found my largest platter in the cupboard. The men's portions were twice the size of the others.

All that was left to do for dinner was take the loaf of crusty bread from the drawer, slice it in half and lather it up with the garlic butter I'd made earlier. This would also be wrapped in foil and added to the embers for just a few short minutes before dinner.

"So, in a nutshell," Teagan began, "Chase and Jensen were best friends in college. I met them both at Clemson, and Chase and I began dating. He had an opportunity to play with Arsenal, in London before we graduated, but I found out I was pregnant just days before he got the offer. I knew he wouldn't take it, so I didn't tell him about the baby. Playing professional soccer was all he wanted."

"Oh, Teagan, I'm sorry." I could see that even though they were so happy now, there was a residual pain behind her eyes.

"It was years ago, but I still get so emotional over it." I could hear her voice tighten up and she dabbed at the corners of her eyes. "Anyway, I planned to follow Chase to London at the end of the semester, but when my father found out I was pregnant, he threatened to smear Chase's name and ruin his career before it even began. My dad was a state senator and knew everyone, so I believed him. I was dumb and terrified. My father basically disowned me. Jensen was my friend, too, and he went to my father and told him that the baby was his. He did it out of loyalty to me, and to Chase."

"Wow." I was mesmerized by her story. I felt so sorry for Chase in that moment and in awe of Jensen.

"Remi was born, and Jensen loved her like his own. We were basically just good friends, but we had Remi to worry about. Then when she was three, she got Leukemia and it was awful."

"Oh, my God! She looks so healthy."

"She is now, thanks to Chase. We were at the end of two rounds of chemo, but she wasn't getting better. He donated bone marrow and she recovered."

I couldn't help asking; "But wasn't Chase heartbroken?"

"We all were, I guess. It's the biggest regret of my life, but it all worked out in the end. Jensen and I got divorced and Chase and I got back together, but we're all still close."

"It was a miracle," Missy added. "In many ways."

"Well, there is much messier explanation I'll tell you about sometime, but that's the gist of it."

"That's an incredible story!" I was still a bit stunned. "So now, Chase and Jensen have reconciled."

"Yes. It wasn't easy, but they put Remi first. That's what parents do, I guess." Teagan was reflective. "Now we have Mace and another one on the way, and Remi spends time with Jensen and Missy, too. My life is so full, I don't know what to do with myself." Her eyes were full of tears and I couldn't help myself; I rose from my chair and went to give her a hug.

"Well, I think your family is special. We have something in common. I lost my parents young and even though it's not the same circumstances, I know what it's like to feel abandoned." Missy and I had abusers in our past, so I felt bonded to both of these women. "I feel like I've known both of you forever."

Missy joined the hug. "And if my brother doesn't marry you, I swear I'll kick him in the balls."

All three of us burst out laughing through our tears.

* * *

Dinner was roasting on the coals and a cooler filled with bottles of water, soda, and beer was sitting next to Ben.

"What will you have?"

"Soda, please," Remi request.

"Water," Teagan said, pointedly. "For me and Mace, too."

"Awww, please?" Remi lamented. "It's vacation."

"You had two sodas already today, Remi."

Remi sighed and took the bottle of water Ben offered. "Okay."

Missy followed suit for herself and Dylan.

"Well, I'm having a beer," Ben said. "Chase? Jensen?"

"Sure, thanks," Chase responded.

Jensen nodded and walked over to take the two beers from Ben. "Thanks, man."

The women were all positioned on logs next to their men, and the children were staying close to their dads. It was clear that Remi missed both of them. Mace was positioned firmly on Chase's knee. The two eight-year-olds chattered on and on about the trail ride. The fire was giving off a golden glow, throwing us all into golden light and purple shadows. The evening was nice, not as cool as the night before.

Ben sat next to me after he'd passed out the drinks and turned the foil packets for the last time on the embers.

"Daddy, isn't Dark so cute?" Remi rambled. "I just love playing with him and look at Gemmy! Isn't she nice? Mommy said I can't have a pony, but can we get a dog?"

The dog was laying between two of the logs on a blanket I'd brought from the house for her. She looked comfy, but tired. The kids wore her out in the past couple of days. I reached down and stroked her silky body.

"You're having a new little sister soon, Remi," Chase soothed, sliding and arm around his daughter and pulling her close to his side. "That's enough for your mom to deal with while I'm on the road."

Chase was fit as a fiddle, but I wondered how long soccer players stayed in the sport before they retired.

"I'll never get a dog," she said sadly.

"We'll talk about it, baby" Teagan said. "Where would the dog be on our vacation if we had it at home? He'd have to be in a kennel and that's not very nice, is it?"

"I could bring her. Auntie Marin wouldn't mind, and she could play with Gemmy."

"That's true, Remi, you could bring her if you came to the ranch."

"See?" Remi exclaimed and ran over to give me an enthusiastic hug which I returned. "I told ya!"

Teagan's eyes widened as she looked at me. It didn't occur to me that I was disagreeing with her, but I wanted to make Remi happy.

"Whoops," Ben said under his breath with a short laugh.

"Well, I think we should all move here," Dylan piped up. "This place is so cool!"

"It would be nice, but you know we can't, buddy," Jensen said. "Ben told me about next summer, though, and we'll work it out." He winked at his son.

"Awesome!"

"Who's hungry?" I asked. "I think the food is finished." I rose to pick up the tongs and placed the foil packets on heavy-duty paper plates. "Missy, can you open the foil around the bread and then everyone can take what they want?"

"Sure. Should I leave it on the rocks? Then it will stay warm."

"Sounds like a great idea, but just make sure to help the little ones get a piece."

Missy helped pass out the bread and opened the foil packets for the children, getting them settled before going to sit down beside Jensen. She didn't take her plate from me but took a seat next to Jensen. "Well, now that we're all here, I have a little announcement."

"What is it, honey?" Jensen asked, glancing up at her.

"Yes, what is it? It must be big if you didn't tell me on the plane?" Teagan interjected. Her husband was sitting close to her with his arm around her. It was clear that these two couples adored each other very much, and their unconventional family dynamic worked wonderfully well. There was no sign of tension between Chase and Jensen, and all four of them were amazing parents.

"Well, I didn't want to spoil this. I wanted to wait until we were with Ben and Marin, and Jensen, you were away on assignment when I found out."

Her husband, who was enjoying his meal, stopped and looked at Missy. He put his plate down on the ground between his feet, then slid an arm around her, his brow furrowed a bit. "Did you need me to come home? I could have found someone else to take the job."

"No, this is perfect." She leaned her head on his shoulder briefly, then took his other hand in hers.

We were all looking on with bated breath.

"Come on, Mom! Spit it out, already!" Dylan commanded, continuing to shovel food into his mouth.

"Well…" she paused dramatically. "We're going to have a baby!" Missy's face was radiant.

Jensen was somewhat stunned for a minute. "Really?" he asked his face broke into a brilliant smile. "Are you serious?"

When Missy nodded, Jensen jumped up and pulled her into his arms and off the ground, holding on for dear life. Their happiness brought a tear to my eyes.

There was a chorus of congratulatory cheers and shouts from the rest of us. Teagan was smiling from ear to ear, and Chase bent to whisper something in her ear before she turned to kiss his lips, gently cupping his jaw.

"This is amazing!" Jensen said, finally setting her on her feet to hold her face with both hands and place a big kiss on her mouth. "How long?" He asked breathlessly.

Missy started to giggle. "Seven weeks. We have a long time to wait."

Jensen laughed and lifted her in his arms again. "I'm so happy!"

"Ugh, more slobbering," Dylan muttered.

"Yay! Now my baby sister will have someone to play with, too!" Remi said.

"I bet you and Dylan will love those babies a lot. You will play with them, too, I think." I winked at Remi.

My heart was warmed by the love radiating among the group. The adults got up and went to congratulate the happy couple. Ben gave his sister a huge hug. "I'm happy for you guys."

"I hope I get a brother," Dylan spouted, still sitting down with his food.

"I don't. I hope it's a girl. Then she can be Mace's damsel." Remi's tone was very matter of fact.

"Gross," Dylan lamented. "Who said he wants one, Remi?"

"You better be quite Dylan Jeffers, or I won't let you be my prince, anymore."

It was an amusing exchange between the two kids.

"Good," he answered, with a wry twist to his expression. "Who wants to be a dumb ole' prince anyway?"

"You'll be jealous when I'm some other prince's damsel! It's a good thing boys grow up, cuz boys are dumb!"

Dylan rolled his eyes. "Yeah? Well, girls are goofy!"

The adults all chuckled at the exchange, though Jensen stepped in. "That's enough, kids."

I laughed out loud at Remi's *boys are dumb* narrative.

Remi went to sit on the end of Jensen and Missy's log, so she was positioned between Jensen and Chase.

I watched her chatter away to them both when Ben's phone vibrated in his back pocket and he took it out and glanced at the screen. Then shut it off and shoved it back inside. He looked to the west at the mountain range, so my eyes followed his. There was smoke billowing up from behind them, showing up in the remnants of the sunset, the sky a bit hazy.

"Ben, what is it?"

"It's just... you know, it's uh..." he continued to look at the mountains.

The others were happily chatting and eating their food, and many compliments came in but my concern for what Ben was thinking reduced them to the background.

"It's a fire," I guessed correctly.

"Yes. Davis texted earlier that they were going, but now it's a lot more out of control. The wind has taken it wild. I have notifications on the police scanner. It's bad."

My stomach clenched. I knew in my heart he wanted to go help. "Ben, they haven't called you in so can't you just enjoy the evening with us? You haven't even had dinner and you've been drinking."

I was suddenly terrified. I could see the stress in his expression, but he nodded and picked up his fork again. I noticed how tense he was. He set his beer down and reached for a water bottle and downed almost all of the contents in one pull. It was a tell.

I inhaled deeply. He was preparing to join the fight. Suddenly the delicious meal I'd prepared tasted like dust in my mouth. I leaned my shoulder against his and lowered my voice so only he could hear me. "I know what you're thinking, but please don't go." I was being selfish but after the nightmares, I didn't care.

His brow furrowed as I implored him. I reached out and wrapped my hand around the inside of his elbow and squeezed. "Please. They haven't called you, so it isn't that bad, is it?"

"It's bad enough to turn the night sky orange, Marin. There are a couple of towns over there. The longer it burns without containing it, the worse it gets."

I sighed and though I understood, I was still scared to death. I could see he was shutting down emotionally. "Your family is here, and we promised to sing campfire songs." I felt the panic rise up and knew it showed in my voice as I gripped his forearm tightly. "The kids have been looking forward to sharing the evening with Chase and Jensen all day."

Ben glanced around the fire to view the scene of all three kids staying close to the two men and Dylan educating Jensen on how to load marshmallows on one of the new sticks Ben had sharpened for this evening's event.

Remi was excitedly retelling about this morning when Dark had basically laid on my lap. She was laughing and Chase was playing along. It was clear that this was a close family.

Ben's jaw was tight as he poked at the chunks of vegetables and hamburger on his plate. "I know, but this is what I do. The rest of you can sing songs and camp out."

I glanced around uneasily, hoping that no one would notice the tension between us, but Missy's eyes were on us. I swallowed hard against the emotion building in my throat. I needed to take a break from the group before I started crying in front of everyone.

"Ben, you're injured. You have this week off."

"I know," he sighed. "My side is healed enough. I should go before it gets worse." The concern in his words and his face was clear.

"If your crew is already gone, how will you get out there?"

"I'll have to drive or meet up with another crew that's called. I don't know." He was getting more and more agitated the more I kept begging, so I decided to stop.

"I'm going to run into the house for a minute," I murmured, releasing my hold on his arm. "I'll be right back."

"Marin," Ben began, putting a hand on my shoulder to stop me.

"I just have to use the bathroom." I stood, knowing I was going to break out crying and didn't want the others to know. I effectively broke the close contact between us as I hurried to get away. I felt like an iron curtain had slammed down between us. It was as if he didn't care how I felt and I knew he would end up going despite what I wanted.

Was this how my entire life would be if we stayed together? Worrying constantly, day and night? As I hurried toward the house, I felt as if there was a gaping hole in my chest that grew with every step away from Ben. How would I get through the rest of this weekend?

Gemmy followed at my heels and up the stairs onto the porch. I was out of sight of the people around the fire, so I bent to pick up the sweet little dog and held her close. I buried my face in her soft fur as a small sob broke from my chest. I gasped and rushed through the door into the house and straight to the couch where I dropped down and continued to cry. I would allow myself just a few minutes of sorrow because I couldn't help it, and because maybe it would give me the release that I needed to suck it up for the rest of the evening. Gemmy looked at me helplessly, then began to lap at the tears on my cheek. I held her tighter and turned my face into her as tears continued to roll down my face.

"Marin?"

Missy's voice snapped my eyes open and lifted my head away from Gem's soft neck. I set Gem down on my lap and quickly wiped at my eyes with one hand. I sniffed.

There was no way I'd be able to hide that I'd been crying.

"Are you okay?" Missy stepped into the living room and sat down on the sofa next to me.

"I don't think so." I couldn't control the tremor in my voice and my face crumpled. I closed my eyes and a new wave of tears squeezed out. "There's a fire and I know Ben will end up going."

"I saw the sky and I wondered about it. He keeps checking his phone. But…" Missy's tone was perplexed. "It's his job. We'll understand if he has to go."

I nodded. "You're right." How could I explain my terror without making Ben's sister think I was psychotic? "It's just I'm afraid for him." Gem had jumped down from my lap and curled up on top of the dog bed I placed for her near the fireplace, her soulful eyes watching me. I curled my arms and hands to my chest and looked away from Missy, hoping to hide my apprehension.

Recognition dawned on Ben's sister's face. "Oh, Marin! I am so insensitive. I should have realized." Her arm snaked around my shoulders as she scooted closer. "Ben is a professional. He's never been hurt, not even once," she reassured.

I nodded, but a shiver ran through me. "My uncle used to say there is a first time for everything."

Missy hugged me tighter. "He sounds like a character." It was clear she was trying to comfort me. "But can I just put it in perspective? I know it sounds like I'm making light of it, but any of us could die at any moment. No one knows how long we have. We can't shut out people we love because we're afraid of losing them. Then you miss out on love."

What she said was true, but she wasn't aware of my nightmares. I'd seen Carter die, and my mind had seen Ben die in the same way. I felt so weak and immature but there was nothing I could do to quell my fear.

"Jensen gets on a plane every week, I fly twice a month minimum, and Chase plays soccer all over the world. Do you think either Teagan or I could stand it if we let it eat us alive?"

The logical part of my mind knew she was right. But heading into an inferno seemed so much more dangerous than getting on a plane. A building fire was one thing, but a forest fire was like a box of matches waiting to strike around him. "I know you're right. Ben thinks I doubt him, but that's not it."

"I know you're just worried. I can see how much he means to you. I'll try to talk him out of going, but if he does, we're all here to keep you company and the time will fly by and he'll be back safe and sound, you'll see."

"Okay," I nodded. Missy patted my hand and stood up. "Come on. The kids will be missing us."

"Congratulations on your baby, Missy. Ben told me you've been trying." I hugged her.

She nodded. "Yes. I was afraid we weren't going to get pregnant. I'm so happy."

"Well, Jensen is over the moon. I'm so happy for you."

She thanked me with a genuine smile and then left the house to return to the campfire.

I followed suit but first went into the bathroom to wash my face. I didn't want it to look all pinched and red. I wanted to support Ben, but as I stood there staring at my own reflection, I silently prayed he would stay at the ranch and that fire would be contained without him.

When I approached the small group, Remi and Dylan both ran forward to hug me around the waist at once. "Are you okay, Auntie Marin?" Remi asked.

I nodded, hugging them both close, each in one of my arms. "Yes. How can I be anything but fine with hugs from the two of you?"

"Look! I made you a s'more!" Dylan said, releasing me and proudly producing a paper plate with the confection in the middle of it. "I roasted the marshmallow just right! I didn't even burn it."

"That's great! Thank you! What would I do without the two of you?" The enthusiasm I injected into my tone was meant to ease their concern as I took the plate from Dylan and touched the top of his head, before glancing in Ben's direction.

His expression was worried, but he stood up and took the plate from me, then slid one arm around me and led me back to our log. "Come on, let's enjoy the rest of the evening."

When we sat down on the log once more, Ben handed me the plate, but kept an arm around me, pulling me close so that our hips and thighs were touching.

We shared my dessert while Ben and Jensen asked Chase about the game he'd won earlier in the day against Peru. I was comforted by the camaraderie the three of them had, though it wasn't long before Remi and Dylan were pressing us about singing cowboy songs. Though Ben tried to be engaged, he was quiet and preoccupied, continually watching the skyline to the west.

Teagan took the opportunity to take young Mace into the house before the singing started.

"Come on kids, let's all go in and get our PJ's on," Missy said, rounding up Remi and Dylan to herd them into the house behind Teagan, who was carrying the sleepy toddler.

I began picking up the paper plates and tossed the recycling into the plastic bag I'd brought outside, then threw the paper products into the fire. I sat down to one side of the men to watch it burn. I stared at it so hard it blurred.

Ben was talking to Chase and Jensen, but his phone began to ring. My heart seized. It wasn't a text, so I knew in my gut they were calling him in. He stood up and walked a few feet away and turned his back to the rest of us.

Chase and Jensen were both watching and murmuring quiet words to each other.

I was straining to hear what Ben was saying into the phone but all I could get was a muffled; "Yeah, okay. Got it. I'll head in."

My heart fell to my stomach and tears stung the back of eyes. I jumped up and rushed to him just as he was shoving his phone back into the back pocket of his jeans.

His hands came up to slide down my arms and his blue eyes begged for my understanding. He was calm, almost eerily so. "I have to go. The fire is getting close to Alta and they've evacuated the town. Davis's team has lost contact, Marin."

I sucked in a deep breath as tears filled my eyes and I shook my head. "Please don't go. You know the bad dreams I've been having? I relive the fire when Carter died, but then he morphs into you. Oh, God, I couldn't survive if you died, Ben! It was you." My chest began to heave in quiet sobs. "Please, don't go."

My hands both lifted to clutch around his forearms as he was holding my upper arms, but he pulled me hard against his chest, and pressed his lips to my temple. I only cried harder.

"I am not Carter, Marin. I swear, I'll come back. Davis is my best friend and he's lost in there with several others. You met them at the bar. One of the water tankers is coming into base to refill, and I'm going out with it to meet up with my crew. I gotta go."

He pushed me back to look into my face. I shook my head, his image blurring from the tears in my eyes.

Ben bent to place a long, deep kiss on my mouth. "I love you. I'm coming back to you. I promise."

"Ben, don't go!" I shook my head again as he backed away. I was desperate to stop him. "I can't take this my entire life. I can't watch you go into fire after fire!"

He stopped, his face getting harder. "I'm happy that you're thinking about us long-term, Marin, but this is what I do. You knew that from day one. If you can't accept it, then I guess you can't, and it means that you don't trust me. You have to let go of the past, and stop being afraid of something that hasn't happened!" Ben was adamant.

I fell to my knees crying, uncaring that the two other men were looking on helplessly, concern clearly etched on both of their faces. "You can't control everything! You don't know what could happen, but you put yourself at risk every time you walk into an inferno."

"You're right, I don't know what might happen, but neither do you! I can't sit here and do nothing, Marin!" Ben glanced at the Jensen and Chase. "My boys are in there and what kind of man would I be if I didn't do what I could to find them?"

"Ben, please!" I begged again.

He stood tall and defiant in front of me. He was proud and strong. I understood why he felt he needed to go, but my heart was exploding inside my chest and I couldn't breathe.

"I understand that my job is dangerous. I get it, but I've been doing it for eight years. I'm damn good at it, and I don't take unnecessary risks. You can't put me in a cage. This is who I am. If you want to throw away everything we're building, it sucks, but I can't stop you. Take care of her," he said, nodding at Jensen and Chase.

Chase nodded. "We will man. You go. I'd come with you to help if you'd let me."

"Sorry, brother," Ben shook his head. "Years of training and all."

"I know. I just wish I could do something."

"You can," Ben said, nodding in my direction. His eyes were pained as he looked at me.

Soon Jensen's arms were around me, lifting me up as I cried. He pressed me into his chest and held the back of my head. "Ben will come back. Marin. We just have to pray and have faith in him."

It all felt surreal. I hoped this was just another of my nightmares, but Jensen's strong arms around me belied that wish. I heard Ben's truck roar to life and lumber down the lane as I melted into a torrent of tears.

everything
HAPPENS FOR
a reason

Chapter 23

Marin

It had been twenty-four hours since Ben had gone to help fight the wildfire. Somehow, I'd managed to stop the tears around the little ones, but only barely. I was a basket case.

Chase and Jensen were camping out with Remi and Dylan tonight because the struggle to put up a good front was wearing thin. I wasn't strong enough to keep it up, and so decided to try to sleep in my room, away from the others.

Teagan had put Mace down in the bedroom they shared, but she and Missy were both sitting with me in the living room. I felt awful. Missy had shared some wonderful news last night and then I had a meltdown afterward, completely overshadowing it. She should have spent the night in the tent with Jensen and doing whatever a couple who just found out they were going to be parents do, but she and Teagan never left my side. Even still.

I sucked in a deep breath and wrapped my hands around the white ceramic mug of hot chamomile tea that Teagan had made for me. She'd brought it with her, and I had to admit, it did have a relaxing effect on me.

We were all sitting in the living room and had switched on the television so we could watch the ten o'clock local news.

The fire was still the headline story, and the aerial pictures showed the raging flames stretching north to south on the western range and licking its way around the small town of Alta, though they managed to keep it from the town. There were airplanes dumping loads of fire retardant in front of the flame wall.

I felt sick. I had my entire life living near mountains and Yellowstone. There had been fires throughout the years and I always felt bad for the animals that lost their lives... and firefighters; there were often firefighters who died. I closed my eyes as the female anchor droned on and on with the details.

Missy moved to sit on the couch next to me. I was curled up in the corner, with my legs beneath me. Her hand reached out to lay a hand on my knee. "Ben's going to be okay. We have to be positive, Marin. It seems more under control, now."

I realized she was only trying to comfort me, but I was terrified. "Aren't you afraid? It's been an entire day."

"Sure, but he loves what he does. I've always known it was risky, but it's his choice. He's well trained and he's strong as an ox. He's taken fire technology training. He knows how fires react to certain situations. He's not walking in blind."

I took another sip of the tea. The lump in my throat made it hard to swallow. "Logically, I know all of that, but I'm still so scared."

Teagan was sitting in the chair to my left, turned toward the two of us on the sofa. "These men we chose to love are complicated, Marin. Chase would have gone with Ben, and so would Jensen, if they were allowed. It's their nature to protect, and isn't that what we love about them?" Her voice was gentle and kind. "I know that Chase's job isn't dangerous like Ben's, but he's in the air flying thousands of miles, almost every week, all season. He's flying more than he's on the ground, and I worry all the time, but he wouldn't be Chase if he couldn't play the game, and Ben wouldn't be Ben without fighting fires."

Tears stung at the back of my eyes and I nodded. "I know. I love that he's brave and always trying to help people, I'm just afraid because Carter died in a fire right in front of me. I hated him at the end, but it was so horrible to watch… and hear." My voice cracked and I fisted the hand not holding my mug and brought it to my mouth.

Missy's hand tightened on my leg. "I'm so sorry, Marin. Ben told me Carter was careless and he'd been drinking. Ben would never be that reckless."

Missy was trying to be reassuring, and I knew she was right. I trusted Ben to be careful, but fires were unpredictable.

"I have this recurring nightmare where I relive the fire and Carter's face as he's screaming, changes into Ben's." My words trembled as they dropped from my lips. "I've seen it in my mind several times. Ben and I haven't known each other very long, but if something happened to him, I don't think I'd survive. I wouldn't want to."

Gemmy jumped up on the couch between us, laid her little head on my lap, and then licked at my hand. Missy smiled gently and began to stroke the puppy down her back. "This little one knows you're sad."

"She's intuitive, but I don't want her to feel sad, too." I put down the tea and gathered Gem onto my lap. The warmth of her against me was comforting. "She loves Ben. She runs after him everywhere he goes."

"He adores her," Missy nodded.

Teagan's eyes were glossy with tears and she quickly dashed a tear from one of her eyes.

The television anchor was reporting that there was a crew missing and they had sent in a rescue team of firefighters and

EMTs with the aerial drops supporting their efforts and making a path.

Every fire crew on the range had been called in and the reporters were kept a good distance away, but their station helicopter had aerial shots of the scene. The red and orange flashing lights of the trucks were scattered up and down the path of the fire, and more of police cars on the roads created barricades so traffic was turned away. There was one reporter who managed to get through and was stationed as close as possible by two of the trucks where there were men and women working to hook up one of the tanker trucks. Water was being pumped at high pressure onto one section of the fire.

The screen flashed with an "exclusive report" logo and the women in the studio transitioned to young woman on scene. I couldn't help but stare at the screen.

"The dark of night might make rescue efforts more difficult, and we will continue to try to talk to one of the firefighters to ask about their progress," the woman said but was soon rebuked.

"Get out of here!" An older man in full fire gear came forward waving his arms. "You news people should not be here."

"Can I just get a statement?" the reporter asked. "Any news on the lost crew?"

"You people. We're kinda busy, lady" he shook his head, clearly disgusted. "Get out of here. We have enough to do without worrying about your crew. They've evacuated the town, so you need to leave and let us alone to do our job! Now!"

"People want to know! Just a couple of questions," the reporter pushed.

"No. Get out of here, now or I'll have you arrested."

Teagan rose and grabbed the remote, changing the channel. "How on earth did those reporters even get in there? The footage showed the roads blocked off by police."

"Reporters are paid to get the story," Missy said. "But when people's lives are at stake they need to back off."

"Thank goodness, you and Jensen only go into locker rooms," Teagan said. "What should we watch? Let's watch a chick flick! It will get help and keep us occupied. Let's get your mind focused on something else. Do you have Netflix?"

I nodded, reaching for the remote. Soon I had Netflix pulled up and was searching through the movies. "What should we watch?"

"Something funny," Missy suggested.

I settled on a romantic comedy about a couple who have a wild one-night stand and the woman won't see the man again and his quest to convince her. I didn't think I'd be able to concentrate, but both of these women were trying so hard to make me feel better, I'd make a concerted effort.

"Thank you, both. I don't know what I'd do without you. If I were here alone, I'd probably be a mess."

"What are friends for?" Teagan asked with a smile, settling in to watch the movie, draping her legs over the arm of the chair as she faced the screen. The big screen TV was the one thing that Uncle Leonard splurged on.

"Friends?" Missy scoffed in amusement. "You two are my sisters! We're family."

Teagan nodded, her smile brightening. "Agreed."

"I'm grateful every day for the circumstances that made us a family, and now you'll be part of it, Marin. The children adore you."

"I feel the same about them. They're great kids."

"Remi would tell us to just have faith in your prince, Marin." Teagan laughed.

The movie was starting but I found the two women more engaging. "What's the story about the damsel thing?" I asked, for the first time feeling a bit more at ease.

"The first time I met her, Remi told me that Jensen needed me to be his damsel," Missy added. "I found her so beguiling. I think I fell in love with her before Jensen!"

"She asked me if I was Ben's damsel, too."

Teagan laughed out loud. "Well, I'm raising a strong young lady, who loves fairy tales. And let's face it, we all want our men to be strong protectors. That's what makes fairy tales great. So, we had a conversation about girls being strong. I told her it's okay to be a damsel occasionally."

"Right! Because the boys need to protect us to feel empowered, so we have to let them," Missy explained. "But I have to be honest, sometimes we really do need them."

"Exactly!" Teagan agreed. "But I want my girls to grow up knowing they can do anything they want on their own."

I found the entire story so perfect. "But they can rely on their fathers."

"Yep," Teagan nodded. "Though, I'm seeing Dylan already take care of Remi already. He's such a little gentleman."

Missy beamed. "I raised him right, but Jensen, Chase, and Ben have all been huge influences on him. I'm thankful for all of them, because his birth dad was such a selfish asshole."

"They're so cute together. They spar a little, but I can tell they adore each other," I said.

"They're best friends and they stand up for each other. I'm very proud of them," Teagan added.

"I'd offer you some wine, but women who are preggers are exempt!" I smiled, my worry easing. "Though I would have advised against the horseback ride, no matter how gentle the horse."

Missy grimaced. "I know, that was why I hesitated today, but as far as the wine, it doesn't mean you can't! Just leave it to me to completely raid your kitchen," All smiles, Missy rose and rushed into the kitchen, soon returning with sodas for her and

364

Teagan, and a glass of chilled white wine for me. She made one more trip, finding a bag of Doritos and a box of Zingers. "Sweet or salty?" She held them up, teasing us with them.

Teagan's face twisted wryly. "Are you kidding? Both. Duh."

Soon we were all passing the snacks around and getting engrossed in the movie. I felt truly thankful for the fire that brought Ben, and now this wonderful family, into my life. I felt blessed for the first time since Uncle Leonard died. I sighed feeling love settle over me. Once again, I found myself wondering if it weren't my uncle working with God that started that fire.

I closed my eyes and offered a silent prayer that Ben, Davis, and everyone else would be protected and the forest fire would soon be contained.

BEN

The fire was raging on all sides of us.

The heat was intense and though my gear protected me, I felt like I was melting inside of it. I hoped Davis and the others had taken shelter in the river as I chopped at the burning trees in front of me that blocked our path. My shoulders were aching as I wielded the ax over and over again.

We'd been out here for hours and dawn was starting to break. I could see the sky above me start to turn purple, and the planes dumping the slurry mixture of water, fire retardant and fertilizer in front of us. Our suits were splattered with the stuff and I wanted to use a gloved hand to wipe it off my visor but resisted. I'd learned in past experience that it would only smear and make it impossible to see.

Marin was on my mind, even though my body was on autopilot. I knew what had to be done. I swung at another tree with everything I had, cracking it under the pressure. It had a pretty thick trunk, but it was weakened; glowing red and black as the fire consumed it, reducing it to glowing embers. The three men with me were doing the same as we carved a path through the burnt forest.

My walkie talkie was clipped to my jacket and I grabbed it. "Any luck finding the guys, Cap?"

"The helicopter found them in the river. Can you get to them? The fire around them is still raging so the copter can't get low enough to air lift them out. The heat plume will turn flip the bird."

"Can you tell me how far we are away? The 'copter is hovering above us right now." I was yelling into the walkie talkie. The fire was still roaring, and the sound of the helicopter was a hindrance, as well as my hat and gas mask I was wearing.

"You're getting closer. Looks like about a mile to the northeast."

Another fucking mile, I thought ruefully. My muscles were already screaming, and I was stronger than some of the other guys with me. We were all exhausted.

Even with four of us hacking away it would take hours and hours. My heart seized for Marin. My mind pictured her crying at my feet while I turned away before I left. I was thankful for my family being there, and hopefully Missy could reason with her. I should have been more empathetic. I was scared shitless when she'd called me from that bathroom stall and I wasn't able to get to her, but all I could think about were Davis and the others trapped out here in this inferno.

Beads of sweat rolled down my face and forehead beneath my gear and stung my eyes.

"Yeah. Just have the pilot keep an eye on us and let me know if we veer off course."

"Sure thing, son," he answered. "You're doing a great thing."

"Just doing my job," I answered. "Is it getting under control?"

"Yeah, it's about sixty percent. They're bringing in some crews from Idaho to help. We'll get it. I'll be in touch," Captain Connors replied.

I let go of the walkie talkie and it fell back into position, hanging from the clip at my side. I put my hand in the air and motioned for the others to continue in the direction we were going. "We're getting close! Keep moving!" I yelled and it was relayed from the man closest to me to the one next to him and so on.

As we continued through the forest, chopping and climbing through what we could, I tried to keep my mind focused on the goal, and allowing only a few minutes here or there to think of Marin. I understood her fear but wished she would have shared the content of her nightmares with me. I'd known something was up the other night in the tent and I chastised myself for not realizing. I was scared that she was still in love with that loser boyfriend, and I was relieved that wasn't it.

I'd never forget the fear on her face when she begged me not to go but I had to find a way to make her understand that fighting fires was what I loved. Though, in this moment when I was weary and sore, and with hours of work in front of me I told myself that I needed my head examined. It would be crazy, except that when Davis and the others finally came into view, all of them in the water to their waists, it was reiterated that it was saving lives that I found the most rewarding.

The men stranded in the river cheered when they saw us, and I almost fell to my knees in relief. I glanced to my right, then left, and saw that the other three men with me were feeling it, too. We needed to rest a bit before we walked out of here, retracing our steps.

We sat down on the bank of the river as Davis, Jake, Mark and three others waded toward us. Davis's gloved hand came down on my shoulder. "It's good to see you, but what took you so fuckin' long?"

I looked up at him. He probably couldn't see the smile on my face, but I lifted a hand to place it on the arm of his coat, grateful we were able to find them. "At least we weren't lounging in a jacuzzi, like you assholes."

I could hear Davis and the others' chorus of laughter and then louder cheers followed.

"I owe you a beer," my friend said.

"Screw that. You owe me a fucking brewery!"

We stood and then the ten of us began the long walk out. My stomach rumbled loudly. Marin would probably be cooking a huge spread for breakfast. I couldn't wait to get home to her.

Home. The word stuck in my head and I smiled. She was home.

* * *

Back at the station, I took a shower and changed into the clean set of clothes I always kept there.

Captain Connors walked into the bunk room as I closed my locker. "I just wanted to say thanks for coming in."

"No problem."

He reached out and offered his hand which I took gladly. "Glad you're part of our crew. You were like a lion leading those men out there. I thought it would take twice as long to get to them."

"I had to get my boys," I said easily. My hair was still wet from the shower, though I'd run a quick comb through it, I could feel the water dripping down the back of my neck.

"Well, you and the others did a stellar job."

"Do you need me to come back for another shift?" I asked, hoping I wouldn't need to.

"No, the boys from Idaho are taking it from here because it's pretty much out. Take the rest of the week off as we agreed."

"Thanks. My sister's family is visiting, and we have a lot planned with the kids."

The captain nodded. "How old are they?"

"Two eight-year-olds and a little boy who is two." Remi wasn't quite eight, but she was close enough.

"Bring 'em by later and we can take the engine out for a ride."

My face split into a huge grin. "I'm sure they'd love that. Thank you."

"Now get the hell out of here," he said jovially. "See you next week."

It was Sunday and half of the day was already wasted. I was sorry that Marin had to work at the diner tomorrow. It was too late for the fishing trip I'd promised Dylan and Remi had been looking forward to the nature walk and treasure hunt with Marin. She was a natural with the kids and I found myself picturing her mothering our kids.

If she wasn't too angry at me, I'd have to speak to her about it when we had a moment alone. I jumped into my truck, fired up the engine and soon, I was rumbling out of town and toward the ranch.

When I pulled in, my brother-in-law and Chase were letting the horses into the pasture. Dylan and Remi must have watched me close enough and were giving instructions to their respective fathers. The men were all smiles as they worked.

Chase, who was holding Mace in his arms, raised a hand to wave at me as the truck came to a stop and I got out of it. Remi and Dylan's heads snapped around and they both took off running in my direction, hitting me with such force, I thought they'd knock me to the ground.

"Uncle Ben!"

"Uncle Ben!"

The two of them were like peas in a pod, hammering me with questions about the fire and what I had to do to get my friends out of trouble.

I gazed down at the two shining faces looking up at me as they both hugged my waist. I ruffled their heads then squeezed them both. "What's for breakfast?"

"Well, it's more like brunch," Remi clarified. "You're kinda late for breakfast." She was so precocious, mature for her young years.

"Mom's making pancakes!" Dylan said.

"With blueberries," Jensen added. "Our favorite, right kids?"

"Yeah!" Dylan answered.

"Unca Ben!" Mace called, waving a chubby toddler hand. "Unca Ben!"

Chase put his young son down who then ran over, so I swooped down to scoop him up in my arms, then tossed him into the air. "Mace!" The little boy squealed with laughter. "Did you have a good sleep?"

"Yup! I hungry."

"Me, too!"

The ranch atmosphere seemed to suit Chase and Jensen well. "Are the horses all fed?" I asked Dylan.

"I showed Dad and Uncle Chase how to do it. We're almost done," he professed proudly.

"Almost," confirmed Jensen. "You go on in. You look like you need a rest."

Truth be told, all I wanted was a meal, sleep, and my arms around Marin.

"Dark even gave me a hug, Uncle Ben!" Remi said. She and Dylan fell in step beside me as I walked toward the farmhouse. "Just like Siri does to Auntie Marin!" The little girl's green eyes sparkled with excitement.

"He did? Where is Aunt Marin?" I asked.

"Oh, she's sleeping. Mommy said we had to let her sleep in, so we gotta be quiet in the house."

By the time we got close to the house the smell of bacon and coffee permeated the air. Missy turned to see who was coming through the door and her face softened in a relief. She put on a brave face, but I knew she was worried whenever I went out to fight a fire.

"Oh, Ben!" Missy lifted a pancake out of the skillet to a waiting plate as Teagan came to take Mace from my arms.

"Welcome back," she said. "Come to Mommy, Mace." Teagan held out her arms and he immediately went to her. "Let's wash up for breakfast. Dylan, you and Remi, too."

Missy walked to me and gave me a big hug as Teagan and the kids disappeared into the mud room to wash up away from the food.

"I don't need to wash up. I just took a shower at the station." I poked her in the ribs with my index finger.

"Cheeky," she said. "Marin is in her room. We were up all-night watching movies, until she was so exhausted that she finally went upstairs around dawn."

"Well, don't you be over-doing it, *Mommy*," I teased, going to the table and grabbing a slice of bacon from a pile waiting on a plate in the center. I devoured it and reached for another.

Missy's lips lifted in a joyful smile. "Sometimes it doesn't feel real. We've been trying for over a year."

"Good things come to those who wait." I winked.

I glanced toward the stairs, grabbing a paper towel and wiping the bacon grease from my fingers.

"Is she still mad?"

My sister shook her head and went back to making pancakes, adding a small handful of fresh blueberries once the batter hit the pan.

"Not mad. She was scared. She told us about the nightmares."

I nodded. "She just told me right before I left, but I still had to go. My best friend was trapped out there with five guys."

"You don't have to explain, Ben. I get it. Go on. I'll feed the kids and when you get down here with Marin, the adults will eat."

I went to the mud room and kicked off my shoes. "Save me some pancakes, Dylan," I instructed.

"You snooze, you lose," he said saucily.

I laughed as he beamed at me. Remi was drying her hands as Dylan stepped up to the sink.

"I do, huh?"

"Yep!" Remi said with a grin.

"What will I do with you, two?"

"Come on, hurry up, Remi," Teagan instructed.

By the time I got to the top of the stairs and stood outside Marin's bedroom door, I was uncharacteristically nervous. My hand closed around the knob and turned. Thankfully, it wasn't locked, and I peered inside. The shades were drawn, but the sun filtered through slightly to cast the room in a golden glow.

Marin was lying on her side, curled up under the covers. The air conditioning kept the house cool despite the summer weather. I walked closer and lifted the edge of the comforter and began to slide underneath and next to the gorgeous woman who had become my entire world.

My arms reached for her as her eyes fluttered open. Happy surprise lit up her face.

"Oh, Ben!" Marin's arms reached for me and I pulled her close, flush against me. I held her tight as her fingers curled into the back of my shirt, and the hair at my nape. "Ben," she whispered against my throat.

"I told you I'd be okay," I said against the side of her face before my lips found purchase on her cheek. She pressed her forehead against my jaw as a sigh of relief left her body. "Do you forgive me?"

"Mmm, huh," she murmured the affirmative.

"You should have told me about the nightmares." I placed a series of soft, teasing kisses on her cheek, jaw, then a gentle open-mouthed kiss on her lips. Her body surged against mine and desire burned bright.

Finally, I kissed her deeply and her mouth opened to me like a flower. My hands slid down her body and I pulled her hips tight against mine, hitching one of her legs over mine. I pressed into her so she could feel the evidence of the effect she had on me.

"I wish we could make love right now, but breakfast is on the table," I said regretfully, but I had to make an admission. "and… I'm so hungry."

Marin's fingers threaded through my hair in the way I'd come to love. "I'm sorry about the way I acted, but I was just so scared. I'll make it up to you."

Our faces were inches apart, our noses almost touching, and sharing each other's breath. As much as I desired her, I was just so damn happy to be in her presence. I loved her beyond anyone I'd ever known, so I was a bit out of my element. I touched the tip of her nose with my finger.

"I wish you didn't have to work at the diner tomorrow. We missed our fishing trip today."

"About that…" she began.

"Yeah?" I asked, hopefully.

"Your sister put it in my head that rather than rebuild the shop, we should turn the ranch into a dude ranch. We could build a few cabins, a larger stable and another paddock."

My eyebrows raised and a grin split my face. "Well, that sounds like a good plan to me."

"But I should still go work at the diner until we get it going. This year would probably just be the build-out."

I was amazed by her. "It sounds like you've given it a lot of thought."

"Well, not that much, but the girls and I talked about it last night after the second movie was over." I could see the idea excited her. "But maybe we could do a bed and breakfast during the winter. Jackson never has enough hotel rooms."

I nodded, still a bit stunned, my brow cocked as I nodded, not breaking her gaze. "We?" I said, pleased that she'd included me.

Marin's eyes widened. "Oh, well, I mean, I guess, me, but I hoped you'd be around."

"Oh, I'll be around, all right," I assured, placing another lingering kiss on her mouth.

"You will?" she whispered as my mouth left hers briefly between kisses.

"I will." I surprised her by rolling her over and pressing her into the bed. "I will. I'll muck out your stalls, feed your horses, exercise them, and any other damn thing you need me to do, for as long as you need me to do it."

Marin's eyes lit up and she giggled in surprise. "Really? Anything?"

I kissed her neck, letting my tongue come out and lick softly, then I sucked on the tender flesh gently. I could feel the effect it had on her and her body arched provocatively into mine. I'd remember this for later. "Anything," I said, nipping at her collarbone.

"Like, what?" she was teasing, and I was delirious with happiness.

"You mean, beyond shoveling manure?" I asked seriously. Marin nodded and my eyes locked with hers. "Well, I thought I might make love to you every night until you couldn't take any more. Maybe I'd marry you and father five or six of your kids." My index finger traced down the side of her face.

I could tell I'd left her speechless. I nudged her top lip with my bottom one. I couldn't help the smile that lifted the corners of my mouth. She was helpless beneath me and as sore as I was, I was loving it as her hands slid down my back and her heels hooked around my calves.

"Only five or six? Who will father the others?" she asked with a little huffed out laugh.

"As many as you want, but I think we'll need to practice, first." I bent to kiss her mouth, my tongue finding its way into the delicious recesses of her mouth. It was a hungry, deep kiss that was beginning to rage out of control. "A lot of practice."

There was a light rap on the door and in a split second I rolled off of Marin and sat up in a flash. My breathing was hard, and I had a huge bulge in my pants. I grabbed a pillow and quickly put it in my lap.

Marin let out a soft giggle. "Yes?" she called out. "Who is it?"

"It's just us, Auntie Marin. Mommy says it's time to eat," Remi said through the door. "All damsels and princes to the table."

"Remi, uh," Dylan's voice was also out in the hallway and his voice carried through the door. "Enough with that mushy stuff. Tough guys don't like it." He sounded irritated. "Uncle Ben's a tough guy."

Marin laughed in utter delight and climbed out of bed, walked around to my side of the bed and sat down beside me.

"Can we come in, please?"

Marin lifted the pillow and checked to see if I had myself under control. I smiled hard and she threw the pillow to the side.

"Yep!" she called.

Both kids barreled through the door in a flurry of excitement, both of them speaking at once. "Mom said we could eat before you, Uncle Ben, but I wanted to hear about the fire. Then Uncle Chase said we can have a soccer game in the fields since we can't go fishing today," Dylan said, diving at the bed and pouncing on it hard enough to bounce us up and down. "If it's okay with you two."

"I wanna show Daddy and Jensey how Dark lays on your lap, Auntie Marin!" Remi moved between us and put one arm around each of our necks.

We both hugged her back and I laid a hand on my nephew's back who was laying on the bed behind Marin. "This is something, isn't it?" I asked the love of my life.

"It's a slice of heaven," she confirmed. Her face was glowing and happy.

I kissed the top of Remi's head as I devoured Marin's beautiful face with my eyes. I'd never forget this day for as long as I lived. I was the luckiest man on earth.

"We might not be able to go fishing today, but I'll need you two to teach me how to play soccer, and then after we need your help with other projects!" Marin said.

"Really? With what?" Dylan asked eagerly.

"Well, your Uncle Ben needs help coming up with a name for our new dude ranch, Dylan."

"Oh, boy! Really? A dude ranch?" He could barely contain his excitement.

"Really!" I confirmed.

"That's awesome!" Dylan exclaimed. "We can ask Uncle Chase to hold a soccer camp, and we can ride horses, and go fishing and have campfires every night!" Dylan was bursting with excitement. "And I'll come here every summer and help!"

"What about me? What can I help with?" Remi asked, looking adoringly up into Marin's face as she took the little girl's hand in hers.

"I need your special help, Remi." Marin free hand touched the little girl's cheek. "Uncle Ben just asked me to marry him, so I need to plan a proper princess event! I hear that you're an expert."

Remi's face lit up. "Yay! Well, the first thing you need is a sparkly dress." She started jumping up and down and squealing, bouncing the bed as badly as Dylan had. Marin and I both burst out laughing at her exuberance. "See, Dylan! I told ya! Even tough guys need their very own damsel!"

"Uh uh," Dylan shook his head. "Damsels need tough guys. You got it backwards."

I grabbed Marin's hand and threaded my fingers through hers. "Hear that?" I asked, my heart so full I could barely stand it. Happiness wrapped its arms around our little group like a warm hug. "Even tough guys need a damsel." I gently nudged her shoulder with my own.

Marin's lips lifted in a brilliant smile. "Well, this damsel needs you." She leaned in toward me, her chin lifting in a silent request. I was more than willing to oblige. Our lips caressed each other's in a soft kiss, I took her lower lip in between both of mine, leaning my forehead on Marin's as the kiss ended.

"Awww, man! More slobbering?" lamented Dylan. "Gross!" He hopped down from the bed and rushed toward the door to head downstairs. "Come on! Let's go eat and then we can go ride the horses and play with Dark!" He ran out of the room and down the stairs.

Remi's frowned, getting a little crinkle over her nose, then rolled her eyes. "This is why boys are dumb. They just gotta grow up to get it, right Uncle Ben?"

"How'd you get so smart?" I smiled and touched Remi's petal soft cheek.

She shrugged. "I was just born that way, I guess."

"I guess!" I agreed.

Laughing, Marin and I stood up from the bed. Remi reached for my hand to tug me forward. I slid an arm around Marin as we headed down to breakfast.

This was the start of the first day in the rest of our lives.

Epilogue

Marin

MThe Teton Valley Guest Ranch would open in just over a month.

It had taken almost a year, but we were almost ready with reservations lined up all summer thanks to Teagan's help with social media marketing. Her baby girl, Bliss, was born six months before Missy and Jensen's baby boy, Joshua, arrived. Dylan got the little brother he'd wished for.

Teagan was at home, caring for the two babies and little Mace, while Jensen and Missy worked full-time, and Chase continued his soccer career. I was still amazed at how well their family dynamic worked. We missed them terribly, but we Skyped often, and they were both adorable.

I Skyped with Dylan and Remi at least twice a week and we texted every day. They were so excited about the ranch and we had arranged for them to spend the entire summer with us. I truly felt like part of their family and it was inexplicable how much I loved each and every one of them.

I'd used the life insurance from Uncle Ben's settlement to pay off the main house mortgage as he would have wanted and the payout from the shop fire as the investment into the dude ranch. The endeavor was much more expensive that we anticipated, and we found out rather quickly that we needed to raise capital from other investors if it was going to become a reality. It might have been a daunting task however, Missy and Jensen chipped in, but the big bucks came from Chase and Teagan. To save money, we did some of the work ourselves but needed to hire most of it done in order to make the deadline. Chase and Jensen flew out whenever they could to help, and it was amazing how it all came together.

The insurance money was enough to build another stable, a huge metal building that would act as storage for feed, supplies and equipment, and a new barn completed with electrical and heat which would be used to hold events like parties and weddings all year long. It was beautiful and magical inside. All wooden beams and stained wooden floors were varnished and glinting, and fairy lights strung all up in the rafters; something my little Remi insisted on. We had to admit, it was perfect. Skylights provided light inside during the day and an amazing view of the star-filled Wyoming sky at night. There were lofts on both ends overlooking the center floor with stairways leading down from both. Our own wedding was scheduled for next December and I was looking forward to working on the final plans with Remi, Missy, and Teagan this summer, but I could already picture it in my mind.

The twelve new cabins had been built out toward the site of my Uncle Leonard's auto shop and were arranged in a half circle around a large bonfire area, but that part of the build required another million-dollar investment.

It had been a joy to design and even put in the hard labor needed to finish in a year. Uncle Leonard's farmhouse had been completely modernized and a new corral and paddock had been added which were built close to the stables. Both of the stables were now filled with horses. All of those we had boarded, but we also acquired twelve more quarter horses at auction. We'd hired two ranch hands, a cook and cleaning crew. It was all finally coming together. I could sense Ben's immense sense of pride every time he spoke about it or came in from a hard day's work.

The insurance company argued the settlement with Carter's family because it was determined, through the fire commissioner's investigation, that he contributed to his own death. The shop was full of flammables as would any auto shop, and it was determined that his own carelessness with a lantern and working during a power outage and lightning storm put most of the liability on him. There was also the issue that he was running the business. The insurance would only pay out a fraction of what the policy provided for, and the family was given a copy of the investigative report. It wasn't ideal, and I was scared of retaliation, but Ben already had an attorney on retainer to file a series of protection orders against Apollo which he'd already violated. Because he was on parole, he was arrested and put back in jail. We both breathed a sigh of relief.

I saddled up Siri and headed out to check on Ben's progress on the main gate archway. Davis was helping and so I had a thermos of cold lemonade and some chocolate chip cookies tucked away in the saddle bags.

"Tkk tkkk. Come on, Siri. Let's go find Daddy. Giddy-up." Siri was still my favorite horse, and she took off in a familiar trot. Her gate was practiced, and I was used to it. It was obvious that she enjoyed getting out on a ride as much as her humans.

Dark was almost a yearling, and close to seven hundred pounds, but he neighed loudly from the pasture, running along the fence until I reached the end of the lane, hoping to follow us.

"Sorry, baby. You can't come yet." When he reached the corner of the fence that separated the pasture from the road going north to the edge of the property, he was forced to stop and neighed loudly. Siri's ears turned toward the sound, but she kept on her course. "One more year and we can start you, Dark. Poor thing. Your baby wants to come with us, Siri."

The colt still had about five hundred pounds to gain before he was fully grown but that wouldn't be until sometime in his second year. He'd grown into a beautiful horse and would be great for breeding, but for ease of training I wanted to geld him. Ben was completely against it. He said he wasn't going to cut the balls off of his boy. Thinking about Ben's expression of shock and utter disgust, I couldn't help but laugh out loud. You'd think I was suggesting cutting *his* balls off.

"Isn't there some sort of birth control pill for horses?" Ben had asked.

"Sure, but it makes them cranky. Dark won't know the difference," I'd argued.

"Look at him? He's so gorgeous, don't you want one of his babies?"

I'd rolled my eyes. "Very, but we can breed Siri with Renegade again and then we'll have another foal like Dark." From my point of view the solution was simple.

Dark was beautiful, no question, but an intact stallion was asking for trouble. Right now, the only intact male we had other than Dark was his sire, Renegade, and Uncle Leonard only agreed to board him in exchange for breeding Siri. Other than that, we had a rule: only geldings.

After a little more ranch experience, Ben would change his mind on such things. In the wild only one stallion would be found with a herd, and the younger males leave or are forced out when they come of age. The last thing we needed was a fight between stallions.

I wanted to start saddle training Dark around twenty months, but left intact he'd be harder to train, and we had to keep him separated from the mares when they were in heat. So far, Ben had won the argument because we could separate the males from the females into separate pastures, and currently, Dark was more like a pet dog, but once he grew up, he'd have to be separated from the females and from his sire, and I didn't want that lonely life for Siri's baby boy.

In fact, we were already planning on breeding Siri one more time so that Remi and Dylan could witness the birthing, but after that, I was considering asking Renegade's owner to find him other accommodations or have him neutered as well. It would be safer and better for all of the horses, including Renegade, because he wouldn't have to be separated so much. I felt bad for him and I totally understood Uncle Leonard's rules. After the business took off, keeping track of which mares needed to be separated from him would get to be too much work due to fluctuating cycles of the females unless we just kept him alone constantly and the thought made me sad.

The new entrance on the north side of the property was almost two miles from the house. Siri could have made it in 15 minutes, but I was using one of the trails and staying off of the road. We switched off between a slow walk and a slow trot. I could sense she wanted to break into a run through some of the fields, but the unevenness of many of the surfaces and possible holes from rabbits or ground hogs meant I couldn't allow her free reign; she might fall into one and break a leg. I kept her to the trails, just to be safe.

Ben's truck finally came into view along with one other big red crew cab truck. Ben, Davis, Mark, and Jake were on scene helping to build a duplicate of the archway they'd already finished on the south side. From the looks of it they were just about finished. They'd made a makeshift scaffolding from the roofs of the two truck cabs, a couple of boards and blankets beneath them to keep from scratching the paint on Davis's new truck.

Jake and Mark were in the bed of Ben's truck handing up the wooden arch complete with the ranch name carved into it. Ben had darkened the lettering with the skillful use of a blowtorch and then sealed it with clear resin to weather-proof it. The effect was rustic and charming. We had similar plaques made for each one of the cabins which had been named for a different breed of horse, the brilliant concoction of Remi and Dylan.

"There she is!" Ben called from his perch atop the truck bridge. "Be down in a minute, babe."

I watched as first Ben, then Davis, took nails from the carpenter aprons they wore and then hammered them in at several places: one side at a time. Jake and Mark stood back and instructed them on adjustments up or down so that both sides were level.

The sign was heavy, and Ben's muscles were bulging with the effort and his skin slick with the sheen of perspiration. Davis was also shirtless and built, but Ben was the focus of my admiration.

"I brought lemonade and cookies!" I called.

Mark and Jake jumped down and approached Siri's flank. I lifted the saddle bags from their position in front of the saddle and handed it over.

Jake took it, lifting one of the flaps pulling and out the Zip-lock bag filled with cookies then handed the leather saddle bags over to Mark. It wasn't long before he had removed the large thermos and a stack of red plastic cups. He lined up four cups on the back of Ben's open tail gate and filled them all, downing his before refilling it.

"What do you think?" Ben asked. He had on a billed hat from the farmer's co-op, his hair longish on the sides and back sticking out beneath it. I couldn't help thinking that my Uncle Leonard would approve. My lips lifted in the start of smile.

He hopped down and walked forward to lay a hand on my thigh. To avoid saddle burn, I never rode horses in shorts, but Ben gave my flesh a squeeze through the denim of my jeans. His face and bare torso were tanned from hours in the sun building fences over the past couple of weeks. He smiled up at me and I covered his hand with my own. "I think it looks incredible."

"Just in time for the grand opening, right?" Mark asked, reaching for a cookie from the bag that Jake still kept as if it were his, and his alone. "Give me one of those."

Jake finally offered the bag.

"Yes. Tomorrow night. I can hardly believe it's here."

"Are you nervous?" Davis asked, finally jumping down to join the other men. Within seconds both he and Ben were downing a full glass of lemonade.

"Not really. I was worried people wouldn't attend, but we've had a lot of RSVPs and it's open to the public. We may even run out of food, the way it's going."

Teagan and I had arranged for a public grand opening event that would include a live country and western band, a pony/horse ride and bouncy houses for little kids, and a bonfire. Though, due to concerns from my personal fireman, we wouldn't be allowing the roasting of hotdogs or marshmallows due to the size of the crowd and the age of the youngsters. Instead, we'd hired Arlene's Diner to cater in a selection of salads, baked beans and she was setting up a large gas grill and serving smoked pulled pork, grilled chicken and burgers. There would be an assortment of cookies and a big tub of watermelon sections on ice for dessert. We had an assortment of soft drinks, tea, coffee and the option of wine or beer for the adults.

"Did the bouncy houses come?" Ben asked, taking three cookies from the bag.

"Yes, they are setting them up right now."

"This is going to be a blast. I can't wait until the family arrives," he said proudly. "Remi and Dylan asked if we could sleep out in one of them tonight." The dimples in his face appeared as he flashed me a smile. "If they are too full of air it will be like sleeping on a basketball."

"It will only be a couple of hours until they arrive," I answered. "I'm excited to see them." We'd seen them a few times throughout the year; they'd come out here twice and we had gone to Atlanta when Missy gave birth to Joshy, and it was the first time we were able to meet little Bliss.

"I'm excited to see them, too. Macey can stay out with us this time, I think. He's three now." His answer confirmed what I already knew; he'd committed us to a camp out in the bouncy house.

"Yes," I agreed.

"Dude," Davis shook his head. "If it were me, I'd be figuring out how I could stay out there with my lady. *Alone.*"

Ben laughed. "Well, that's because you haven't met those kids. They are amazing!" He reached up and patted my behind. Siri snorted. "Okay, girl. You get some love, too." He rubbed the side of her neck with his other hand, never letting go of me. "I think that's a good idea, though."

A slow smile slid across my lips. Ben's eyes were hidden by his Ray-Bans, but I knew the blue eyes held a mischievous glint, as he openly flirted with me.

"I gotta say," Davis began, "Working out here is hard, but not as hard as fighting fires. Maybe Ben had the right idea." He took off his cowboy hat and ran a hand through his dark hair before replacing it on his head. I could see it was damp with sweat.

I nodded, my hand reaching down to wrap around Ben's forearm. His hand was still resting on the back of my saddle by my lower back. Touching each other whenever we were close had become natural and second nature; like breathing.

"I'm thankful," I admitted. Ben had quit the fire department and was working with me to build the ranch full-time but was still a member of the volunteer squad and did go out when needed. It was still a worry, but I'd come to accept that fighting fires, and being a hero, was just part of who Ben was, and I loved all of him. My heart was full, and I was proud of the man he was. I felt cherished every day.

"Just say the word, buddy," Ben said, giving my butt a pat, then walking over to the bed of his truck to remove four shovels and a post hole digger. "If this first season is anything to go by, we're going to be busy as hell, and if we have to expand, who knows? God willing, we'll need a shit load of help. That goes for you two, too." He nodded at Jake and Mark. "Right, boss lady?"

Ben was teasing me, but I had to admit there was a certain satisfaction to seeing this all come together. "I couldn't have done it without you," I said.

"Oh, Ben, I love you, Ben," Davis teased in a sing-songy voice. The men burst out laughing. "Ben, you're so strong!"

I couldn't help but smile and roll my eyes. "Okay, Davis, enough of you. I meant any of you! If you're not careful, I'll tell Gina you're into Ben and not her." They started dating a few months ago after a few more of our group nights at the Moose.

"She knows better," he chuckled. "Believe me!"

The men still had several evergreens to plant beside the huge boulders we'd had delivered to make the entrances more elaborate. Siri shifted beneath me, anxious to move around. "It's time for me to get back. I need to make sure the cabins are in order for our guests." We'd invited some of our friends to stay at the cabins for the weekend after the grand opening celebration.

Teagan and Chase would share one with Mace and Bliss, Missy and Jensen with Joshy, Gina with Davis, and Mark with his girlfriend. Jake was still single, so he'd have his own, but Chase had also invited his parents and siblings who would round out the trial group. It was designed as a test run for the staff.

Remi and Dylan had requested a campout in the bouncy houses tonight, but Saturday night would be spent in the cabins with their parents. Ben and I would have our own. I was looking forward to both of the coming evenings.

"Don't stress. It's just our family and friends. It doesn't have to be perfect, tonight."

"But I'd like it to be," I answered.

"I know, but don't stress. I'll see you later, sweetheart," Ben walked over to say goodbye, and I leaned down to kiss him. He removed his hat and once again his arm slid around my hips, and he offered a pat. "Be careful."

"Thanks for the refreshments," Jake called, stuffing one last cookie into his mouth.

"You're welcome." As I turned to leave, the men were already unloading the evergreens from the back of Davis's truck. They were less than four feet now, but they'd still look good now and even more so in the future when they were taller. "You guys are doing a great job."

I turned Siri around and decided to let her run for a short distance to burn some of her energy. "Tkk Tkk. Let's go Siri." I barely touched her side with my heel, and she knew I was going to let her gallop.

The terrain was flat on this side of the entrance for about a quarter mile, and she took off like a rocket when I gave her the lead. Her gallop was smooth, and I was used to being in sync with her strides. I felt happy and free with the wind blowing my hair back. I knew by the time I arrived back at the house; our family would be arriving. I couldn't wait to see them.

* * *

"Auntie Marin!" Remi yelled, bounding toward me with Dylan, as I Siri and I trotted into the yard.

She and Dylan were both a couple inches taller, their features a slightly more mature.

"Whoa, Siri." I stopped the horse near the two SUV's that were parked in front of the house. I dismounted from Siri as the two kids ran toward me. I still held Siri's reins, but did my best to hug them both tight. I kissed first one, then the other on the top of their heads. "You two are so big! Will you stop growing, please? Has it only been a month?"

I smiled down into their shining faces. They were gorgeous and a sight for sore eyes.

"Come on, Aunt Marin, you know we can't," Dylan said.

I cupped his cheek, then Remi's. "I know. I'm so happy to see you! Are you hungry? I made chocolate chip cookies, or I can make you a sandwich or maybe mac and cheese?" The caterers were already on site and had a large smoker going for the pulled pork. The air smelled delicious, but it wouldn't be ready for four or five more hours.

"Okay," Dylan agreed to it all. I couldn't help but laugh. That would have been Ben's answer, too.

The adults were watching from a short distance away, still near the cars. Missy and Teagan were both holding their babies, and Chase was just getting Mace out of the car seat in the back. He was three now, and he'd grown the most. He ran toward us as fast as his little legs could carry him once Chase set him on his feet. I handed Siri's reigns to Dylan and bent to scoop him up in my arms. "My! Who is this big handsome boy?"

"It's me, Auntie Marin!" He hugged my neck with his little arms. "Can I ride your horsey? Can I?" His green eyes were wide with wonder as he watched Siri snort and bob her head.

"Mace, give Aunt Marin a chance to say hello," Chase said stepping forward to reclaim his son. "Sorry."

"Oh, no, it's fine. Siri's all saddled up and I'll be happy to give them all a ride. But I'd like to say hello to the babies."

Missy and Teagan approached. "You look wonderful, Marin," Missy said. She held her month-old baby boy dressed in a white and blue onesie. There was a blanket beneath him, but he was not wrapped in it due to the warm weather. "Here's Joshy," she said, beaming. I looked down at the sleeping baby, palming the top of his head. He had silky fine hair, but it was blond and short.

"He's precious. Two boys will have your hands full."

Jensen was standing beside his wife and I hugged him. He was the epitome of a proud father. "In a good way." He smirked at me. "I'm loving every minute of it."

"It's so good to see you guys," I said sincerely, even though it had only been a month since we'd been in Atlanta.

Turning to Teagan, who was holding the little replica of Remi. "Hello, Bliss," I said. Her green eyes stared at me and her dark hair was sticking up all over her head, save a little gathered in a barrette with a pink ribbon bow. I reached out and held her plump little hand. It was only been a month since we'd seen them, but the two babies had changed so much. "You're just beautiful, aren't you?"

"Mommy says she looks like me!" Remi piped up. "I'm gonna teach her all about being a princess when she grows up a little!"

I smiled. "Well, you're certainly the expert on princesses," I agreed. "And also, beautiful!"

"Yep!" She nodded her head, and her long dark ponytail bounced up and down. "Where's Gemmy?"

"In the house, but what'd ya say we take our rides then get some lunch? We've got lots to do to get ready for tonight! You can play with her in the new barn, after. Wait until you see the fairy lights, Remi. They are gorgeous!"

Remi clasped her hands together at the same time as a huge grin broke out on her beautiful face. "Yay! My idea!"

Missy and Teagan took the babies into the house while I climbed back up into the saddle and then Chase handed Mace up into my arms. I settled the little boy in front of me, using my arms as a cage around his body as I held onto the reigns and the saddle horn.

"You and Dylan will have a turn when Mace is done, okay?" I smiled at Remi.

"Sure, Auntie Marin!" She agreed happily as Chase lifted his daughter up and over his head until she was sitting on top of his shoulders. Dylan climbed on to the corral fence and Jensen opened the gate for me, so I'd be able to lead Siri through.

"Gid yap! Gid yap!" Mace called out happily, and I laughed out loud with Chase and Jensen.

"You heard him, Siri. Giddy-up!" I nudged her and she started into a slow walk. Jensen closed the gate behind us and leaned on it near his son.

Mace's giggles filled the open air as I urged Siri into a slow trot. His squeals of delight filled my heart with joy as I held him securely to me. I hoped one day that my own child would be in the very place he was sitting; on Siri's saddle in front of me as I took him or her on their first horseback ride. Chase and Teagan, and Missy and Jensen, had exactly what I wanted. A family of my own that fit right in with the bigger picture of theirs.

I wished Ben had been around to share this moment, but we both had work to do to make sure the celebration tonight was absolutely perfect.

BEN

The inside of the barn was like a magical place.

Marin had not delegated the decorating or the planning of the party, other than a little help from Remi and Teagan, and the result was outstanding. I stood in the center of the huge event space we'd created, looking around and just taking it all in.

There were votives scattered around; on the tables, the bar, and on several little recessed shelves that had been built into the walls near the stairs on the way up to the lofts. I had to admit that the twinkling lights that I'd complained about stringing through the log beams that crossed the building every four feet were the best part. The live band was playing soft instrumentals during dinner, but later the dance party would begin.

I had plans for the evening, and I couldn't have picked a better place. My mother had flown in with Chase's parents, his brother and sister and their kids. They'd all rented cars and shown up right after Missy's group. We'd invited our caterer, Arlene, her husband and her kids. Gina had a sister, and her family would be here, too. They would all be staying in the cabins until Sunday, but tonight, we were open to the public.

Remi and Dylan had been stuck to me like glue, and I loved it. They were both dressed up, though Dylan complained when he had to change out of his play clothes. Remi was wearing a pretty white sundress and Dylan had on nice jeans and short sleeved button down in soft shade of blue. They both had on new cowboy boots, which I knew would be off their feet and shoved under a table in short order. I planned to show them how to break them in but even then, it would take more than a week of wear before they didn't hurt their feet. "This is a ranch, Uncle Ben. How come we had to dress up?"

I laid a hand on his shoulder. "Because we want the people of Jackson to see that while it's a dude ranch, it's still a classy place to hold weddings and other parties. Besides, you might meet a pretty girl to dance with," I teased.

"Uncle Ben!" Remi admonished. "I'm his damsel, so he has to dance with me!"

My nephew rolled his eyes and I chuckled.

"I don't wanna dance right now, Remi. I wanna eat." Dylan walked over to where the food was set up with several uniformed people to assist with the serving. Remi crossed her arms and stood firm. "Aren't you coming?" Dylan asked, pausing to look over his shoulder when he realized she hadn't come with him.

"Not until you admit I'm your damsel," she was adamant, her face resolute.

Dylan's head lolled back; his hands dropped to his side in defeat. "Ugh," he groaned. "Fine. You're my damsel. But only because I'm starving."

"Give it time, Remi. Boys don't start looking at girls until they're at least twelve. Even then, it's iffy." I patted her between her shoulder blades. "You'll see."

"Well, I might find a new prince before then."

"I bet you could, too. You look like Rapunzel." Her dark hair was flowing down her back in a cascade of curls. "But wait a few years. You've got a lot of time. Let's just concentrate on tonight, then having a great summer, okay?"

At the end of the week when their families left for home, Remi and Dylan were staying behind until just a week before they had to be back at school. Mace was too young, but I hoped that this would become a tradition, even when Marin and I started our own family.

"Okay. Will you dance with us later, Uncle Ben? Auntie Marin said she'd teach us some of those country line dances. I mean more of them," She giggled a little.

"I remember. Thank you for helping Auntie Marin, Remi. She told me these beautiful lights were your idea."

"Yep, cuz you told me what you told me."

"Well, thank you for keeping my secret."

"I told the band when I do this, they have'ta start playing that song you told me about." She pointed her finger.

"Okay but wait until I do the thing we talked about."

"I will, Uncle Ben. After the watermelon song. I got it."

In secret, I'd taught my entire family The Watermelon Crawl over Skype so we could surprise Marin, sort of like a flash mob. It was the first line dance we'd even danced to and I thought it would be fun for her if everyone knew it. Especially Remi and Dylan. They adored Marin and I knew she already loved them as if they were her own.

"Remi! Are you coming or what?" Dylan called from across the room. He was waiting for her to come take a plate in front of him, holding her place in line.

"See? I am his damsel, right?" she said wryly shaking her head, swishing her long hair across her back. "Boys are dumb."

I laughed and nodded my agreement as she took off toward where Dylan waited.

Everyone looked perfect. I noticed the crowd were wearing dressy casual, as if they were going to a club or summer wedding as my eyes scanned for Marin. Chase and Teagan were already swaying together on the dance floor, Mace and Bliss secure with their grandparents at one of the tables. Missy and Jensen were there, too, deep in conversation with Chase's sister Kat while her husband managed their brood in the buffet line.

Finally, my eyes landed on Marin. She was standing upstairs, looking down from one of the lofts. She looked ethereal, just like an angel. She had on a pale pink dress, with a low-cut sweetheart neckline that was trimmed in white lace with more on the short cap sleeves. The dress flared out and finished with a five-inch ruffle that ended just above the knee. She paired it with her old cowboy boots and the effect had my heart literally flipping inside my chest. I found my hand coming up to rest over it as if it could ease the ache the sight of her caused.

I felt a hand on my arm and turned to find my mother there. I bent down to hug her. "Hi, Mom! I'm so happy you could make it." She'd flown in with Chase's family and while I knew she was here, I was busy planting trees until I had just enough time to feed and water the horses, then hop in the shower. This was the first time I'd seen her this time. She lived in Atlanta near Jensen and Missy.

"I wouldn't miss it. Marin has been an absolute doll since we arrived, and you look so handsome. So happy."

"I am," I said, sobering. "And you look very beautiful," I returned her compliment.

"I think I'm the only one not wearing cowboy boots."

"Nah, Teagan and Missy aren't either. Can't take the city out of those two."

"Are you ready for this?" Mom asked, a gentle smile curing her face. She looked like a slightly older version of my sister, but still stunning as hell.

I nodded. "So ready." *More ready for this than any other moment of my life.*

She reached up and patted my cheek, then presented me with a small dark blue box. "I had it cleaned, and it looks perfect."

I wanted to look inside, but I glanced up to where I'd last seen Marin and she was now watching us. She'd found me in the crowd and was smiling down. "Okay. Thank you for doing that."

"Don't be nervous, son."

Was I nervous? Marin had already agreed to marry me, but I had to acknowledge the butterflies in my stomach. "I'm trying not to."

"Well, the place looks great, and you couldn't have picked a more perfect night. You and Marin have done an amazing job." She hugged me tightly, once more, and then patted my shoulders with both hands that ended with a hard squeeze. I could hear the tears in her voice as she struggled to keep her composure. "You make me very proud."

My arms tightened around her waist for a moment and then released her. "Are you ready to dance?"

She laughed through her tears. "Are you kidding? Remi and Dylan have been practicing in whichever living room happens to be closet. I think I've done that damn thing a thousand times. Missy's done it many times with little Josh strapped to her belly like a sack of potatoes."

I let out an uproarious laugh. I could totally picture it in my mind, and if their enthusiasm was anything to judge by then tonight would be super fun, and totally perfect. "That's hilarious! I bet the kids pestered the hell out of them."

"Oh, they did. You should have seen Jensen. He couldn't stop laughing for the first five run-throughs."

Marin made her way down the stairs across the mostly empty dance floor to where I stood with my mom. It was an easy habit to slide my arm around the back of her waist whenever she was near. I bent to kiss her temple.

She smiled brilliantly at my mother. "Are you all settled in?"

"Oh, my goodness, yes! The cabin is so quaint. Everything is perfect. You must be so proud of everything you've accomplished in such a short time."

"We are," Marin beamed. "Thank you." Her arm went behind my waist, she was tucked perfectly into place at my side. We fit so easily, in so many ways.

"Are you both ready to grab some food? Maybe we should eat before more people begin to show up." I suggested.

Marin and my mother agreed, and it wasn't long before we were all seated at a long table that had been set up to accommodate all of us. My mother started a conversation with Chase's parents the minute she sat down next to them.

The food was delicious but when people began to file in, Marin and I took our place at the door to shake hands and thank everyone for coming.

At sundown, the bonfire was started outside and the band turned up the amps, switching to covers of popular country songs that spilled into the open air around the fire. It was turning out to be a great party, and everyone was having a blast.

We had a book set up on a table near the entrance where guests could sign in and inquire about any dates they wanted to book for future events. I'd gone over to glance at it a couple of times throughout the evening and it was filling up fast. There were already two full pages of reservation requests.

I was checking it out for the last time when Gina and Davis arrived.

"Wow, this is incredible! This place is going to be such a big success and another big draw for Jackson," Gina exclaimed.

I leaned down and kissed her on the cheek. "Glad you two could make it. You look great."

"Make it? Dude, I never left! I just showered in the cabin and Gina brought me a change of clothes. Where is Marin?" Davis asked.

I pointed to the dance floor. She was dancing with Remi and Dylan and holding little Mace on her hip. "Over there." She looked deliriously happy.

"I can see motherhood all over her," Davis teased, with a cock of one eyebrow.

"And what's wrong with that?" Gina poked him in the chest.

"Ow! Did I say anything was wrong with it?" Davis protested.

I couldn't help the grin that graced my face. I couldn't be happier that things were working out with Gina and Davis. Her fiery spirit was just what my best friend needed.

"Marin and I are planning on making a thank you toast soon, so grab a drink from the bar."

When the pair left my side, I walked up to the band and nodded at Marin. When the song they were playing ended, the band waited for us to come up to the stage. My hand reached for Marin's and my fingers threaded through hers. The lead singer handed me the microphone, but I passed it off to my girl. Jensen walked forward and handed us each a glass of wine as if on cue.

"Ladies and gentlemen, may we have your attention? We just wanted to say thank you for making tonight such a wonderful evening and such a success! I hope my Uncle Leonard is looking down from Heaven and proud of what we've done with the place. We look forward to hosting your events and seeing your families with us for a stay at the ranch. We're so excited for what the future holds for the Teton Valley Ranch."

Marin handed the mic back to me as the crowd clapped.

"Also, we've had a lot of support from our family and friends, and we'd be remiss if we didn't thank all of you. We couldn't have done it without you. Thanks to my friends, Davis, Jake and Mark who have put in a lot of sweat into the build, and to our family who have offered financial and moral support, we are truly grateful, especially Remi and Dylan who offered so many incredible ideas."

The crowd cheered and clapped again, the sound echoing through the large space.

"Free weekends for life!" Davis shouted from the back of the room. "And we'll consider it even!"

"That's what I'm talking about!" Jensen added.

"Hey, hey now," I answered. My words admonished but my tone was teasing. "Let's not get crazy."

The room burst into another round of uproarious laughter.

"Now, we have a surprise for Marin. If you'll be so kind as to indulge us for about three and a half minutes. If you know this one, join in."

Marin's eyes widened, full of questions. "What's going on?"

Chase, holding Mace on his hip, along with Missy, Teagan, Remi, Dylan, Davis, Gina and the rest of my firefighter friends all joined us on the dance floor, making lines in behind us. Chase's brother and sister's families all joined in, as well. Apparently, Remi and Dylan had made it a mission to teach everyone possible the fun line dance.

"Tell them Dylan," I said, holding the mic down for him.

"We all learned a line dance for my new Aunt Marin. Uncle Ben says it's an oldie, but a goody! She learned it from her Uncle Leonard when she was about our age, so we gotta keep it in the family. But friends are okay, too."

Remi, who was standing beside Dylan, leaned forward. "It's the first line dance Uncle Ben did with Auntie Marin, too, so we've all been practicing and practicing so we could show her how much we love her!"

The crowd all burst into a chorus of exclamations.

"It's the watermelon song!" Dylan announced gleefully.

"He means, The Watermelon Crawl," Remi corrected, excitement lacing her voice.

Marin's mouth dropped open and her hands came up to her mouth before her eyes filled with tears. I stood next to Marin and she gave me a tight hug. "Did you teach them?"

"Yeah. On Skype, no less." I laughed and she smiled up at me, her eyes glassy.

"Thank you," Marin whispered. "I love you."

"Back at you." I winked at her, lifting her hand to kiss it just as the music started when Remi and Dylan rushed up to the stage to be in the front line. It was apparent they'd decided that they would lead the dancing. Others in the crowed recognized the song, knew the dance and were soon joining in.

Happiness showed like a beacon from Marin's eyes and bright smile as the band played the quirky song and we all danced. Mace was giggling as Chase held him in his arms, dancing regardless. Even my mother joined in, standing between her two grandchildren at the front. When the song ended everyone shouted and clapped. Marin hugged me, then went down on one knee in front of Remi and Dylan and hugged each of them with one arm. "This was so special. Thank you, so much."

"Aw it was nothing," Dylan said, casually. "It was even kinda fun."

"Kinda?" Remi lamented with a grunt.

Marin laughed out loud. "Well, I think it was completely amazing." She kissed each one on the cheek.

Remi pointed at the lead singer of the band and the soft instrumental version of a song I'd picked out just for tonight began to play.

"Ladies and Gentlemen, before we resume the dancing, Ben wanted to say one more thing." He took the microphone off of the stand and handed it back to me.

I was holding Marin's hand so she wouldn't leave the dance floor as it cleared off; everyone resumed their seats or places at the bar.

I rubbed the top of her hand with my left thumb. She looked at me expectantly as turned to face her.

"Marin, I know I shouldn't be thankful for a fire that changed your life so drastically, but I can't help it, because it changed mine, too. The minute I laid eyes on you in the back of that ambulance, I knew you'd change me in ways I never imagined. It was love at first sight."

The candlelight made her light grey eyes sparkle as tears filled them. I was sure she knew what was happening because her throat constricted as she swallowed and that little crinkle between her brows appeared. It happened when she was thinking hard or trying not cry and was just another thing that I loved about her. The soft smile on my face deepened but the emotion of the moment overwhelmed me.

"There are so many things I want to say to you. I wish I would have met your Uncle Leonard, but I know he had to be one hell of a man to raise a little girl on his own, especially because you turned into the woman you are. I wish I could thank him; I wish I could ask his permission to marry you. Since I can't, I have to hope that he'd approve of me."

A tear dropped from her eye and tumbled down her cheek, followed by another as she nodded. "He would."

"I want to say thank you for your heart, your kindness, for letting me protect you, and for protecting me, too. Thank you for loving me and letting me love you…. For trusting me with your today and your tomorrows. You know that I love you more than anything in the world, and I want to take care of you for the rest of our lives. I can't even fathom growing old without you."

I took the box my mother had given me earlier in the evening out of my pocket and opened it, then knelt down on one knee. The vintage ring was a large cushion cut stone mounted in a white gold filigree band. The matching wedding ring would remain in the box for now.

"This is my grandmother's ring, Marin. I've been waiting for the right person to give it to, and I know with all my heart and soul that person is you. So, Marin Marie Landry, will you do me the honor of becoming my bride?"

The room was silent except for the super soft strains of the song. "I will. Yes!" she cried brokenly. I slipped the ring onto the third finger of her left hand before standing to lift her off of the floor and take her mouth in a passionate kiss.

The room erupted in shouts, cheers and thunderous clapping. My heart felt as if it would burst. She'd already said yes, but now, in front of all of our family and friends it was official.

The song the band was playing got louder and I realized I was still holding the microphone in one hand even as I held Marin close and kissed her.

I pulled my mouth from hers and she buried her face into the front of my shirt and chest. I was grinning from ear to ear as I leaned over and handed it back to the front man of the band.

"This song is dedicated to Ben and Marin and it's called 'Better Today.'"

It was a country song that I loved and that I felt would suit the moment. I never let go of Marin as the song began and we started to sway. I cupped her face with one hand and used my thumb to tilt her chin upward. "I figured I'd better make it official, since our wedding is in December." I grinned down at her, before sobering. She was so beautiful, and she was mine. "I love you so much," I murmured, before I lowered my mouth to kiss her again. I nudged her upper lip with my lower one, wishing I could devour her, increase the pressure and let my tongue dance with hers.

"Ben," she sighed, her fingers gently sliding down the line of my jaw. "Later. The kids."

"I know," I agreed, placing my forehead on her own. I was rethinking my decision to sleep in the bouncy house with the kids tonight. I bent and kissed the side of her neck since she was denying me her mouth. She smelled like spring and vanilla. "I wish we could be alone tonight. I should have thought this through a little better."

"We have years of nights to make love to each other. I adore these children and they helped you make this evening so special." Her lips found purchase on my jaw and I wished the rest of the world would disappear and we were alone. "We can't take this away from them. They are so precious to me. You, too."

"You're right, but I guarantee nothing once they're asleep." Marin let out a soft giggle. "I'm glad you love kids so much."

"Yeah, I remember. Five or six, you said?"

Happiness exploded inside me like a bomb. I smiled as she nuzzled into the open neckline of my shirt.

"Oh, at least."

She nodded and looked up at me; a lazy smile gracing her lips. "At least."

Marin

The crowds had gone home, and our family and friends were all delivered to their respective cabins to bed down for the night.

Ben and Dylan made sure the fire was out while Remi and I went inside to get ready for bed. Ben and Dylan came in to wash up before I sprayed all of our long-sleeved T-shirts, leggings and sweats with bug repellant before loading up with blankets, pillows and sleeping bags, then heading out to one of the bouncy houses still set up in the yard. Ben had shut the generator off on the second one and it was deflated, so the whir of one was the only thing that interrupted the sounds of crickets, grasshoppers and the occasional bird or the hooting of the Barn Owl that lived in the stable. After ghost stories and fairy tales, and a full day of excitement, Remi and Dylan were finally asleep.

As I lay in Ben's arms, I remembered the words he whispered on the dance floor, I relived every magical moment of the evening. After our slow dance, we went outside by the fire for a few minutes alone, then he had spirited me away from spying eyes until we were around the back of the stable, out of earshot of the party.

"Remember, the first time we made love was in this stable," he'd whispered. I closed my eyes, remembering the perfection of the next few minutes as we made-out against the wall. Ben had turned so it was his back against the rough wood as we got lost in a torrent of passion; kissing and petting that couldn't culminate in making love. Without the fire, there were too many bugs to contend with and we both knew that, as hosts, we couldn't leave the party for too long.

Now, we were spooning, my head resting on his arm and his other wrapped around me. My fingers traced a light pattern on his strong forearm as we lay together in silence.

I was content just to lay with him to be in his arms, knowing he was mine. I'd never felt like this with Carter. I finally trusted that God would watch over Ben whenever he was out fighting an occasional fire. The ranch was the compromise, and I felt sure that my Uncle Leonard had been whispering in God's ear to create a plan that would keep me happy and keep Ben safe.

"What are you thinking about?" Ben's sultry voice whispered in my ear.

I smiled and placed my arm down to cover his. "Oh, just happy. You're my prince."

I could feel Ben's smile against the skin of my neck and his warm breath washed over my skin when he spoke. "You're spending too much time with Remi."

I shook my head. He didn't know how perfect he was. "You are. You take care of me in so many ways. Everything I could ever want in a man."

He paused for a split second. "It's mutual, Marin. I don't think I'd survive without you, now."

His words filled me with love and pride that he could want me this much. "You're not gonna start slobbering on me now, are you?" I teased to keep myself from tearing up.

Ben chuckled, sliding one thigh between both of mine and pressing into me. "Try and stop me," he murmured. His arm tightened and pulled me tighter back against him as he began a slow seduction that began with delicious and languid open mouth kisses along the back of my neck. I could feel he was already aroused. His mouth worked magic that caused goosebumps over every inch of my skin and began the familiar ache down low in my belly that only he could command.

My breath left me, and I arched back against him as his hand cupped the fullness of my left breast. He tweaked the nipple softly tugging and rolling it between his thumb and index finger. "Uhhh," I sighed as his other hand reached down into my leggings to the part of me that was craving his touch. His fingers slid down to part the slick flesh and begin to play. His breathing started to increase as his hips pressed forward in rhythm with his kisses and the delight his touch was creating. "Mmmm, Ben," I moaned softly.

"Shhh, we have to be quiet. This will only work if we are absolutely silent," Ben whispered. He began to push down the black leggings I wore and finished the job with his foot, and I kicked one leg free of them. He pushed down his sweats just far enough and moved until he was on top of me, using his elbows to take most of his weight. My knees lifted and my hips arched toward his of their own violation, knowing what delights awaited. I could feel his erection hard and strong, probing between my legs. He found my entrance and pushed inside. I sucked in my breath as my body expanded to except the fullness of his. I bit my lip. It felt amazing, but the entire air-filled structure moved with us.

"Fuck," Ben whispered. "I didn't really think this through."

I used my vaginal muscles and squeezed around him, not wanting him to pull out.

"God, Marin." Ben moaned softly, but in the silence of the night it was loud. I squeezed again and he dropped his head into my neck, pulling out then pushing back in.

"Now who's being loud?"

His hands cupped the side of my head and he raised his to look down into my face. "You have no idea how badly I want to go at it right now. Like wild and crazy," Ben whispered, trying to move his hips without making the bouncy house rock and roll. "But we might literally be caught with our pants down."

I bit my lip, trying hard not to burst into a giggle and my arms tightened around him as I buried my face into his chest. I swallowed to stop myself.

"We can do this. Just go slow and if they wake up, we're under covers," he whispered in my ear.

My answer was to squeeze around him and arch my hips toward his. His mouth settled on mine as his body began to thrust ever so slowly into me. We began a gentle push and pull, the squeeze of my muscles every time he thrust forward, was getting both of us closer. My fingers curled into his shoulders and he hoisted my left knee higher by hooking it over his right arm. The position allowed deeper penetration, and harder pressure where I needed it.

Our kisses grew deeper and more impassioned as we moved together, our tongues laving and worshiping each other's. He tasted and felt so good, I never wanted it to end. Our breathing increased in speed and got shallower, but somehow, we kept from bouncing up and down, and thankfully our movements only caused a gentle sway of the balloon-like structure. I sucked his tongue inside my mouth then his top lip, then his mouth moved up my cheek to my temple and he pressed a kiss there.

"Do you know how much I love you?" The words were so softly spoken, I barely heard.

"I hope as much as I love you," was my answer.

I could feel myself getting close and I pressed a hand beneath his sweats to close around his hard butt. I pressed him closer, my heel hooking around his knee.

Our bodies worked perfectly together, and I felt the shudder begin and spread throughout my entire body. My hands clutched at his hard back as I reached my climax.

Ben's kisses swallowed my cries of passion, and his muscles all flexed. I knew he was coming inside me, his orgasm rocking him in wave after wave, yet miraculously, he remained completely silent.

I crossed my feet behind his back, not wanting him to leave me yet. His breathing was hard as he lifted his head and looked at me. I touched his face gently, stroking back his hair and cupping his cheeks. "I never wanted it to end," I admitted in another whisper. I closed my eyes, trying to catch my breath.

"It won't."

My eyes flashed open and we both glanced over at the two kids. Thankfully, they were sleeping soundly.

I smiled up at Ben. His eyes were sparkling in the moonlight a slight smirk graced his luscious mouth. "My hero," I whispered.

Ben bent to kiss me tenderly, brushing the hair back from one side of my face. "Don't forget it."

"Never," I hugged him and closed my eyes, again.

Gem, who was lying next to Remi, whined.

Ben's mouth pressed into a smile as he separated from me, pulling up his sweats as he moved. I struggled to replace my left leg back into my leggings beneath the covers.

"Come here, Gemmy," I called. Instantly, the now full-sized black lab stood up and walked over to us, then plopped down on top of our quilt to take up her much-prized position between her two humans.

The bouncy house wobbled and rocked much more than it had while we were making love. Ben laid an arm across Gem and held my hand. "Go figure," he said, amused that Remi and Dylan were not roused.

We lay in the silence, still touching until Gem began to snore in between us.

"Just don't go anywhere, Ben," I said sleepily.

His fingers threaded through mine. "I won't," he assured. "What was it Remi said? Even tough guys need their damsel. You're mine, babe. Forever."

The End

Thank you for reading!

If you enjoyed this story, please consider leaving an honest review at
https://amzn.to/41Ksp0A

If you enjoyed this book, continue the series with *Forever & Always*, Remi and Dylan's story!

Visit this link for a sneak peak:
https://dl.bookfunnel.com/kww2jdqk96

About the Author

Kahlen Aymes is a USA Today bestselling author who writes steamy romance novels that cross genre lines between New Adult, Adult Contemporary, and Erotica.

Kahlen has been on several bestseller lists including Barnes & Noble, Amazon, Smashwords, Publisher's Weekly, iBooks and USA Today! She began her writing career without ever planning on publishing a single word and won multiple awards in the world's second largest fan fiction community, including BEST Author, BEST RPF, Best All-Human that Knocks You Off Your Feet, and several others! Her reader's encouragement and support are what prompted publication.

Kahlen enjoys reading, as well as writing, theater arts, cooking, roller skating and going for long walks. She is the proud mom to one teenage daughter and two golden retrievers, who basically rule her world.

With a strong love of writing and romance, you can count on her to deliver strong, relatable characters, deep and detailed plots, sexy love scenes, and emotion overflow!

CONNECT with KAHLEN

Facebook
Facebook.com/kahlen.aymes.author

Goodreads
Goodreads.com/author/show/5768062.Kahlen_Aymes

Twitter
@Kahlen_Aymes: Twitter.com/Kahlen_Aymes

Instagram
Kahlen.Aymes
Instagram.com/kahlen.aymes/

Pinterest
Pinterest.com/kahlenaymes/

TikTok
Tiktok.com/@kahlenaymesauthor

Amazon
http://bit.ly/3sNpBxoKAAmzn

Bookbub
Bookbub.com/authors/kahlen-aymes

OFFICIAL WEBSITE

For merchandise, signed copies, Julia's recipes, missing scenes, appearances & events, Kahlen's Blog, series playlists and more, visit **KahlenAymes.com**

For exciting news, giveaways, appearances, and book discussion sign-up for Kahlen and many more of your favorite authors, **sign up for our newsletter**: https://landing.mailerlite.com/webforms/landing/i7w8k4 (We won't spam you, PROMISE!)

Kahlen Aymes Book Babes Group on Facebook Facebook.com/groups/252301134873105

Kindle Unlimited readers, find the KU Romance Explosion Reader Group on Facebook! Facebook.com/groups/1271577439678148

Request an eBook autograph at: Authorgraph.com/authors/Kahlen_Aymes

If you have interest in joining **Kahlen's STREET TEAM**, please contact us at Info@KahlenAymes.com